Pra

The Sweeth

"Brings together two flawed yet appealing single parents searching for love . . . [a] heartwarming and charming story."
—*Publishers Weekly*

"As always, Jump's storytelling is a warm, irresistible invitation into a romance that will hold you rapt, and into a community you can't help but care deeply for. Her characters lure you in from line one, as does her clever, unassuming humor."
—*USA Today*

"Jump's expert storytelling shines. . . . A solid plot, strong tension and steady pacing draws the reader into this delightful read."
—*RT Book Reviews*

"I wish Ms. Jump's books weren't so darn addictive, because I just have to read them all! *The Sweetheart Rules* is snappy, seriously sensitive, and delightfully delicious."
—*Romance Junkies*

The Sweetheart Bargain

"Shirley Jump's stories sparkle with warmth and wit and glow with strong, heartfelt emotions. This is real romance."
—Jayne Ann Krentz, *New York Times* bestselling author

continued . . .

"A fun, heartwarming, small-town romance that you'll fall in love with . . . Shirley Jump is a true talent."
— Jill Shalvis, *New York Times* bestselling author

"Emotional and unforgettable, thumbs up for Jump."
— Lori Wilde, *New York Times* bestselling author

"Shirley Jump packs lots of sweet and plenty of heat in this heartwarming first book of her promising new series."
— Virginia Kantra, *New York Times* bestselling author of *Carolina Man*

"Fans will enjoy following the sisters' paths to love and the quaint and quirky setting." — *Booklist*

"The story is inviting, intriguing, heart-tugging, and splendid in its sexiness." — *USA Today*

Praise for the novels of Shirley Jump

"Fast-paced and filled with emotion and larger-than-life characters, this is a beautifully written, heartwarming story." — *RT Book Reviews*

"Shirley Jump weaves a story that hypnotizes from the first page . . . I love it, absolutely love it."
— *Coffee Time Romance*

"Lots of sizzle, wit, love, and romance."
— *A Romance Review*

"A hilarious and passionate contemporary romance that I found impossible to put down." — *Romance Junkies*

Berkley Sensation titles by Shirley Jump

THE SWEETHEART BARGAIN
THE SWEETHEART RULES
THE SWEETHEART SECRET

The Sweetheart Secret

SHIRLEY JUMP

BERKLEY SENSATION, NEW YORK

THE BERKLEY PUBLISHING GROUP
Published by the Penguin Group
Penguin Group (USA) LLC
375 Hudson Street, New York, New York 10014

USA • Canada • UK • Ireland • Australia • New Zealand • India • South Africa • China

penguin.com

A Penguin Random House Company

THE SWEETHEART SECRET

A Berkley Sensation Book / published by arrangement with the author

Copyright © 2014 by Shirley Jump.
Excerpt from *When Somebody Loves You* by Shirley Jump copyright © 2014 by Shirley Jump.
Penguin supports copyright. Copyright fuels creativity, encourages diverse voices,
promotes free speech, and creates a vibrant culture. Thank you for buying an authorized
edition of this book and for complying with copyright laws by not reproducing, scanning,
or distributing any part of it in any form without permission. You are supporting writers
and allowing Penguin to continue to publish books for every reader.

Berkley Sensation Books are published by The Berkley Publishing Group.
BERKLEY SENSATION® is a registered trademark of Penguin Group (USA) LLC.
The "B" design is a trademark of Penguin Group (USA) LLC.

For information, address: The Berkley Publishing Group,
a division of Penguin Group (USA) LLC,
375 Hudson Street, New York, New York 10014.

ISBN: 978-0-425-26452-2

PUBLISHING HISTORY
Berkley Sensation mass-market edition / September 2014

PRINTED IN THE UNITED STATES OF AMERICA

10 9 8 7 6 5 4 3 2 1

Cover photos © Shutterstock/Thinkstock.
Cover design by MN Studios.
Interior text design by Laura K. Corless.

*To my children, who changed my life in a thousand ways,
and who make me proud to be their mom
every day of my life.*

Acknowledgments

Writing a book is such a solitary venture, at least the writing part of it. The research, though, sometimes takes a whole lot of people who know a little of this, a little of that, or a whole lot about things I know nothing about. Like the life of a doctor. The symptoms an elderly patient might exhibit. I can barely diagnose a cold versus a fever (is it starve a cold, feed a fever? Or feed a fever, starve a cold? Ah, well, I'll just eat all the time and that'll solve it). Huge thanks to Bernie Moye, ARNP, who listened to all my stupid questions and gave me lots of great advice on how Colt would treat his grandpa. Thank you also to authors Kate Hardy and Scarlet Wilson who gave me all kinds of details on the moments in the hospital and what it's like to deal with geriatric patients.

Major Pain's name came from a reader—Melissa Swanson— who proposed the name in a dog naming conversation I had on my Shirley Jump author page on Facebook. It was so much fun and I loved the inventiveness of my readers!

Thank you to my family, because they are the ones who pick up the slack and throw some food my way when I'm on deadline and rarely emerge from the writer cave. My husband holds the house together and makes sure all the animals and people are fed and dispersed to their various activities. He's not such a bad short-order cook, either, and an amazing grillmaster.

Thank you also to the fabulous art department at Berkley. I love, love, love the way they've designed the covers for the Sweetheart Sisters series. And to my editor, Kate, who is an absolute dream to work with.

A huge thank you to my running buddies, Eileen, Kathryn, Pauline, and Sharon, who have listened to me spin wild plot variations on our long runs and (hardly) ever told me to stop talking about the book. Those long runs and girl chatter kept me sane during the book-writing process, and you all make those miles pass by in a blip of time. Not to mention, the well-deserved pancake breakfasts we have afterwards!

If you are reading this, then I want to thank YOU, too. My readers are my favorite people, and I adore each and every one of you. Your letters and e-mails make my day, and it is truly an honor to bring you stories and hear that you enjoyed them, or that a laugh at Greta's antics helped you during a difficult time. Thank you—for without you, there would be no books to buy.

One

There were days when Colt Harper swore Greta Winslow had been put on earth solely to test his commitment to the Hippocratic oath.

Greta was an eighty-three-year-old firecracker —petite and wiry, but determined to sneak bourbon into her morning coffee and avoid all things green and leafy. She disproved his constant healthy-living lectures by having the constitution of a thoroughbred mare. He always saved her appointments for the end of the day, because if he started a Monday with a visit from the stubborn Greta, he'd end up barking at everyone else who followed.

And this week, he definitely didn't need the extra stress. His plan was to just get through the appointment, get out the door, and hope for the best when he got home tonight— to his other most frustrating patient.

Colt drew in a breath and refocused on Greta. "I'm sorry, Mrs. Winslow, what did you say?"

"I asked if it was possible to be allergic to someone." Greta leaned forward and arched a thin gray brow. "As in the mere sight of his blindingly white head and ugly moon-pie face gives you the dry heaves."

Colt bit back a laugh. No doubt, Greta was referring to her much-maligned neighbor, Harold Twohig. The feud between the two residents of Golden Years Retirement Village was part and parcel of Rescue Bay's daily gossip chatter. The sleepy Florida coastal town had a vibrant senior population, which kept Colt busy in his practice, but also insured a little soap-opera-worthy drama from time to time. Especially when it came to Greta and Harold's love-hate relationship. "As far as I know, that is not medically possible."

"As far as *you* know. Which means there is still a possibility it could be true." Greta sat back, crossed her arms over her pale blue sweater, and harrumphed. "Which means I need a prescription."

He glanced down at Greta's chart—hard copy today because his tablet had met with an unfortunate family accident yesterday. As had the tablet he'd owned before that one. And his laptop. And his iPhone. Colt either needed to stop bringing electronics home or buy better accidental breakage coverage. Either that, or find a way to stop every conversation with his grandfather from derailing into electronic shrapnel.

"Prescription for what?" he said to Greta. "You seem to be doing pretty well lately."

"A prescription ordering me to stay away from Harold Twohig for my mental and gastrointestinal health." Greta put out her palm, expectant. "Just write that out, Doc. I'll sign it for you, save you some time."

He chuckled. "All you need to do is turn the other way when you see him coming. He'll get the hint." Rumor had it that Greta had a soft spot for Harold, even if she professed the opposite.

Greta pshawed. "That man is as dense as a butternut squash. He's got it in his head that he is in love with me. Lord help me, I think he's delusional."

"Nothing wrong with a man determined to be with the woman he loves." As he said the words, they sent a tremor of memory through him, a little earthquake fissuring another break in Colt's concentration. One woman, who had turned Colt's life upside down twice, once fourteen years ago, and then again a few months ago, after a bad day had led him to a New Orleans diner and a chance meeting with his past.

All followed by a bottle of wine, a platter of blazin' hot buffalo wings, and one night in a king-sized bed at a hotel on Bourbon Street. One misstep—but it was done, over, in the past, and he was moving forward, back on the pre-scribed, planned, straight path where he was simply Doctor Colton Harper, upstanding citizen of Rescue Bay.

Not Colt Harper, the motorcycle-riding dropout with a checkered past. No, not him. Never again.

That other Colt Harper had made a lot of mistakes, mis-takes that haunted him to this day, hovered over what was left of his family like thunderclouds. Mistakes he was de-termined not to repeat.

Uh-huh. Then what had that been three months ago, if not a repeat of mistakes best left in the past?

"Doc? Did you hear me?"

Damn. Once again, he'd lost track of his thoughts. "I'm sorry, Mrs. Winslow. What did you say?"

"My goodness, you are distracted today. I said that Har-old Twohig isn't in love with anything besides his mirror."

Colt bit back a laugh, then scanned the top sheet of the chart, double-checking he'd covered all the basics for Greta's checkup. Doing so forced his brain back into work mode, into the world of medical tests, diagnoses, and practicality. He glanced at his watch, and did a mental calculation of the minutes until he was home. If Colt was lucky, things would go well tonight.

Okay, given the way the last six months had gone, *well* wouldn't be a word to describe his evenings with Grandpa Earl. They were like two battering rams—with one of them being stubborn, uncooperative, and cranky.

And then there was Grandpa Earl, who was all that times two.

Maybe he should just face facts and find Grandpa Earl a bed in an assisted living home. Maybe living with his only grandson wasn't the best choice. For either of them.

And maybe Colt was trying to restore a past that was

beyond resurrecting. Too many years, too many hurts, just . . . too many everythings to put it all back to rights again.

Despite all the arguments and broken electronics, though, Colt still had hope that he could build a bridge, one that would get them past the painful wounds of the past and maybe, just maybe, give Grandpa a way to forgive Colt. Maybe then Colt could forgive himself.

Maybe.

Colt signed off on the bottom of Greta's paperwork, then handed her the orange sheet, with an extra note scribbled at the bottom. "Good job on the walking. Same recommendation as last time—"

"Eat more vegetables, drink less bourbon." Greta made a face. "You are a party pooper, Doc. You know, you really should try letting loose once in a while. Have some bourbon. Cheat at a game of cards. Not that *I* cheat, of course."

"Of course not." He grinned.

She flicked at his tie. "I just think you should loosen the reins. Step outside all those straight lines that do nothing but box you in."

"Straight lines?" Colt scoffed. "I think straight lines keep you in order, which is a good thing."

"How can they? Heck, lines aren't even a shape, for goodness' sake. In my considerable life experience, straight lines leave no room for fun, and we all need a little fun." She leaned in and gave him a nod. "Some of us more than others."

"I don't know about that." Since the day he'd entered medical school, Colt had done his best to never deviate outside the lines and columns and tidy spaces where he lived his life.

That day, he'd finally grown up, instead of leaving common sense in the exhaust fumes of a '93 Harley Softail. He'd wiped his past clean, become a doctor, and buried all traces of the Colton Harper he used to be.

Until he'd found part of his past waiting tables in a diner in New Orleans, and upended his world. He wondered what Greta would say if she knew that three months ago her buttoned-up, straightlaced physician had done all the things he'd told his patients not to do. At the time, Colt had convinced himself he'd had a good reason to let loose, to have a little fun—

To take a trip down memory lane. More than a trip, more like an all-night journey.

"You are truly no fun, Doctor Harper." Greta pouted.

"I'm your doctor, Mrs. Winslow. I'm supposed to be serious and attentive."

"Serious and attentive, not the human version of *War and Peace*."

"I'm sorry, Mrs. Winslow, but I like things quiet and serious." As soon as he'd returned back to Rescue Bay, he had thrown himself into the predictable routine of shingles vaccinations, blood pressure checks, and glucose level tests, because the more he organized himself into straight lines, the further that one crazy weekend disappeared into his memory. The more he could tell himself it had been an aberration, nothing more. A crazy sidestep into a past he had left far behind him. A past filled with secrets no one here knew. Or ever would, if he had anything to say about it.

So he focused on his practice and his grandfather, and told himself he was happy. One day after another, following a predictable routine, with no surprises. Just the way Colt liked things.

"Okay, Mrs. Winslow," Colt said, "don't forget to make an appointment with Frannie for—"

The exam room burst open. Colt started to chastise his nurse—a new one, who had started just last week and often ran around like a harried chicken—and stopped himself when he saw who it was. Just like that, Colt's mostly predictable, mostly perfect life turned upside down, the chart in his hands fluttered to the floor, the pile of multicolored papers scattering like leaves in the wind, scuttling beneath the swivel chair, the exam table.

In the doorway stood the last woman in the world he expected to see, the one woman he'd vowed never to see again after that night in New Orleans. Judging by the fury on her face, he wasn't high on her friends and family list, either.

"What the hell is this?" She waved a manila envelope in his face.

"Daisy? How did you . . . where did you . . . what are you . . . ?" His brain misfired and the words got lost in his throat.

Frannie, Colt's receptionist/assistant/right-hand woman, squeezed past Daisy and into the room. Her florid face was blotched with red and her normally neat auburn chignon had come undone. "Doc, I'm sorry. I tried to stop her, but she was like a wildcat—"

Wildcat. That was the perfect word for Daisy Barton. She stood there, brunette hair cascading down her shoulders, a figure-hugging red dress that made the word *hourglass* seem like a sin, and full crimson lips that could tempt a man into doing things he knew he shouldn't.

Colt knew that firsthand. He'd tangled with Daisy— *willingly*—twice. Even though he knew any encounter with her was bound to end with a fight and regrets, seeing her again made his chest tighten and those straight lines begin to curve. Damn.

He cleared his throat. "It's okay, Frannie. I'll handle this." He returned his attention to Daisy. "Please wait outside. We can talk about this later."

Daisy put her hands on his hips. "Talk? Honey, you were never interested in *talking* with me."

Across from him, Greta's mouth formed a surprised O. She glanced at Daisy, then at Colt. "Why, Doc Harper, it seems I have misjudged you. You have surprised me, and so few people do that at my age. No wonder you've been so distracted lately."

Damn. If he knew Greta, this little encounter with Daisy was going to be all over the Rescue Bay gossip channel before the end of the day. That was the last thing he needed.

"I'm with a patient right now, Daisy," he said, forcing a cool, detached, professional tone to his voice, when all his brain could do was picture her naked and on top of him, that wild tangle of hair kissing the tops of her breasts, and tickling against his hands. "Please wait for me in the lobby."

She eyed him, her big brown eyes like pools of molten chocolate. "You're going to make your *wife* wait?"

Oh, shit. Now he knew why Daisy had come in like a tornado.

"Hold the phone. Did you say . . . *wife*?" Greta kept glancing between Daisy and Colt, as if she'd just realized Big Foot and the Abominable Snowman were involved in a clandestine affair.

Colt could feel those straight lines dissolving into a tangled, messy web. He glared at Daisy. "Please. Wait. In. The. Lobby."

Daisy took a step forward, placed the envelope in his hand, then pressed a hard, short, ice-cold kiss to his cheek. "I'll be outside, dear," she said, with a slash of sarcasm on the *dear*. "But I won't wait long."

Then she was gone. The door shut, leaving behind the faintest trace of her dark, smoldering perfume. Colt jerked into action. He bent down, gathering the papers he'd dropped earlier, stuffing the envelope Daisy had given him to the back of the pile. He straightened, then let out an *oomph* when something—or someone—slapped him on the back. "What the—"

"How could you not tell me you're married?" Greta asked. "And to a beautiful girl like that, too."

"I'm *not* married. Well, technically, maybe I still am, but . . ." He pushed his glasses up his nose. What was he doing? Confiding in Greta Winslow? "I don't share my personal life with my patients, Mrs. Winslow."

"I think your personal life just shared itself, Doc." Greta waved toward the closed door. "Where have you been hiding her anyway?"

"It's . . . complicated." Yeah, that was the word for it. *Complicated.* And crazy. And a mess he didn't need right now. "I would appreciate it if this . . . incident stayed between us."

She propped a fist on her waist and eyed him. "Are you

going to give me a prescription to keep Harold Twohig away?"

"Are you blackmailing me?"

"I'm bargaining. That's different." She shrugged. "And legal."

"Mrs. Winslow, I have no doubt you can handle Mr. Twohig on your own. You are a smart and resourceful woman."

She snorted. "You're the one with the fancy degree. And if you ask me, you're a blooming idiot."

"Mrs. Winslow—"

She hopped off the exam table and stood in front of him, hands on her hips, her chin upturned in defiant argument. "Women like that don't come along every day. Heck, God doesn't even *make* females that look like that every day. I don't know what you did to let her get away, but you need to go get her, and keep her this time."

"Mrs. Winslow, we're in the middle of—"

"We're done. I'm the last patient of the day. Don't think I don't know you save me for last." She wagged a finger at him. "Now go after that girl and apologize for whatever you did wrong. She's your *wife*."

"She's not. She's . . ." He let out a gust. How could he even begin to explain the push-pull that defined his relationship with Daisy Barton? "It's complicated."

"No, it's not. You *make* it complicated. If you ask me, the secret to life is easy. Go for what makes you happy." She gave him a light jab on the shoulder, which required quite the stretch from her five-foot-three frame to reach his six-foot-one height. "Even if it's bourbon in your coffee. Take my advice, Doc. Before your life gets sucked into a whirling drain filled with crappy food and pesky old men."

The door shut behind Greta. Colt stood there, the chart in his hands, all organized and tidy again. The rest of him, though, was a rat's nest. What the hell was Daisy doing here? She could have simply signed the papers and put them in the pre-addressed, stamped envelope he'd included. Instead, she'd come all the way from Louisiana to Rescue Bay and dropped a bomb in his lap.

He'd never thought Daisy would return to Rescue Bay. He should have known better than to try to predict the very unpredictable Daisy Barton. She'd never done or said what he anticipated. When he'd been young and determined to flip off the world, he'd found that quality exciting. Intriguing. But now, today, as a man cemented in the community and in his job, he didn't need surprises.

Especially a surprise like her.

He dropped the chart on the exam table, then exited the room. The lobby was empty, save for Frannie, who was still sputtering an apology. Colt waved it off, then exited through the side door, skirting the small brick building that housed his practice. He caught up to Daisy just as she was climbing into a dented gray Toyota sedan.

He put a hand on the door before she could shut it. Her perfume, dark and rich like a good coffee, wafted up to tease at his senses, urge him to lean in closer, to linger along the curve of her neck. He gripped the hard metal of the door instead. "What the hell are you doing here, Daisy? Why didn't you simply sign the papers and mail them back to me?"

"Because I don't want a divorce."

The words hung in the air, six words he never expected to hear. Hell, he hadn't expected to find out he was still married to her when he asked his lawyer to unearth a copy of the divorce decree. *A mistake in the filing,* his lawyer had said, and sent a new set of divorce papers off to Daisy. *A quick, easy process,* his lawyer had promised.

Apparently his lawyer had never met Daisy Barton.

"Daisy, we haven't been together in fourteen years—"

"What was that back in June?"

"An . . . aberration."

She snorted. "Is that what you call it?"

"We had one night,"—one crazy, hot, turn-a-man-inside-out night—"and that was it. It was wrong and when I realized that our divorce was never final, I sent you the papers. I don't understand the problem, Daisy. We both wanted that divorce. Besides, we never had a real marriage to begin with."

"Well we do now, my dear husband. All legal and every-thing. In fact, next month is our fifteenth anniversary. Maybe we should think of doing something." The ice in her voice chilled the warm Florida air.

Was she insane? There was no way he was going to cele-brate their anniversary or anything of the sort. He thrust the envelope of divorce papers at her, but she ignored them. "Just sign, and we can be done with this insanity. I'm dating someone else." Well, technically, he wasn't dating anyone, but Daisy didn't need to know that.

"So sorry to put a crimp in your social life with our mar-riage." She turned away from him, facing the windshield, her features cold and stony.

"A marriage that has been over since we were nineteen. A marriage that only lasted three weeks. A marriage we ended by mutual agreement years ago."

"Mutual agreement? You walked out and never returned. I'd call that a one-sided decision on your part."

He wasn't about to retread all that again. He'd had his reasons for leaving, reasons she didn't need to know. Telling Daisy wouldn't change a thing. "Just sign, Daisy. We'll be rid of each other once and for all. Isn't that what you want, too?"

She bit her lip, and the gesture sent a fire roaring through him that nearly made him groan. Damn. This was why he didn't want to be with Daisy. Because every time he got close to her, his brain turned into a pile of useless goo. "No, I don't," she said. "Not yet."

"What do you mean—*not yet*?"

She blew her bangs out of her face and stared straight ahead, her hands resting on the steering wheel, key in the ignition. A tiny pair of bright pink plastic dice dangled from the ring, tick-tocking back and forth against the metal keys. "It's complicated."

He'd said the same thing to Greta. He laid his palms on the roof of the car and bit back a gust of frustration. "That's the understatement of the year. Everything about you is complicated."

She jerked her attention toward him, fire sparking in the set of her mouth. "There used to be a time when you liked that."

"There used to be a time when we both liked each other's faults."

"Yeah, well we were young and stupid then. We were different people then." She shook her head, then fiddled with the dice again, her keys jangling softly together. Her shoulders sagged a little and her voice dropped into a softer range. "Do you remember when we bought these?"

Remember? Hell, it was one of those memories that lingered in the back of a man's mind like taffy. He started to lie, then let out a sigh and said, "Yeah, I do."

"We were walking down the street in New Orleans, with what, ten dollars between us?"

They'd been too broke to even consider themselves poor, but hadn't cared at all. They'd both been infatuated and naïve enough to think the world would work out just because they wanted it to. "Back then neither of us cared about how we were going to pay the rent or buy a winter coat. We lived every day by the seat of our pants."

Impractical and spontaneous. Two words that no longer described Colt, but had always come attached to Daisy. There'd been a day when he thought that was attractive. Intoxicating even.

"I saw those dice in one of those tourist-trap stores on Bourbon Street, and told you I had to have them." She fiddled with them some more and a smile stole across her face. "You asked me why and I said so that we always remember to take chances. Do you remember that, Colt?"

The memory hit him like a tidal wave. The crowded, busy street. The eager vendors hawking everything from beer to beads. And in the middle of all that, Daisy. He'd fished the last couple dollars out of his pocket, bought the dice, and dangled them in front of her. She'd let out a joyous squeal, then risen on her tiptoes to press a kiss to his lips, a honeyed kiss that had made everything else pale in comparison. He'd swooped her into his arms, then made the most insane decision of his life, all because of a pair of dice and a kiss.

They'd lasted three whole weeks together, three tumultuous weeks as filled with fights as they had been with wild, hot nights, until Colt called home and was hit by a hard, fast, and tragic reminder of where irresponsibility landed him. That day, he'd left Daisy and those crazy weeks behind. He'd started all over again, become a respectable, dependable doctor, a man with principles and expectations. Far, far from the Colt Harper he'd been in Louisiana.

Then this past summer, a medical conference had taken him back to New Orleans. The moment he'd seen Daisy, waiting tables at a cheesy diner near the convention center, he'd been standing there with the dice and the ten dollars all over again. Before he knew it, he'd invited Daisy back to his hotel, and for a few hours, it had been like old times. And ended like old times, too. With a fight, a promise to never see each other again, and one of them stomping out of the room. He'd thought that was it. He'd been wrong.

She looked up at him now, her eyes hidden by dark sunglasses. "What happened to you, Colt?"

"Nothing. I told you I had to go back to—"

"I didn't mean that morning. I meant in the last fourteen years." She reached out and flicked the navy satin tie he wore, as if it was a spider crawling down his shirt. "Look at you. All pressed and neat as a pin. You're wearing a tie. Khaki pants. *Khakis*, for God's sake. The Colt I used to know wore leather jackets and jeans and didn't even own an iron."

"I've changed since then."

She dropped the sunglasses and let her gaze roam over him. "Well, at least you give off the aura of a respectable husband."

"I'm not your husband, Daisy." He tried again to get her to take the divorce papers. The last thing he needed to do was fall for that smile because of nostalgia. "So just sign this."

She pushed them back in his direction. "I don't want a divorce. I want a fresh start."

"A . . . a what?"

"You owe me that much at least, Colt. I need to start over, and I have a chance here, in this town. But it turns out I need a little help to do that, and you know it pains me to even admit that. But I was hoping *my husband* would give me a little assistance. Then we can quietly get divorced."

Twice in the space of ten minutes, he'd been blackmailed. To think he had once been head over heels for this woman. A mistake, of monumental proportions. "You want money? Is that it? How much, Daisy?"

"I don't want any money. I want a name." Her lower lip quivered for a moment and made him feel like a heel, then she blew out a breath and she was all steel and sass again. Whatever had been behind the comment was gone now, replaced by that impenetrable wall that made Daisy both infuriating and mysterious. "Give me a few weeks and then I'll be out of your life."

"Weeks? Why?"

She turned the key in the ignition and the car roared to life. "You don't get to ask why, Colt. You gave up that right a long time ago."

"You can't come into this town and tell everyone we're married. I have a life here, Daisy. A life that doesn't include a wife." People had forgotten about the Colt he used to be. The town had moved on, changed. Everyone here knew him only as a respectable doctor, not the headstrong teen who had run out of town, tossing aside school and his family, for what had amounted to a fling. An unforgettable fling, but a fling nonetheless.

"That life includes a wife now." Daisy jerked the door shut, then propped an elbow on the open window and looked up at him. "Listen, I'm not here to make your life miserable. Maybe we can work out some kind of deal. Quid pro quo. Maybe there's something you want—"

His mind rocketed back to that night in New Orleans. Daisy climbing on top of him, pinning his wrists to the bed—

Okay, that wasn't helping anything. At all.

"There's nothing I want. Except a divorce."

"I can't do that. I need you, Colt. Just for a few weeks. Please." She bit her lip, and he sensed she hated having to beg. "There's got to be something I can do for you. Something, uh, other than what happened in New Orleans."

Meaning no sex. Not that he'd even considered that.

Liar.

What was with this woman? She turned him inside out and upside down in the space of five minutes.

"Think about my offer, Colt. I'm staying at the Rescue Bay Inn for a few days. Room one twelve." She handed him a slip of paper. "My cell."

He stepped back and she pulled away. A moment later, her car was gone. Three months ago, they'd been tangled in soft-as-butter sheets. She'd had her legs wrapped around his waist, her nails clutching at his back, her teeth nibbling his ear, and he'd been lost, in the moment, in her. Now they were exchanging numbers and making appointments, as if none of that had ever happened. That was what he'd wanted, how he'd left things three months ago. But it didn't make words like *quid pro quo* sting any less.

A pair of seagulls flew overhead, squawking disapproval or agreement or the location of the nearest fish shack, Colt didn't know. A breeze skated across the lot, making palm fronds shiver and the thick green grass yield. Daisy's car disappeared around the corner with a red taillight flicker, and Colt stood there, empty, cold.

He started back toward his office, then stopped when he saw Greta Winslow, standing under the overhang on the corner of the building, out of earshot but still watching the whole thing. Great. Now this was going to be on the front page of the Rescue Bay paper: LOCAL DOC HIDING SECRET MARRIAGE WITH MYSTERY WOMAN.

"Here, Doc," Greta said, marching up to him and thrusting a paper at his chest. "I think you need this more than I do."

He glanced down at the orange sheet he'd handed her earlier. Beneath his signature he'd written: *Doctor's Advice: Embrace the things that scare you, from broccoli to love.*

"That was just a joke, Greta. I didn't mean—"

"Sometimes your subconscious is smarter than all those fancy medical degrees put together, Doc. And sometimes"—she laid a hand on his arm—"an old woman with eighty-plus years of life experience has a thing or two to teach her too-smart-for-his-own-good physician."

"I appreciate the advice, Mrs. Winslow, I really do. But Daisy and I are just friends. Acquaintances, really. This whole marriage thing is a misunderstanding."

She eyed him, her pale blue eyes squinting against the sun. "You should take a dose of your own medicine. Eat more broccoli, drink less bourbon, and most of all, don't be afraid of love. Because in the end, it's sure as hell better than the alternative."

He arched a brow. "What's the alternative?"

"Dying alone, drooling into your Wheaties." She grinned, then patted him on the arm. "See, Doc? It could always be worse."

Two

When Daisy Barton was five years old, her mother had enrolled her in kindergarten, dropped her off in front of the James K. Polk Elementary School, and told her to be a good girl. Daisy had gone inside the building alone, scared, and overwhelmed, wearing the hand-me-down red plaid jumper and white buckle shoes she had chosen with such care that morning. Before the heavy metal-and-glass door shut behind her, she heard the high-pitched squeal of tires against the pavement, and her mother was gone. Off to pursue needlepoint in the Ozarks or meditation in the desert, or whatever lark had captured Willow Barton's attention that month.

Aunt Clara had been the one to pick Daisy up at the end of the day, to wipe away Daisy's tears, and to mend the tear in Daisy's dress. Aunt Clara had filled in as Daisy's mother, in between Willow's "adventures." Aunt Clara, long married to Willow's brother Lou, had been the closest thing Daisy had to a maternal figure, and when she'd moved away from Jacksonville and down to Rescue Bay for a few years, Daisy had felt as if her right arm was severed.

She'd called Aunt Clara regularly, and spent one summer here at the Hideaway Inn, but missed those family ties something fierce. Even from miles away, Aunt Clara had been the voice of reason and support, a steady foundation for Daisy to stand on when her life got too crazy. Which was like every other week.

So when Aunt Clara had asked something of Daisy in return, there'd been no doubt that Daisy's answer would be yes.

The problem? Daisy had no clue how big of a task Aunt Clara's request would be. Or how impossible it would be to bring to fruition. Or how Colt Harper would become the one monkey wrench she hadn't expected.

Two weeks ago, Aunt Clara had laid in that big white hospital bed in Jacksonville, taken Daisy's hand in one of hers, Cousin Emma's in the other, and said, "I only ask one thing of you two girls. That you don't let my family legacy crumble into the sea. It's time I faced facts. I'm too sick and too old to get back to running the B&B, so I'm handing you girls the keys."

And now Daisy was here in Rescue Bay, and hoping that if she got started, Emma would follow along. Turned out, though, that Aunt Clara's "family legacy" needed more than just a spit and polish to get it back up and running. Nine years of being empty had damaged the wooden building housing the Hideaway Inn. The building had suffered serious storm and saltwater damage, along with plumbing and electrical issues, according to the contractor she'd had look at the place. Which meant money—something that wasn't growing on trees or sprouting leaves in Daisy's paltry wallet.

With Aunt Clara already financially strapped and Emma refusing to have anything to do with the inn, that left Daisy to come up with a miracle. For the first time in Daisy's life, she needed someone else's help to get what she wanted. Specifically, Colt Harper's help.

If your husband signs off on the loan, the banker had said, *I could get this approved without a problem.*

The banker apparently didn't know Colt. Or know that anything between her and Colt came wrapped with a double-knotted problem bow. Which was what had had her blasting into his office like a pissed-off hornet, because she'd seen the divorce papers and panicked.

Without a husband, she had zero chance at the loan. And without the loan, she had zero chance at fulfilling Aunt Clara's wish. There was too much at stake to let that happen.

When she'd applied for the loan, Daisy had had no idea she was still married to Colt, or still connected via credit reports. It had taken her a good thirty seconds to process the words from the banker.

Your husband.

Her potential financial anchor, too. Assuming, that was, that she could convince him to cosign for the loan. Considering the way she'd burst into his office today, she hadn't exactly won him over with honey. She needed to try again, but in a calm, collected manner. Or something close to that, considering nothing about Daisy Barton had ever been calm or collected. Either way, before she disturbed that particular hornet's nest again, Daisy decided to see firsthand what she was getting herself into.

Daisy left her car keys on the scarred, rickety wood laminate nightstand—that Toyota was on its last breath as it was—and changed into comfortable flats, then headed outside. The warm sun hit her like a wave, and she turned her face to greet it. She closed her eyes, and thought if heaven had a temperature, this was it.

She started walking, inhaling the sweet salty tang of the ocean air, marveling at the palm trees and bright flowering shrubs that lined the streets, the way everything was so green and bright and pretty. For the first time in a long time, Daisy was filled with hope. Hope that things could be truly different—that *she* would be truly different.

Oh, how she had missed this place.

Daisy hadn't been back to Rescue Bay in more than a dozen years. Her one stay here—that wonderful, crazy, amazing summer she'd spent at the inn—had been the best summer of Daisy's life. For a little while, her world had been perfect, normal, and she'd thought—

No, *prayed*, that it would last.

Then Willow had pulled up in her beat-up Lincoln to uproot Daisy like a dandelion hiding among the roses. Daisy had never returned to the Hideaway. The following summer, Uncle Lou had died and Aunt Clara had moved back to Jacksonville. The Hideaway had withered away, managed from afar by a woman who couldn't face carrying on the business without her husband.

Despite all the time that had passed, Daisy still remembered the route to the inn. Her feet took the same streets, made the same turns. Even though the landscape had changed, populated with more houses and more businesses, the route felt as familiar as her own hand.

She rounded the corner onto Gulfview Boulevard. The Gulf of Mexico spread before her in all its glistening blue glory, enticing, warm, gently whooshing in and out against the sandy beach. To her left lay the boardwalk that made up most of the touristy area of Rescue Bay. An ice cream shop, bakery, coffee shop, and T-shirt store sat in squat, sherbert-colored buildings, their doors propped open to catch the ocean breeze.

Daisy turned right, passing a long line of tall palm trees, their fronds swaying like lazy hula dancers in the breeze. Around the next curve in the road lay the Hideaway Inn. Daisy stopped walking, tugged her phone out of her pocket, then dialed a number she knew as well as her own. A moment later, the connection was answered. "I'm almost to the inn. And I wanted to share the moment I saw it again with you, even though you're not, well, technically here."

Emma let out a long sigh. "We've had this discussion, Dase."

"Come on, don't you miss the place, just a little?"

"No." Emma bit off the word, succinct and cold. There'd been a time when Emma had loved the Hideaway as much as Daisy. Then something had changed, something Emma wouldn't talk about, a dark shadow she kept behind closed doors, and she'd never returned. Daisy had thought about coming to the Hideaway over the years, but knew it would never be the same, not without Emma.

Had Daisy made a mistake? She'd been so sure that if she

just took the bull by the horns and came here, getting the renovation wheels spinning, so to speak, that Emma would follow.

"We used to have so much fun here, Em," Daisy said. "Don't you remember that summer we spent on the beach? The—"

"Daisy, I'm not interested in that place. I don't know why my mother thinks I should be. It's a family albatross. All it did was drag my grandparents down, then my parents when they took it over, and now it's got you wrapped up in its tentacles." She let out a low curse under her breath. "Why are you so intent on getting it up and running again?"

"Because Aunt Clara asked us to."

Emma sighed. "I know that, and for the life of me, I can't figure out why. You would think my mother would just let that place go after . . . everything."

"What do you mean? Aunt Clara loves the Hideaway."

"*Used* to love it," Emma said. "Now it's just . . ."

"Just what?" Daisy sensed that shadow again, the closed door. She waited, but Emma didn't explain.

"It's just another disaster," Emma said. "Do you know how much work it needs?" Daisy turned the corner and for a moment, she saw the old Hideaway Inn, the two stories of sky blue siding with soft white trim, the wide front porch that stretched from one end to the other, the lush green lawn, the gauzy kitchen curtains drifting lazily in the breeze. Then the mirage cleared and she saw the reality.

A faded building with broken shutters dangling like missing teeth in a welterweight's smile. The lush lawn had gone brown and dead. The kitchen windows were boarded up, and the front porch sagged to one side.

"One hundred and ninety-two thousand dollars worth of work," Daisy said and let out a sigh. She'd been hoping the contractor had been wrong, that maybe he'd overestimated, to scare her off from such a giant project. "I got an estimate."

Though seeing the inn now, Daisy had to wonder if the contractor had instead *under*estimated. A lot. The vacation retreat she remembered from childhood had become a sad, rundown ghost.

"You did? When?"

"I called someone the day I left the hospital. I told you I was serious about this, Em."

Emma laughed. "Dase, I've known you all my life. You've never been serious about anything. I'm the one who overanalyzes and overschedules and over-everythings. You're the one who lives on the edge."

Emma was right. Maybe it had been a part of being raised in an untraditional house. Maybe her mother had instilled some kind of wanderlust or need for spontaneity in her only child. Daisy had dropped out of school at seventeen, got her GED at twenty, but had flitted from job to job all her life. She'd never lived in one apartment long enough to celebrate two holidays. She didn't balance her checkbook, didn't bake cookies, didn't make friends with the neighbors.

And yet, here she was, in a town as traditional as turkey on Thanksgiving. Trying to be a dependable, mortgage-paying, tax-filing grown-up.

"Even if we wanted to fix up the Hideaway, where are we supposed to get *two hundred* grand?" Emma asked. "That place has sucked my mom's bank account dry. What money she had left from when she and my dad took over for my grandparents was wiped away in the years that she let it go."

"I'm working on getting a loan, Em. We can get it up and running, just like it was before. Don't you remember how much fun we had here? How for a little while, everything was"—Daisy took in the depressing sight before her, and tried her best to remember the way the inn used to be—"perfect?"

"Daisy, you're living in a fairy tale. Nothing is ever perfect." Emma's voice held low, sad notes. "Not one place, not one person."

"Emma—"

"I can't do this. I'm sorry," Emma said. "I . . . I just can't."

The connection ended, leaving Daisy with silence. She stared up at the inn, seeing the bright, cheery building that had once housed two girls on the brink of being women, two girls who had believed in fairy tales and princes on white horses. The inn held a special magic, Daisy had always believed, and if she could restore it to its former glory, maybe Emma would find that magic again, too.

That meant Daisy needed that loan. And if the money wasn't going to come to her, she was going to go get it. No matter what it took. Or who it meant asking.

Three

"You . . . are gonna . . . kill yourself. Or . . . me." Nick Patterson bent at the waist and heaved in a few deep breaths. Sweat poured from his brow, plastered his faded gray T-shirt to his chest. "Jesus, Colt, what's . . . with you . . . today?"

"Nothing." Colt stepped back, aimed his shot, and let the ball fly toward the netless hoop. It missed its target, pinging off the battered orange rim and bouncing outside the chalked foul line. Colt's concentration had been zero all day, ever since Daisy came storming into his office, disrupting his life. He'd hoped a few rounds of hoops with Nick would ease this tension in his gut, but so far, the frustrating game was having the opposite effect. "Damn it."

Nick jerked to the right, grabbed the ball on a rebound, but didn't shoot. His childhood friend stood a few inches taller than Colt. On the court, Nick had the height advantage, but most days, Colt moved faster, which made for nicely competitive games. On the days when Colt's mind was on basketball, that was.

"Nothing's wrong? Bullshit." Nick tucked the ball under one arm. "Is it your grandpa again? My grandpa's been asking about Earl. Said something about missing him at the card games lately."

"It's not my grandpa." Colt put out his hand. "Just throw me the ball, Nick."

"I will when you tell me why you are turning a friendly game of one-on-one into a death match."

Colt swiped off the sweat beading on his forehead, then crossed to the sidelines and grabbed a bottle of water out of the cooler. He twisted off the top, handed it to Nick, and grabbed a second for himself. The two men sat on the old, faded bench and faced the pockmarked basketball court that had long ago been forgotten by Rescue Bay's teenagers.

He and Nick had been coming to this court for twenty-plus years, to shoot a few hoops and talk, in the way that guys talked—between beers and points. Of all the people in Rescue Bay, Nick was the only one who had known Colt all his life. They'd suffered through the same parochial school in a nearby town, lived on the same block, and fished the same lake with their grandfathers. And when Colt had needed a friend, needed someone who wouldn't judge him or condemn him—

Nick had been there.

Colt took a long swig of water and waited for the cool liquid to slide down his throat. "It's Daisy."

The water bottle popped out of Nick's mouth. "Daisy? As in . . . *Daisy*? Holy shit. Now there's a blast from the past."

"And apparently a blast into the present, too. She's in town. I found out when she came roaring into my office earlier today when I was with a patient. Pissed off as all hell, and ready to rip me a new one."

Nick chuckled. "Sounds like your entire marriage. As short-lived as it was."

Colt snorted and took another swig of water. "You can say that again."

"Well, that sure as hell explains why you're killing yourself on the court. Working off a little frustration?"

"Just a little." Understatement of the year. Seeing Daisy

again had woken a beast inside his gut, the same one that had sent him straight to her bed when he'd seen her in New Orleans. There was something about Daisy Barton. Something irresistible. Exactly why he should try to avoid her. Quit thinking about her. And most of all, talking about her.

Yeah, and look how that plan was going so far.

Colt got to his feet, picked up the ball, went to line up his shot, then stopped. All he saw in his head was Daisy's curves, Daisy's lips, just . . . Daisy. He shook his head.

"Damn it. I don't want to think about her," he said more to himself than to his friend.

Nick put down the water bottle and crossed in front of Colt. He bent at the knees, and fanned out his hands, shifting his weight back and forth, playing defense, waiting on Colt's next move. "Give me one good reason why any straight man with a pulse wouldn't think about Daisy in some seriously unholy ways."

"Because we're not getting involved again. Or ever." Colt dribbled a few times, stepped right, lined up again. Focus on the ball, on the shot, instead of on one horrific day fourteen years ago. A day when Colt realized what happened when he put himself ahead of those he loved. He wouldn't do it again. "Daisy and I are like iron pills and milk. The two don't work well together. At all."

Nick swiped the ball out of Colt's hands, pivoted, then sent the ball sailing through the basket. "Only you would turn a conversation about Daisy, who is, I have to say, one of the hottest-looking women God ever put on earth, into a lecture about multivitamins."

Because if Colt thought of Daisy in terms of RDAs of ferritin and calcium, maybe it wouldn't make him drive over to the Rescue Bay Inn and finish what they had started back in New Orleans. Wouldn't make him want to tangle himself again with the one woman on earth who drove him crazy, in more ways than one. The one woman who made him forget his responsibilities and his promises. No. Never again.

"I already learned my lesson," Colt said. "I married her, remember?"

"So? Doesn't mean you can't do it better now that you're older, wiser." Nick grabbed the rebounding ball, made another three-pointer, as easy as tossing pennies into a pond. "More experienced."

"Apparently not wiser. Turns out"—Colt stepped in, grabbed the ball, and pivoted in front of Nick—"I'm still married to her."

The ball pinged off the rim and back into Nick's hands. He didn't dribble, didn't shoot. Just stared at Colt, mouth agape. "What the hell? *Still* married? How's that?"

"When we got divorced, someone didn't finish filing the paperwork." Colt shrugged.

"Someone . . . like you?"

Colt gave a half nod. He'd always prided himself on being organized and detail oriented, but when it came to Daisy, all those little charts and checklists flew out the window. They'd been in a rush to get married, and he'd been in a rush to get divorced. Apparently such a rush that he hadn't made sure the paperwork got to the courthouse. Some psychologist would probably call it a Freudian desire to stay attached to Daisy or something, but Colt would disagree.

"I was young and stupid then," he said, echoing Daisy's words.

It was more than that, but Colt didn't want to talk about it. He never talked about the day he returned to Rescue Bay, and found the family he had left behind, the family he had been in such a rush to leave, irreparably destroyed. Because of one foolish decision. Because of Colt's selfish choices.

Will you be here, Colt, when I get back?

Of course. I'm always here for you, buddy.

A grin, then a light jab to his arm. *You're a good big brother.*

You're not so bad yourself, for a pesky little brother.

Laughter, always laughter. When Colt's thoughts wandered to Henry, they were filled with the merry sound of Henry's laughter. Then, just as quickly, that laughter evaporated and a hollow, aching pain filled the spaces in Colt's heart.

Because Colt hadn't been there. He'd broken his promise, and Henry had been the one to pay the price.

He'd thrown himself into making amends from that day forward, but it hadn't been enough. Would never be enough. He sucked in a breath, but it didn't ease the searing pain in his heart. Damn it, why did Daisy have to come back here? Just seeing her reopened a wound that had never healed.

"You've never been someone who missed a paperwork deadline, or had so much as a file folder out of place," Nick said, dragging Colt back into the present. "How did you miss something as important as your *divorce*?"

Colt reached for the ball. "Come on, we gonna play or what?"

Nick circled the ball around to his back. "I think you've got some subconscious desire to stay with Daisy."

The last thing he needed was Nick playing pop psychologist. "Of course not. It was a mistake, plain and simple. I was busy then. It was right after—"

Nick's features softened. "Yeah. I forgot it was at the same time. No wonder you forgot to file."

Colt shrugged, and let out a long, slow breath, until his chest stopped aching and he could pretend he wasn't affected by any of it anymore. "Either way, I thought I was divorced all these years. Then I ran into her a few months ago—"

"Whoa. Hold on, cowboy. You never told me you saw her a few months ago."

Okay, so maybe he hadn't shared *everything* with his best friend. "I was at a medical convention, and she was working at a diner I stopped at. One thing led to another and . . ." Colt reached for the ball, but Nick whisked it away again. "Anyway, when I got home, I realized I never did get a copy of my final divorce decree, so I called my lawyer and found out I hadn't filed way back when."

"Why would seeing Daisy make you think of your divorce decree? Oh, wait, I know." Nick held the ball out of Colt's reach, half taunting him. "Because you were dating Maryanne."

"And considering marrying her." Until Maryanne had

broken up with him to move back to Tulsa and date her high school sweetheart. At the time, Colt had been more relieved than disappointed, which surprised him. He'd always thought Maryanne would be the perfect doctor's wife. Tidy, good-natured, organized.

And not a woman who lit a fire in his belly or made him forget details. Made him lose focus. Just the fact that seeing Daisy in that diner had put Maryanne far from his mind should have been a clue that the quiet, introverted insurance adjuster he'd been dating wasn't Miss Right. Maybe that was what the night with Daisy had been about—a test for him to see if he was making the right choice with Maryanne.

When the answer was already there before he'd even walked into Nero's and said hello to Daisy.

Nick mocked a yawn. "Maryanne is a nice woman and all, but if you ask me, it'd be like an eighteenth-century marriage. All tea and embroidery and *how was your day, dear.*"

"And what's wrong with that?"

"What's *right* with that? Who wants to come home and stare at each other every night? What you want is a woman who makes you break the land-speed record to get home. A woman who drives you crazy, in a good way."

Colt snorted. "And have you met any women like that?"

"Hell no. Which is why I'm still single." He raised his hands and gave the ball an easy push, up and over and into the net. "And still beating your ass at basketball."

"Lucky shot." Like the first ten shots had been. And the five before that.

Colt had a lot on his mind, that was all. With any luck, Daisy would leave town by the end of the week, and he could get back to focusing on his patients and his grandfather. On getting all those straight lines back into alignment. Uh-huh. As long as he stayed at least one state away from Daisy Barton, maybe that would work.

"Just admit it." Nick stepped forward, retrieved the ball, gave it a bounce, and aimed at the basket again.

"Admit what?"

"That you still like Daisy." Nick shot an easy layup that swooshed through the hoop. "Heck, maybe still love her."

"When did I ever say I loved her?"

Nick arched a brow. "When you ran off and eloped with her?"

"That was the insane decision of a couple of teenagers. It wasn't about love."

"If you say so." Nick caught the ball again. "All I know is that your game is off and your mind is somewhere else. I'd bet a year's salary that *somewhere* is with a gorgeous brunette. Either way, the ball is now in your court." He pressed the ball into Colt's hands. "Don't waste the last good shot you have."

Four

"What on God's green earth is *that*?"

Esther glanced up from the pile of brown yarn in her lap and gave Greta a quizzical look. Esther's purple polka-dotted granny glasses perched at a precarious angle on the bridge of her nose, as if they wanted to swan dive into the bodice of her neon paisley housedress.

"What is what?" Esther asked.

"That." Greta waved at the tangled, stringy mess. Esther and Greta were sitting in the morning room while Greta sipped a mug of bourbon-spiked coffee and Esther worked her one-woman craft fair. "It looks like a dog died in your lap."

"Well, it is a dog. But he's not dead. He's just not finished." Esther grinned and held up a flat four-legged knitted Frankenpupster. "It's a knit-your-own-dog kit. Once I finish knitting Rooney here, I'll stuff him, and voila, a pet."

Oh Lord, Esther really was beginning to lose it. So sad to see her friends slip into early dementia. "Esther dear, it's a stuffed animal. The kind of thing three-year-olds play with."

Esther pouted. "Rooney is more than that. He's a low-maintenance pet. You'll see. As soon as I'm done with

Rooney, you're going to want one of your very own. I can make a golden retriever or a Lhasa apso or—"

"My sweet Greta doesn't need a pet of her own. Not when she has me to keep her company." Harold Twohig's overly minty, hot-as-lava breath trickled down the side of Greta's head. Lord Almighty, that man sprang out of nowhere, like a spider slithering under the floorboards. She spun around and shot him a glare.

"There's a law against stalking, you know. And sneaking up on old ladies who were busy. Very busy."

He just grinned, the damned fool.

"Go back to your cave, Harold." Greta waved in the general direction of the exit. Any exit. Preferably one that led to Mars.

Harold leaned back and crossed his arms over his chest. He gave Greta a long, assessing look, followed by a toothy smile. "Is that all you've got today? I have to say, I'm a little disappointed."

"You want me to be meaner?"

"The harder you try to insult me, Greta dear," Harold said, reaching down to lay a sweaty palm against her cheek for a brief second, "the more I know you care."

She started to huff out a response, but Harold just turned on his past-Labor-Day white golf shoes and headed out of the morning room. Greta resisted the urge to throw Esther's half-stuffed dead dog after him and let it smack Harold in the back of his oversized egg head.

"Harold sure does like you, Greta," Esther said, her gaze on the knitting needles and giant skein of brown yarn working together in furious movements. "I don't see why you keep resisting his attentions."

Greta signaled to the waitstaff for a fresh cup of coffee. Lord knew she was going to need one. Not to mention a second jigger full of the supplemental beverage tucked in the pocket of her sweater. "Esther, I do not cavort with evil, especially in human form."

Pauline hurried up to the table in her usual cyclone of stuff. She dumped her purse, coat, and hat into a chair, followed by a set of keys, a bundle of newspapers, and a thick manila envelope. It all poured out of her arms and into a teetering mountain that dwarfed the high-backed chair. Every time Pauline entered a room, she was like a passel of clowns exploding from a VW bug.

"Who's evil in a human form?" Pauline said.

"Harold Twohig." The words burned past Greta's lips. Why did the man insist on plaguing her so? She didn't have the stomach for him. Not today. Heck, not any day.

"You say his name with such vehemence," Pauline said. "And here I thought you two were getting along."

Pauline slipped into a cushioned seat across from Esther and her growing bundle of furry yarn. Esther kept on knitting away, a woman on a mission to fill her tiny Golden Years apartment with a faux menagerie.

"Harold and I never got along," Greta said. "I merely formed a temporary alliance with that spawn of Satan so I could work some magic between Diana and Mike. As painful as it was to be in Harold's presence, it warms my heart to see those two engaged."

Two happy endings already this year. Her grandson Luke and darling Olivia, set to get married next month. Now Luke's friend Mike and Olivia's sister Diana, engaged and setting up house together in Rescue Bay with Mike's adorable little girls. At the end of the day, that was the kind of thing that gave Greta comfort and told her that when her time to go came, she'd be leaving a legacy of happily ever afters.

Except for Edward. Her only child had yet to do so much as glance in the direction of any of the women Greta had tried to set him up with. He'd been widowed so long, it was as if he'd forgotten how to date. She worried about her son, and about him living the rest of his days as a workaholic hermit.

Pauline cleared her throat. "Speaking of Harold—"

Greta grimaced.

"Did he say if Earl was joining the guys for their card game today?"

"I didn't ask, Pauline. I try never to talk to Harold.

Especially immediately after eating." Greta leaned in and eyed Pauline. "Why do you care what Earl Harper is doing today?"

"No reason. I was just hoping to get a chance to pick his brain. My Cadillac is acting up a bit and I thought he might know why."

"The man's retired, Pauline. Let him live in peace."

"I'll run by the garage this afternoon instead." Pauline retrieved the envelope from the chair, and undid the metal clasp. "Okay, girls. Time for us to get to work. I've got the latest letters for our Common Sense Carla column. Let me read a few and we can decide which one we're going to tackle this week. We have several doozies in this batch. I'm thinking a secret lover would be good to spice things up."

"I like the idea of a secret lover. Or spouse." Greta grinned.

Pauline shuffled through the stack of letters in the envelope and pulled out a pale blue sheet. In the year the three women had been writing the local advice column, they'd covered the gamut of topics. Several local papers were carrying the Common Sense Carla column now—part of Esther's attempt at world domination. Either way, Greta enjoyed helping with the column, if only because it provided a ready excuse for some meddling—well-meaning, of course. That gave her another reason to get out of bed in the morning, and at Greta's age, sometimes that required the addition of a good shove and an industrial crane.

"I don't see a secret spouse letter," Pauline said. "I have a woman secretly in love with her irritating neighbor. What about that?"

Greta yanked the paper out of Pauline's scrawny hand. "That would only give other people ideas."

"Like the idea that *you* wrote it?" Pauline grinned.

"Lord, no." Greta put up her hands to ward off the idea. "Why would I write such a thing?"

"Who would Greta be secretly in love with?" Esther asked.

Pauline rolled her eyes. "Esther, you really need to pay more attention."

"I can't. I'm knitting. There's a lot of counting involved. Or Rooney will end up with one leg longer than the other."

Pauline looked at Greta. "Rooney?"

"Don't ask. Trust me, you don't want to know." Greta shook her head. One of the waitstaff came over with a trio of coffee mugs, deposited them in front of the ladies, then left. As soon as the nurses weren't looking, Greta tugged the bottle of Maker's Mark out of her pocket, unscrewed the top, and added a little sweetness to her coffee. Esther tsk-tsked. Pauline bit back a laugh.

Greta ignored them both. Her daddy had started every day with a little shot of the hard stuff, and he'd lived to ninety-seven, which made all the case Greta needed for her morning Maker's Mark. Clearly, there were some things about longevity that Doc Harper didn't know. "Before we get to our next letter, I think we need to discuss our next mission."

"Mission? That sounds dangerous," Esther said. "I'm too old for dangerous."

"You are also too old for a stuffed dog, but that sure as sunshine isn't stopping you today."

Esther stuck out her tongue at Greta, then went back to work on Frankenpup. Pauline mouthed *stuffed dog*? Greta just shook her head. Esther was a hopeless case when it came to crafts. The only plus to Esther's knitting frenzy was that she'd forgotten all about her quilting fetish. Which kept Greta from having to pretend she liked quilting just so she could sit at quilting club and drink bourbon.

"We have a new resident in Rescue Bay," Greta began. "And I'm thinking she should be our next project."

"Wait. I thought we were looking for a mission." Esther blinked. "Now we have a project, too? I have my hands full of projects, if you need one, Greta. Why there's a cross-stitch I started back in 1982 that—"

"Mission. Project. Same thing. And the day I do cross-stitch is the day you shoot me in the head, Esther."

"I thought you said that about the day you kiss Harold Twohig." Pauline gave Greta a grin.

Greta's cheeks flamed. She pressed a palm to her stomach.

Just the thought of that man made her inner workings churn like a lethal case of indigestion. Okay, yes, maybe they had shared a single, solitary, *almost* kiss. Thankfully thwarted at the last second by Greta's quick thinking. Didn't change a thing about how she despised Harold Twohig and his over-zealous stalking. Even if he did seem to be growing on her, like invasive ivy on a brick facade. "You have a way of making even my morning coffee taste horrible, Pauline."

Pauline's gaze narrowed. "I'll bet dollars to donuts that you have an ulterior motive in this little project."

"My only ulterior motive is to keep our little local economy rolling along. I'm just doing my part."

Pauline snorted, a sound that was just south of a curse. "Okay, so what's your mission? And how exactly does it help the 'local economy'?" She put air quotes around the last two words.

Greta took a long sip of coffee while she weighed her next words. She was in possession of some very interesting information—information that Doc Harper definitely didn't want shared—and she wanted to be smart about when or if she used it. Perhaps the next time the man prescribed vegetables, she'd remind him of what a good friend she'd been, not telling about his secret wife. But that didn't mean she couldn't hint at the truth. "I think our new resident knows Doc Harper, from way back. And that means that maybe our next happy ending could be his. Which means we get a new taxpayer in town, and maybe some future taxpayers in another nine months or so."

"I thought you hated Doc Harper," Pauline said. "I've always liked him, personally. He's a smart cookie. And after all he and his family have been through, too. I don't blame his parents for moving away. Where'd they go again?"

"Arizona, I think," Esther said. "To live with the cactuses. Or is it cacti?"

Greta waved off Esther's plural debate. "What are you talking about, Pauline?"

"Don't you remember? When Doc Harper was just a kid himself, his little brother died. Some kind of tragic accident, though I don't recall what. Six months later, the Harpers up and moved to—"

"Tucson," Esther cut in. "With the cacti."

"And Doc was here by himself," Pauline said. "I guess that's when he went to college, got his degree, all that business."

Greta had forgotten about that. Used to be, she knew every single thing that happened in this town. Now, her brain had become a sieve, sprouting more holes every day. "That must have been a long time ago."

Pauline nodded. "At least twelve years, maybe more."

"Poor Doc Harper," Esther chimed in. "That's probably why he has such a lovely bedside manner. Plus he has the sweetest eyes, don't you think?"

"I think if he's happy, then he's not going to be such a fussbudget when it comes time for my checkups," Greta said. Maybe all this past history explained why Doc Harper was such a stickler for healthy living. Either way, it would be a good idea to keep him smiling. "And in the end, a happy ending for Doc Harper is really . . ."

"A happy ending for you," Pauline finished. She sat back in her chair and laughed. "Why would I expect anything else from you, Greta dear?"

"I'm just trying to be neighborly, Pauline. If I happen to benefit out of all this . . ." She sipped her coffee and thought of her daddy for a moment and how he had always been the first to offer a helping hand, a listening ear, or just an ice-cold beer when a neighbor was in trouble. She hoped he'd be proud of her, continuing a legacy of helping others, in her own little way. "Well, that's just a bow tie on the package of life, isn't it?"

Five

A squat blue coffee cup whipped by Colt's head, so fast and so close, it made his hair flicker. The words *Fishermen Hook 'Em Faster* spiraled by in a blur, before the nearly empty mug crashed into the wall and shattered on the tile floor. The cup fractured into an alphabet soup, and the remaining dregs of coffee bloomed a brown daisy onto the beige wall. "Grandpa, what the hell—"

"I told you I'm not going for any more tests. Quit making those damned appointments." Grandpa Earl stood in the kitchen and hoisted the cordless phone by one end, like a snake he'd yanked out of the garden. Even at eighty-two, Earl Harper had the same wiry frame and close-cropped hair of his military days, but age and illness had stooped his posture and hollowed the contours of his face. His dark hair had gone gray, nearly white, and his blue eyes had softened to a pale sky.

Grandpa Earl, once a man who Colt had thought could beat anything, conquer any obstacle, was sick. Early onset Parkinson's, coupled with the gradual wear down of congestive heart failure, had eroded the hearty Earl Harper, a little more every day. Something Grandpa had refused to accept.

Hell, even Colt was having trouble with the concept, and he was the one who had made the initial diagnosis.

Colt sighed. "Grandpa, you need to at least see a specialist. I'm a general practitioner. Not an expert in Parkinson's or heart disease."

"I don't need an expert. I know what's wrong with me." Earl scowled. "So leave me be, will you?"

"At least get out of the house once in a while." Colt loosened his tie, tucked his glasses in his pocket. "Go back to the card games at Golden Years. Nick said his grandpa was asking about you."

"That rat bastard. The day I play cards with him is the day I roll over and die. And don't start asking me why. I don't need to talk about it or get my feelings on the table or any such Dr. Phil foolishness. What I need is to be left the hell alone." Grandpa Earl tossed the phone onto the counter, then crossed to the living room and returned to his seat in the ugly La-Z-Boy recliner that sat in direct line with the television screen. With a grunted exclamation point, Grandpa pulled the lever and flipped out the footrest. The brown leather chair had seen better days—hell, better decades—and sported duct tape bandages on all major appendages. Grandpa's La-Z-Boy had been in Earl's house on Bayberry Lane for as long as Colt could remember. When Colt insisted his grandfather give up the old, rundown house and move into Colt's bungalow, the chair had been the one non-negotiable on Grandpa's list.

As much as he hated that hideous chair, Colt had agreed. Grandpa Earl needed to be in a safer environment, one where Colt could be sure that his elderly grandfather was getting the care he needed. Care that involved making sure he took his medications every day, and ate three squares. Colt had thought it would be easy.

He'd been wrong. Grandpa Earl had never been one for convention, and apparently not one for following doctor's orders—especially when that doctor was his grandson. Hence the coffee shrapnel. Right beside the dent in the wall from yesterday's soup bowl. And the triangular hole made by Colt's iPad the day before.

When Colt had been a kid, Grandpa Earl had been the closest thing to a parental role model in Colt's life. Grandpa had taken Colt and his brother fishing, taught the boys how to tie a gossamer thin line into a lure, how to reel in a silvery-green bass before it slipped the hook, and how to have patience as the sun marched lazily across the sky and the fish hovered beneath the lake's placid surface. His grandfather had served two decades in the military, then worked forty-five years under a hood, fixing anything with an engine, until he was forced to retire when he lost his grip on his tools and his patience.

Then Grandma Nancy had died a little over a year ago, and the busy, brimming life that Grandpa Earl had once had ground to a halt, except for the weekly card games with Walt Patterson, which came to an abrupt end earlier in the year. From that day forward, Grandpa Earl had fully withdrawn into a hermit-like life, ignoring medical advice and doctor recommendations. As his illness progressed and loneliness took over the four-bedroom house where he and Nancy had raised their sons, the once vital, energetic grandfather Colt had known slipped away.

There were days when Colt would do anything to get those moments back. To have one last fishing trip, one last memory on the banks of the Whistler's Lake. One last day of wisdom and laughter, the kind of days Colt had never treasured—until they were gone.

Because of Colt's mistakes. Mistakes Grandpa had never forgiven. For fourteen years, Colt had been doing his level best to atone, but the wall remained between Colt and Grandpa Earl. Two stubborn men, hurting in their own ways, and refusing to be the first to yield.

Colt laid his briefcase by the door, dropped his keys into the wooden bowl on the credenza. He bit back a comment about the dirty dishes littering the kitchen counter and table, the empty ice cream container sitting beside, instead of in,

the trash. In the weeks since Grandpa Earl had moved in
with Colt, the daily silent battle between them about maintaining order had grown in proportion. It wasn't an argument
Colt wanted to have today. Or any day. "Grandpa, I'm not
trying to hurt you—"

"No, worse. You're trying to kill me. I don't need any of
those fancy medicines you keep trying to shove down my
throat. And I don't need to be living here, like a prisoner on
death row. Let me go back to my own house and my own
ways of treating these damned shakes."

The house his Grandpa had no longer been able to main-
tain on his own was now on the market, but Colt chose not to
remind Grandpa of that fact. "Those shakes are called Parkinson's, Grandpa. There are medications that can help and
treatments that can ease the symptoms. You can't just—"

"I can and I will. It's a free goddamn country. Something
you'd know if you'd gone to war, like I did, instead of going
to that fancy college." Grandpa thumbed the remote and
turned up the volume until Alex Trebek's voice boomed in
the tiny space.

That fancy college had given Colt a medical degree,
something his grandfather conveniently ignored every time
the subject of his failing health came up. What was that
saying about *physician, heal thyself*? Right now, Colt was
having a hell of a time just *healing thy family*.

The doorbell rang, cutting off Colt's next argument.
Didn't matter. Some days, it felt like he was just rehashing
the words from the day before. Maybe he was crazy for trying
to restore the past—for trying to get close again to the man
who blamed Colt for the death of his youngest grandchild.
Hell, Colt still blamed himself.

If he couldn't find a way to forgive himself, how could
he expect to find a way for Grandpa to do the same?

The doorbell rang again, and Colt shook off the thoughts.
Grandpa gestured toward the door with a remote. "I bet
that's the pizza I ordered for dinner. Thank God."

Pizza? Again? After the Chinese food yesterday and subs
the day before? Seemed like Grandpa had every delivery

place in a ten-mile radius on speed dial. Colt threw up his hands. "What are you ordering pizza for? I had a perfectly healthy dinner planned."

"Let me guess. More rubber chicken and tasteless broccoli?" Grandpa scoffed. "I'd rather chew off my own hand."

"That can be arranged," Colt muttered. He crossed to the door, debating whether to send the pizza guy away or just buy a few moments of peace with a large pepperoni. But when he pulled open the front door, he found something far more tempting and dangerous standing on his front stoop. Colt sucked in a breath, told himself he wasn't at all rocked by the sight of Daisy on his front step, looking radiant in a bright yellow dress that flared at the waist and showed off shapely legs that could erase a man's willpower in the blink of an eye. "Daisy. What are you doing here?"

Gee, way to start with a stellar conversational opener. He'd basically just repeated what he'd said earlier.

"I handled our first meeting poorly and I wanted to try talking to you again," she said. "Calmly this time."

Colt heard the TV volume descend, followed by the click of the La-Z-Boy's footrest going down, then the shuffle of his grandfather's feet on the tile floor. "Is that my pizza?"

"No, Grandpa, it's not. It's . . ." Colt hesitated. How to describe Daisy? *Friend* didn't fit, neither did *wife*. *Trouble* might be more apt, but that would open a door to questions that Colt didn't want to answer. "Someone here to see me."

She glanced at the coffee cup shards. "Uh, is this a bad time?"

"No, no . . . it's fine." Colt started to step through the door and usher Daisy out onto the porch, when he saw a familiar hand grip the door frame above his head.

"You didn't tell me this someone was a woman. Invite her in, boy, before someone scoops her up and you're left holding nothing but your regrets in one hand and your Johnson in the other."

Daisy arched a brow and covered up a laugh. Colt rolled his eyes. "Grandpa!"

Grandpa sidled around Colt's side and stuck out a hand.

"I'm Earl Harper. Colt's grandfather. The friendlier Harper man."

Colt snorted.

Daisy smiled, a smile that Colt knew could sock a man in the gut and leave him weak in the knees. "Nice to meet you. I'm Daisy. Colt's—"

"Friend," Colt supplied. At least until he came up with a better alternative to describe their complicated, on/off relationship. Something with less than ten syllables.

"Friend," Daisy affirmed.

Somehow, hearing the word coming from Daisy made his gut ache. Just friends was what he wanted, wasn't it? Exes who remained on friendly terms, friendly enough to sleep together three months ago? Friendly enough that she lingered in his mind like a favorite song stuck on repeat? Or friendly enough that they'd send a Christmas card each year, maybe check in once in a while on social media?

Yes, *complicated* was the word for it.

"Well, come in, come in," Grandpa said. "It's been so damned long since we had any company here, I thought we were living on the moon. We're having pizza, if you're hungry."

"Oh, I'm not staying long. I just needed to talk to Colt for a minute."

Grandpa waved that off. "It's near supper time. Come in, have a few bites. I promise to be sociable, though I can't say the same for my grumpy grandson."

"*I'm* the grumpy one?" Colt said. And what was up with Grandpa Earl? Since when did he want company? Or make jokes? Maybe it was a diversionary tactic. To keep Colt from focusing on the canceled doctor's appointment and the roughage revolution. "Grandpa, I think—"

"Why, would you lookie there. My pizza. Right on time." Grandpa waved at a beat-up two-door Chevy jerking its way up the drive. A faded RAY'S PIZZA sign sat askew on the roof. "Give him a good tip, Colt, will you?"

Colt reached for his wallet. It was either that or send the pizza guy away and right now, that was a battle Colt didn't want to have. Grandpa had stopped throwing coffee cups and that was reason enough to relent on the pizza. "Seems my grandfather is sticking me with the bill for his dietary indiscretions."

Daisy grinned. "As far as indiscretions go, I'd have to say pizza is a pretty inexpensive one. Don't you agree?"

Something went hot in Colt's gut. Hotter than any pizza the pimply kid coming up the walk was holding. A few words, and he was rocketed back to the night in the hotel with Daisy, when he'd forgotten his life, his responsibilities, and most of all, his reasons for walking away all those years ago.

He cleared his throat and reminded himself there'd been more than one reason why he and Daisy didn't work outside the bedroom. "Depends on who's footing the bill."

"For God's sake, quit your chatting and start your paying," Grandpa shouted. "My stomach isn't getting any fuller standing here waiting."

Colt fished some money out of his wallet, then exchanged the bills for a large warm cardboard box. The kid thanked him with a grunt, then trotted back down the steps. Loud rock music thumped out of the speakers when he hopped in the car and pulled away.

Daisy laid a hand on Colt's. Just a momentary touch, but it sent a sizzling flicker down his veins. "I should let you have dinner. I'll come back another time."

"Have you eaten?" Colt asked, before he could think about the wisdom of inviting her in. That touch had frazzled his brain. Not to mention what the dress, and that smile of hers, had done to the rest of him.

He was as bad as his patients. He knew what was right for him, what was best for his health and sanity, yet he craved the very woman who made him run from all those smart choices. Insane.

What was it about Daisy Barton that drove him crazy? From the first time he'd seen her, sitting on the steps outside of the Hideaway Inn, she'd invaded his thoughts and his better judgment like honeysuckle.

When Daisy's mother had shown up that summer and whisked Daisy back to her home in Jacksonville, Colt had been unable to focus on anything. College applications, homework assignments, all got forgotten. One day he hopped on his motorcycle, roared up the state, and showed up on her doorstep. Five minutes later, Daisy had her arms clasped tight around his waist and they'd been on their way—to anywhere that they could be together. Back then, his only thought was being with her. Now he was presumably smarter and more grounded. Until he looked at her, and everything inside him flipped again.

"I haven't eaten since lunch when I had something masquerading as meatloaf." Daisy pressed a hand to her belly. "I think that diner next to the motel is a little loose with their descriptions."

Colt chuckled. "The Drop Inn isn't known for its cuisine. It does, however, sport forty-four different beers, which is what brings in most of the local traffic, from what I hear."

"For God's sake, Colton, invite the woman in and quit jabbering on the porch. What kind of host are you, anyway?" Grandpa Earl opened the cabinets, withdrew a trio of plates, and put them on the kitchen table. "Look. I'll even use a napkin this time." He sat in a chair, tugged a napkin out of the holder on the table, and spread it across his lap.

A meal at the table. With Grandpa Earl in something approximating a good mood. That was enough reason to invite Daisy to stay. If she could inspire a good mood in Grandpa, even for a few minutes, it was worth the price Colt would pay to have a momentary peaceful lull in this ongoing battle. A way to forget all the things that Colt did a good job of shoving under the carpet.

"Why don't you stay for dinner? We can talk after we eat," Colt said. She hesitated, so he gave her a smile. "I promise, we don't bite."

"Pity, because I sometimes do." She flashed him a smile that was half vixen, half sex kitten. As Daisy whispered by him in a soft cloud of tempting perfume, Colt had to wonder if he'd invited her in because he wanted his grandfather to behave—

Or because Colt wanted an excuse to misbehave. Again.

Six

The dissolution of Emma Barton Jennings's marriage had been as slow as molasses dripping into a bowl. One day, her relationship with Roger had all been perfect and shiny and wonderful, and then bit by bit, each day, the union that had started so bright began to dim. She'd made one last-ditch effort to resurrect their marriage, a weekend getaway, and instead ended up inadvertently driving the last nail in the coffin. The second they got back, Roger had packed the last of his bags and moved the rest of the way out.

But if there was one thing Emma excelled at, it was maintaining a fiction. She'd done it all her life, and she wasn't about to change now. No one knew Roger had left; no one knew her marriage was on life support. She kept thinking that maybe if she pretended it wasn't happening . . . it wouldn't.

"Hi, Momma." Emma placed a kiss on her mother's cheek, then smoothed the blanket lying across Clara's chest. Her mother was in her favorite spot—on the chaise lounge in the living room, where the big screen TV held court over the fireplace and the sun streamed in from the sliding glass doors leading to the lanai. She'd been home from the hospital in Jacksonville for over a week now, and except for lingering cough and exhaustion, seemed recovered from that scary bout with pneumonia last month. For a while there, Emma hadn't been sure her sixty-year-old mother was strong enough to survive, but in the end, Clara had surprised everyone, including the doctors. "How are you doing today?"

"I'm still breathing. Always a positive." Clara pushed up on the pillows behind her head and sat up straighter. "How's my favorite daughter?"

Emma laughed at the familiar joke. "I'm your only daughter. Always have been, always will be. And Jack is your favorite son, also your only son."

"All the more reason to be my favorites." Clara grabbed Emma's hand and met her daughter's gaze with direct green eyes. Her mother had always had that ability to zero in on any little detail. Maybe that was why Emma had always talked in vague terms about her marriage to Roger. If she dropped even the slightest hint of trouble, her mother would have been all over it. And now . . .

Well now Emma had problems of her own to deal with. Problems she didn't need to add to her mother's plate.

Don't you miss the place, just a little?

Daisy's question came back to Emma, offering a way out, but also a return to the very place where Emma's memories had been destroyed and her mother's heart had been broken. Lord knew why her mother had held on to that place, given what all had happened there. Going to the Hideaway would mean answering Daisy's questions—questions that Emma had yet to answer for herself.

"You didn't answer the question, missy," Momma said, as if reading Emma's mind.

"I'm fine." Emma shrugged. "Roger's getting ready for another school year, so he's been on campus often."

"Which means you're alone a lot and Roger is gone twelve hours a day."

Emma shrugged again, as if it didn't matter. As if she hadn't been alone for months, heck, years. Her husband had used the hectic school years at Jacksonville U as an excuse to spend less and less time at home. Then he started filling up his summers with golf games and research projects, or anything that kept him away. Then he'd landed a book deal after years of writing in his spare time, and he'd disappeared into his office every spare minute he had to work on his novels. He'd become a part-time husband, making an effort just often enough to make Emma believe they still had a chance.

Emma thought of telling her mother about the impending divorce, then decided Clara would worry too much, and end up sick again. Later, when Momma was stronger, and when Emma had figured out what the heck she was going to do with her life. "With Roger busy at school, I get the house to myself again," Emma said, putting on a bright, happy smile that made her cheeks hurt. "I was even thinking of switching to working full-time at the insurance company."

"You hate that job. Besides, I thought you were doing well working on your own, with the photography."

"I need a steady job, Momma, not one that fluctuates between baptisms and bridal season. I can't just sit around all day and stare at the walls." Walls that seemed to close in more every day. Walls that echoed with emptiness, a cavern that had once been a home.

Or had she just been fooling herself all this time?

"You should go down to Rescue Bay and—"

"Momma, I'm not going there. Not while you still need me."

Clara shifted on the lounge and gave her daughter a smile. On the TV, credits rolled over the screen for the movie that had just ended. Outside, the pool glistened in the sun and geckos darted among the shadows beneath the lanai screen.

"I'm just fine," Momma said. "If I need help, I'll call one of my friends or call your aunt Willow, assuming she's back from whatever adventure she's off on now. You go, take care of you. And help Daisy. She can't handle that place all on her own, you know."

Emma tugged a magazine out from the pile on the end table. She flashed the cover in her mother's direction. "Want to see what Kanye and Kim are up to this week? I hear they redecorated the nursery again."

Clara waved that off. "Tell me when *you'll* be decorating a nursery. That's newsworthy."

A weight sank to the pit of Emma's stomach. The truth bubbled inside her, like a witch's brew, toxic and deadly. If she spoke it aloud, it would make it true, and she wasn't ready to face that yet. She knew she couldn't put it off forever, but right now, with her mother still pale and thin, putting off the truth was the best choice for everyone. She put the magazine back on the pile. "I have to go. I forgot I'm supposed to pick up Roger's dry cleaning before five."

She hadn't picked up Roger's dry cleaning in four months. Hadn't made him a dinner in three. And hadn't had a husband to go home to in two. But she didn't say any of that to her mother.

Momma reached out a hand and touched her daughter's knee. "Are you feeling all right, honey? You look a little pale."

"I'm fine, Momma. Just fine." Maybe if she said that enough times, it would become the truth. Or maybe it would just become one more lie in a growing falsehood mountain. "Just fine."

Then she hurried out of the room before the tears welling in her eyes told the truth.

Daisy had told herself she'd accepted Colt's invitation to dinner because it was a good opportunity to make her case about the loan. Except she hadn't brought up the loan or the Hideaway Inn one time. Instead, she'd sat at the small round table in Colt's kitchen, trying to figure out this new Colt, a man who surprised her in more ways than one.

She'd expected to find him living in a tidy little modern style condo, all organized and sterile. Maybe something downtown, near his office. Instead, he shared a cozy beachside bungalow with his grandfather, a small house that could have been one of a hundred similar bungalows fronting a private section of Rescue Bay's three-mile-long beach, just north of the Hideaway Inn. The furniture was a mishmash of recycled pieces, most of them older than Colt, but worn in a way that spoke of family memories and long evening chats. Everything, from the antique brass umbrella stand by the door to the wide-bellied cedar chest across from the kitchen table, seemed to hold histories, secrets, mysteries waiting to be uncovered.

The second they sat down at the table—Colt with a salad he'd assembled, Daisy and Earl with the ooey-gooey pizza— Colt's cell phone started ringing. He glanced at the screen. "It's a consult I've been waiting on. I need to take this."

"Take away," Earl said, waving a hand in dismissal. "It's not like we eat dinner together every day."

"Grandpa—"

"It's fine. I'll sit here with Daisy and enjoy my pizza. She's probably better company than you anyway." Earl slid a spatula under the pizza. "How many slices, Daisy?"

"Just one, thank you." She grinned. "But I'll be back for more soon."

"A woman after my own heart." Earl slid a slice onto her plate, then took two for himself before getting to his feet, crossing to the fridge, and pulling a beer out of the bottom drawer. Colt tensed, but didn't say anything to his grandfather.

The phone trilled again. Colt glanced between Daisy at the table and Earl by the fridge, clearly torn about leaving the room. He started to walk away, then turned back and paused to lean down and whisper in Daisy's ear. "Just warning you. My grandpa can be . . . difficult."

"Oh, I can handle difficult," she said, trying to pretend his nearness had no impact on her. Whatsoever. "I used to live with you, remember?"

"*I* was never the difficult one." The words were hot and low, sending a tremor through Daisy. He held her gaze for one long moment, then he straightened and pressed a button on his phone, issuing a short, professional greeting before striding from the room. In an instant, Colt had gone from the man she remembered to the man in the khakis and tie.

Earl returned to the table, and took a long swig of his beer. "I love my grandson, but most days he has a hornet up his ass the size of a pterodactyl."

Daisy laughed. "I get the feeling he likes things the way he likes things."

"All neat and tidy and without any unnecessary carbohydrates." Earl gestured toward Colt's salad and made a face. Then he lifted the spatula again. "Meanwhile, want another piece?"

"Definitely." She held out her plate.

She and Earl ate and chatted, an easy conversation about the crazy neighbors down the street, the benefits of classic crust over pan pizza, which then segued into a conversation about her cantankerous car. Between the food and the chatting, Daisy settled in at the small maple table as if she'd always been there.

It was what Daisy had imagined having a grandparent would be like. The kind of atmosphere she'd found at Emma's raucous, warm house during holidays and school recital nights, before Daisy went home to a house where the words *dependable* and *family* didn't exist.

Daisy had grown up with a mostly absent mother, an always absent father, but no real grandparents. Her father's parents lived in Texas, and the handful of times they had come to visit had resulted in stiff, awkward conversations that ended almost as quickly as they began. Her mother's parents had died long ago, long before Daisy was born, and had been nothing more than photographs in an album that Daisy had found on a shelf.

She'd imagined, in those days when she'd been young and craving family like some women craved sugar, that her grandfather would be like Earl Harper. A mix of grumpy and wise, a man with enough years behind him to color his sentences with history and insight.

"You know, if your car is sputtering like that," Earl said, bringing her back to the conversation, "you might want to get the air filter checked. Could be a little clogged. And don't take it to one of those chain places that turn a simple oil change into a full body paint job. Take it to a mechanic who's been in business more than five minutes. Someone with some grease under his nails and experience under his belt."

"Thanks, I will." She lifted the pie knife in Earl's direction. "Do you want another slice of pizza?"

Earl put a hand on his stomach and shook his head. "I've had about all this old belly can fit for now. Which means there's going to be room for a snack later."

Daisy laughed. "Smart thinking. I'm all about snacks. And second helpings. And especially dessert."

"Good to see a girl with an appetite. Nothing more annoying than those salad-only girls. Colt's grandma, now that was a woman who could eat. And cook." Earl leaned in toward Daisy, his pale blue eyes assessing her. "Can you cook? Because Colt sure can't. A man could starve to death in this house."

"Quit exaggerating, Grandpa. You're not starving," Colt said, as he walked back into the room and tucked his phone away. "I serve plenty of healthy food around here, but you choose not to eat it."

"Which is another way of asking a man to starve." Earl scowled.

Tension stiffened Colt's stance. "I'm just trying to take care of you."

"I don't need anyone to do a goddamn thing for me." Earl started to get to his feet, then his face paled, a tremor shook his body, and he reached for the edge of the table. In an instant, Colt was there, with one hand under Earl's elbow, and another on his back. Earl jerked away from Colt's touch. "You know what would make me feel better? You, leaving me the hell alone. You hover over me like I'm some kind of invalid."

"Grandpa, I'm not trying to hover. You have some issues—"

"What I have is a pain in the ass grandson who thinks he knows it all just because he's got an MD next to his name. Goddamn doctors do nothing but make people sicker." Earl pushed off from the table then crossed to the sink. Sweat beaded on his brow and his breath came in shaky bursts.

Concern filled Colt's features and erased all traces of irritation. He stood there, looking lost and frustrated, one hand on the back of the chair, one extended out, as if he could reach his grandfather, now several feet away. Daisy ached to soothe the waters somehow, to make it easier for Colt.

Only because she wanted him in a good mood before she talked to him about the loan. Not because that worried look in his face softened something deep inside of Daisy. Something that transported her back, back, back in time, to the days when she and Colt had found common ground in escaping the disappointments behind their own front doors.

In the old days, she would have grabbed Colt by the hand, and dashed away from their responsibilities. They would have bought a six-pack of PBR with a fake ID, climbed the fence for the private beach, built a little fire in the cove beside the dunes, and whiled away the hours until the moon marched across the sky and the sun began to crest again.

But this wasn't the old days, and she suspected *Doctor* Colt wasn't one for fake IDs or trespassing anymore.

"Grandpa, why don't you sit down?" Colt said. "I'll clean up."

"I'm not a baby. I can clean up my own damned messes." Earl gripped the edge of the sink with one hand, and shooed Colt away with the other.

Daisy bit back a smile. She recognized that stubborn spirit. Apparently a few things were passed down in the Harper DNA.

Frustration and concern filled Colt's eyes. Daisy decided to step in, even if it meant Colt ended up hating her later, not thanking her.

"Hey, Earl, why don't you and I knock out these dishes?" Daisy said. "Save Colt the trouble and the dishpan hands. Afterward, maybe we could sit on the porch and talk some smack about that crazy neighbor next door." Before Earl could protest, Daisy slipped into place beside him, turned on the water, and squirted some soap over the dishes. She handed Earl a dish towel. "Here, you dry. And don't complain one bit, because I'm doing the hard part."

"Okay, okay. How can I turn down an offer like that from a pretty woman like you?" Earl grinned, then leaned one hip against the counter. He made it look like a nonchalant move, as if he didn't need the extra support. After a while, the tension in his face eased and the color returned to his cheeks.

Daisy kept up a constant chatter with Earl while she washed and he dried. Colt finished his salad, then joined them in the kitchen, taking the dishes his grandfather dried and putting them away. The tension between the men eased. They joked and chatted with her as they worked, and the three of them whipped through the cleanup in record time. The whole thing was so domestic, so ordinary, that for a little while Daisy fell into the fantasy of being in a family. A home.

When the last dish was washed, she pulled the plug and watched the water drain, taking along a swirl of soap bubbles. With it, the light feeling she'd had before disappeared, and she remembered.

She wasn't here for some warm and cozy memories. She wasn't here to act out some missing component of her childhood or pretend she was in some traditional two-point-five kids and white-picket-fence world. She was here for business reasons—and nothing more.

"Well, kids, it's about time for *Dancing with the Stars*. I'm going to call it an early night." Earl put the towel on the counter, then laid a hand on Daisy's shoulder. His kind blue eyes filled with warmth. "We'll make fun of the neighbors another time, young lady."

Daisy nodded. "No problem."

Though Daisy had no intentions of coming back here. Too bad, really, because she liked Earl. And had enjoyed the pizza more than she wanted to admit.

Earl left the room, his steps slow and shuffling. Leaving Daisy alone with Colt, with the perfect opportunity to bring up why she was here. But for some reason the same woman who could tell off a rude customer in five seconds flat, level a grope-hungry boss with one look, and take on every challenge handed to her, had gone tongue-tied.

It wasn't the pizza or the homey environment. Every breath she took brought with it a whiff of Colt's cologne, dark, woodsy, tempting. She wanted to curve into his height, lean her head on his broad shoulders, and hell, yes, jump his bones and take him upstairs to what she hoped was a king-sized bed.

She wanted to grab Colt's tie, unbutton his shirt, and get to the man beneath the starch. She wanted to hear his voice, growling deep against her throat, telling her everything that he was planning on doing to her in bed. Just like he had oh, so many years ago.

Those thoughts were not helping anything. She shook her head and refocused on the topic at hand. "I enjoyed talking to your grandpa. He's a really interesting man."

"Thank you," Colt said. "You really have a nice way with him. He's never that nice to me, not lately anyway."

"Well, maybe it was just the change in conversational partners. You can be a little . . ."

"What?" He came a little closer. That dark cologne wafted between them. Enticing. "I can be a little what? Go ahead, you can say it."

A smile curved up her face. "A little . . . stuffy."

"Me?"

She danced her fingers along that tie, the buttons, the still-fresh panels of button-down. "Yes, Mr. Khakis, you."

He caught her hand, and her breath lodged in her throat. "I do own other clothes, you know."

"Oh yeah?" she said, pretending she didn't notice how warm her hand felt against his. "Then prove it."

"Come by on a weekend and you'll see me in jeans and a ratty T-shirt."

"*You* own a ratty T-shirt?"

"Well, technically"—a sheepish grin filled his face—"I'd need to poke a hole in the fabric, maybe tear a seam or two, but yes, I *can* own a ratty T-shirt."

She laughed. "Oooh, you are living on the edge, Colt."

He released her hand and stepped away. Something shifted in his eyes, a shadow dropping over his features. "Yeah, that's me all right." He cleared his throat. "Anyway, what did you want to talk to me about?"

She reached for the dish towel, put her back to the sink,

and busied her hands with folding it into thirds. The light mood between them had dissipated, reminding her to get back to why she was here, but she couldn't find the words. Asking someone else for help—especially financial help— wasn't something Daisy did. Ever. She'd been on her own since she was eighteen, and the thought of having to go outside for assistance rankled.

But what choice did she have? Emma needed this new start, needed it even more than Daisy did. And maybe, just maybe, if she brought her cousin here, back to where their lives had once been light and happy, she'd get Emma back, too.

"I, uh, didn't come by for pizza." Daisy draped the towel over the edge of the counter, then pushed off from the sink. "I came here to ask you to be a cosigner on a loan. That's why I'm here in Rescue Bay."

"A loan?" Colt blinked. "For what? Why?"

"Because . . ." She gritted her teeth, then pushed the words through. "You have better credit than I do and it turns out the bank won't loan me the money without your signature. I thought I could get it just by staying married, but now they want you to sign for the loan, too."

"Wait a minute." He stepped back. "Is that why you really came roaring into my office yesterday, pissed off about the divorce papers? Were you using my credit without letting me know?"

"No, I wasn't doing that at all. You happened to come up, though, when I applied for the loan. Seems we're still attached financially, since we're still attached legally. For the record, I didn't want to use you at all. But . . . I have to." She bit back a curse. Damn. She hated admitting that.

"How much of a loan are we talking about?"

Okay, so he hadn't said no. Yet. She took a breath, then exhaled it with the next words. "A hundred and ninety thousand dollars. More or less."

Colt let out a low whistle. "That's a hell of a lot of money. What are you buying? A small castle?"

A happy ending. But Daisy didn't say that out loud. The less Colt knew about Daisy's personal life, the better. Opening up to him all those years ago had left her alone and heartbroken. She was older now, wiser, and not the same starry-eyed girl who had run off and eloped with Colt, nor was she the hormone-addled Daisy who had slept with him three months ago. She was a woman with a mission now, a very important mission. "I've decided to reopen the Hideaway Inn."

"What? When did you decide that?"

She didn't want to get into all the reasons why she had decided to run the inn. Doing so would open a vein, and that was something Daisy didn't do, not with Colt, not with anybody. If she did, she'd be forced to admit that a part of her, a crazy part, craved Colt's ordered, grounded world with a grandpa who ordered pizza, and a cozy bungalow on the ocean.

The idea of a life like that was what had made her jump in her car, move back to this town, and take a major leap of faith with the inn. She'd changed every aspect of her world in an instant and yet the thought of staying here after the renovations were done, both terrified and tempted her. So instead she defaulted to her usual live-by-the-seat-of-herpants attitude, far easier than puzzling out why the very thing she wanted nearly drove her to panic attacks.

"I decided two weeks ago." She shrugged. "I woke up one day, quit my job, and—"

"You quit your job, applied for a two hundred grand loan, and moved down here, on a . . . whim?"

"Yeah, basically." She parked her fists on her hips. Okay, so that sounded irresponsible and rash and a thousand other mistakes waiting to happen, but Daisy wasn't about to justify or explain her choices to Colt, of all people. "So, will you cosign for me?"

He snorted. "And that would make sound financial sense . . . how? You don't exactly have staying power, Daisy."

"Look who's talking. You left after three weeks."

"And you went through three jobs in three weeks."

"Hence, the poor credit." She wasn't going to rehash her financial missteps. She'd had enough lectures on fiscal responsibility from the bankers she'd talked to. "Now will you please sign the papers for me?"

He shook his head and walked away. "You're incredible. I don't see you for years. Then we have a chance, one night together, and next thing I know, you're in town, wanting money out of me."

"I don't need any actual money from you. Just your signature. And I wouldn't ask if I had *any* other option, believe me."

He scoffed. "Gee, way to make me feel wanted."

"You want me to make you feel wanted?" She closed the distance between them again and raised her chin until her lips were inches from his. Her heart fluttered. Heat pooled in her gut. She watched the pulse in his throat start to speed up, *boom-boom-boom*. The air between them charged with heated memories, unanswered desire. It had always been that way when she got close to Colt, as if he was a magnet that she couldn't resist.

"Is that what you want, Colt?" she said, her voice low and dark. "A little more sex, a little less commitment? Because you are very, very good at that."

"I'm not the man I used to be."

Her gaze raked over him. He still had the same blue eyes, the same dark hair with one pesky lock that dusted his forehead, the one that made her think of Clark Kent when she'd first met him. But then her gaze dropped lower, to the parts of Colt that had changed. The leather jackets and ripped jeans of years ago were gone. Instead now, a tie, loosened a little, but still with a stranglehold on his neck. The buttoned-down shirt, the pressed pants, the glasses tucked in his shirt pocket. The cell phone tethering him to a job 24/7.

"No. You're not. And that's too bad." She shook her head. She didn't need this. Didn't need his intrusiveness. His questions. His input. She could do this on her own. Somehow. "Forget I even asked you."

Then she walked out the door, leaving behind a few forgotten slices of stone-cold pizza. And her best chance at changing her future.

Seven

It was official. Daisy Barton was a naïve dreamer who didn't know when to walk away. A whole day of phone calls and e-mails, and all she had to show for it was a bigger pile of refusals from every bank in a fifty-mile radius.

Maybe quitting her job hadn't been the smartest decision. Turned out bankers liked people who were employed.

Damn Colt for being right. Planning ahead had never been her strong suit. She didn't put money aside for rainy days, didn't make five-year plans or think about when she was going to retire. She lived one day at a time, never dwelling on the shadows behind her, or the unseen curves in the road ahead. Which meant every once in a while she got caught in the rain without an umbrella.

"Okay then," she said to herself, to the dreary, rundown, taupe world of Room 112 at the Rescue Bay Inn—a glorified title for a motel that looked like something straight out of a Hitchcock movie. "It's time to grow up."

The trouble? Daisy Barton hadn't the first clue how a settled, dependable, grown-up thirty-two-year-old woman should behave. It was as if she'd gotten stuck at twenty-one and hadn't shifted into the next gear. The very things she had always wanted—a life, a home, a *purpose*—kept eluding her.

She'd start with getting the hell out of this depressing room for a while. Then figure the rest out from there.

Two blocks into her walk, she hit Main Street. A collection of pastel-colored shops, like cupcakes in a display, lined the quaint downtown area of Rescue Bay. The familiar boardwalk fronting the Gulf was still filled with the same tourist attractions, as if nothing had changed in almost two decades. Sure, the awnings were newer, the wares inside changed to fit the times, but overall, the beachfront looked as it had years ago.

Downtown Rescue Bay, however, had become a little more congested and a little busier than she remembered. Here, the landscape yielded to more traditional stores and homes, as if the Walnut Grove from the *Little House on the Prairie* books Daisy had read years ago had been brought into the twenty-first century—only with palm trees and cocoa butter. She'd always loved that about Rescue Bay, how it felt like it had walked out of the pages of a novel. She'd lived in cities most of her life, but there was just something . . . warm about Rescue Bay, like a handmade quilt draped over her shoulders.

Being near the water calmed Daisy's soul, made her feel rooted. Daisy had spent far too many years hopping from job to job, moving from place to place. The day Aunt Clara asked her to go to the inn, Daisy had realized a horrifying truth—

She had turned into Willow, her flighty, irresponsible, spontaneous mother.

No more. Things were changing for Daisy, one way or another. Even if the very thought of staying put made her panic.

She bought a newspaper at the Quick 'N Go, then sat down at a bright red circular table outside the quaint Shoebox Café and began to scan the classifieds. Around her, the town bustled and moved, people walking by, bicyclists whipping past, cars slowing to say hello to a friend on the corner. It was . . .

Perfect.

Exactly the kind of place Daisy needed. In more ways than one.

She'd only had one summer here, one too-fast, too-short summer, living in Rescue Bay, staying at the Hideaway Inn and spending every day with Emma, the two of them "two peas in a pod," according to Aunt Clara. Then Emma had met a boy, and Daisy had met Colt, and perfection stepped up a notch or ten.

Saving the Hideaway Inn wasn't about restoring a business, or fulfilling Aunt Clara's request. No, deep down inside, Daisy knew that restoring the inn was about restoring something that had died. Something that she hoped still existed, in her, in Emma.

She dug in her purse for a pen, but came up empty. Yet another sign she needed to change her life. She wasn't even prepared enough to look for a job.

Instead, she improvised, swirling a red lipstick upward, and using the waxy color to circle anything she remotely qualified for. Dog walker. Beauty shop assistant. Diner waitress.

The door behind her opened, and the spry elderly lady Daisy had seen the other day in Colt's office came outside, followed by two men—one older, one younger—who looked so much alike they had to be father and son. The scent of fresh-baked bread and apple pie wafted from the café's interior.

"Why hello again," the woman said. She had an easy smile, and a friendly manner packed into her five-foot-three frame.

Daisy returned the greeting, then offered up an apologetic smile. "I'm so sorry I burst in on your appointment. I was in a rush and didn't think."

The woman waved it off. "Don't think another thing about it, dear. You saved me yet another lecture about brussel sprouts and Metamucil."

Daisy laughed. "That doesn't sound like fun."

"Tell Doc Harper. He thinks brussel sprouts cure everything. If I were a doctor, I'd prescribe cookies all around."

Daisy could just imagine Colt's reaction to that. The man she'd met and married all those years ago would have endorsed cookies for dinner, pancakes for lunch, or ditching work to hit the beach. He'd been fun and adventurous, sexy and dangerous, the kind of man who made breaking the rules into a tempting game.

Then he'd changed, swinging a hundred and eighty degrees in the opposite direction. In the years since, he'd taken that change to the nth degree. The Colt she had met three months ago had been as buttoned up as a butler, all scheduled and organized. The second she saw him sitting alone at a table in Nero's, she'd decided to make it a personal mission to loosen him up and give him a taste of what he'd been missing.

The trouble was where that taste had led. Right here, right now, in a muddy web that would only get muddier if she got close to Colt again. She'd focus on getting the loan, getting Emma down here, and only then, when Emma was here and Daisy had set their worlds to rights again, only then would she be able to move forward.

"Oh my, I completely forgot my manners." The woman beside Daisy turned toward the two men on her right side. "I'm Greta Winslow, and these two handsome men are my son, Edward, and my grandson, Luke."

Daisy rose and shook with each of the men. Luke was tall and trim, with the build and haircut of a military man, while his father had the buttoned-up suit and tie of a businessman. If not for the dark hair and deep blue eyes, she would have sworn they weren't related. "Nice to meet you both. I'm Daisy Barton."

"New to Rescue Bay?" Luke asked. Beside him, his father stepped away, scrolling through messages on his phone with Type-A intensity. Daisy had met dozens of men like Edward over the years, men who had little interest in anything beyond their career. But his son and mother were likeable, friendly, and open, as if the two of them could make up for Edward's indifference.

"Sort of. I stayed here one summer, years ago," Daisy said to Luke. "But the town is pretty much the way I remember it."

"You did?" Greta said. "Where?"

"At the Hideaway Inn. Some of my relatives owned it. They still do, in fact."

"Really? I remember the Hideaway Inn," Greta said. "Such a lovely place for a vacation. My Edward and I would go there sometimes for dinner. A lovely woman used to own it with her husband. Harriet and . . . George, I think."

"They were my cousin's grandparents, on her mother's side. My aunt and uncle took over after they retired. But then my uncle died and my aunt . . . she just didn't want to be there without him. Now, my cousin and I are looking at reopening it."

"That would be a wonderful thing for Rescue Bay. Why, I remember the days when there were weddings out at the Hideaway every weekend." She turned to her grandson. "Luke, you should talk to Olivia about having your wedding there. It's right on the beach and has this lovely outdoor patio that faces the water."

"Sounds perfect. Is it available?" Luke asked Daisy.

"Well, it's currently being renovated." A white lie, but if Daisy got the loan, it would be the truth. "When were you planning on getting married?"

"Next month." Luke grinned. "Grandma here keeps trying to get us to pin down a place, but really, all Olivia and I want is something simple and done, especially since we keep procrastinating on the planning. To us, the marriage is the important part, not the wedding."

"Such wisdom." Greta beamed and gave Luke's hand a pat. "Every so often, you reflect the good genes I gave you."

Luke laughed. "Easy to do with you spouting wisdom at me every other minute."

"Some people call that meddling," Greta said to Daisy, sotto voce.

"Meddling is your middle name, Grandma." Luke gave his grandmother a gentle one-armed hug. A wave of affection showed in that gesture, the kind of affection Daisy had craved nearly all her life. What was with this town? Was everybody here part of the same inviting little family?

"Be sure to stay away from this one," Luke continued. "My grandmother will have you married off before you can look both ways to cross the street."

"Oh, I don't have to marry off this one," Greta said. "She's already married. To Doc Harper."

The world stilled. The streets quieted and it seemed as if everyone on the sidewalk stopped what they were doing and held their breath.

"Oh, darn. I didn't mean to spill those particular beans," Greta said.

Luke arched a brow. "Doc Harper has a *wife*?"

Damn. Daisy hadn't wanted that to be public knowledge. But it was her own fault for bursting into Colt's office and not thinking before she spoke—or yelled, rather. Impulsive—that was going to be inscribed on her tombstone: IF ONLY SHE HAD THOUGHT BEFORE SHE ACTED.

No one had ever accused Daisy Barton of being too cautious. Which was how she ended up in this whole mess in the first place.

"Yes, but we've been . . . separated," Daisy said.

"And now you both are together again. I'm sure Doc Harper is just over the moon to have you nearby." Greta smiled, as if just saying those words made it a fact.

Daisy wouldn't call Colt's reaction "over the moon." More like over the top. Okay, maybe not that bad. But he definitely wasn't happy to see her.

There'd been a time . . .

Those days were over, Daisy reminded herself. Far in the past. Colt and she had changed—that night three months ago had told her that—and dwelling on what used to be only kept her stuck. She was moving forward, not back. Never, ever back.

Greta turned to the men beside her. "You two scoot. I can walk back to Golden Years from here."

Edward scowled, and thumbed a remote toward a Mercedes parked alongside them. It chirped a happy, polished greeting in return. "Mother, you're probably tired. I can drive you—"

"Edward Winslow, I am old enough to know when I need a ride and when I can hoof it back home by myself." Greta gave him a glare, then nodded toward Daisy. "Besides, I want to get to know Rescue Bay's newest resident. It's my duty to welcome all new people to town."

"I thought Patty Simon was the Welcome Wagon president," Luke said.

Greta's face pursed like a lemon. "That woman couldn't be president of a Girl Scout troop. She almost gave everyone at Golden Years food poisoning with her undercooked muffins."

Luke chuckled. "I detect a little jealousy in your voice, Grandma." He leaned toward Daisy and lowered his tone to a conspiratorial whisper. "My grandma doesn't like the fact that Patty has the hots for Harold Twohig. Don't let her fool you about retirement being boring. It's quite the little soap opera over there at Golden Years."

Greta gave Luke a not-so-gentle swat. "I have no interest in that pox on society. Stop filling Daisy's head with lies."

Daisy watched the exchange, and tried to quell the envy bubbling inside her. They all seemed so normal, so warm and friendly, like the kind of families on TV. Good God, she was over thirty. She shouldn't be envious of something as simple as a little family teasing.

But she was. More than she wanted to admit. That envy bumped up against all the things Daisy kept tucked deep inside her, the past she never visited, the home she had run away from because it had never been home, not for a moment. For a few weeks, she'd thought she'd found what she'd been seeking, no, what she'd *craved*—

But then it was gone, and she wised up to the fact that putting stock in fantasies only led to heartbreak.

"I'm just teasing. We all know you love to hate Harold." Luke bent down and kissed his grandmother's cheek. "I'll see you later, Grandma." Then he turned to Daisy. "It was nice to meet you. Best of luck with the Hideaway. And if you do start doing weddings, just let me or Olivia know. Or my grandmother. She'll be sure to spread the word."

"Thank you," Daisy said. Already, a potential customer? It had to be a sign that the inn was meant to be resurrected. "I will."

The two men climbed into the car and headed down the street. Greta slid into the seat opposite Daisy. Daisy found herself warming to Greta. The older woman had a friendly face, with inquisitive light blue eyes that sparkled with a touch of mischief. She was spry and strong, the kind of woman Daisy would have loved to have had as a grandmother when she was a little girl.

"Now that the Meddlesome Twins are gone, why don't you tell me all about Doc Harper?" Greta gave Daisy a smile. An open-up-to-me smile.

Daisy shrugged. "There's really nothing to tell, Mrs. Winslow. We haven't seen each other in a long time."

Unless you counted three months ago. And last night. And the pizza. The tension between them as thick as wool.

"Call me Greta, please. Mrs. Winslow makes me sound like I'm one step closer to being the Crypt Keeper."

"Greta it is, then." Yes, indeed, she liked this woman. A smile found its way across Daisy's face, and for the first time since she'd arrived in Rescue Bay, she began to think maybe her idea of starting over here wasn't so crazy after all. At least for Emma. Daisy . . .

Well, Daisy had never been much for putting down roots. At her age, maybe it was too late for the leopard to change her spots. Maybe she should just move on, find a new adventure, after Emma was settled and running the inn.

"So, if you haven't seen each other in a long time," Greta began, interrupting Daisy's thoughts, "how can you be husband and wife? A proper husband and wife, that is?"

"It's . . . complicated. And honestly, I'd rather it didn't become public knowledge." Though Daisy suspected Greta had already told half the town. So much for coming to Rescue Bay in a calm, deliberate manner.

Ha. Nothing about Daisy had ever been calm or deliberate. Starting today—okay, tomorrow—she was going to aim for calm and deliberate. There was no sense in trying to get a fresh start if she kept making the same old mistakes of the past.

Greta leaned over the paper that Daisy had spread across

the table. "My, that is an awful lot of red. Are you looking for a job or giving the paper a little love?"

Daisy's bright crimson lipstick circles dotted the classifieds like giant measles. "Oh, that. I didn't have a pen."

Greta fished in a tiny purse beside her and came up with a ballpoint that she handed to Daisy. On the navy-colored barrel sat a white text ad for Colt's practice. Coincidence? Or hint?

Greta leaned closer. "So, what kind of job are you looking for? I might be able to help."

"Anything, really. I'm not picky." Given the few jobs Daisy had seen in the paper, "not picky" was going to have to become her life motto. She'd hoped to find something that would pay well, and not require being on her feet for twelve hours a day, but apparently not having a degree cut her chances of that to almost zero. "I've been a waitress and a delivery driver, a short order cook and pretty much anything they paid me to do. Anything legal, that is."

"Hmm . . . let me ponder on that." Greta sat back against the bright blue-and-white-striped chair, a finger to her lips, while her gaze assessed Daisy. "Are you planning on staying in town long?"

Greta was clearly fishing for information, Daisy realized. A little neighborly prying. "Just long enough," Daisy said with a smile, "to finish what I started."

"What's that?"

"I moved here, thinking I'd reopen the Hideaway Inn with my cousin, but . . ." She sighed and closed up the paper. None of the jobs she'd seen paid enough to finance the loan, or to allow her to pay for the renovations on her own. Daisy needed to face reality. She'd bitten off more than she could chew. That's what she got for being too impulsive. "I can't get a loan to repair the inn without a job, and even if I did, I don't know if I can afford the repayment schedule. The amount the contractor quoted me is way out of my range."

"Finally, something I can help with, and something I'd be delighted to be a part of." Greta patted Daisy's hand. "I know a contractor. He's fair, honest, quite a good-looking man, too, and happens to be almost family."

"*Almost* family?"

"He's marrying Diana, who is my granddaughter-in-law-to-be's sister."

Small town connections. Daisy bit back a laugh. "Luke's fiancée's sister?"

"The exact one. She's also the town veterinarian, and she runs the local animal shelter with Olivia. Oh, and if you know anyone looking for a pet, the shelter is having a little adoption fair in the park this Friday afternoon."

Greta seemed determined to get Daisy plugged into this town. Probably a good thing for someone looking to reopen a local business, but still a little overwhelming for someone who'd never been part of anything larger than an apartment-building Labor Day barbecue before. "I'd appreciate the recommendation for a contractor, Mrs. Winslow—"

"Greta, please. Remember, I'm not old enough to be called Mrs. Winslow."

"Greta," Daisy corrected with a smile, "but I can't promise that I'm going to get the financing to pay for the work. I've run into a . . . snag with the bank, and I'm debating whether it's just a sign that I'm doing the wrong thing."

Greta's hand covered hers. "No, it's a sign that you need to work harder, my dear. Everything worth having is worth fighting for."

If she had fought harder for Colt all those years ago, would they still be together? Or would she have realized sooner that they were a mistake that never should have been? And what if she fought like hell to save the Hideaway Inn, but never got her cousin back?

"What if you fight," Daisy said softly, "and still lose?"

"Don't let a little defeat stop you. My daddy always said that a closed door is really just an invitation to break in through the window." Greta winked, then got to her feet. "So find yourself a window, my dear, and if you need to throw a brick through it, well, just make sure you sweep up any broken glass afterward. After all, you're going to be keeping that contractor busy enough."

Eight

As soon as that infernal woman pulled out of the driveway, Earl picked up the phone so he could get the hell out of here before that visiting nurse got it in her foolish head to come back—or worse, send reinforcements. The second the nurse had shown up, Earl was ready for her. Nothing said *I'm not interested in being poked and prodded* like a man on the porch with a twenty-two. The dust cloud from her hasty exit was just settling when the phone call connected. "Pete, it's Earl. Need a favor."

Pete didn't question. Never had, never would. Earl had worked on Pete's fleet—if one could call three taxis for the only taxi service in Rescue Bay a fleet—for more than two decades. In twenty years, Pete had never lost a day of work, or a dollar of wages, because Earl had kept his good friend's cars running in tip-top shape. "Be there in five minutes."

True to his word, Pete showed up, waiting in the drive, the bright yellow and white Taurus idling softly. Earl descended the few stairs of the bungalow, cursing that he had to grip the handrail. It was the little things that told a man he was getting old. The tremors that knocked a fresh cup of coffee to the floor. The shortness of breath after a walk in the summer heat.

The trepidation about something as simple as descending a flight of stairs. He'd never been a man to rely on help from anyone or anything.

And that—that was what pissed him off the most about his age. That he needed help. Earl Harper prided himself on being a man who paid his own bills, pulled up his own bootstraps, and ran his own ship. Now he was living in someone else's house, following someone else's orders, and waiting on someone else to come and tell him what to do all over again.

He climbed into the cab and shut the door. Relief at being out of the house filled him, but was chased by the emptiness that followed Earl, no matter where he went or how hard he tried to escape. "Hey, Pete."

Pete tossed him a grin. "You know, you can sit up front."

"Feels more official this way."

Pete chuckled, then tugged his ball cap brim a little lower. "If there's one thing you've never been, Earl Harper, it's official." He put the car in reverse and began to back out of the driveway. "Same destination?"

Pete asked the question as if he didn't know the answer. Maybe he thought it made Earl feel less pitiful that he'd been going to the same spot for the last seven hundred Wednesday afternoons and had yet to find what he was seeking.

"Yeah. Thanks."

Pete just nodded and started driving. He kept up a constant patter of conversation as he wove his way through Rescue Bay's streets, talking about his wife, his kids, his grandkids. Didn't matter to Pete that Earl didn't respond. Their decades-long friendship came with an understanding that if one man didn't want to talk, the other just filled in the gaps. Earl had done a lot of chattering when Pete was going through his divorce, then he'd done a lot of listening when Pete and Colleen reunited. For the past fourteen years, though, Earl had done a lot of listening and not much talking.

Finally, Pete pulled into a grassy lot, and shut off the car. He sat back, closed his eyes, and prepared to wait.

Earl climbed out of the car and shut the door. His steps moved slow, but sure, guided by the memory of a well-worn path that he'd been traversing since he could walk. He'd come here with his grandfather, his father, and then his son and his grandsons. He knew every tree, every rock, every curve in the water. He knew the best spots for fishing and the best spots for thinking. And he knew the one spot that made his heart ache like a phantom limb.

The birds chirped happy songs, flitting from tree to tree. A heron paused on the bank, alert and still. Earl eased onto a tree stump, his feet settling into a well-trampled space where the grass no longer grew. A fish flipped in the water, scaring the heron into flight, and sending a flutter of ripples across the lake's placid surface.

Earl sat on that stump until his legs grew numb. He sat there and he listened to the quiet song made by the trees and the wind. He sat there and he watched Mother Nature paint the world in blues and greens, then kiss it all with gold. He sat there until he couldn't sit there anymore, because it hurt too much.

Then he hung his head and he sat there some more, until tears moistened his cheeks and the day grew long. Peace stayed just out of reach, a fickle, mean mistress.

Break in through a window.

Now that was something Daisy had experience with. Granted, not since she was a teenager trying to avoid getting caught coming home in the middle of the night, but still a skill she knew well.

If your husband signs off on the loan, I could get this approved without a problem.

Which meant she needed to find a way to convince her "husband" to remain married. And add his signature to some loan documents.

Yeah, should be about as easy as negotiating peace in the Middle East. Considering Colt hadn't answered her calls, and hadn't come by the motel yet to see her, or called her cell. Clearly, he wasn't planning on negotiating.

Last night . . . well, last night had been crazy and wonderful and bittersweet. She'd enjoyed stepping into that homey world, where there were squabbles over what to eat for dinner and who did the dishes. For a moment, Daisy had felt . . . warm.

Not just when Colt was standing close, either. That hadn't been warm—that had been hot and tempting and a thousand other things Daisy was determined to avoid. She needed to get involved with Colt about as much as she needed a wolverine for a pet.

He was no longer the Colt she had fallen in love with and never would be again. He was the kind of man she ran from—buttoned up and organized and dull.

Okay, maybe not dull, but not the Colt she remembered.

The man Daisy had known years ago had been a risk taker. The kind of guy who would hop on his motorcycle, blast out of Florida with Daisy on the back, and elope, without a second thought. She had no idea where that man had gone, but if there was a chance she could get through to that side of him long enough to convince him to sign off on the loan—

Well, she was going to pull out all the negotiation tactics she knew.

Which was what had Daisy making two stops that Thursday morning. For ammunition that she knew Colt Harper would not be able to ignore. And a little secret weapon.

A little after nine, she parked in front of his office, and strode inside the squat brick building, a white box in one hand. The tidy, tastefully decorated waiting room was empty. A blessing, to be sure, since the last thing Daisy wanted to do was interrupt another appointment and really aggravate Colt. Daisy plastered a smile on her face, then strode up to the reception desk.

Frannie got to her feet, putting out her hands. The tall, buxom, auburn-haired woman cut an imposing figure, and her stony face said this was her front office, her domain, and there was no way Daisy was gaining the upper hand again. "I can't let you back there, unless you have an appointment. Direct orders from Doc Harper."

"I totally understand. Frannie, is it? I was out of line the other day. Way out of line. I stopped by to apologize." Daisy lifted the lid, and tipped the box forward a little. "And what

better way to do that than with beignets? They're a specialty
in New Orleans."

"Beignets?" Frannie's eyes grew round. She leaned in,
inhaled the scent of fresh baked goods. "Oh my. Where did
you find those in Rescue Bay?"

"I asked the local bakery to do me a favor and make
some." Actually, begged them to do her a favor was a more
apt description. She'd paid twice as much for the beignets
because they'd been a last minute request, but if a few dollars of pastries helped Daisy save the Hideaway Inn, then it
was a worthy investment. A business expense, of sorts.

Daisy moved the box closer to Frannie. "I have been
craving them ever since I left Louisiana. They smell so di-
vine, I almost ate one in the car, but then that wouldn't be
much of an apology gift, would it?"

"They're still warm?" Frannie shot a glance at the exam
room area, then back toward the beignets. Melting confec-
tionary sugar added a sheen to the top of the fried dough,
and the sweet, warm scent wafted temptation across the
desk. She bit her lip, considering. "No one is due in for the
next few minutes. And it *is* almost time for my coffee break.
I'd hate for these to get cold. Why don't we go back to the
break room and just have a couple bites?"

"I think that is a brilliant idea."

Frannie opened the door separating the waiting area from
the exam rooms and waved Daisy down the green carpeted
hall and into a small room at the back of the building. A
round laminate table took up the center of the space, while
boxes of supplies lined the shelves against the far wall.
White, sterile, and boring, the break room had all the per-
sonality of a ream of paper.

A young woman dressed in nurse's scrubs came into the
room. "Oh, wow. Dessert?"

"Don't tell Doc Harper, Suzie. He'll have a cow." Frannie
shut the door behind the nurse, then opened a cabinet, withdrew some paper plates and a plastic knife, then sat down
at the table. "Just one, really fast. Doc Harper has this thing
about eating healthy. He's not a fan of the carbohydrate, and

he's very anti fried food. Lectures everyone about what it does to your arteries. But what he doesn't know we eat can't hurt us." Frannie had a beignet halfway to the plate when the break room door opened.

"Frannie, are we—" Colt's words jerked to a halt.

Daisy did a slow, easy pivot toward him, and waited while his gaze took her in. She gave him time, a couple heartbeats, for the full effect of the deep green dress she'd bought in a local dress shop to work its magic. The jersey material fit her like a glove, curving in all the right places, then showing a slight peek of thigh with a bias cut slit up one side. She'd swept her hair up into a bun, then released a few tendrils, to give it that messy, tumbled look. It wasn't a brick through a window, but it was as close as Daisy could get.

"Hi, Colt," she said, as friendly as a long-time neighbor. "I didn't mean to bother you again. I was just stopping by to apologize to Frannie for bursting in the other day. It was wrong of me and I brought her a little something to make up for my craziness."

"Well . . . thank you." But he scowled as he said it, clearly not pleased to see her in his break room. Despite the dress and the hair.

Okay, so maybe he wasn't as attracted to her as she thought. Maybe she didn't make his heart skip a beat anymore. Maybe she'd just compounded her problems instead of making them better. Or maybe he just needed a little . . . sweetening up.

"I felt so bad, I brought along a little New Orleans apology." Daisy held the box toward him. "Beignets."

For a moment, she thought she'd made a mistake. The scowl lingered on his face, then, one degree at a time, his gaze softened, his features lightened and yielded to a small smile, then a step forward, then an inhale. "Beignets, did you say? I haven't had one of those since . . ."

His gaze settled on hers. In the space of a heartbeat, a loose thread between them tied in a knot.

"That time you ran out and bought me a dozen for breakfast," she said softly. She still remembered being snug in the bed, waiting for Colt. He'd come back with a big white box, similar to the one she held today, then climbed under the covers with her and fed her a beignet, one tempting bite at a time. "We were so hungry, we ate them all."

"I think it was the *only* thing we ate that day." His blue eyes locked on hers. The heat in the room arced up a few degrees.

She thought of the bed, the beignets, the crumbs that had dusted her chest. The way Colt had licked each one off, then devoured her. "We were . . . busy."

Frannie looked from Colt to Daisy. Then back again. "Uh, I think Suzie and I are going to take this to my desk. I think we have something . . . to do or talk about or something." A moment later, the two women bustled out of the room. Daisy hardly noticed them leave.

"Would you like one?" Daisy asked Colt.

"I shouldn't. They're like fat pills and very bad for your heart and . . ."

"A little indulgence once in a while never hurt anyone, Colt." She broke off a piece of the dough, and held it out to him, just as he had with her years ago. "Just one bite."

"Along with a trip down Memory Lane?"

Was he thinking of that day in the bed? Their honeymoon, filled with days and days of nothing but making love and eating as fast as they could, then slipping beneath the sheets again and finally, blissfully, into each other. Did he remember those amazing days? Those exquisite nights? When the only piece of furniture they'd had—or wanted—was a king-sized mattress on the floor of their fifth-floor walk-up.

"Not a trip, exactly." She took another step closer to him, her skirt swirling around her legs and brushing against his. The bite of dough kissed against his lips. "Just a quick detour."

"What are you doing, Daisy?"

She wasn't sure. She'd come here to try to entice him into signing the loan documents, but her mind kept circling back to the early days of their marriage. To that bubble of a fairy tale she'd lived in for a few short weeks. She was tempted, so tempted, to go back there, to let Colt into her heart again.

No. She'd made that mistake before. Fourteen years ago, and again, three months ago. Not again. She stepped back.

"Eating breakfast." She popped the bite into her mouth, and tried to pretend his mere presence had no effect on her. Colt's gaze stayed on her mouth, watching her chew, swallow. Her heart raced, her pulse skittered, but she stayed where she was.

No one had told her that breaking the window would put her at risk, too. She'd come here, thinking she would be in charge, and she could entice Colt and convince him to sign the loan papers with a little fattening pastry and some feminine wiles. But as he continued to watch her, his gaze intense and dark, she had to wonder who was really in charge.

He lifted a hand to touch her face and something turned to lava deep inside her. "You have a little powdered sugar right"—he brushed her lower lip with his thumb—"there."

Daisy opened her mouth against his touch. Fire roared in her belly, wound a tight coil inside her. "Do you remember the beignets, Colt?"

Hope fluttered in the space between the question and the answer. The part of her that missed the old Colt, missed what they had once had. The part of her that had forgotten how he had roared out of her life with nothing more than a note on the table, and never explained why he broke her heart. The part of her that had vowed to forget him, but never had. That foolish, hope-riddled part of her that she couldn't kill no matter how hard she tried.

"I remember everything, Daisy."

Lord help her, so did she. She looked at his mouth, his hands, his chest, and wanted to kiss him, touch him, feel him against her again. Oh, this was a dangerous game she was playing. And for what? She wasn't even sure her cousin wanted the Hideaway.

All she knew for sure was that she didn't want to fall for Colt again. He'd broken her heart and left her twice. Why couldn't she learn her lesson, move on from her mistakes? Why did she keep returning to the one man who was so wrong for her?

"We used to take risks, Colt," she said. Maybe she was searching for the whys, the explanations for why they hadn't worked out. Maybe then she'd stop caring about what might have been. "Leap off bridges without knowing what was waiting below. I want to feel that again, Colt, and that's partly why I'm here, why I'm taking a risk on the Hideaway. I want to grab life by the reins and hold on for the ride. I'm tired of working jobs that go nowhere, serving hash to people who don't care, and dreading Mondays because it means another retread of the same thing day in and day out. Don't you want that, too?"

"I'm happy here, Daisy. It's comfortable. Predictable."

Comfortable. Predictable. Two words she would never have associated with Colton Harper. "Who are you? What happened to the Colt I met?"

"I grew up." His words were cold and short. All these years later, and still, he wouldn't open up to her. Tell her why he had changed, why he had cut her from his life like a dead branch.

Instead, his gaze shifted, and she got the feeling he was hiding something. As he had years ago. Shutting her out, pushing her to the side.

"No. Something changed with you. Something you have never told me," she said. "Something that drove you away and never brought you back. And keeps you there, even now."

He shook his head and stepped back. "We are done, Daisy. We have been for years. What happened a few months ago was . . . an aberration. A mistake."

"Yeah, and so was all of this." She dropped the box on the table, then walked away from the beignets and the memories. She'd tried to break a window and gotten nowhere closer to what she needed. Either it was time to come up with a better plan—or cut her losses and leave this town and this crazy plan in her rearview mirror.

Nine

Okay, so maybe Greta Winslow *was* a closet romantic like Pauline kept saying. Not that Greta would admit that out loud, of course. She'd never hear the end of it from the old biddies at Golden Years. She'd lose all respectability as a grumpy old lady.

But as she watched Olivia shop for a wedding dress, Greta had to admit there were few things in this world that could make her happier. How she loved this girl, soon to be her granddaughter. She was smart and sassy, strong and sweet, the perfect balance for Greta's loving but stubborn former military grandson.

"Greta, what do you think of this one?" Olivia held up a simple cap sleeve white dress that skimmed her ankles. No lace, no beading, just a smooth expanse of white satiny fabric. On Olivia, it would be beautiful, but Greta thought an occasion like marrying the love of one's life needed a bit more *ka-pow*.

"I think you need one with a little bling." Greta reached for the next dress on the rack and held it in front of Olivia. "Same style as what you picked, but it has sparkle. My daddy always said a little sparkle makes everything look better. Of course, he was talking about the ice cubes in his bourbon, not dresses, but the principle works the same."

Olivia laughed. "Okay. I'll try them both on." She disappeared into the fitting room of the dress shop, with the two dresses slung over her shoulder.

Greta lowered herself onto one of the bright pink cushioned chairs flanking the fitting rooms. Lord, but she was tired. Some days, it seemed Old Age was doing its best to pick on her and remind her she'd passed her twenties a long, long time ago.

The shop door rang, letting in a burst of sunshine, a whoosh of September heat, and Daisy Barton. She had a bag over one arm, and a pair of sunglasses propped atop her head. A beautiful green dress showed off her figure, making a few women shoot Daisy envious glances. Goodness, what was wrong with Doc Harper? The man had to be blind not to be head over heels in love with her.

Greta got to her feet and crossed to Daisy, detouring the girl before she reached the sales counter. "Well, hello, dear. Fancy seeing you here."

Greta wanted to add, *Shopping for a vow renewal dress?* but thought perhaps it might be a tad soon to spring that question on Daisy. Given the sparks between those two the other day, it was clear not all was well in Harper-relationship world. Though Greta was sure, given enough time and gentle nudges, Daisy and Colt would fall back in love again. And a happy, madly in love doctor would mean less vegetable lectures for Greta. Win all around.

"Hello, Greta." A genuine smile filled Daisy's face. "So nice to see you again."

Greta gestured to the bag on Daisy's shoulder. "Shopping spree or shopping atoning?"

Daisy laughed. "Atoning. I bought two dresses today, but decided to return the second one."

"If I still had a figure like yours, I'd wear every dress I could get my hands on." Greta wagged a finger at her. "Flaunt what God gave you, dear, and if God makes a dress that flaunts it even more, buy it."

"Well, I already did that." She waved a hand down the figure hugging green dress. "Unfortunately, it didn't have the intended effect. I figured I might as well return the other one I bought in red, and use the money toward the renovations instead."

"Now, that's no fun." Greta put an arm around Daisy and drew her deeper into the shop, and away from the register. Once again, she questioned her doctor's intelligence level and visual acuity. If he hadn't been swayed by this beauty, then there had to be something seriously defective with him. Lord only knew why she'd take medical advice from a man who clearly had a screw loose. "Why don't you hang out with Olivia and me? We're shopping for wedding dresses."

"Oh, I shouldn't," Daisy said. "Olivia doesn't even know me and—"

"What do you think, Grandma?" Olivia stepped from the dressing room and spread her arms. The dress Greta had chosen nicely accented Olivia's trim figure. It was a pale white, almost ethereal, with delicate beading that traced the scoop neck and sparkled along the empire waist. It fell to her calves in a fabric cloud, but hung light enough to spin when she pivoted.

Tears sprang to Greta's eyes. She pressed a finger to her nose, and told herself not to get emotional. For once, she didn't listen to herself. She dug a handkerchief out of her purse and pressed it to the tears. "Oh, Olivia, that is . . . beautiful. You are beautiful. Just breathtaking."

Olivia gathered Greta into her arms with a warm, gentle hug. "If this one makes you cry, then it's the right one."

Greta drew back. "Are you sure? Do you love it, too?"

Olivia nodded. An excited, happy light shone in her eyes. "It's perfect. You have excellent taste, Grandma."

"Of course I do. I picked you to be my granddaughter." Greta gave Olivia a grin, then stepped back to grab Daisy's hand and pull her closer, before she got it in her head to leave. For a second there, she'd forgotten all about poor Daisy. "My goodness, sometimes I lose my manners. Olivia, I want you to meet Daisy Barton. Daisy, meet Olivia, the best granddaughter I could ever ask for. Daisy is the one renovating the Hideaway Inn."

Olivia shook with Daisy. "Luke told me about that. He said there might be a possibility we could have our wedding there. It sounds wonderful. My grandma-to-be here has been singing the Hideaway Inn's praises. When are you reopening?"

"Soon. My cousin and I are working on the logistics of that," Daisy said. "I have to talk to the contractor before I can be sure that I can make a wedding next month work, but I definitely want to try and make it happen for you and Luke. We want to get the Hideaway Inn back in business as soon as possible."

Aha. There was the key to getting Daisy to stay—talking about the inn. Maybe Greta wasn't going to win Daisy over with romantic wedding shopping, but if she was lucky, a little conversation about the Hideaway would get some wedding fever to rub off on her. If Greta was doubly lucky, Doc Harper would wander in and she could get the two of them to be in a marriage mood.

Instead, the door to the shop opened again and Harold Twohig strode in, bold as a peacock. He beelined past the circular racks, didn't slow to look at the mannequin displays of wedding dresses, and didn't stop moving until he reached Greta. "If I'd known you wanted a wedding dress, I would have proposed, my little bumblebee."

She slugged him. Hard as an eighty-three-year-old could slug an eighty-four-year-old lecherous old man. "I am not here for me. I am not interested in getting married again. And I am definitely not your bumblebee, you old fool."

Harold chuckled. "Hide our love all you want, Greta. I know it's there." He leaned in closer and lowered his voice. "Especially when you share a plate of lasagna with me."

"That was an anomaly. I was hungry. And overcome by the scent of cheese."

Olivia grinned. "Did you have dinner with Harold, Grandma?"

That man might as well be going around with a megaphone. Blaring her personal life in public, like a town crier with a hot bit of gossip.

"I most certainly did not." Greta paused. "Willingly."

Harold just laughed again. "Well, perhaps I will see you later tonight when I put some artery-clogging rib eyes on the grill. Say, around six? Right now, I'm heading out of town to help my sister bring in her boat for repairs. I have to reschedule my checkup with Doc Harper, but I'll be back before dinner."

"You have a sister?" She knew little about Harold's personal life. By choice, of course, because if she knew about his family and friends and all his past triumphs and tragedies, she'd build a relationship with him. That was akin to raising the enemy's flag on her roof.

"A younger sister at that. Which means my mother thought I was so perfect, she'd have another just like me." He winked.

"Or she was so disappointed in the results with the first baby, she popped out a backup. Optimism in childbirth."

"Optimism. I always have that." Harold leaned over, pressed a kiss to Greta's forehead, quick, like an inoculation shot, then shifted away before she could land another blow. "I'll see you later today, honey bun."

Greta made a gagging sound as Harold walked away. He just toodled a wave over his shoulder and ignored her. "That man is ridiculously blind to my signals," she said.

Olivia laughed. "Grandma, if you eat lasagna with the man, he's going to think you're interested."

"I was simply taking advantage of a free meal. What he reads into that is not my concern." She turned to Daisy. She was the one Greta wanted to get a man interested in — specifically one man who had altogether too many rules for healthy living. Luke and Olivia were happy now, same with Mike and Diana. All that Greta needed for a trifecta of happy endings was to resurrect Colt and Daisy's till-death-do-us-part. "Now, let's all grab some cupcakes. Lord knows I need something to settle my stomach after a visit from Harold Too-Clueless Twohig."

Olivia laughed and draped an arm around Greta's shoulders. "Some would call that butterflies, Grandma. Maybe Harold is starting to rub off on you."

"That's just his dandruff flaking onto my collar." Greta held her head high, and led the way out of the dress shop. One cupcake wasn't going to be enough, she decided. To eradicate all traces of Harold's touch, she was going to need a full dozen.

Ten

Colt lasted four hours.

He made it through the rest of his morning patients, choked down a lunch he didn't taste, and entered chart notes he hardly remembered. He barely answered Suzie's questions, and had the nurse take vitals since he couldn't concentrate long enough to remember the numbers he saw. The box of beignets sat on the break room table, always in the back of his mind. He'd gone in there at least three times to eat one, then changed his mind. Finally, he tossed them in the trash, and told himself it was a healthy choice.

But it didn't make him feel any better. Didn't ease his thoughts.

At one, he came out of his office and headed for the front desk. "What's the schedule look like for the rest of the day?" he asked Frannie.

She leaned back in her chair and arched a sharp auburn brow in his direction. Frannie had been with him for more than six years now and knew him better than he knew himself. She was a mother of four grown sons and grandmother to three more boys, and the one thing she didn't do was take crap from anyone. She ran his office like a well-oiled machine.

"You're asking me?" she said. "Half the time you know your schedule better than I do, Doc. You are freakishly well organized. Makes me feel like a hoarder."

Colt glanced at Frannie's desk, neat as a pin save for the stack of patient folders waiting in a wicker basket to be processed for insurance and then filing. "You? You are the most efficient assistant I've ever had."

Frannie laughed. "I'm the only assistant you've ever had, but I'll take the compliment." She turned to her computer, clicked on the scheduling program, then ran a finger down the screen. "Mrs. Ward canceled and Mr. Twohig rescheduled. That leaves just one other appointment for the day, a physical with Mrs. Cook."

"Mrs. Cook. Okay." He stood there, shifted his weight. His mind wandered back to Daisy. Had she really thought he'd sign off on a two-hundred-thousand-dollar loan, just for a beignet? Okay, a beignet and a killer dress that had been starring in a striptease fantasy in his head for hours. He refocused on his assistant. "Uh . . . what's Mrs. Cook coming in for again?"

Frannie met his gaze with direct, assessing green eyes that could diagnose a lie as well as he could diagnose pneumonia. "Nothing big. Just a physical. You know, I can easily reschedule that appointment for you, Doc. You look a little . . . distracted."

"I'm fine," Colt said. He fiddled with the pens on the counter, resorting them into blues on one side, reds on the other. "Just fine."

Frannie's hand covered his, stopping his ballpoint OCD. "You are far from fine."

He crossed to the window, then back again to Frannie's desk. Nervous energy coiled tight in his chest, a spring held back by a weakening pin. His mind kept straying to Daisy. He'd been so tempted by the beignets, by her. Truth be told, he hadn't thought about a single other thing the rest of the day. "When did you say my next appointment was? Who canceled again?"

The office door opened and Greta bustled into the room.
She wasn't on the schedule, which meant she was either here
on a fact-finding mission or to give Colt a piece of her mind
about broccoli. "Why, if it isn't Doc Harper. Just the man I
wanted to see."

He did not have the patience for this today. Heck, he barely
had the brainpower to function. "Mrs. Winslow, I'm—"

"There's not a car in the parking lot, and I know Harold
Twohig rescheduled his one o'clock."

"How do you know Harold Twohig rescheduled?"

"He told me as much when—" Her face reddened and
she waved a hand. "That's neither here nor there. What matters is that I am here on an urgent matter."

Colt took a step closer, ran a quick scan over Greta's
features. "Are you feeling all right?"

"I'm perfectly fine. I am in outstanding health." She
parked her fists on her hips, as if daring him to disagree.
"I'm not here to talk about me, or God forbid, Harold
Twohig. I want to talk about Daisy."

"Daisy?" What was with the universe today? Every time
he tried to stop thinking about Daisy, there was a reminder
of her. And *wham*, his mind was right back where it started.
On the beignets. On Daisy's dress. And most of all, on how
damned much he'd wanted to kiss her in the break room.
And still did, damn it.

"Daisy is a lovely woman," Greta said. "Olivia and I
spent most of the afternoon with her. Daisy is sweet and
warm and just a delightful addition to Rescue Bay. Especially since she's a budding entrepreneur, about to reopen a
long-standing business in this town. In my book, that's an
extra check in the plus-Daisy column." Greta raised her chin.
"I have no idea what kind of . . . foolishness you are embark-
ing upon with her, but I think it would be smart of you to
give her a reason to stay around."

"Mrs. Winslow—"

"A little birdie told me she needs a job. And since you
have connections within this community, I'm sure you can

help her out." Greta patted his arm. "Now I know you might think I'm meddling, but I'm merely trying to help strengthen our local economy by maintaining our workforce."

Frannie snorted out a laugh. Colt coughed to cover a laugh of his own. Of all the justifications he'd heard from Greta for her various machinations, this one was the boldest of all. "Helping the local economy?"

"Why, of course. It's part of my civic duty." She gave his arm a pat. "Anyway, you think about it. I'm sure something will come to you."

After Greta left, Colt stood by the window for a long time while Muzak played on the sound system and the A/C blew cool air into the room. He should have been thinking about his grandfather, about finding a way to bring Grandpa Earl out of that dark cave he'd retreated to, a way to restore what family Colt had left. Colt should have been thinking about his practice, his patients, hell, his taxes. But instead, his mind lingered on one thing.

Daisy.

If Greta was right and Daisy was looking to settle down, stay here, did that mean she had changed? And if she had, what did that mean to him?

Frannie came up behind him and handed him a note. "Doctor Kepler called. Your grandfather canceled his appointment and refused to reschedule. And I forgot to tell you earlier, but the visiting nurse left a rather angry voicemail this morning. Apparently your grandpa ran her off with a shotgun."

Colt ran a hand through his hair. "Great. Just what I need."

"It'll be fine." Frannie gave him a gentle smile. "My mom was like that after she got really sick with cancer. Wouldn't let anyone do a darned thing for her. She hated being weak and hated asking for help. It'll take some time, but I'm sure your grandpa will come around and you'll find a nurse who won't take any guff from Earl. You, though, *you* need a break."

"I'm fine, I'm fine." But he lingered by the window, trying to settle the thoughts that rushed through his mind like tumbleweeds.

After a moment, Frannie got to her feet, crossed into his

office, and returned with his briefcase. She pressed the leather satchel into his hands. "See you tomorrow, Doc."

"What? I still have patients."

"Your mind is as far from work as Earth is from the moon. You know it, and I know it."

"Frannie, I don't leave early. I don't take days off. I don't cancel."

"Which is exactly why you should do it today. Saints don't make good doctors, Doc Harper." She put a hand to his back and gave him a gentle nudge toward the door. "Now go take some time to clear your head. Work will be here tomorrow."

Colt wanted to argue, to tell Frannie work was the only thing he needed right now, but he would have been lying. She was right. He *was* distracted. The sooner he rid himself of that distraction, the better. Then he could focus on patient care. Instead of what had brought a five-foot-six curvy blast of his past hurtling into his well-ordered, carefully constructed life. The last thing he needed was Daisy bursting into town and shaking the snow globe of his world.

If she really was planning on staying and running the Hideaway Inn, that meant she'd be reopening the past Colt had tried so hard to put behind him. Exposing not just the man he used to be, but the mistakes he had made, too.

People in this town saw him as a respectable, conscientious doctor. But a responsible man didn't run off and elope with a woman he barely knew. A responsible man didn't walk out on his wife of three weeks. A responsible man didn't abandon the brother who was counting on him. A brother who—

Will you be here, Colt, when I get back?

Of course. I'm always here for you, buddy.

You're a good big brother.

Colt closed his eyes and drew in a shaky breath. He forced his thoughts back, tucking the past deeper into the recesses of his mind, something he had done a thousand times before. Because if he did that enough times, maybe one of these days it wouldn't hurt so bad. He took another breath, then another, until the dark receded.

Then he thanked Frannie and headed outside, to go home,

spend some time updating charts or analyzing spreadsheets or something equally predictable and safe. Something that would refocus his mind on work. Instead, when he reached in his pocket for his car keys, his fingers brushed against the slip of paper Daisy had given him.

Her familiar slanted handwriting stared back at him. Just her name, followed by the ten digits of her cell phone number. The *D* in Daisy as dominant as a sequoia, followed by a long scribble of the other four letters. The last time he'd seen her name written like that had been on a marriage license in Louisiana, with his name paired along hers, two signatures filled with hope and naïveté.

He got in his car, started the engine, and headed to the eastern side of Rescue Bay. He passed the turn for his own street, turned left, then right, before arriving at the destination that had been inevitable since Frannie handed him his briefcase.

The Rescue Bay Inn.

Daisy's dusty crimson Toyota was parked in front of Room 112 of the rundown, sun-paled building. No other cars sat in the lot, and the outdoor pool had only one visitor: a long-legged brunette in a navy blue one-piece swimsuit that molded to her curves like hot fudge on a sundae.

Damn.

He stood there for a long moment, feeling like a stalker, watching her lie in the sun, face upturned to greet the Florida rays, giant dark sunglasses masking her brown eyes. A *People* magazine lay on the concrete beside her, anchored in place by a half-full water bottle and an open package of cookies.

He unlatched the gate, and when the hinges creaked in complaint, Daisy sat up, and pivoted toward him. No expression betrayed her thoughts, but her shoulders stiffened and her hand curled tight around the aluminum frame of the chair.

All he noticed was the way the swimsuit hugged her body, the dark fabric ten times more dramatic against her pale skin. The way the neckline—a sweetheart neckline, some remote reach of his brain supplied—outlined the generous swells of her breasts, then dipped in a tantalizing V in the center. Her hair was undone, loose around her shoulders, and the breeze toyed with the dark tresses, as if taunting him with what he couldn't have.

He'd had an entire speech planned on the way over here. A list of a half dozen reasons why she should sign the divorce papers and go back to New Orleans. But every one of those thoughts flitted away, and all he managed instead was, "Enjoying the sun? It's a nice warm day for it."

Lame small talk. What was he, sixteen again? What was it about Daisy Barton that muddled Colt's mind? She made him feel like a geeky, stumbling fool.

She leaned back against the chair and studied him, her own eyes unreadable behind the oversized dark sunglasses. "Did you really come here to discuss the weather, Colt?"

"No, I didn't." He cleared his throat, then took a seat on the edge of the lounge chair beside her. He propped his elbows on his knees, and forced his gaze away from her cleavage and back to her face. "I came here to talk about us. Well, you. And me. And . . ." He cursed. "What the hell are you doing here, Daisy?"

Three times he'd asked her that same question. Maybe because he still couldn't put the words *Daisy, here,* and *back in his life* together.

"I'm enjoying the sun." She lay back against the chair and turned her face to the sky again.

"Goddammit, Daisy, don't play games with me. We had an understanding years ago—"

"An understanding? I thought it was a marriage."

"A marriage we ended, by mutual agreement," he said. "Until you came to New Orleans and thought you'd screw my brains out, for what, old times' sake?"

The harsh words iced the air between them. "That wasn't what that was."

"No?" She turned to him again, lowered the sunglasses, and met his gaze head-on. "Then what do you call it when you flirt with me, tell me you still care, take me back to your hotel room, have mind-blowing sex with me, and then FedEx divorce papers to me three months later?"

"I'm sorry I misled you."

She got to her feet, ripped off the sunglasses, and glared down at him. "*Misled* me? Is that how you're justifying it?" She shook her head, snatched up her towel, the cookies, and water, then jammed her feet into a pair of flip-flops. "You know what, Colt? You were right. It *was* a nice day to enjoy the sun. Until you came by."

Then she brushed past him and out through the gate. The metal swung back, clanged against a pole, and stayed there. Daisy marched across the lot, into Room 112, and slammed the door.

Well, hell.

Colt stood there, while the pool gurgled and traffic went by on the street a few feet away. He knew he should let her go. He should get in his damned car and go home or go back to work or go get a beer and put her out of his mind. Daisy Barton had never been one to be tamed or corralled. The sooner he quit trying to tell her what to do, the sooner she would get bored with whatever game she was playing here, and be on her way.

Or maybe . . . if he was smart, he could find a way to sever the ties with Daisy once and for all, and also restore order to his own life. He grabbed the magazine and crossed the lot to knock on the flimsy motel room door. An instant later, Daisy flung it open, still wearing the bathing suit, the towel discarded on the floor by the door.

"You forgot your magazine," he said, and held it out.

Once again, another brilliant sentence. What the hell was wrong with him?

She held his gaze for a minute, then looked away and bit her lip. She jerked the magazine out of his hand and started to close the door.

He reached for the edge, and stopped her. "And . . . I wanted to apologize. Can I come in?"

She considered that for a long moment, then stepped back and waved him into the room. They stood there, staring at each other, two people who once used to talk so much it seemed they'd run out of breath before they ran out of words, now mute and at an impasse.

"It wasn't mine," she said.

"What wasn't?"

"The magazine. I found it there. It was someone else's. I should take it back to the pool in case whoever left it comes back." She started to go past him, but he caught her arm. When she looked up at Colt, he realized that for all her bravado and anger, Daisy was scared.

Why? Did he make her as nervous and discombobulated as she did him? Maybe she was having trouble, too, trying to figure out what this was—or wasn't—between them.

"The magazine can wait," Colt said. "There's no one else at the pool."

"Still, I should . . ." She glanced down at his hand on her arm. He released her and stepped back, but the warmth of her flesh had left an invisible imprint on his palm.

"I'm sorry," Colt said. "For New Orleans. I never should have made you think there was something between us still. I was drunk and lonely and there was a part of me that . . ."

"That what, Colt?"

He didn't have an answer. He never did when it came to Daisy. That was the problem with her. She was the kind of woman who made a man forget his priorities and his plan. Every time he got within ten feet of her, his brain cells misfired.

"I . . . don't know," he said.

"Then why are you here? I thought we settled all this back in your office. You don't want me in Rescue Bay and you don't want to help me with the loan. So why did you come to the motel, and even more, why follow me to my room?"

"Oreo cookies." He shook his head and let out a little laugh. Who was he kidding? This wasn't just about restoring order to his life. It was about trying to make sense of why he was still drawn to the one woman who didn't make sense for him. "It was the damned Oreo cookies."

Confusion filled her eyes. "Oreo cookies?"

He picked up the opened package she had tossed on the nightstand. Dark chocolate crumbs littered the veneer surface like ants at a picnic. Inside the package, chocolate wafers rustled together. "The first time I met you, you were eating Oreos. I'd never seen anyone eat an Oreo like you do."

He could remember the day like yesterday. She'd been seventeen, sitting on the wide porch steps outside of the Hideaway Inn. He'd been in a hurry, rushing to his summer job at the paddleboard shop down the beach, but he'd stopped when he'd seen the pretty brunette sitting in the sunshine, with a half-eaten package of Oreos. She'd smiled up at him, a smile as bright and warm as the sun, and said, "Want one?"

That was it. Two words. It had stopped Colt in his rush to get to work. For that moment, he couldn't think of a single thing in the world that sounded better than sitting in the warm summer air with a pretty girl, eating cookies for breakfast. He'd dropped onto the step beside her, and *wham*, that was it. He'd been hooked, on the cookies, on her.

An embarrassed smile danced on her lips now, flushed her cheeks a pretty pink. "I only like the middle."

"And I only like the cookie part."

"I remember." Her voice was soft in the dim room, her eyes wide mysterious pools.

A long time ago, he'd found those differences between them sexy and endearing. He'd thought their wild, headstrong relationship, with all its clashes and drama, was a sign of meant-to-be. Now he knew better, or at least he told himself he did. Because right now, in the quiet solitude of a crappy motel room on the eastern side of Rescue Bay, Colt was having trouble thinking about anything more than how beautiful Daisy looked right now.

He put down the package and moved until he was inches away from her, until the dark floral scent of her perfume teased at his senses, awakening memories that haunted his nights, made him remember the backseat of his father's Grand Marquis and a squeaky bed in a fifth-floor walk-up.

It made him wonder about possibilities, like what might have happened if he had opened up to her years ago, instead of enduring those dark, horrible days alone. If he had called her and said *I need you, Daisy,* would she have come? And most important of all, would she have stayed?

That's what he wanted to know, the question that had drawn him to her in that diner three months ago. Once again, instead of asking it and opening doors he'd kept shut for fourteen years, he said, "Why are you really here, Daisy?"

"I told you. Because I need"—she took a breath and in that moment, he thought she'd say *I need you,* but then the breath passed and instead she said—"a new beginning."

The vulnerability in her words chipped away at his resolve. "Why here? Why now?"

She paused a long time. Then she turned away, crossed to the window, and looked out at the pool, sparkling in the sun. When she spoke again, her voice was low, quiet. "This place was the only place that ever felt like home. I know I was only here for a summer, but it was a *perfect* summer. I mean, look at this town. Gulf breezes, palm trees swaying in the wind, egrets that perch sedately on the edge of the water. It's like living in the middle of a Jimmy Buffet song."

"I don't know if it's quite as perfect as all that."

She shrugged. A melancholy smile curved up her face. "At the time my aunt asked me and Emma to take over the inn, I was so tired of working in dives, so tired of having men old enough to be my grandfather grab my ass when I brought them a menu," she went on. "And so, so tired of feeling like I was a hamster on a wheel, getting nowhere fast. Then when the chance came to resurrect the inn . . . well, it was time for a change, and maybe a chance to find that Jimmy Buffet world. So I came here."

He took a half step closer, and turned her to face him. Her chest rose and fell with her breath. The heat from her barely clad body drifted down his skin.

"That's all you want from me, Daisy? A cosigner on a loan?"

"You owe me that much, Colt, after . . ." Her eyes welled. She bit her lip, drew in a breath, and the tears receded. "Don't you think?"

She wasn't talking about that night three months ago in New Orleans. She was talking about how he had left her the first time, just up and walked away, a scared kid who hadn't cared how the chips fell behind him. He'd been focused on getting home, on making amends for leaving, and he'd never thought about how cruel it was to leave nothing more than a note behind.

He'd never told her why he'd left, why he hadn't returned. Why he'd excised his wife from his life after that day, like a tumor.

"I owe you more than that," he said, his voice suddenly rough against his throat. Every ounce of him was hyperaware of the tiny scraps of fabric covering her curves, the scent of cocoa butter tempting him like a siren at the edge of a rocky cliff. The bed a few feet away. The wild, headstrong rush that always enveloped them every time they were in close proximity, like magnets that couldn't resist the pull.

A cookie crumb dotted the edge of her lips. It made him think of the beignets. Of the first time he'd met her. Of all the times he'd wanted her and kissed her, and how much he still wanted to do just that.

"Won't your girlfriend be mad you're in a motel room alone with me?"

"I don't have a girlfriend, Daisy," he said. "I don't know what made me say that."

Her brown eyes were wide and dark, as rich as good coffee, and just as unreadable. "I don't know what made it bother me."

"It bothered you?"

She smiled. "A little."

"I'm glad." He reached up, and whisked the crumb away with his thumb, then let his touch linger against her sweet, tempting mouth. Her lips parted in surprise.

"What are you doing?" she whispered.

"I don't know." Then he leaned in and kissed her. His hand cupped the back of her head, tangling in the dark wall of silk, and his body surged against hers, while his other arm wrapped around her waist and pulled her even closer. She stiffened for a half second, then went liquid in his arms, opening her mouth to his. She tasted of sugar and cream, of sunshine and heat.

The kiss deepened, her tongue dancing a familiar tango with his. His mind became a foggy blur of memories and fantasies, stored up in their years apart. She nipped gently at his bottom lip, then soothed it with a sweet and tender kiss, the combination that had always sent his pulse into overdrive, and now had him grabbing her, yanking her closer, until he forgot where she began and he ended.

She curved into him with a familiar ease, breasts to chest, waist to waist, her legs pressing against his. He didn't think, didn't pause to find one of those straight lines. His hands roamed down her back, skipping over the tied straps holding the top of the swimsuit in place. The strings teased against his fingers, a thick bow waiting like a gift. He caught a loop, gave it a gentle tug, and the straps unfurled with a soft whisper. There was a hitch in Daisy's breath, and then she stepped back, her eyes locked on his, a half smile playing on her lips. The fabric held its position for one long second, then waltzed down her skin and slid over her breasts. She stood there, a woman confident in her own skin, her own sexuality, those glorious breasts round and firm and achingly perfect.

"Daisy. Dear God, Daisy." Anything more intelligent couldn't find purchase in his thoughts. He had a vague thought that he hadn't meant to do this, to come here, to get wrapped up in her again, but just as fast, the thought left him. "You are . . ."

"The same as I always was." The smile curved a little higher.

"Always incredible and always very, very beautiful." He had a whole other list of adjectives that could be applied to Daisy, but they fell away when he lifted his palms to cup her breasts. Three months ago, they'd been in such a rush, a hurried, frenzied, too-many-years-apart demand to have each other. Now all he wanted was time. Lots of time.

She mewed, then arched against his hands when his thumbs circled her nipples. "Colt, oh . . . we can't, we shouldn't . . ."

"I know," he said, pressing his lips to her throat, to the warm pulse ticking wildly beneath her skin. He reached around to the back of her suit, to tug down the rest, to have all of her, have her now, have her—

No.

He could write this ending in his sleep. What was he doing? He'd struggled for years to get what he had right now—a nice, quiet, predictable existence. The opposite of life with Daisy.

Then there was his grandfather. His priority was Earl Harper. Grandpa was the last tie Colt had to—

To what mattered most. What had always mattered most. *That* was what he needed to remember. Not this . . . fleeting moment of lust. Yeah, that's all it was. Fleeting lust, gone as soon as it started.

He stepped back. His body screamed *no*, his pulse raced like a horse in the final stretch. He shook his head, took another step. "I'm sorry. That got out of hand."

Yeah, maybe it would be easier if he put it that way, all calm and measured like the whole thing was just a momentary lapse in judgment, not a detonated rocket grenade in his solar plexus.

Daisy was already backing away from him, and retying the top of her suit, covering her chest. He couldn't tell if she was angry or relieved that he had stopped them.

"It always does between us. And that's the problem." She whispered a curse under her breath. "I shouldn't have gone along with it. I had no intentions of letting things get out of hand between us ever again."

"Neither did I." What was wrong with him? The second he'd seen her, he'd forgotten his reason for coming. Forgotten anything existed outside of Room 112 at the Rescue Bay Motel. That alone was a sign he'd made a mistake coming here. Colt was a planner, a man who didn't go off course.

Except he did. Every time he was around Daisy. And when he did that, people got hurt. People he loved.

She took a step toward him. "Then what the hell are you doing here, Colt?"

He had come here for a reason, a reason he seemed to have forgotten somewhere between the car and the motel room and her breasts. "You, uh, offered me a deal. Quid pro quo. Remember?"

"I'm not sleeping with you just to get a loan."

"I don't want to sleep with you. Well, I do—" Damn, his mouth kept running away from his brain. "But it wouldn't be a smart thing to do. For either of us."

She scoffed. "You can say that again."

He didn't know whether to be hurt or relieved that she felt the same way. Either way, sleeping with Daisy would make things messier, and if there was one thing he hated, it was messy. "Mrs. Winslow said you need a job. I need an . . . assistant."

"You already have one. And I have no medical training."

"Not for my office. For my grandfather. He fired the last two aides I hired. One of them before she even crossed the threshold. The two before that quit within the first two days. He refuses to listen to me, blows off his doctor appointments, refuses to take his medications, and eats like crap. If he doesn't start taking care of himself . . ." Colt had delivered bad news a thousand times, but never did it burn on its way up his throat like acid. "He could . . . die."

Concern filled her brown eyes. "Your grandfather is that sick?"

"He's on his way there. Early onset Parkinson's and heart disease. Both are conditions that require a change in lifestyle and habits, and he just doesn't want to change. It's like he's determined to . . ." Colt shook his head. He refused to speak that three-letter word again. "I can't let him do that to himself."

"But I wouldn't know what to do if there was a medical emergency."

"He just needs someone who makes sure he eats well and he takes his medication. Maybe get him out for a walk once in a while. He's . . . difficult. And you are the only person who has made him even come close to smiling in at least two years." Colt could still remember the Grandpa Earl who had joked and fished with his grandsons, the man Earl used to be—before.

That was how Colt divided his life. Before. And After. But no matter how hard Colt had worked to try to restore the Before, he had failed. Maybe with Daisy around, Earl would regain the jovial spirit he'd had years ago. Would once again be the grandfather who had taken Colt and Henry fishing and camping. Who had taught them how to change a flat and shoot an arrow. It wouldn't be the same as Before—there was no way to ever get those days back, no matter how much Colt tried—but it would be something. A chance at what he had lost fourteen years ago. That alone would be worth whatever deal Colt had to make. A deal that would keep Daisy here, disrupting his life, his sleep, his world. Maybe with enough time he'd become immune to her and his heart would stop stuttering every time she was near.

"In exchange for helping my grandpa," Colt said, "I'll sign the loan papers."

"You . . . you will?"

"And I'll pay you. What I would have paid an aide anyway."

Confusion knitted Daisy's brow. "Why not just have your family pitch in and help? Your parents, your brother?"

Colt's jaw hardened. He wasn't about to explain that his parents had moved to Arizona immediately After, after their lives had changed, after the family Colt once had was irrevocably broken. That his father would rather die than return to Rescue Bay. "They're not . . . here to help."

He didn't elaborate, and she didn't press the subject. "You're the one who got through to him the other day," he said, before she asked any more of the questions he didn't want to answer. "I need you, Daisy."

She eyed him, her chocolate eyes assessing and probing. "Why are you doing all this?"

"Because my grandfather matters more to me than anything in the world. He's . . ." Colt exhaled, trying to push the memories away, but they lingered, persistent, strong. The hole in Colt's heart had never really healed, and never really would, he suspected. He ached to return to the past, to have a do-over, a second chance to right the terrible wrongs of fourteen years ago. "He's all I have left. And I can't . . . I can't lose him, too."

"Too? What are you talking about?"

He didn't want to answer that question. He'd closed that chapter of his life a long time ago, and all he could do now was hold on to what he had left. "Will you help me or not?"

She hesitated a moment longer, then nodded. "Okay. I'll do it. Do you want me to start tomorrow morning or—"

"Now."

"Now?"

"You can't live in this . . ." He waved at the threadbare, depressing room. "Hellhole. And I can't leave my grandfather alone. Sometimes I get called out in the middle of the night because a patient falls ill. Sometimes my day runs longer than I expect. The only solution is someone who is always there. For this to work, I need you to . . ." He paused, questioning the wisdom of his plan. Especially in light of that kiss. But what choice did he have? He needed help, and so did she. "You need to move in."

"Move in?" She considered that for a moment, her gaze skipping over the room, then lingering on his face.

His heart stilled. He held his breath, sure she was going to say no. Half of him wanted her to say no, because he wasn't so sure he had the strength to live in the same house as Daisy and not want to carry her off to his bed.

"Okay. I'll move in tonight. But this"—she waved a hand over her body—"is off limits. You leave me, and my Oreos, alone, Colt Harper, and we'll get along just fine."

Eleven

Emma was ripping weeds out of the front flowerbeds when Roger's car pulled into the driveway. She was on her hands and knees, covered in clumps of dirt and sweat. Of course. He couldn't show up when she was wearing a killer dress and a slinky pair of heels or had her hair at least brushed, not tangled in a messy ponytail using the rubber band that had come wrapped around the Sunday paper.

"What are you doing?" he asked.

His voice was smooth and dark, like coffee on a cold morning, and even after everything that had happened and everything she had long ago given up on, his voice still slid through her with the same warmth as the day she'd met him, nine years ago. She felt that same flutter of attraction, the lilt of hope, that he was here for her, that he wanted her. Just as he had all those years ago. They'd met when he'd come up to her in a bookstore in downtown Jacksonville, holding up two cookbooks, one by Bobby Flay and one by Julia Child, and asked Emma which one was a better gift.

For a girlfriend? she'd asked.

He'd laughed, a rich, deep sound that seemed to come

from somewhere deep inside him. *My mother. I don't have a girlfriend.*

For the first time in Emma's life, she'd been flirtatious, spontaneous. It had been because of his eyes, wide and kind and almost ebony, and that delicious voice of his. *I'll tell you over a cup of coffee,* she'd said, and that had been it. One latte later, she was in love.

"Pulling weeds," she said to him now and turned back to the gangly green plants trying to take over her flowers. "Getting rid of what doesn't belong here."

Roger didn't say anything for a moment. "I came by to get my golf shoes. I went to play golf with Larry this morning and realized they were still . . ."

"In the garage. Second shelf. I . . . moved them out of your closet." She'd moved everything out of his closet and put it in the box on the shelf because it was easier to do that than to see his things still there, mocking her.

"Thanks." Roger headed into the open garage, disappearing for a moment in the darkened interior, then emerged a few minutes later with a shoebox and a statue. "Why is my samurai in the garage?"

She yanked out a plant, and too late realized it wasn't a weed. "It didn't match."

"I thought you loved this statue. Remember when we bought it? That day in—"

"Chinatown." She yanked another plant but her vision was starting to blur and again, she grabbed the wrong stalk. She sighed, sat back, and put her hands on her knees. She sucked back the tears, because she refused to let him see how much this bothered her, how much she still cared, damn it. "I remember us buying that samurai in a little shop from that owner who barely spoke English, and shipping it home in enough bubble wrap to hold a collection of Fabergé eggs. We said it was to remind us of the sushi and the music and the hills and everything we loved about San Francisco. I remember all of it, Roger. I remember us dating, I remember us getting married, I remember us promising forever and ever." She turned to him. He looked good, damn him, in a pressed blue shirt and faded jeans. But looking good and sounding good didn't make up for the fact that he had checked out of their marriage a long time ago, and then moved out when she'd tried to save them. Two months ago they'd had one night, one wonderful night when she'd thought everything was finally coming together for them, and then like turning off a switch, Roger was gone. "It's too bad you forgot."

"I didn't forget, Emma. We drifted apart."

"I hate when people say that. It makes it sound so soft and easy, like two boats in the water. We didn't drift apart, Roger. You changed." She propped a hand on her knee and looked up at him. "When is it enough? When have you made enough, worked enough, done enough? All along, you kept saying, once I sell the book, I'll take a sabbatical, we'll work on having a family . . ." She shook her head. "Instead, you work more. You're gone more. Now, you're gone entirely."

"Do you think I want to work all these hours? It's about security, Emma. Knowing we have something to fall back on, if things go south."

"You had me to fall back on," she said softly. "And you chose your job."

She went back to the plants, yanking and adding to the pile of refuse beside her, not caring what she was pulling out. "Don't forget to get the rest of your things."

He hesitated for a long time, so long she thought she might run out of weeds before he left. "What happened to us, Emma?"

She reached into the garden and wrapped her fist around a thick clump of goosegrass. "A weed grew in the flower-beds, Roger. And nobody bothered to take it out before it killed everything that was good."

Insane.

That was the only word for what Daisy was about to do. Insane, or desperate. Or both. She parked her Toyota in

Colt's driveway on Thursday night, grabbed the two bags of her belongings from the back—trying not to think about what it meant to be over thirty and have her entire life enclosed in two beat-up suitcases—then headed up the walkway. Colt's Honda wasn't here, which meant he had most likely gone back to work after he'd come to the motel.

Part of her was relieved not to see him. Part was disappointed.

She was doing this entirely to secure funding to renovate the Hideaway Inn. This wasn't about rekindling her relationship with Colt or giving their marriage the old college try. It was business, plain and simple. So she shouldn't care one way or another if he was here, at work, or harvesting rocks on the moon.

Uh-huh. Tell that to the stone of disappointment in her gut.

She needed to stop indulging in some decade-old romantic fantasy of riding off into the sunset with Colt. It was as if a part of her had never gotten past that day on the steps when he'd dropped down beside her, shared her package of cookies, and made her feel, for the first time in her life, like a smart, pretty, interesting person. Like someone who mattered.

Until he left her, alone and crying. Twice.

Only a fool had to get three strikes before calling an out.

She stood on the crushed shell walkway, holding one bag in each hand and debated—should she ring the bell? Or just go in?

She was saved from that choice when Earl emerged, holding the door for her. He was tall, a couple inches taller than Colt, and filled the doorframe with the authority of a man who had earned his place in the world. In the bright sunlight, she could see the wear in his features, the toll taken by getting old and battling illness. She could also see kindness in his eyes, and laugh lines around his mouth that spoke of a good man who'd lived a good life.

"Welcome to the bachelor pad, such as it is," he said.

"Home of late-night pizza and bad manners?"

"Of course. It's just like being in college, only with doctor's visits and medication alarms. Old men really know how to have fun." Earl let go of the door to reach for one of her bags, but Daisy shooed him away.

"You know very well that I'm here to help you, not vice versa."

"Doesn't mean I can't be a gentleman." He gave her an imaginary tip of his hat. "I'm not so old and decrepit that I can't be chivalrous, you know."

"Okay, then. But you get the light one." She handed him the smaller of the two bags, and followed him into the house. They were heading down the hall toward the bedrooms when the back door opened and Colt stepped inside.

"What are you doing? Why is my grandfather carrying your bags?" Colt rushed up, took the bag out of Earl's hands, and pivoted toward Daisy. Anger flared in his eyes, set in the tension of his jaw. "Didn't I tell you that you were here to care for *him*, not for him to wait on you hand and foot?"

Earl stepped between them and wagged a finger at Colt's chest. "Colton, don't you lecture her."

"Stay out of this, Grandpa."

"Who lit your beans on fire? You're even grumpier than usual, and that's saying something." Earl turned around and waved a hand in dismissal. "I give up. Have it your way, Captain Colt. I'm going to go watch the UFC fight on TV. Something civilized."

After Earl had gone down the hall and into the living room, Daisy whirled on Colt. She lowered her voice to a harsh whisper. "I am not treating your grandfather like a bellhop, Colt. He offered, and so I let him carry one little bag. He wants to feel useful, not put out to pasture."

"He shouldn't be doing anything, regardless of what he wants." Colt shook his head and cursed under his breath. "I knew this was going to be a mistake."

"Gee, way to trust me. I've been here ten seconds so far." She reached out, yanked the bag out of his hands, and strode past him. "Give me an hour and maybe I can really give you a reason to fire me."

She marched into the bedroom on the right—the one she assumed was meant to be hers, because there was a freshly made bed and a vase of brightly colored flowers on the nightstand. The flowers caused a stutter in her step. What had Colt been thinking when he'd put the vase at her bedside? Why was she touched? She was mad at Colt, and a few buds in a vase weren't going to change that.

She dumped the bags on the chair in the corner, then spun around to shut the door. She would have given it a nice good slam—oh, just like the old days with Colt—but he was there, his hand on the oak door, his tall frame blocking the doorway.

"I'm not trying to fight with you, Daisy. I just want you to make sure my grandpa takes it easy."

From the room down the hall, she could hear the soft undertow of Earl's television. Still, she kept her voice low. "I know that. And if you're going to question me every five seconds, this isn't going to work." She crossed her arms over her chest. "You need to trust me, Colt. I'm not going to hurt your grandpa. I like him."

"I'm not saying you'll hurt him on purpose." He shook his head again. "Okay, maybe I inferred that. But I didn't mean it."

Colt crossed into the room and took a seat on the edge of the bed. He braced his hands on his knees and let out a long breath. "I worry about him. He won't listen to me, won't take my advice. He needs to take care of himself, and as much as I wish I could, I can't force him to be smart about his health. God . . . if I lost him . . ."

She didn't want to care. Didn't want the raw notes in Colt's voice to weaken her. But they did. She crossed to the bed, sat down beside him, and placed her hand over one of his. "I'll take care of him. I'll boss him around and make him eat his vegetables and get him out on a walk once in a while. I promise."

Colt lifted his gaze to hers. He seemed so weary, so ready for someone else to step in and ease the burdens he carried. He searched her face for a long time, then nodded. The weariness ebbed a little. "I'm counting on you, Daisy."

No one had ever said that to her before. No one had ever

depended on Daisy Barton for anything. The enormity of the responsibility hit her like a weight. In an instant, this had gone from being a deal for a mortgage to something much bigger than she'd expected.

Something with hopes tied on the end, like strings trailing from a balloon. She wanted to say no, wanted to tell him he was putting his stock in the wrong girl. She'd never settled down, never been responsible for anything more complicated than a houseplant—and even those had withered and died within a week.

She needed this job, needed the loan. Needed to help Emma find whatever Emma had lost. And right now, Colt needed her.

In an instant, she'd gone from living a life where she answered to no one, to one with a whole lot of people tying expectations onto her. People, including herself, depending on her to make a difference.

"You can count on me," she said. Though the promise sounded shaky to her ears.

Colt's phone started buzzing. He flipped it out and glanced at the screen. "I gotta go. Patient emergency. Can you just . . . just stay and we'll talk later?"

"I'm not going anywhere."

Colt got to his feet, the phone in one hand, but paused in the doorway. His tie was loosened, the top button of his shirt undone, his hair a little mussed. And so was he. Those notes of vulnerability touched her, drew her closer.

"Listen, my grandfather can be difficult," Colt said, "and that's putting it mildly. Just make sure he takes his medicine and at least gets outside once in a while. Bribe him if you need to—the exercise will do him good, so will getting dressed and seeing the sun for a little bit."

"Will do. And if he refuses, I'll dangle a piece of pizza as an incentive. It'll be fine, Colt. I promise," she said again.

Relief flooded Colt's face and curved into a smile. "Thank you, Daisy."

"No need to thank me. I'm just doing my job." Though

it was the only job she'd ever had where resisting the boss was going to be tougher than the work itself.

The evening settled around Colt's shoulders like a warm, dark blanket. The moon hung high in the sky, full bellied and bright. A few night birds called to each other, and from somewhere far off came the hoot of an owl. The ocean whooshed in and out, kissing the sand before retreating again.

He thought of Daisy, asleep inside the house. Already, she tempted him and lured him, simply by being inside the same four walls. He'd told himself when he hired her to be his grandfather's live-in caretaker that he'd treat her like any other nurse.

Yeah, not so much. Five minutes in and he had already broken his own rules. He hadn't bought flowers for any other nurse. Hadn't made sure the room was stocked with fresh linens and that the pillows were fluffed. He hadn't wondered if any other nurse wanted Folgers or Starbucks in the morning. He hadn't fantasized about any other nurse, and stayed up half the night, hoping she'd wander out for a snack in something tiny and see-through.

He ran a hand through his hair and let out a long breath. Why did he want the one woman who reminded him of his biggest mistakes? His deepest pain? Every time she was around, she reminded him of what he had lost—

And why.

He had put his family on the backburner. Turned his back on them so he could run away and marry a woman he barely knew. And when the call had come, the call asking him to come back, he had ignored it.

Will you be here, Colt, when I get back?

Of course. I'm always here for you, buddy.

Colt drew in a breath, but it sliced through his chest like a machete. Damn it. Damn it. *Damn it.*

The caws of the night birds turned accusatory, the moon's light dropped a spotlight over Colt, as if the heavens themselves were asking him why he hadn't been there. Why he had promised Henry, then not shown up.

And Henry had gone alone to the lake. Fallen off the boat. And drowned.

Colt's heart fractured, and the breath in his chest shuddered in and out. "I'm sorry," he whispered, to the night birds, to the moon, but they didn't care. They didn't respond.

They never had. Colt tipped his head and took a long drag off the beer. It didn't help.

The back door opened and Grandpa Earl stepped onto the porch. "Sorry. I didn't know you were out here." He started to duck back inside but Colt put out a hand.

"It's okay. Have a seat." Colt gestured to the spot beside him on the porch. He had been alone with his own thoughts long enough and welcomed the company, if only because it would make his mind stop playing the endless loop of Henry's voice. Hell, he'd even welcome an argument with Grandpa if it would divert his thoughts from Henry's last words to him.

"Have a seat," Colt said again.

"Nah, it's all right. It's late. I should go inside." Grandpa turned to open the door again. When had they gotten to this point? To being strangers, barely even roommates? Colt missed the days when his grandfather had been his best friend, the one Colt could turn to for advice about cars and girls. Before his grandfather had started looking at Colt with disappointment and grief.

"Grandpa, wait."

His grandfather paused, his back to Colt, his hand on the knob.

"Come outside and sit with me." Colt swallowed. "Please."

Grandpa Earl hesitated some more. Then he let go of the door and lowered himself to the opposite side of the step. There was a good two feet of space between them, but it felt like a mile. He didn't say anything for a long while, then he nodded toward the sky. "Nice night."

Okay, so it wasn't a conversational milestone, but Grandpa was at least tethering a line between them again.

"Yeah. I love this time of year. Still pretty warm but not so hot you feel like you're living in an oven."

"The breeze off the water is always nice, too."

Here they sat, two men who used to be close, exchanging small talk about the weather. It frustrated Colt, made him want to get up and go in the house, giving up like he had done a hundred times before. Instead, he reached to the right and grabbed a beer from the box he'd grabbed earlier from the fridge, then held it out to his grandfather. "Want one?"

Grandpa Earl raised a brow in surprise. "You're offering me a beer?"

"Once in a while, a beer is okay. And besides, these are non-alcoholic." Colt picked up a second bottle. Regardless of all his lectures about healthy eating and living, right now what he wanted more than anything was a connection with the man who was more like a father than a grandfather.

Grandpa chuckled. "Non-alcoholic? What's the point?"

"Pretending they're real beers is almost the same thing as drinking one."

"Almost. Thanks." Grandpa took the bottle, popped the top, then clinked the bottle against Colt's. "Cheers."

The action brought back the memory of toasting with soda cans when he was a boy. Grandpa, Colt, and Henry, sitting on the wooden skiff that Grandpa used for fishing on the lake, drinking sodas in the sun and eating peanut butter sandwiches that Colt's mom had made for the boys. "What was it you used to say? To big fish and bigger tales?"

Grandpa Earl chuckled. "Something like that."

Colt spun the bottle between his hands. It cooled his palms, eased the tension in his shoulders. How he missed those days, missed the sun on his back, the suspense of a line in the water. It wasn't just the fishing that he missed, though, it was the time with his grandfather, when Grandpa Earl would ramble on about his childhood in a post-war world, or the best ways to deal with girls who still held an

ick factor for young Henry and Colt. He missed the camaraderie, the closeness. The bond.

For years, Colt had tiptoed around the subject of Henry,
avoiding that painful minefield with every breath he took.
Still, the unspoken words had sat in the background of every
conversation, like a festering wound. Maybe if they finally
talked about Henry, about what they had lost, it would be
that first step back to . . . somewhere other than here. Maybe
if he started with fishing, the one thing that used to bind
them all, it would help. "You know, Grandpa, if you ever
want to grab a pole, head for the lake, it might be a way to
remember him—"

The mood between them shifted in an instant. Grandpa
Earl let out a curse and put his bottle on the step. "Goddamn
it. Quit asking me, Colton."

"Why don't you ever want to talk about it?"

"Talking doesn't do anyone any good. It just fills the
world with more hot air." Earl drank from the beer, and
stared out at the ocean.

Colt sighed. "I miss him, too, you know. I'd do anything
to bring him back."

"Yeah, well, there isn't anything you can do to make that
right. There never will be." Grandpa Earl got to his feet and
went to the door. He opened it, then stood there, his head
hung low. "You keep talking to me about me having heart
disease, and about taking care of myself. Well, if you ask
me, my heart's been broken for fourteen years. There isn't
a drug in the world that's gonna heal that, so quit trying to
mend what's never getting better."

Then he went inside, leaving Colt alone in the dark.

Twelve

The next morning, Daisy realized what Colt had been talking about when he called Earl "difficult." Within ten minutes of Colt leaving for work, she'd had three arguments with Earl about taking his medication, the last one ending with him stomping off, slamming the door to his room, and raising the TV volume to deafening.

Daisy waited ten minutes, then strode down the hall and knocked twice on Earl's door. "Get your walking shoes on."

"I'm not going for a walk," he said through the closed door.

"We both are. And if you walk far enough, there's ice cream at the end of our route." The earlier pizza incentive hadn't moved Earl one inch, so Daisy decided to up the ante. A bowl of ice cream—well, frozen yogurt masquerading as ice cream, she decided—would motivate her to do about anything, so she figured it'd work on Earl's sweet tooth, too.

It reminded her of the beignets and Colt. Of how tempting and alluring a simple bite of fried pastry could be. And how much trouble it could get a woman in if she wasn't careful.

A second passed, then the door unlatched and Earl stuck his head out. The TV had been muted, and that told Daisy she'd already halfway won the battle.

"That ice cream offer wouldn't be a bribe, would it?" Earl asked.

"I prefer to call it a reward. I don't know about you, but I am a reward motivated kind of girl. Put a bonus at the end of a paycheck, or a great pair of shoes at the end of a tedious shopping trip, and I'm in, a hundred percent."

"I don't need bonuses, and I prefer a decent pair of Timberlands over any other kind of shoes. But ice cream . . ." A smile curved across Earl's face. "You know my grandson will read you the riot act for that one."

"Then I say we destroy all the evidence before we get back." She bent and picked up a pair of sneakers, sitting just inside his door, far easier to walk in than his beloved boots. She dangled them in front of Earl. "Chocolate chip or vanilla?"

On Friday night, Colt stood in his living room, looking down at the giant brown-and-white ball of fur sprawled at his feet, then up again at the two guilty parties, one sitting in the La-Z-Boy and the other on the edge of the sofa. Neither had the slightest bit of contrition in their features.

"What the hell is this?" Colt said.

"You went to college. I'm sure you can figure it out." Earl harrumphed, then flipped out his footrest and leaned back in the chair.

"I'm not asking literally, Grandpa. I mean, what is it doing in my living room and whose idea was it?" Not even twenty-four hours after Daisy moved in, Colt's perfectly ordered life was in disarray. He shouldn't have been surprised. Daisy never had been one for asking permission or thinking a decision through. But this choice . . . this one impacted Colt, not just today, but for years to come. "Well?"

No one answered him. Grandpa Earl fiddled with the remote, while Daisy just sat on the edge of the sofa, with a smile on her face. The kind that said she knew she was breaking the rules, and didn't care. There'd been a time when he had loved that about her, and been as much of a

party to rebellion as she was. Skipping school, blowing off
work, partying in public places—Colt and Daisy had done
what they wanted, when they wanted, and when his father
had disapproved, Colt had hopped on his Harley, with Daisy
on the back, and blown off everything and everyone.

And look where it had gotten him.

"Well, either way, it goes back." Colt waved a hand at the
door, but still no one moved or said a word. "Immediately.
I don't have time or space or—"

The floppy-eared beast on the floor got to its feet, then
nosed Colt's pant leg. A long brown tail wagged a happy
beat, then the dog lifted his head, pressed it beneath Colt's
hand. Seeking attention, approval?

The stone resolve in Colt's chest eased a little. How could
it not? The dog looked up at him as if he was saying *Just
give me a chance to worm my way into your heart.* The dog's
tail kept on wagging, and his head bopped beneath Colt's
palm. *Love me, love me.*

Colt gave the dog's head a half a pat. Seemed kinda mean
not to at least respond. It was a silly-looking dog, half-brown,
half-white, two giant ears flopping to the side. As hairy and
big as he was, the dog had to be a mix of some kind of
sheepdog or mountain dog, and something else that Colt
couldn't figure out. He didn't know much about dogs, and
especially not this dog.

"We were thinking of calling him Major. You know, because he kind of looks . . . authoritative," Daisy said.

"He looks like a Major Pain, is what he looks like." Colt
gave the dog another pat, which apparently provided an
open-ended invitation to be his new best friend. The dog
started panting, then sat squarely beside Colt's foot, his tail
swishing a half circle in the carpet. "We're not keeping
him." Colt tried to keep his voice firm and resolute, even as
the dog pressed his furry head against Colt's hand again.
Love me, love me, I'm nice. "I don't have time or room for
a dog."

"You said that already," Daisy said, with that knowing
smile.

"Because apparently neither of you thought of that before you brought Major Pain here home." Didn't they realize how much he already had on his shoulders? His grandfather, his practice, his . . . whatever this was between himself and Daisy? The last thing Colt Harper needed was something else with a heartbeat depending on him.

"A dog takes up no room at all," Grandpa said. "Besides, he's my dog now, and I'm keeping him. You want him out, you'll have to kick me out first. Major and I are a package deal." He thumbed the remote, and the TV sprang to life with some show about digging for gold in Alaska.

Daisy got to her feet. She was wearing short white shorts that showed off her incredible legs, already beginning to tan. Her feet were bare and there was something that seemed both carefree and intimate about that. She had on a dark blue T-shirt that dipped in an enticing V in the front, with a floral pattern running down the sides that encouraged his gaze to dip lower, to linger on her curves. For a second, he forgot about the dog, forgot he was irritated by the newly adopted furbeast in his living room, forgot everything but how awesome her legs looked.

When Daisy put a soft hand on his shoulder, it seemed to sizzle and spark, down his arm, through his veins, like the wick on a stick of dynamite. "Colt, will you come help me set the table for dinner?"

Colt started to say no—his to-do list was as long as his arm and getting longer by the minute—but then he glanced at her amazing legs again and thought he could follow those legs to Mars, if need be. "Sure. No problem."

They headed into the kitchen, Major Pain—already, Colt was thinking of the dog with a name, which was a dangerous thing—bringing up the rear, with a hopeful wag of his tail. He settled in the corner by the back door, head on his paws, his brown eyes watching the humans.

"Tell me again . . . Why is there a dog in my house?" Colt asked. He kept his voice low, to keep it from carrying into the living room. Grandpa Earl had changed the channel to

Wheel of Fortune, and Colt could hear Pat Sajak congratulating someone on winning a trip to Greece.

Daisy shrugged. "It's an incentive."

"Incentive? For what?"

"For walking. Your grandpa and I went for a walk today—"

"Wait." Colt put up a hand. "You got him out of the house? Like *out* of the house, out of the house? Not just onto the porch or into the yard for five seconds?"

She nodded. "All the way out of the house and into town. We walked down to the boardwalk, then downtown, and back again. We stopped for breaks often and—"

Colt shook his head. He glanced at Grandpa's sneakers, sitting by the back door instead of in his room or in a closet. A few blades of grass clung to the soles. "He hasn't left the house in six months. He hasn't done *anything* for six months."

Actually, it had been longer than that since the Grandpa Earl that Colt knew and loved had made an appearance. More than a decade since his grandfather had done anything more than work and lock himself in his garage to putter with his tools. Or so he claimed. Colt suspected Earl used the garage door as a wall, a way to disengage from the rest of the world.

Hell, Colt couldn't blame him. He'd done the same thing, only with medical texts and college classes. Immersed himself in staying busy so he wouldn't have time to think, to breathe, to answer the questions in his own mind.

Now here was Grandpa Earl, finally, after all these years, making the first steps back to building connections, getting out in the world. All because of a dumb dog, and a very smart woman.

"That is . . . amazing, Daisy," he said.

She shrugged, as if it was no big deal. "We walked about a mile all together, I'd say. We had lunch on the boardwalk and then when we headed downtown, there was a little event in the park for the local shelter, and Olivia had some dogs out for adoption, and . . ." Daisy threw up her hands and gave Colt another smile, the kind that said *Forgive me, but*

I couldn't help it. "Your grandpa was going on and on about how much he missed his old dog Beau, and how his life hadn't been the same, and when he saw Major there"—the dog flopped his tail in agreement—"I saw his face light up. He looked ten years younger." She leaned in closer, her eyes bright. "He was smiling, Colt. An honest to God smile."

In less than a single day, Daisy had been able to do what Colt couldn't do in fourteen years. With a walk in the park and a stowaway dog. An odd mixture of gratitude and jealousy rolled through Colt. "I can't remember the last time I saw my grandfather smile."

Daisy put a hand on his arm, and met his gaze with her own. Her brown eyes softened with sympathy, understanding, as if she knew what it was like to lose something precious, and then have a glimpse of that magic again.

Once again, it had him wondering if maybe he'd made a mistake years ago, keeping his pain to himself, shutting her out. Letting her go.

"Then let him keep the dog," she said softly.

"I've never owned a dog. I don't know the first thing about taking care of one." As far as excuses went, that one was pretty lame. *Yeah, I don't know how to feed something every day and let it outside, so take it away before I get attached.*

"I'll make sure your grandpa gets out and walks Major/ Major Pain here every day, plus do anything else the dog needs."

"And after you're gone? Who'll do it then?"

Was he just asking about the dog? Or was he already starting to worry about how he would accomplish the miracles this woman had brought to his life in a mere twenty-four hours? The Daisy he had met—the Daisy he had married—hadn't been the kind of woman who would patiently walk around town with an elderly man. Who would find the one thing that would make that man smile—and fight for him to become a part of the family.

Had he been wrong about her? Or had she changed in the years they'd spent apart?

"You looking to get rid of me already?" She said,

bringing him back to the question he'd asked. She grinned. "I've only been here for one day."

He inhaled, and caught the scent of baking bread, roast turkey. It was as if he'd walked into a restaurant. A really good restaurant, not the slap it together short-order cooking place that Colt had created here in the last few months. Not only that, but the dishes were done, the windows open to let in the breeze, and there were fresh-cut flowers from the yard in a vase on the kitchen table.

He shook his head, inhaled again. "Are you . . . are you making dinner?"

She glanced at the stove. "Yup. Honey-orange basted turkey, whole wheat bread, and oven-roasted broccoli. Healthy, but still delicious."

He opened the oven and peeked inside. The turkey glistened, brown and juicy, beside a tray of broccoli just beginning to soften. The bread plumped in a golden brown arch, ready for a thick pat of butter. His stomach rumbled, and the salad he'd had for lunch seemed a very distant memory. "That looks amazing. I didn't even know you could cook."

"I can do a lot of things that you don't know about, Colt." She slipped on a pair of pot holders, then took the meal out of the oven and put it on top of the stove. For a minute, she seemed as domestic as Betty Crocker—only a decidedly sexier version of the cooking icon, with those amazing legs and endless curves. "You're not the only one who's changed in the last few years. And if you keep me around, I might just surprise you."

He thought of the dog and the dinner and the smile on his grandfather's face. "You already have, Daisy. You already have."

Thirteen

Unnerving. That was the best word for that moment back in the kitchen. She'd hurried through the meal and cleanup, then claimed to be tired and headed off to bed. Sleep hadn't come, and now, several hours later, Daisy sat in her room, watching the moonlight fall over the Gulf of Mexico, and wondered if she'd been crazy to agree to this deal with Colt. Yes, she needed the loan. Yes, she needed the income—

But at what cost?

That soft tone in his voice, that smile on his face, that wonder in his eyes when he realized the changes in his grandfather and in his house, all spoke of a man who was counting on her. She sucked at being the one people counted on. And yet, like a glutton for punishment, she kept throwing herself into positions that required responsibility and dependability.

Not to mention that little domestic scene earlier, where Daisy was Harriet Homemaker with an apron, some pot-holders, and fresh bread. If she didn't watch out, she'd get used to that role—used to pretending she was Colt's little wife, with dinner and a smile waiting at the end of the day.

No way was she getting sucked into that fantasy again. No ever-loving way.

Soon as Emma got here, Daisy was handing over the keys and hitting the road. Going back to the kind of jobs that required nothing more than an ability to write down *cheeseburger, medium rare, hold the mayo, side of fries*.

Except a part of her didn't want to leave. A part of her wanted to stay right here, in this place that had once been so magical, and try to find that same wonderful feeling again. It was the price she might end up paying for trying to set down roots that she couldn't abide.

Because there would be a price. Daisy knew that too well. Hadn't she learned over and over again with Willow that settling down was a fairy tale reserved for others? Heck, Daisy's own marriage hadn't even lasted as long as the Christmas buying season.

Yet she'd still had hope, even after Colt left her. The first time, she'd held on to hope for a long, long time, staying in that apartment and the city, figuring he'd be back. That same hope was what had brought her back to New Orleans years later, after dozens of jobs and address changes. Then, like Sleeping Beauty, that hope had fluttered to life again when Colt had stopped in the diner fourteen years after she'd last seen him. For one crazy night, she'd believed they had a second chance.

Foolish. That should be her middle name. Colt wasn't any better at settling down and building a relationship than she was. Even if he gave off the appearance of being Joe Homebody with those damned khakis. The Colt she knew didn't open up and share at the end of the day. He didn't let her into his thoughts, or his heart. Even now, even after all these years, and that stung.

Daisy turned on her phone, and pulled up the messaging program. Her hand hovered over the keys for a long time. Outside her open window, the ocean whispered a soft caress against the sand, and a light, warm breeze clicked through the palms. Nostalgia washed over her, and when she closed her eyes, she was seventeen again and lying in one of the twin beds in the back bedroom of the Hideaway Inn, trading secrets in a hushed voice.

Before she could think twice, Daisy typed in Emma's name. *Can't sleep*, she texted. *Remember that time we snuck out with a bottle of wine to the beach in the middle of the night?*

There was a pause, then a *ping*. *OMG. I remember that. That wine was so disgusting. We got sick right after we drank it.*

But it was fun while it lasted, wasn't it? She added a smiley face, then hit send.

It was. And then a second later, a smiley face from Emma.

Daisy itched to press the issue, to ask Emma to come to Rescue Bay, to try to find those memories that were as scattered as the shells on the beach, but hesitated. What if she pushed and Emma withdrew even more?

This is almost like staying up all night in that tiny bedroom we shared.

Talking about boys, LOL.

Daisy hesitated, then typed, *Speaking of boys . . . remember Colt?*

An immediate text back. *Of course. Why?*

I'm sort of staying at his house. It's a long story, and we're not involved—Okay, maybe that kiss in her motel room told a different story—*I'm sort of helping him out.*

A moment passed, and then Daisy's phone rang. She pressed the button and sat back against the pillows. "How'd I guess that mentioning I was sort of living with Colt would make you call?"

Emma laughed. "Well, you can't just drop a bomb like that on me through text. That kind of news *demands* a phone call."

For a moment, Daisy just enjoyed the sounds of laughter in Emma's voice. Once, Emma had been Daisy's best friend, the closest thing to a sister she had ever known. Over the years, Daisy had let that relationship lapse. She hadn't realized how much she had missed Emma until she heard that laugh. "I saved the biggest news for last."

"Bigger news than reuniting with the one man who trips your trigger?"

"The man I am also still"—Daisy toyed with the edge of the blanket—"married to."

Emma gasped. "Wait. Whoa. Still married? Really?"

"Yup, in name at least. It's a long story about paperwork that never got filed. Now I'm living with him. But not living with him, living with him, if that makes sense."

"Not screwing his brains out, I take it?"

"No, definitely not. No." Not that Daisy hadn't thought about doing that, oh, a thousand times. Pretty much with every waking breath. Knowing a mere flight of stairs separated her from Colt made heat rise in her gut, sent her pulse skittering. In a few seconds, she could be upstairs, in his room, in his bed, in his arms. "No way."

Emma laughed. "That's a lot of negatives, Dase. Does that mean you're *thinking* about screwing his brains out?"

"Not at all. I'm just here to help him with his grandpa, until he finds a full-time caretaker."

"You are a sucky liar. You know that, right?"

"Either that or you're a great detective." Daisy settled against her pillows and drew the blanket to her chest. She clutched the phone tighter, as if doing so would erase the distance between her and her cousin. "Emma, I've missed talking to you."

"Same here, Dase. Same here." Something in Emma's tone, though, trended toward deeper shades of melancholy. Whatever it was, she didn't elaborate, just let the silence stretch across the phone connection.

When had they gone from being best friends to being distant relatives? Daisy well remembered the days when Emma had told her every minute detail about her life, and Daisy had done the same. Aunt Clara used to say the two girls lived in each other's pockets, and for a long time, it seemed that way. Then Emma had gotten married to Roger and she'd begun to drift away, a little more each year.

Maybe it was just Emma being married, caught up in a different kind of life than Daisy's. Daisy had lived here and there, jumped from job to job, letting more and more time lapse between phone calls and visits to Jacksonville. After a while, she and her cousin had lost track of the things they had in common.

Deep down, though, Daisy knew there was more than just a few missed connections eroding her relationship with Emma. Something that lurked in the shadows of every conversation, but that Emma wouldn't voice.

"By the way, I'm meeting a contractor at the inn tomorrow," Daisy said, forcing the worry from her voice and replacing it with bright optimism. "A friend of a friend, who says he'll cut me a break on the price. Maybe that'll take the estimate from astronomical to affordable. Which means together, we could handle the payments. And there's a couple here in town who want to hold their wedding at the inn next month. The Hideaway Inn is coming back to life, Emma."

Emma sighed. "I don't want to run that place, Daisy. I wish you'd let it go."

"You used to love it here. You loved it here more than I did."

"That was . . . before."

"Before what?"

A long pause. "You know, it's late. I better get some sleep. I have a photo shoot tomorrow at the crack of dawn."

And in those words, Daisy saw an opportunity. A small window. If she could just get Emma to come to Rescue Bay, maybe she could find a way to bridge this gap between them. A way to ease the sadness that hung on the end of every syllable Emma spoke. "You know, you really are a fabulous photographer, Em."

"Thanks."

"Why don't you come down to see the inn, take a few pictures, and let me use them for marketing? You don't have to stay long. Just a few days, a weekend even. If you like how the place is coming together, then stay. If not, go back to Jacksonville and to your job." Daisy pressed on, hoping that if she kept talking enough, Emma would just say yes. "At least give me the chance to show you what it can be, and in exchange, you try to capture a little of that magic on film. A win all around, not to mention a cheap vacation. Plus, as soon as the kitchen's up and running, I'll bake those chocolate chip cookies you love."

"Daisy, I don't know . . ."

"Then you can tell your mom you at least came down here and saw the place. That'll make her happy and get her off your back." Daisy caught her breath. "See? Win all around."

Another long pause. This one stretched so long, Daisy checked to make sure the connection was still intact.

"I'll think about it," Emma said finally. "That's all I can promise."

"That's all I ask." Daisy held tight to the phone and decided that she would stay, as long as it took. Emma needed a new start—whether she knew it or not—and Daisy wasn't going anywhere until she got it. Not yet.

Colt paced his room, back and forth, between the view of the Gulf and the view of the neighbor's roof. The small bedroom on the second floor of the bungalow had gables at either end, making Colt's pacing more of a short shuffle.

Every step, he was aware of Daisy, sleeping just one floor below him. Did she still sleep in the nude? Or did she wear a ratty old T-shirt? A sexy nightgown?

Then his oh-so-helpful insomniac brain flashed back to lying in bed with her, naked and warm beneath the covers, legs intertwined. One touch led to two, led to him climbing on top of her and sinking into her deep, wet warmth, again and again and—

Okay, that was not productive thinking. At all. Now he not only couldn't sleep, but he also needed an ice-cold shower. He threw on a pair of baggy sweats, then headed downstairs. The kitchen was dark, save for the light coming in from the moon outside the window.

He paced a little more. Didn't make the thoughts recede. He opened up the fridge. Golden light spilled onto the floor, stretching across the tiles, skipping over the furniture, then revealing two long shadows. Two long, shapely shadows that had been starring in his fantasies a second ago.

Colt cleared his throat. "Daisy. What are you doing up?"

"I couldn't sleep." She ran a hand through her hair, which displaced the dark waves, until they tumbled into place again over her shoulders and her oversized T-shirt. The tee sported the logo from the diner where he'd seen her three months ago, and a giant coffee cup in the center. She had on loose-fitting pink-and-white-striped pajama pants, and her feet were again bare, revealing those crimson toes. Not naked, but still sexy in a rumpled, come-hither way.

"I guess I'm not the only one with insomnia," she said.

Major Pain padded out to the kitchen with him, his tail in overdrive. Daisy gave the dog's head a little pat, then opened the back door and let the dog out.

Colt stood there like an idiot, with the fridge door open and blasting cold air into the room, staring at Daisy's T-shirt and thinking about that night he'd walked by the diner, seen Daisy inside, and instead of turning left and avoiding her, he'd turned right, gone inside, and gotten a table at her station. He'd told himself it was because he was curious about how she was doing, when in reality, he knew better.

It was because she was the only woman he'd ever met who could turn him inside out with nothing more than a smile. At the time, he'd been debating whether to propose to Maryanne, to settle down in a predictable, boring life with a nice but dull woman. Then he'd seen Daisy, and known deep in his heart that he'd never be happy in that predictable, boring, safe life.

Why was it that what his brain wanted and what his body craved diverged on two very different paths? He kept going left when he knew he should turn right. Did she feel the same? Was that why she was here, awake like him?

"Do you want to talk about what's keeping you from sleeping?" he said.

She smiled. "How'd you know I had something on my mind?"

He might not have lived with Daisy in over a decade, but he still remembered their late-night conversations. So many of them, it seemed like they spent more time in the dark than in the light of day. "Remember the night before you had that job interview, back in New Orleans. You were up until, what two? Three?"

"Three thirty."

He remembered that night, the space beside him in the bed, finding Daisy in the next room, clad in one of his shirts and nothing more. "I got up, because the bed was cold, and you were wearing down a path between the door and the television."

The smile widened. "You told me not to worry about the job interview because if that door shut, it meant a better one was going to open for me. It set my mind at ease, and I went back to sleep."

Was that why he hadn't been able to sleep? Because the space beside him in his bed was empty? Or because a part of him was still so tuned to Daisy that he sensed when she was awake? "So what door are you worried about today?"

"The fridge door. You planning on eating anything?" Daisy nodded toward the open refrigerator. "Because I'm thinking that leftover pizza sounds really good right now."

"Oh, that's not a healthy option. I should have an apple or . . . something." Though none of that appealed to Colt, either. He wondered why she didn't want to open up to him, why she was keeping her worries to herself, then realized that he did the same thing, and had been for years.

She was working for him, nothing more. He wasn't here to solve her problems or ease her stresses. Or wonder what it would be like to have her warm his bed at night. But he did, damn it. More than he wanted to admit to her, or to himself.

Daisy reached past him, the soft cotton of her T-shirt gliding against his arm with a whisper. She grabbed the plate with the pizza, then looked up at him. "Come on, Colt. Live a little."

"I'll, uh, have an apple instead." He pivoted to the right and grabbed a Red Delicious out of the bowl on the counter. And tried not to think of the irony of him trying to avoid Daisy's temptations by opting for the biblically famous symbol of temptation.

"Suit yourself." Daisy put the pizza in the microwave. While the food heated, she let the dog back in, then reached into the fridge for one of Grandpa Earl's beers. "Is it okay if I have one?"

"I won't mind, but Grandpa Earl might."

"It's only been a day. I think he still likes me." She popped the top and leaned against the counter, drinking from the bottle. "Might as well take advantage of that while I can." She hoisted the beer in Colt's direction. "Cheers."

"Cheers." He tapped the bottle with his apple, then took a bite. The microwave dinged. Daisy withdrew the pizza and leaned against the counter again. She picked off a piece of pepperoni and popped it in her mouth.

"Don't you, uh, want to sit down and eat that?" Colt gestured toward the kitchen table, with its napkins and place mats and civility.

She shook her head, a soft, sexy smile on her face. "It feels so much more decadent when you're standing up."

Colt swallowed. Took another bite of the apple. It tasted flat and plain on his tongue, like it was made of cardboard. He moved a couple inches closer to Daisy, drawn to her, as he had been that first day with the cookies. She broke the rules, in every element of her life, and the part of Colt that chafed under his straight lines and organization, wanted more of that side of Daisy. Always had. To hell with the rules and his plans, and everything else. *It feels so much more decadent when you're standing up.*

That made him think of sex—hell, being in the same zip code as Daisy made him think of sex—and the time they'd rushed into their apartment, hot and ready for each other, and he'd lifted her onto the counter and plunged into her. It had been fiery and furious, one of those moments when common sense flew south of the border. So many of their days together had been like that—as if they were combustibles that exploded when they were brought together. And yes, many, many times, they had explored standing-up decadence.

Damn.

"Everything does," he said.

And he didn't mean eating.

She dangled a slice of pepperoni in front of him. In the dim light, her eyes seemed wider and bigger, her smile sexier. "Are you sure I can't tempt you to try some?"

"My apple is . . ." He shook his head and let out a little laugh. Who was he fooling? "Okay. Not nearly as tempting as that pizza."

"Oh, I don't know. Maybe we should each try a bite and see. If you're willing to share, that is." She leaned forward and opened her mouth.

God, this woman made everything around her pale in comparison. In the dark, intimate world of the kitchen, Colt could barely think, hardly breathe. His every thought centered around Daisy. Kissing Daisy. Touching Daisy. And holy hell, yes, fucking Daisy.

He moved the apple to her lips, and watched as she took a bite. He swallowed a groan. Damned good thing his sweats were baggy, or she would know how much that simple act had affected him.

"Now it's your turn, Colt," she said, her voice soft and dark.

His gaze never left hers as he moved his mouth to eat the tiny pizza morsel. When he did, his lips met her fingers, and a fire roared to life in his gut. He swallowed. "Yours is, uh, definitely better."

Another smile. "The bad things always are."

Bad things, like Daisy Barton. A woman who made him want to run out on his obligations and head for a private beach where the only thing they had to wear was sunscreen.

"Want some more?" she asked.

Oh, he wanted more all right. Not just more pizza, but more of her. More of what had happened three months ago. More of what had happened back in her motel room. But more led to mistakes, and he was older, wiser now. Meaning he should know better. "I, uh, should get some sleep. My grandpa has a doctor appointment in the morning, and then I have rounds at Golden Years. It makes for a long Saturday."

"Don't you take weekends off?"

"Not very often."

"Then take this weekend off, or at least don't work Sunday. How about we pack a picnic lunch and eat on the beach this Sunday afternoon? You, me, your grandpa, and Major." At the sound of his name, the dog thumped his tail.

A tempting thought, but then Colt remembered his standing Sunday date, and shook his head. "I . . . I can't. I have plans."

"Plans? Like what? Maybe we can tag along. You said you wanted more family time, and this can be a way to get it."

Colt shook his head again. "It's something I have to do alone."

Hurt flashed in her eyes. "Oh. Okay."

He wanted to explain, to tell her, but that would mean also telling her about what had happened to Henry, and Colt wasn't ready to do that. Not yet. Maybe not ever. Opening that door meant accepting the blame he held, and of all the burdens he carried, that was the one that could topple him. "Maybe another day we can do a picnic on the beach."

"Okay." She tore off a piece of pizza and ate it, but now there was a distinct sense of distance between them. "I can take your grandpa to the doctor, if you want. That's my job, after all."

He gave up pretending he wanted the apple and tossed the remains into the trash. "Don't you have that meeting with Mike at the property?" Daisy had mentioned it to him at dinner earlier tonight. It was nice to see a local contractor getting the work, and from what he knew about Mike, the job would be fair and reasonable.

"I can reschedule."

"No, you keep that meeting. I like to go to my grandfather's appointments with him. Make sure they cover all the bases, that he understands what they tell him, and that any follow-up appointments get made."

She smiled. "Still a control freak?"

"Not me." He put up his hands. "I'm just . . . conscientious."

"Oh yeah? Then what would happen if I turned the tables on you?"

She did that just by being here. She did it with the pizza and the dog and her smile. She did it by the way she invaded his thoughts, made him crave the unfettered, uncomplicated life they'd once had. "You already have, Daisy."

"Oh, Colton Harper, I can do so much more than that." She tipped her beer toward him, then turned on her heel and headed down the hall to her room. The dog padded along behind her, leaving Colt standing in the kitchen, feeling jealous and hungry. And not just for pizza.

Fourteen

"The good news is—it's not a total teardown," Mike Stark said. The tall, dark-haired contractor stood in the lobby of the Hideaway Inn on Saturday morning, a clipboard in one hand, a pen in the other. The once grand entryway was decaying before Daisy's eyes. The striped wallpaper hung from the wall like limp spaghetti, and the staircase was missing treads, like gaps in a smile. The carpets had a musty, damp smell, there was a dark water spot on the ceiling, and nearly every square inch was coated with cobwebs and dust.

And that was just the lobby. What she'd seen in the other rooms, from leaky pipes to crumbling walls, all spelled disaster. Emma was right. This place was an albatross.

"Is it salvageable?" Daisy asked.

Mike took a look around the space. "What you see here is mostly cosmetic. There are some plumbing issues, and some updates that should be made to make it more efficient and eliminate problems down the road, but overall, the building has great bones. The other contractor was either incompetent or trying to milk you for more money. After looking around, I'm positive I can do the job for a whole lot less than the other contractor quoted you."

Daisy smiled. "Really?"

Mike studied the papers on the clipboard and nodded. "Yup. Plus, I'll be doing this for close to cost, since you're a friend of the family, such as it is." He looked up and grinned. "And just so you know, Greta is always looking to expand that family. So if you're not already married, she'll be finding you a Prince Charming faster than you can sneeze."

"Oh, I'm not looking for a Prince Charming. Not now, maybe not ever." She'd done the marriage route once—one very long marriage, it turned out—and it hadn't worked out. At all. It wasn't exactly called a success story to be married to the same man for fourteen years and only spending three weeks and one night with him.

Except she'd been tempted last night to take him back to her room and taste a lot more than just his Red Delicious. Thank God she'd come to her senses before she fell for the same foolish fairy tale that had her eloping in the first place. She really needed to learn to stay in bed at night. *Nothing good happens after eleven between a boy and a girl,* Aunt Clara had always said, and she'd been right.

"Don't say you're not looking for Prince Charming out loud in front of Greta." Mike chuckled. "She'll make it her mission to convince you that everyone deserves to be paired up, like on Noah's Ark."

Instead of responding, Daisy changed the subject. Back to her reason for being here—which had nothing to do with some two-by-two mission. Although, she needed to try to remember that when she was around Colt, too. Damn the man for bringing up that night all those years ago. It was one of her sweeter memories from their short-lived marriage. Colt, holding her tight and telling her it would all be fine, that she'd ace the interview and if they didn't give her the job, they were the ones losing out, not her. Colt had been a rock and an anchor for a girl who had never had a steady foundation to stand upon. And then, just when she'd begun to count on him, he was gone.

"Uh, Mike, when do you think you can start the work?"

Daisy said. "I was hoping to reopen before the tourist season starts in January. And there's always demand for weddings on the beach."

"You're in luck, because my crew just finished up a job this week, and if you give the go-ahead, they can get started on Monday. You'll mostly be talking to my partner, Nick Patterson. I'm still full-time in the Coast Guard, so he oversees the business for me. But he's got great experience, and he knows his way around power tools. You can trust him to do a high-quality job."

"I remember Nick. He's a friend of . . . a friend." She didn't go into specifics, hoping Greta hadn't told Mike she was still married to Colt. The fewer people who knew about that, the better. It would just invite questions that Daisy didn't want to answer.

"You know Nick?" Mike said. "Small world."

She nodded. "I spent a summer in Rescue Bay, at the Hideaway Inn, helping my aunt. He was friends with some of the people I hung out with. Teenagers partying on the beach and all that."

"Nick's a great guy, and an amazing carpenter. He'll take care of this building as if it were his own."

"That's good to hear. This is my family's legacy . . ." Though the word *legacy* sounded odd to Daisy, who wouldn't call anything she'd gotten from Willow a legacy. ". . . and I want it done right. Now about financing—"

Mike waved that off. "I have an inkling of the issues you're facing. Greta said you're a close personal friend of Colt Harper's, and that to me is a good enough bond, until the bank loan is in your hands."

"Thank you very much, Mr. Stark." She put out her hand and they shook. The feeling of completing a deal, one that could transform her future, Emma's, maybe even this town's, sent a strange sense of accomplishment through Daisy. She'd taken the first and biggest step toward reopening the Hideaway Inn, and it felt good. Damned good. "Greta was right about you. She said you were fair and honest. Not to mention, almost family."

Mike grinned. "An endorsement from Greta Winslow is akin to a USDA stamp around here. You must be pretty good stock yourself, since all she did was rave about you."

"I don't know about that," Daisy said, hugging her arms to her chest and looking around at the place that was finally on its way to becoming the home she remembered. "But I'm working on it."

"Aren't we all?" Mike grinned again. He tore off the top sheet from his clipboard and handed it to her. He looked around the lobby and nodded. "I'm looking forward to seeing this place come to life again. You know, it seems like it's just been holding its breath, waiting for someone to come along and resurrect it."

"That's a good way to look at it," Daisy said. "A much more positive view than this place is falling down around our ears."

"Well, it's also doing that." Mike chuckled. "But that can all be fixed, and before you know it, it'll be back up and running."

They walked toward the double front doors. Daisy scuffed at a piece of plaster on the wood floor. "I was thinking . . . what if you started on the outdoor area first, just cleaned it up, got the pavement power-washed . . . that kind of thing. Is that possible?"

Mike glanced down at his long list of projects for the bed and breakfast. "Most projects work from the roof on down, then from the inside out, with the landscaping being left for last. Why would you want to do that?"

"Luke mentioned that he and Olivia are looking for a place to hold their wedding. I know it'll be too early to have a full event here, but maybe it would be a nice test run for the Hideaway Inn." And a way to get Emma down here. If Daisy called her cousin with an actual booked event—one that would need all hands on deck and a photographer to capture every moment—then maybe that would be just enough to get Emma to drive down.

Mike thought about it for a second, mulling his list and then glancing around the first floor. "You'd want to get the kitchen work started, and get this first-floor restroom renovated, but those should be doable. We can tackle the common areas first, work on the outside projects, then start hitting each guest room. The exterior needs to be shored up before the winter comes, anyway, so I don't think it'll take much adjusting of our timeline. Let me talk to Nick and see if that works for him."

She liked Mike Stark, liked him a lot. She could see why Greta had sung his praises. He was fair and honest and easy to work with. "Thank you."

"No, thank *you*. Rescue Bay needs a little shot in the tourism arm, and the Hideaway Inn is the first step toward making this town the destination it used to be."

Daisy looked out the window at the deep blue green Gulf of Mexico, and the lush white sands lying empty, just waiting for life to return. "For more than just visitors," she said softly. "And for more than just a weekend."

Sunday morning rolled in as both a blessing and a curse. A blessing, because it freed Colt from his daily schedule, and a curse, because it left him at home with far too much free time to kill with Daisy close by. Colt had enough frustration in his life, just with taking Grandpa to his appointments.

Yesterday's visit to the heart specialist in Tampa had gone about as well as wrangling pigs into a chute. Grandpa had let the doctor take his blood pressure and listen to his heart, then resorted to grunted answers after that. He'd refused to go for another EKG, refused to do any blood work, and just generally refused to cooperate. Eventually, Colt had thrown up his hands, thanked the doctor for his time, and driven Grandpa Earl home.

Colt had spent the rest of the day doing rounds, then getting caught up on paperwork back in his office. He hadn't gone home until well after dark, when Daisy and Grandpa were already asleep. He'd opened the fridge to find a dinner waiting for him, some kind of chicken sauté, with another slice of that amazing homemade bread. The dishes were done, the floor swept, the house quiet and clean.

He'd eaten alone at the kitchen table, wondering how he was going to keep on living with the woman who tortured him with scenes of domesticity. If theirs had been an ordinary marriage, he would have ended his day with climbing into bed with Daisy, hauling her close, and making warm, sweet, wonderful love to her. Instead he went upstairs to his own cold sheets and a vow to find a full-time nurse who didn't make him want to drizzle warm honey down her belly and take his time licking off every drop.

Damn.

Sunday morning, he got up at five, strapped on his running shoes, and pounded out a hard, fast six miles. If he thought the run would ease the tension in his chest, the constant craving for Daisy, he was wrong. As he turned the corner for his street, he saw a motorcycle parked outside his neighbor's house, sporting a FOR SALE sign.

He'd slowed his pace, and thought of the day he'd roared up to Daisy's house in Jacksonville, told her he couldn't live another moment without her, then zoomed out of Florida with Daisy clutching his waist. All bright-eyed and sure that if they were together, everything would be perfect from that day forward.

When he got back inside the house after his run, Daisy was in the kitchen, wearing a soft pink robe that fell to her knees, her feet bare. She was making coffee, seeming as at home in his house as he was. The dog sat at her feet, wagging his tail with hope for a snack.

It was like a scene out of a Rockwell painting, and for the hundredth time he wondered if it was also an image of the life he could have had—if he had stayed with Daisy all these years. Would they have been one of those couples who had Sunday breakfast together while the kids dashed around the table? One of those couples who held each other in bed while watching silly late-night movies? Or would Daisy be flitting away, as she had years ago? Off to another home, another job . . . another life?

She turned when he entered the kitchen, a half smile on her lips, and a mug in her hands. Colt's craving for her erupted again. Half of him wanted to turn around, buy that motorcycle, and roar on down the road with Daisy, until they found a place to be alone for a very, very long time.

This was why she was bad for him. She made him want the very life that had driven a wedge between them. That carefree, answering to no one, detached from everyone but each other. That was who Daisy was—and who Colt would never be. He'd detoured down that road once already. Not again.

"Want a cup?" she said.

He shook off the thoughts of motorcycles and running away. He had responsibilities here. A practice. A life. He couldn't indulge in crazy fantasies like that. "After I have some water. Damn, it's warm out there this morning." He swiped the sweat off his brow and bent to take off his running shoes. When he straightened, he found Daisy standing before him, an icy glass in her hands. "Thanks."

"You're welcome." She thumbed toward the stove. "Your grandpa is finishing up in the bathroom, and I'm making him some eggs and turkey bacon. Do you want some?"

It was so damned domestic. So . . . married. "Daisy, you don't have to wait on me. I hired you to help my grandpa. I can take care of myself."

"I know you can." She smiled. "But if I'm making something for your grandfather and me to eat, it's no trouble to make something for you, too. You can always pay me extra, if it makes you feel guilty."

"Deal." He sat at the kitchen table, sipping the water, and watching Daisy move around his kitchen. He hadn't had a woman in his kitchen in years.

Fourteen years, to be exact. During their short-lived marriage, there'd been more takeout than real meals, food they could grab and consume as fast as possible. They spent more time making sparks in the bedroom than worrying about what might be cooking in the oven. He'd never seen this nurturing side of Daisy and he had to admit he liked it, very much.

He couldn't remember the last time anyone had cooked for him—unless he counted the endless parade of pies and muffins that his patients brought him. A full meal, start to finish . . .

Well, it was nice. Very nice. Something he was becoming accustomed to.

A dozen times, he got up to help, but Daisy waved him back into his seat. "You just ran, what, a gazillion miles? I've got this."

"Not quite a gazillion. Just six."

She laughed. "That's six more than I'll ever run. I prefer my workouts to be on a mat. As in Pilates or yoga, not sex, just in case your hormones were thinking I meant something else," she added, wagging a spatula at him.

"Why would I think that?" But she was right. The minute she put the words *workout* and *mat* together, he'd been thinking sex, on the floor, on a bed, hell, anywhere that she was.

How on earth was he going to live with this woman? Why had he thought this was a good idea? A sound idea? Clearly, he'd been thinking with the part of his body lacking in brain cells.

"Here you go." She slid a plate in front of him. Fluffy scrambled eggs sat beside buttered wheat toast and two lean strips of turkey bacon. A small bunch of plump red grapes sat to one side. "Coffee now?"

"Yes, thank you." Before she even returned with a mug, he dug in and had half the eggs and all of the bacon consumed. "Sorry. Guess running builds up an appetite."

"So do workouts on a mat." She grinned, a sparkle in her eye that could have been read as flirting or maybe just teasing. The pink robe had opened slightly above the belt, exposing a snippet of a red satin short nightgown, which sent his mind down a whole other path that didn't involve Pilates, but did involve some interesting body contortions.

"Well, this is sure a sight better than corn flakes." Grandpa Earl came into the kitchen, already dressed in jeans and a dark blue T-shirt.

Colt swallowed his surprise. For months, he'd been trying to get Grandpa to start the day dressed in something other than the day before's sweatpants. And here he was, up for breakfast, showered, shaved, his hair combed. Once again, Colt marveled at the changes Daisy had made. All for the better. "Good morning, Grandpa."

"Good morning to you, too." Grandpa sat down across from Colt, and thanked Daisy for the plate of food she laid before him.

It was all a complete one-eighty from the past few months that Grandpa had been living with Colt. Daisy filled in the seat between the two men, with a smaller version of the same breakfast for herself. The dog sat beside Grandpa, waiting and hoping for scraps.

Grandpa tossed a crust to Major Pain, who thumped his appreciation on the floor with his tail. The moment reminded Colt of when he'd been a kid, and Grandpa had done the same thing with his dog Beau.

Colt felt a hitch in his chest as the memories flooded back. Him and Henry, sitting at Grandma and Grandpa's kitchen table on Sunday mornings. Grandma would fill "her boys" with a healthy breakfast, then send them off for a day of fishing in the bright afternoon sun. Colt half expected to see Grandpa's tackle box by the door, his fishing cap perched on the arm of the chair. His heart waited to hear Henry's voice. *Colt, hurry up! The fish are bitin'!* Followed by Grandpa's indulgent chuckles as he wrapped up the remains of his breakfast in a napkin and headed out the door with the boys. Grandma, standing on the porch, watching them go, her arms wrapped around her body, her smile wide and proud, and her heart full.

Grandpa tossed the dog another piece of crust. "I saw that one and the one before, Grandpa." Colt grinned. "Dogs shouldn't eat people food, you know."

"Ah, he'll be fine. He's not getting any of my eggs or bacon. So don't be getting any ideas there, Major." Earl shot Major Pain a serious nod. "Damned good breakfast, Daisy. Thank you."

"Oh, you're welcome, Mr. Harper."

"Earl, please. Mr. Harper makes me sound old. And Lord

knows I'm not ready for that yet. Got plenty of years left in this old tank." He tapped a fist against his chest.

"Speaking of keeping the tank filled," Colt said. "Did you take your meds this morning? You know—"

"Damn it, Colton." Grandpa Earl scowled. The light mood from earlier evaporated and the familiar arguments dropped into the empty seat at the table. "Can't a man enjoy his breakfast before you start reminding him of his mortality? I'll take those stupid pills when I'm good and ready."

Colt started to argue back, when Daisy put a hand over his. "I'll take care of it," she said. "Don't worry."

He wanted to tell her that all he did was worry about Grandpa Earl. Then his phone buzzed and drew his attention away. He thought about muting it, but when he looked up and saw Grandpa smiling at something Daisy said to him, Colt felt like an intruder in his own house. He was the practical one, raining on the party.

"Thanks for breakfast." He got to his feet, scraped the crumbs off his plate, then loaded the dish in the dishwasher. He drained his coffee mug, then poured a refill. "I have to go."

"We were going on that picnic lunch today, Colt. Remember? A little time in the sand and surf? I thought you might find time to join us, even for a few minutes."

He glanced at his grandfather, but Grandpa Earl was concentrating on his eggs. Clearly, Grandpa didn't want Colt to tag along. The thought pained Colt. "I . . . I have to go."

"Colt, it'd be nice if you—"

"I have to go. Sorry." He headed down the hall to the bathroom. A few minutes later, Daisy heard the sound of the shower running. Colt had shut her out again. Shut them both out.

"He's always off and running somewhere." Earl scowled. "Gets to feeling like he doesn't want to be here."

"I'm sure he does want to be here. He's just . . . busy." She put the dishes in the dishwasher, added detergent, and started the cycle. Still, it hurt that Colt had left. She shouldn't be surprised. He'd done it to her before, after all. She needed to remember she was his employee, not his wife, and she was here as a caretaker, not to build some fairy tale family. Like a fool, she still had hope that Colt could change. Probably the same naïveté that had her believing in the Easter Bunny until she was in middle school. "I'll leave him a note, in case he changes his mind."

Earl got up to pour another cup of coffee. "You sure do have a lot of hope that things can change, Daisy."

"And what's wrong with hope?"

"It hurts like hell when you lose it." Earl put down the mug and glanced toward the hallway that Colt had gone down. "And hurts even more when you try to get it back. And you can't."

Fifteen

Greta Winslow was concocting a plan. Which meant she'd had to break out the windmill cookies, the Maker's Mark, and a few favors. When her doorbell rang shortly after ten that morning, she popped to her feet. "Goodness, I do appreciate punctuality. At my age, every minute counts."

"Who's on time?" Pauline asked. Esther sat beside her, still knitting, but not really paying attention to the conversation. The fur body underneath Esther's needle was starting to take shape. Sort of like a melted King Kong.

"My archenemy. And spy in training." Greta hurried down the hall and opened the door. Harold Twohig stood on her doorstep, all spit and polish in a button-down beige shirt and black trousers, as if she'd invited him to the opera. For Pete's sake, the man had no concept of the words *informal meeting*. "Let me guess. You also wore a tux on casual Fridays?"

"My dear Greta, if all it takes to get your heart racing is a penguin suit, I'll break out my Brooks Brothers this very afternoon." He grinned.

She shook her head and waved off the idea. "I have hardly digested my breakfast, Harold. It is far too early for that kind of an image in my head."

He just laughed. "Then what, pray tell, did you invite me over for? A little early morning canoodling?"

"Lord Almighty, I'm going to have to take some Pepto just to get through a conversation with you." She grabbed him by the button-down and tugged him into her house. This had been a mistake. Every time she involved Harold in anything, he took it as a sign that she was interested in him. "Now get in here quick before the neighbors start talking."

"Ooh, I do like an aggressive woman." He reached for her but she smacked his hand away.

"You unbutton or unfasten or unzip anything on that scrawny, hairy, albino body of yours and I will take a butcher knife to your appendages."

"Aggressive *and* rough." He leaned down to her ear and whispered. "You really know how to flirt, my dear Greta."

She shuddered, and just hauled him the rest of the way down the hall and into the kitchen. Pauline and Esther gasped. Esther almost dropped a stitch. For a second, no one said anything, just stared and gawked, like seeing Harold in Greta's kitchen was some kind of roadside industrial accident.

"Harold?" Esther blinked. "What are you doing here? And in Greta's house?"

"Greta, are you two dating?" Pauline said, with a sly smile on her face.

"Lord, no. He's our secret weapon."

"I like the sound of that," Harold said. "It sounds sexy."

"Don't make me do something I'm going to regret. Or get arrested for." She pointed at a chair and ignored Harold's incessant smiling. Lord Almighty, she was already regretting this five seconds into it. "Have a seat, and if you quit with the double entendres, I might even pour you a cup of coffee."

Harold patted his stomach. "Sounds like just the thing to go along with those cookies you baked—"

She thwacked him in the back of the head. Goodness, that man was a sputtering fool. "Quit talking, Harold, or the coffee will be in your lap instead of in a mug."

He just grinned, the idiot. Greta poured a mug for him, then refilled Pauline and Esther's cups before sitting down herself. She shielded her eyes against the glare from the southeast corner of the room. "Lord Almighty, Esther, that dress is bright. What kind of spying do you expect to do when you're dressed like a highway marker?"

"Greta, florals are in this year. Especially bright florals." Esther pressed a palm to her orange and yellow patterned dress. The thing glared like a bus in fog.

"So is wearing your pants down to the ground, but you don't see me doing that," Greta said. "Everything I wear is securely buttoned and belted."

"And challenging." Harold grinned again.

She wanted to hit him, but instead just balled up her hands into fists and gave him a glare. Which Harold ignored. Lord, give her patience, or Greta was going to severely maim someone before the day was through.

Pauline and Esther leaned in as if Harold was a specimen under a microscope. "So, Harold, how are things with you and Greta?" Pauline said. "She won't say a word about you. I have absolutely no idea why."

"Goodness, Pauline, are you part of the Spanish Inquisition? Let the man breathe." Greta reached behind her to the counter, and retrieved a platter overflowing with windmill cookies to put in the center of the table. "We have work to do."

"Work? But I haven't finished my dog yet." Esther held up Rooney in Harold's direction. "Isn't it clever, Harold? Knit your own dog. If you want, I could make you one, too."

"Esther, Harold has his own real-life dog. He doesn't want your yarn knockoffs."

"I think it's adorable, Esther," Harold said, shooting Greta a grin. "And if you want to make one for me, I would display it with pride."

Esther beamed. Greta fought the urge to gag. What was wrong with Esther? Since when did she think it was okay to suck up to Harold Twohig?

"Ladies, can we focus?" She crossed her hands in front of her and looked at Harold. "I need the scoop on Daisy and Doc Harper, and I know you have it because you're friends with Walt Patterson, whose grandson is best friends with Doc Harper."

"Good gracious, Greta, you have more people in that sentence than a Smith family reunion. And just because I see Walt a few times a week doesn't mean that Walt and I talk about what's going on with his grandson's friend and Daisy." Harold sipped at his coffee and reached for a cookie. "These are my favorite kind of cookies, Greta. How'd you know?"

She wasn't going to answer the favorite cookies question. Because if she did, Pauline and Esther would think something was up between Greta and Harold and nothing was up. At all.

"You're old men. What else do you have to talk about besides what your families are up to? Your golf game?" She mocked a yawn.

"We might just be talking about *you*, my dear Greta." He arched a caterpillar brow.

Greta rolled her eyes. "Get a grip on your knickers, you lecher. Focus, Harold. There are happy endings at stake here and I'm not getting any younger waiting for you to mature."

Esther reached for a cookie, but Pauline put a hand on hers. Pauline arched a brow and nodded toward Harold. "Hey, Esther, don't we have a bingo game to go to?"

Esther made a face. "Bingo? Since when?"

"What Bingo?" Greta asked. What was Pauline doing? She had called the women here specifically to work on her Colt-Daisy plan, and Pauline was dashing out as quickly as she could.

"Since now," Pauline said, with another hint-hint nod in Greta and Harold's direction.

"But I didn't get to eat a cookie yet," Esther said.

Greta wheeled on Pauline. What was wrong with these two? Leaving at the worst possible time, too. "Where are you two going? We have work to do."

"You and Harold can handle it. I'm sure he'll love being your minion, Greta. Or love slave, whatever term you want to slap on the job." Pauline laughed.

What was this? A mutiny in her three-woman army? And since when did Pauline turn the tables on Greta Winslow?

Greta's face flushed and she waved off the sudden heat in the room. "Harold is not my . . . anything."

"I don't know. I kinda like the term love slave." Harold put out his wrists. "Shackle me, Greta."

"You're lucky it's still illegal to murder someone in your own kitchen," Greta said. "And even more illegal to murder more than one someone at a time."

"That's my cue." Pauline grinned, then got to her feet and pressed two cookies into Esther's palm. "Here are your cookies. One for the road, and one for on the way out the door."

"But, but—"

"Come on, Esther, it is time to go," Pauline said, taking Esther's elbow. "I promise, we'll even stop at the craft store."

"Really? Because last time you said we were going to the craft store, we ended up at the DMV and I had to wait in line with you for an hour."

"I have my Michael's coupons all ready to go, I swear," Pauline said, patting her purse. She leaned down and gave Greta a one-armed hug. She swore she could hear Pauline laughing as she did it. "Bye, Greta. Don't do anything I wouldn't do. Which actually leaves the field quite open."

"What are you doing?" Greta whispered to Pauline. "You know I don't want to be alone with that ogre."

"Oh, for goodness' sake, just admit you find him hot. Everyone knows you like Harold."

"Pauline, I do not like him. Not one bit."

"Whatever you say, Greta." Then she straightened, toodled a wave at Harold, and hurried out the door with Esther. Had Greta spiked the wrong coffee this morning? What was up with Pauline and Esther? Some friends they turned out to be, leaving her with the troll who lived under the Golden Years bridge.

"Well, well, my dear. Seems we are alone at last." Harold leaned across the table. "What do you have planned for me?"

Since she'd been deserted by her best soldiers, it looked like the only option Greta had left was to align herself with the devil's spawn. Or Harold Twohig. Whoever came with the least amount of headaches. And prosecutable offenses.

Sixteen

The straw that broke the camel's back in Emma's world popped up in her Facebook newsfeed like a weed in a rose garden. *Roger Jennings is separated.*

Her husband. No longer. If there was one evil about social media, it was its ability to put a public and undeniable stamp on things. Denial was harder to hold on to when the words were there in black and white.

Emma stared at the sentence for a good five minutes, but the words didn't disappear. She stared at that singular sentence until her eyes blurred and reality smacked her hard. Her marriage was over. As over as a relationship could get.

Why had she thought otherwise? He had moved out over two months ago. They'd been physically separated all that time, and now he was simply making it official. But for some reason, until she'd seen the actual truth in print, Emma had retained this little nugget of hope that they could fix things, regain what they had lost. That that one night before he'd moved out meant there was still a foundation to fall back on.

By the end of the day, Emma had packed her bags, loaded her car, and called her mother. "Daisy wanted me to take a few pictures of the Hideaway, to use in a brochure. I'll be back soon. Will you be okay?"

"I'll be fine, totally fine. If I need anything, Masie next door can come by if I need her. Willow is out of town again"—Clara let out a dramatic sigh at Willow's constant whim indulging—"but Masie is nearby. Besides, I'm feeling better every day."

Emma thought her mother's voice sounded stronger, and her spirits were high. At her doctor appointment yesterday, she'd gotten a clean bill of health, as long as she didn't push herself too hard and cause a recurrence. All good signs, which made it easier for Emma to justify leaving for a few days. A weekend, no more. Just long enough to stop obsessively sending the Facebook dagger a little deeper into Emma's heart.

The whole drive down to the Hideaway, Emma debated detouring from her path and holing up in a hotel instead. But her mother would have asked questions, and as much as Emma was maintaining a fiction about her marriage, she wasn't about to outright lie. A sin of omission, like failing to mention Roger had moved out, was far better than a sin of commission, and telling a bald-faced lie to her mother's face.

A little after eleven on Monday morning, Emma pulled into the circular drive that fronted the Hideaway Inn. Weeds covered the gravel surface, and the once grand wraparound porch sagged in a frown, but to her, it still looked the same. She'd always loved the Hideaway, with its rustic charm and expansive views of the Gulf. For the last five years, those sweet memories had been intertwined with heartbreak, though. As much as Emma wanted to leap out of the car and embrace the Hideaway like an old friend, another part of her wanted to peel out of the driveway and never see the place again.

It held too many bittersweet memories, too many hurts that she had tried to put away. Like her father having a heart attack at the Hideaway the year after Emma's wedding at the inn. Her mother had left the Hideaway after her husband died and never found the heart to return.

Like the fact that she had thought returning to the inn would work some kind of magic. Two months ago, after one sweet and wonderful night with her husband in her bed, she'd woken up with the crazy idea that if she brought Roger to the Hideaway, to the place where they had been married years ago, maybe she could get over the past, and at the same time reignite the dying flame in her marriage. But she and Roger never even made it out of their Jacksonville driveway. He'd broken up with her, in between taking one suitcase to the car and another to the bedroom, then climbed in his own car and driven away. By the time she got home from work the next day, his things were gone and her marriage was over.

He'd only left one thing behind—and that was the one thing that Emma was going to keep, no matter what.

She got out of her car, and looked up at the building, this time with more critical eyes. Daisy had made the situation sound a lot better than it was. Geez, this place was going to need a bulldozer and a miracle to get it running again.

A pale blue pickup truck emblazoned with STARK CONTRACTING pulled into the drive, followed by Daisy's ancient Toyota. Daisy was barreling out of her car before she fully had it in Park, and running across the drive to grab Emma in a tight, fierce hug. "You're here!"

The embrace was like coming home. Emma hadn't realized how much she had missed her cousin until she was enveloped in Daisy's warmth again. It was like being a teenager all over again, with Daisy coming to stay for a weekend of late-night conversations and pizza gorging. It made Emma want to pour out the entire awful story about the demise of her marriage, the mistake she had made in hanging on too long to a dying animal. Instead, she said simply, "Oh, Dase, I'm glad to see you."

"Not as happy as I am to see you." Daisy gave Emma a second tight hug, then stepped back and waved at the couple getting out of the pickup truck. Daisy exchanged small talk with the man, who looked familiar to Emma. A second later, Emma recognized him as a friend of Colt's. The summer

Daisy had stayed at the Inn, Colt and his friends had been frequent visitors to the wide swath of beach in front of the inn.

Daisy greeted Nick with a quick, friendly hug, then waved toward Emma. "Nick, I don't know if you remember my cousin, but this is Emma."

"Nice to meet you," he said. She could still see the Nick she had met in the boyish charm in his face. "And this is my right-hand woman on the project, M. J. Reynolds."

"Maggie," the woman corrected with a smile. "He calls me M.J. so I sound more like a brawny carpenter."

Emma shook with the tall, sandy-haired Nick and the athletic brunette Maggie. The carpenters sported twin tool belts and scuffed work boots, but there was something in the air between them, a chemistry that charged the space, that seemed to say they were more than friends, or would be soon.

Damn. Couldn't she get a break? Everywhere she turned, there were happy couples. *Roger Jennings is separated.*

Emma forced a polite smile to her face. Maybe she was just reading things that weren't there, just another jaded divorcée-to-be seeing the world as some kind of two-by-two conspiracy. "Nice to meet you, Maggie, and nice to see you again, Nick." She shaded her eyes, then took in the decaying inn again. "I think you're going to have your work cut out for you here."

"Nothing we can't handle." Nick grinned. "Would you two like to take a tour, see what we're going to be tackling, before we get started today?"

If Emma did that, she'd be getting more involved with the Hideaway, with securing its future, and she didn't want to do that. Daisy could handle the renovations, and Emma could go back to Jacksonville and make some tough decisions. As for the future of the Hideaway, once it was done being refurbished, that was a choice to make down the road. If Emma could talk Daisy and her mother into selling it, then this place would be in her past once and for all.

Exactly how she wanted it. No more reminders of what might have been.

"That's okay. We can do that later," Emma said. "I don't want to tie up your workday."

"No problem. We'll get started. The sooner we get to work, the sooner this place can be a Rescue Bay destination again." Nick nodded toward Maggie, and the two of them reached into the back of the truck and began loading up with supplies.

"Let's go down to the beach, and I'll tell you about what I have planned." Daisy looped an arm through Emma's. "Are you hungry? I bought a sandwich and some sodas on the way over here, but it's way too much food for just me, so I'd be thrilled to share. Besides, it's a perfect day for a Pick-Me-Up Picnic. Don't you think?"

A smile curved up Emma's face. It was as if Daisy had read her mind. She shouldn't be surprised. When the two of them had been together, they'd been more like twins than cousins. "I can't believe you remembered those."

"I remember it all, Emma." Daisy squeezed her cousin's hand. "Now, come on, let's go re-create some memories."

They skirted the building, and picked their way down the rotting steps that led to the beach, with Daisy's dog following at their heels. All the while, Daisy talked about the changes ahead for the inn, about the outdoor renovations starting today, followed by new plumbing and electrical, some kitchen updates, repairs to the roof . . .

Emma let Daisy talk while her own mind whirled along a different path. *Roger Jennings is separated.*

Her marriage, her life, crumbling as if it were made out of the soft sand lining the beach. And here she was, hours away and powerless to change any of it. It was as if she was a spectator, watching an especially awful showing of *This Is Your Life, Emma Jennings.*

They settled on the beach, on a blanket Daisy had grabbed out of her trunk and spread across the sand. Major turned around three times, twisting one corner of the plaid blanket, then curled himself into a ball and fell asleep. Daisy divvied up the lunch, and kept on talking about the inn between bites.

"Now that I finally have the loan from the bank, I don't have to worry about funding the renovations. And, having those little loan repayment coupons makes me even more determined to make the inn profitable. The inn has a second chance at life, and I want to take it. Which brings me to Olivia and Luke's wedding. It's a great opportunity for the Hideaway, and if you came back for that next month, then that might help you get a photography business going down here, too. I know running the inn is going to take a lot of time, but during the slow season, it might be a way to get some extra income and since you are an *amazing* photographer, it'd be crazy for you not to keep that going."

"Whoa, whoa." Emma put up a hand to ward off Daisy's enthusiasm. "I'm only here for the weekend. Just to take the pictures you needed."

"Okay." Daisy leaned back on her elbows and turned her face to greet the warm sun. "But if you fall in love with this place again and want to stay, I'll be the first to say I told you so."

"I'm not falling in love again. With anyone."

Daisy leaned over and opened her eyes. "Did something happen between you and Roger?"

"I'm just . . . talking out loud," Emma said. Too fast, too defensive. Damn. She picked at her sandwich, trying to avoid Daisy's assessing gaze. A family settled on a blanket on a spot further down the beach. A husband, wife, with two little girls wearing bright white bonnets to block the sun's rays. The girls laughed and charged down the beach, then gasped and ran back when the cold water hit their toes. The couple held hands, with the children on either side, and started strolling along the sandy shore. Emma's chest hurt and she looked away.

"Do you remember the first Pick-Me-Up Picnic?" Daisy said.

Emma nodded. "We were, what . . . five? Six?"

"My mom had gone off on another one of her adventures. She missed my acting debut in the first-grade play."

"I remember that. You were a spectacular broccoli."

"Not half as talented as your rutabaga." Daisy grinned.

"Well, not to be a braggart, but I did have that one hilarious root cellar line." Emma blew on her fingers.

Daisy laughed. "After the play, I rode home with you. I was so sad and your mom said it was an occasion for a Pick-Me-Up Picnic."

Emma's mother was always doing things like that. Making up holidays or special occasions, because either Emma or Jack had had a bad day. She'd welcomed Daisy into that family circle, like a mother eagle bringing one more eaglet under her wing. Daisy had eaten those days up, loving the normalcy, the warmth of them, such a departure from the chaos of her own home. Emma had often felt bad for her cousin and her unorthodox mother, rarely home, rarely plugged in. More often than not, Daisy had been at Emma's house, like an extra sister.

"We got fast food and ice creams and sat on the beach until the sun went down," Emma said. "It was one of the best days ever."

"There's nothing like a Pick-Me-Up Picnic," Daisy said. "And the ones that we had when we were older that involved alcohol. Though that's probably not what your mom had in mind when she started the tradition."

"But so much more fun than milkshakes and diet sodas." Emma toasted Daisy with her bottle of diet cola, and the two of them shared a laugh. Just like old times. For a second, Emma imagined the future if she stayed here, if she and Daisy partnered on the Hideaway Inn and ended every day with a Pick-Me-Up Picnic and the kind of conversations that came from practically being sisters since birth.

Then she thought of the mess she'd left back in Jacksonville, the life half done. *Roger Jennings is separated.*

Was Emma strong enough to go back and deal with that? Or would it just draw out the agonizing foregone conclusion? Maybe it was time to cut her losses and move down here. Start all over again, far from the reminders of the marriage that had died when she hadn't been looking.

"You still living with Colt?" Emma asked. After all, she'd

come down here to *not* dwell on the Facebook status. Better to dwell on someone else's love life than her own.

A blush filled Daisy's cheeks, something Emma hadn't seen on her cousin's face in years. For a second, Emma envied that blush, that flush of excitement about a special person. Clearly, Daisy wasn't as over Colt or as uninterested as she had professed. "Yes."

"So . . . how are things going between you two?"

"They're . . . complicated." Then Daisy smiled, the kind of private smile that said she was thinking of something that only she and Colt shared.

Again that envy ran through Emma. She tried to brush it off, but the feeling lingered. She wanted to run, to get far, far from people sharing private conversations and special little smiles. "Listen, thanks for lunch. I'm going to get my camera and get some pictures taken. The light's good right now"—it was a lie; at lunchtime, the light was too high, too bright, but Emma didn't want to be here another second—"and I want to see what I can capture."

"Emma, wait—"

But Emma was already on her feet and heading up the beach, away from that happy look in Daisy's eyes, away from the very thing that she'd once had and lost. Or maybe never really had at all—and had only been deluding herself into thinking she had.

Seventeen

For fourteen years, Colt Harper had loved his job, loved arriving at the office, and loved interacting with his patients. He'd enjoyed helping people get healthy, and the puzzle solving of health care. There'd been the inevitable heartbreaking endings, but for the most part, Colt prided himself on doing a good job, and being an involved, caring physician.

Until Daisy Barton arrived in town and upset his perfect world. Now he spent his days glancing at the clock, counting down the hours until his last appointment, and hurrying home to see what might be cooking in the oven. Even Grandpa Earl had started joking and laughing, especially with Daisy, which made Colt's homecomings far less stressful, and, for days, free of broken dishes.

So when Harold Twohig came in at eleven that Monday morning, Colt was already itching to be done for the day. Mondays were his early days, with the second half of the day spent at the local hospital, checking on anyone who had been hospitalized over the weekend, and doing follow-ups on any others receiving long-term care. As far as Colt knew, the weekend had been uneventful, which meant he had a good chance of getting home before the sun set.

"Howdy, Doc." Harold Twohig sat on the paper-covered exam table, patient and still, while Colt checked his vitals and ran through the standard questions about sleeping, eating, and overall health. Beside them, Suzie took notes, and filled in the chart. "How am I doing?"

"You're doing great, Harold. Looks like the blood pressure medicine is doing its job. I think we can reduce your dose. Great job."

"It's the dog." Harold grinned. "I adopted myself a dog a few months back, and I tell you, there's nothing like a wagging tail to get me up off my lazy butt and out for a walk. That and the love of a good woman."

"I hope having a dog works with my grandpa, too," Colt said. If Major Pain got Grandpa Earl to live healthier, then Colt would welcome the giant furball with open arms. At this point, Colt was willing to hire Bigfoot to be a walking companion if it motivated his grandpa. "He adopted a dog a few days ago, but I wouldn't say it's changed his mind much about taking his meds."

Harold chuckled. "Earl can be a pain in the ass, and I'm saying that as one of his oldest friends. But he'll come around."

The exam done, Suzie excused herself and left the room. Colt dropped his attention to the chart, comparing Harold's last year's physical to this one. His patient was definitely making good strides in the right direction. "I hope you're right. He hasn't been the same in a long time."

"I went through the same thing myself, after my wife died. I didn't want to talk to anyone, get close to anyone, and I didn't give a crap about whether I ate or walked or took my damned vitamins." He shrugged. "Took me some time to realize that taking care of myself didn't take away from what I felt about losing my wife. The grief and guilt of not being there enough for her had gotten to me, made me into a damned zombie. But then I realized that taking care of myself, in a weird way, made all that easier to bear."

Colt perched on the edge of the counter and rested his foot on the stool beside him. "You think it was the guilt that kept you from doing the right things?"

"I *know* it was guilt." Harold's face sobered and he took his time putting his words together. "My wife was a good woman, Doc. One of the best. She took care of dogs and people, as if saving the whole world was her mission. She never said a mean word to anyone, and put up with my bad habits like she was Mother Teresa. But when she died . . . hell"—he shook his head—"I felt like I hadn't done enough, taken care of her enough. My Lenore, bless her heart, would have said I did plenty, but I knew I could have done more. I guess I didn't feel I deserved to be healthy and strong after that."

Was that what it was? Grandpa Earl didn't feel like he deserved to be the one who lived? Colt had wrestled with those same demons himself for years. The guilt over not being here, over leaving Henry alone, and the overpowering guilt about not being able to undo what had been done. It had spurred his entry into medicine, as if he could atone with a thousand patients for what he had missed with his brother.

"What changed your mind, Harold?" Colt asked. "If you don't mind me asking."

"I don't mind at all." Harold slid his arms into the sleeves of his shirt and began buttoning the panels shut. "For me, it was finding what value I had to offer. To know that I mattered, even without my saintly wife by my side." He slid off the table, and put a hand on Colt's shoulder. "Let Earl know why you need him. And what it would do to you if you lost him."

Colt thought about Harold's words all the way home. He sat in the driveway for a while, wondering if maybe he was too late to build a bridge with his grandpa. They barely had civilized conversations now. Unless Daisy was around. She seemed to bring out the best in the two of them. Somehow, without Daisy as an intermediary, Colt was going to have to find a way to get from throwing coffee cups to calm chats.

He stared at the house for a long time. Grandpa Earl came to the window and looked out, a tall frame silhouetted against the glass, thin, solitary. The glass might as well have been a cement wall, Colt thought.

A hundred times, Colt reached for the door handle, to go inside, to finally confront those demons standing between them. A hundred times, his hand brushed against the metal handle, then slipped away.

He thought of all those fishing trips, those lazy, serene afternoons floating in the skiff. The hours he had spent helping Grandpa at the garage, the two of them lying underneath a car, staring up at the gray intestines of a Chevy or a Ford. He missed that. A hell of a lot.

No, not just missed it. Needed it. And if Colt needed his grandpa, there was a chance maybe Grandpa Earl needed his grandson, too.

Colt got out of the car, took two steps up the walkway. He saw Grandpa turn away, and leave an empty space behind the window. The words Colt needed to say refused to push past the lump in his throat, so instead of going inside, he chickened out.

Damn. What kind of doctor couldn't take good advice?

One who wasn't so sure he had the strength to deal with the consequences of such a conversation. He was doing the same thing as Harold, as his grandpa. Putting off his own healing because he hadn't dealt with the guilt of what had scarred him.

Dealing with it meant talking about Henry's death. Something Colt had never really done, with anyone. Last night, he'd come so close . . . so very close to telling Daisy what had happened to his little brother, then he'd stopped himself because he knew the truth would forever dim the way Daisy looked at him.

Frustration and guilt built in Colt's chest, clawed up his throat. He kicked off his shoes, but it didn't help. He loosened his tie; it didn't ease the feeling. He broke into a run, as if he could ever put enough miles between himself and the past. The sand was soft, yielding beneath his feet, requiring more effort. He pushed forward, until the beach curved

and the residential area ended, and the two-story Hideaway
Inn peeked over the treetops.

He slowed his pace, then switched to a walk when he saw
Daisy lying on a blanket, her legs out straight, arms bent,
face upturned to the sun. Another woman sat beside her,
talking, while Major Pain napped in the sun on the corner
of the blanket.

Something in Colt's heart clenched. He envied the easy
way Daisy sat in the sun, as if there was nothing to worry
about, nothing on her shoulders. He envied that someone
else, even a friend, was making her smile and laugh. He
even envied the damned dog, so close to Daisy.

The other woman, a lighter brunette than Daisy, but with
similar features, said something, then got to her feet and
headed up the sand a moment later. After she had left, Daisy
noticed him, and sat up, a smile winging its way across her
face. Daisy got to her feet and headed down the sand toward
him, with Major Pain bringing up the rear.

Colt's heart skipped a beat as she approached. Everything
about Daisy seemed so free and easy, the bare feet in the
sand, the dress skimming her ankles, her hair loose along
her shoulders. She made him want to skip out on work for
the rest of the week and just spend the days dashing in and
out of the surf.

God, he was turning into a walking, talking romance
novel.

"Hey, what are you doing here?" She leaned in, and her
brows wrinkled. "And why are you so sweaty?"

"I left work early to grab lunch before I have to go on
rounds. And I decided to try to fit in a run." He shrugged.

"In your khakis and button-down shirt?" She stepped
forward, flicked at the loosened tie. "Didn't even have time
to take off the tie?"

"I, uh, was a little stressed today."

"So you got to it as fast as possible?" She winked, and
heat burned deep in his gut. She danced her fingers down
the tie, a tease lighting her face. A memory quickened in
his mind, of them making love, half-dressed, half-undressed,

in too much of a rush to do anything more than have each other, to ease that bone-deep need.

"Seems you're in a rush for a lot of things lately," she said. "For a man who thinks everything through and draws all those little lines and charts, that's a big one-eighty. If I didn't know better, I'd say you were becoming more like the Colt I remembered."

"It was . . . an aberration."

"You? An aberration? You are far from that, Colt." She laughed, then fell into place beside him and started walking down the beach. The dog tagged along, darting in and out of the surf, nipping at the incoming waves. "Although . . . your house is definitely an aberration, which makes it all that much more interesting. Why is your house so different from you?"

"My house? How's that?"

"I would have expected you to be living in one of those ultra-modern, all-white condos or town houses or something. Not a cozy bungalow on the beach filled with eclectic furniture and a view of the water." She stopped walking and turned toward him, raising her chin to meet his. "So why is a khakis and tie, organizational-freak doctor living on the beach, with the sand and the wind and the water?"

He shrugged. "I missed the beach."

"Missed it? You've lived in Rescue Bay all your life."

"I missed this because I rarely had it, even living so close to it." He waved a hand toward the blue-green expanse before them. "When I was a kid, I didn't go to the beach that much. I can count on one hand the number of times my parents took me there. I always had homework to do, or chores to complete, or something else on the long list of things they wanted me to do. I took that summer job at the paddleboard shop because it gave me an excuse to spend time on the water. Then I met you and"—his gaze softened, his eyes locked with hers, and a heartbeat passed between them—"and that summer, I made a lot of really good memories on this beach."

A smile curved up her face. "Really good . . . as in the day we lost our virginity together?"

That wasn't just Colt's best memory of the beach, but the best memory he had, hands down. A moonlit night, a blanket, and a bottle of wine purloined from the Hideaway Inn's dining room. They'd laid the blanket in a protected cove beside a low dune on the beach, and as the moon kissed the sand and them, he had gone from a nervous high school boy to a man with Daisy Barton. Not in the slow, easy manner they wrote about in novels, but in a fiery rush that left them both spent and sweaty. He'd made love many times since then, and to other women besides Daisy, but few moments even came close to comparing in perfection to that night. "Okay, yeah, that was an incredible night."

"Not bad for a first time, huh?" She leaned into him, teasing him with her mouth, her voice.

"Not bad, period." His lips brushed against hers when he spoke, and heat roared through his veins. All he could think about, all he could see, was her lithe body beneath his, kissed by moonlight, so eager, so willing, and so happy. He reached up now and captured her jaw with his hand, ran a thumb over her bottom lip. She inhaled, and her lips parted, her gaze intent on his. The steady drumbeat of his pulse urged him closer, nearer, and before he could think twice, he was kissing her, a hard, fast, ravenous kiss, with his fingers tangling in her hair and Daisy surging against him.

The dog barked, and Colt pulled back, struggling to find his footing, his common sense again. "I'm sorry. I didn't mean . . ."

"To kiss me? Yet it keeps happening, and I keep kissing you back." She kicked at a shell on the sand. "Some psychologist might say we have unresolved feelings for each other."

"Unresolved." He snorted. "I think that's the second best word to describe us."

"Right after complicated."

He nodded. "Unresolved and complicated."

"Goes together, sort of like chocolate wafers and cream filling." She grinned.

He chuckled. "Yeah, it does." He cleared his throat and

then started walking again, with Daisy by his side. "And for the record, I wasn't just talking about memories from that one night on the beach. I meant all those walks along the water that we took, those late nights when we watched the sun set and stayed here until it rose again. That's why I moved here, to have a little of that again."

Damn, he was sounding like a sentimental fool. Must have been the conversation with Harold today. Or the heat. Or something.

She cocked her head and studied him. "Are you saying you live on the beach because it reminds you of . . . me?"

That was Daisy, direct and to the point. There was no dancing around the subject. She came right out and nailed the issue like a dart champion hitting the bull's-eye.

"No, of course not. There were other considerations. Like the price of the house, the size. The location." He said the words too fast, and he saw the disappointment shimmer in her eyes.

He wanted to take it back, to tell her he was lying, that he was afraid if he told her the truth—that she was right, he lived here because so many of his happy memories centered around this beach and those idyllic summer days with Daisy—then she would see something between them that couldn't be. Because tangled with those memories of Daisy was the reality that when he thought of her and their time together, he also remembered the most painful days of his life.

"We're not good together, Daisy. You know that. I know that. Just because I'm guilty of living here, and once in a while indulging in a little reminiscing, doesn't mean that this"—he waved a hand between them—"can work. If we keep on pretending it might, then someone's going to get hurt."

The light in her eyes dimmed even more, and he knew, just by the words he had said, that he had hurt her. Maybe it was better this way. End it quickly, before things got out of hand. Well, any more out of hand than they already were, with that hell-fire kiss in her motel room, the one just now, and the thousand other times he'd come within inches of touching her, kissing her, taking her to his bedroom.

"Bullshit," she said. The hurt washed away, replaced by anger. The fiery temper that came attached to Daisy roared to life. She stalked forward and poked a finger at his chest. "Do you know what your problem is, Colt? You're a coward. You told me years ago that you wanted to run away, to get away from this town and from all the expectations on your shoulders. So we did that, and then what did you do? You ran right back here and right back to everything you wanted to leave. And yet, you still won't admit that you're terrified as hell of getting close to someone. Of committing to something more lasting than a mortgage."

"That was different. *I* was different then."

"And then you run into me fourteen years later, we have one hell of an amazing night, and *wham*, you're out the door again as fast as your feet can carry you. I keep being stupid enough to believe that the old Colt is in there somewhere, because you're living in a house on a beach, and talking about that one crazy summer we had. Then just as quickly, you make sure to remind me that you're a tie and khakis guy. And not getting involved with the likes of me." She flicked at his tie like it was a roach on his shirt.

"And what is wrong with being a tie and khakis guy? What is wrong with settling down, being responsible, sticking to one place for longer than five minutes?"

"Nothing. If you're doing it for the right reasons." She crossed her arms over her chest. "And not just because you're too scared to take a risk."

"You want to talk about risk? You think just because you're always jetting off on this adventure, or that trip, quitting your job and landing in Rescue Bay for a week, a month, a year, that it makes you a risk taker? It doesn't." He caught her chin, made her hold his gaze. "You do it because you are a bigger coward than I am."

She tried to wrest her jaw away, but he held firm. "I'm not scared."

"You're so scared, you're ready to run right now. Run as far and as fast as you can go."

"I'm here for the inn, for my cousin."

"And once the inn is done? What then?"

He saw the answer in the tremble in her jaw, in the way she cut her gaze away. "I don't know, Colt. I haven't thought that far ahead. All I know is that right now, my cousin and my aunt need me. They're all the family I have and I can't imagine doing anything that would let them down. That, to me, is risk. Putting everything I have on the line for the people I love, even if it scares the hell out of me." Her brown eyes met his. "Would you do that? Risk everything for the people you love? Even if it scared you to do so?"

He released her and stepped away. The truth to what really stood between them had come in the way she looked away, and in the words she'd said, driving home the reality about who Colt Harper was.

A man, who when push came to shove, had let down those he loved. He wanted to tell her what had happened, why he was so terrified of being the shoulders for someone else, but in the end, words failed him.

"I guess we're both cowards then," he said. "Which is reason number seven-hundred and twenty-two why we'd be idiots to get involved again."

Eighteen

Daisy bounded out of bed the next morning, more excited to start her day than she could ever remember feeling. Emma was here in town, the loan was in place, the construction was underway, and her life finally felt like it was getting on an even keel.

Well, everything except her relationship with Colt. Her marriage, such as it was. If it really ever was one.

Colt's question from yesterday came back to her. Once the inn was done, what then? Was she going to put in the months, maybe years, necessary to get it running and profitable again? Or would she run out the door and onto something else? He'd nailed her with his words. She *was* terrified of staying, of being dependable. A part of her did want to run as far and as fast as she could.

Leaving Emma to deal with the inn, just as Daisy's mother had left her to deal with a thousand other things when she was growing up? Would it be so bad to stay? To make this cozy beachside town her home?

Even if it meant seeing Colt every day? Or *especially* if it meant seeing Colt every single day?

She'd taken Aunt Clara up on the invitation to run the

inn, and run down here as fast as she could, yet another spontaneous move in a life filled with them, without ever thinking through what that commitment would entail. The Hideaway Inn wasn't some greasy-spoon diner that could replace her five minutes after she threw down her apron and walked out the door.

Colt was right. She hated that about him, but he was right. She was scared of staying put, of shouldering responsibilities bigger than herself. And most of all, scared of letting down the two people in the world who meant the most to her.

Her cell phone rang. Daisy dove across the bed to unleash it from the charger and answer. "Hello?"

"Daisy? This is Olivia, Greta's soon-to-be-granddaughter. We met a few days ago, remember?"

Daisy settled against the headboard, shoving a pillow behind her back. "Yes, yes, of course. How are you?"

Olivia laughed. "Much less stressed now that I finally nailed down a wedding location."

Daisy held her breath, afraid to ask the question.

"That is, if the Hideaway Inn is still available," Olivia went on. "We're thinking just thirty or forty people, three Saturdays from now?"

Joy exploded in Daisy's heart. She'd had no idea until she had that first booking how excited it would make her. "Absolutely! That would be perfect. I talked to the contractor and everything is on track for having the outdoor work done before then. We can handle a wedding by then, no problem."

"Excellent. One more thing off my list. I know you don't have catering services yet, and Luke and I just wanted something simple, so we're going with a buffet from the Shoebox Café, if that works. Finger foods, mostly, things people can eat easily in an outdoor setting."

Daisy appreciated Olivia thinking of that detail. Daisy hadn't even considered food or silverware or decorations. Okay, so maybe she wasn't as prepared to host events as she thought. "We have plenty of tables and linens still," Daisy said, grateful that she'd checked the inn's storage building yesterday, "and some nice folding wooden chairs. We can set those up on the sand if you want, or on the patio, if it's a little breezy."

"Sounds perfect." The two of them set a date to meet at the inn and go over final details, then Olivia said good-bye. Daisy held the phone to her chest for a long time after the call ended, a big goofy smile on her face.

Maybe it was the sun in the sky. The birds chirping outside. The ocean breeze blowing through the open windows. But Daisy was filled with hope and optimism, and a thought that maybe, just maybe, she could change everything in her world if she stayed still long enough to try.

It was an odd feeling. One Daisy had never had before. Permanence. Stability. The words hung around her like ill-fitting clothes. She'd married Colt in an unconventional way, vowing to have an unconventional marriage—one where they weren't beholden to the stereotype of a three-bedroom, two-bath house, and jobs and dental plans.

Look how that had worked out—nothing was more unconventional than eloping with a man, and forgetting to dissolve the marriage. She'd always thought she was happy that way, making rules and plans that didn't account for anyone but herself. But as soon as she realized that the Hideaway Inn was returning to business, a business that Daisy would need to stay and helm, there came an excitement about the future. An anticipation about what could happen if she stayed put.

She got dressed, ate a quick breakfast of toast and coffee, then headed into the living room to find Earl, already in his recliner, the remote cemented in his hand.

"Okay, Earl, let's get your exercises done."

"You're not Jane Fonda, and I'm not a pretzel." He flipped out the footrest on his chair and leaned back.

"And you're not doing your heart one bit of good sitting in that chair again today." She clapped her hands together. "So come on, let's get to work."

He harrumphed and turned on the television.

Daisy parked her fists on her hips and stood between Earl

and the television screen. "You're not going to sit here all day. In fact, we're leaving the house today."

"Why? We've got food and television here. There's no reason to go anywhere else."

She shifted to the left when he tried to peer around her. "Number one, you have a dog now and that dog comes with responsibility. Which means a walk, at least once a day. So first thing today, we're heading downtown."

"Downtown? But that's far—"

"While we're there, we might even do a little shopping."

Earl put up a hand. "No, no shopping. Absolutely no—"

"And we're going out to lunch, too. To have something healthy, at the Shoebox Café, which welcomes dogs, as long as their humans eat outside."

Earl readied another objection, then a smile eased onto his face and became a chuckle. "All right, all right. But no shopping."

"If you're an entertaining companion on our walk, then I won't have to amuse myself stopping at a shoe sale." Funny how alike Colt and Earl were. They were both stubborn but personable, strong and smart. She could definitely see the Harper DNA in their words and their actions.

"If it means I'll get out of shopping, then I'll talk your ear off, missy." Earl snapped a leash onto Major, and a few minutes later they headed into a perfect Florida fall day. Temperatures hovered in the low seventies, with a slight breeze off the Gulf. The humidity had eased, and the warmth washed over them with a gentle touch.

It made Daisy think about her conversation with Colt yesterday. How he had moved to the beach partly because he'd rarely been allowed here as a kid. She couldn't imagine that, living so close to something she loved and never being allowed to be there.

"Tell me a story about Colt," Daisy said, as they ambled down the palm-shaded streets that led to downtown. Who was the Colt who had existed before she met him that summer? He'd never talked much about his childhood, and she realized it was a missing piece that she wanted to fill. Maybe then it would help her understand the tie and khakis guy he had become. "About when he was a little boy."

Earl rubbed his chin. "He wasn't the one who left lots of stories behind, if that makes sense. Colt was the one who never misbehaved, never got in trouble. He followed the rules, got good grades."

Although he hadn't been like that when she met him, she could see that side of him in the tidy, efficient doctor he had become. The stickler for rules and order. Something had made him detour from those rules and good grades, though, because the Colt she'd met had ridden a motorcycle and thumbed his nose at his job. "The perfect child, huh?"

"Well, yeah, but he had a lot of expectations on his shoulders. My son and his wife were hard on Colt. My son had this perfectionist streak in him, and it extended to his kids. Colt did his best to live up to that, but you know, that kind of pressure takes a toll."

Daisy ducked under a low-hanging branch. "What do you mean?"

"By the time Colt got to the end of junior year, he'd maxed out on all the high level classes at high school, won 'bout every award a kid could win, and was already getting letters from colleges, before he even applied to them. But that summer, he got his license and a job, and got himself some freedom and . . ."

"And met me."

Earl nodded. "I don't think I ever said this before, but I think you were the best thing that ever happened to Colt. I was always worried that he was like a grenade, about to go off at the slightest bit of extra pressure. Then he met you and next thing we know, he's got a motorcycle and an attitude." Earl chuckled. "A regular teenager, and if you ask me, it was about damned time. It was good for him."

She kept her gaze on Major, plodding along in front of them. "Even when we ran off to New Orleans?"

"Oh, you mean that elopement?"

She shot him a look of surprise but Earl just grinned.

"Bet you thought I didn't know about that," he said. "I know Colt thinks I don't because he never told anyone. But I suspected as much, when my son told me you two blew out of town the day after you turned eighteen. I thought Colt's father was going to have a stroke right there in my kitchen, he was so ticked. I suggested Colt ran off to get married—because I would have done the same thing—and my son was having none of that. Even if you called him today and told him you two got hitched, I bet he'd disagree and tell you that you didn't."

"He sounds like a difficult man."

"My son would argue the sky was pink till he was blue in the face, but that's what made him a great lawyer." Earl shrugged. "I love him, believe me, but I never did have much in common with him, though Lord knows I tried. My grandsons, now they were my best buddies."

Earl's love for his grandsons showed in the soft tones in his voice, the smile on his face. "I bet you spoiled them rotten."

Earl chuckled as they rounded the corner onto Main Street. "You know it. Mostly, I spoiled them with guy things. Fishing trips, go-kart rides, that kind of thing. Their grandma was the one who made them pancakes and cookies and cupcakes. Drove my health-nut son crazy, but hey, that's what grandparents are supposed to do."

"I never really knew my grandparents. I would have loved to have had grandparents like you and your wife."

Earl reached out and drew Daisy into a one-armed hug. "And I would have loved a granddaughter like you. If things work out with you and Colt, maybe I'll gain a granddaughter, and some great-grandkids, in the bargain. And if they don't, I'll make you my honorary granddaughter anyway."

Tears rushed to Daisy's eyes. She swiped them away with her fingers and smiled at Earl. "I'd like that."

"Good. Means I get more Christmas presents now." He winked at her, then started walking again.

They scored one of the empty tables outside the Shoebox Café and ordered iced teas. Major lay in the shaded area beneath the table, his tail patting a happy beat against the ground.

Greta, Esther, and Pauline headed toward the diner, chatting as they walked, trailed by an elderly gentleman with white hair. Earl glanced down the street, then away, as if he was trying to pretend he hadn't seen the three women.

"When I was a boy, we used to avoid that house," he said, pointing to a gray Victorian-style home on the corner. "Folks said it was haunted. 'Course, it was no such thing, just one of those empty places that needed some TLC, but it gave us boys something to wonder about. Ten years ago, some history buff came in, bought it for a song, and renovated it back to what it used to be. He even got himself some kind of a plaque designating it as an important place or some such thing."

"What made it so important?"

Earl kept his attention on the house, but his gaze flickered back to the women every few seconds. "Rumor has it, one of the pirates who settled here in Rescue Bay built it with all his plundered gold. I don't know how true that is, but I do know the house has been here forever. It's practically an institution."

"I think it's romantic."

Earl scoffed. "I think it's a maintenance headache waiting for some sucker to buy it."

That made Daisy laugh. "Oh, I think you need to meet a woman, Earl. Someone to bring out the romantic side of you."

He flicked a hand at the idea. "I am too old for such foolishness."

"Oh really? Even with Pauline?" As they approached a nearby table, Greta and the girls sent a wave in Daisy and Earl's direction. Daisy returned the gesture.

Earl snorted. "What about Pauline?"

"Oh, I've heard you mention her a time or two." Daisy grinned. "And, you've been sneaking little glances at her ever since we sat down."

He jerked his gaze to the table. "She's in my line of vision. Nothing more."

As if reading Earl's mind, Greta and the others came

over to the table. Daisy bit back a smile. Luke was right. The folks at Golden Years were as busy as a soap opera. Daisy could only hope she was as spry and engaged when she was in her eighties.

"Good afternoon, ladies," Daisy said. "Out for lunch?"

"Why yes, we are," Greta said. "What a coincidence, running into you here."

"Coincidence? I saw you in Pauline's giant Caddy five minutes ago. You smacked her in the head and told her to park so you could go to the Shoebox." Earl shook his head and muttered, "Bunch of stalkers."

Greta introduced Pauline, Esther, and Harold to Daisy, then invited herself to sit at the table with Earl and Daisy. Earl scowled and crossed his arms over his chest. Pauline and Esther sat at the next table, picked up menus, and began discussing the lunch options.

"Hey, Earl," Harold said, filling the awkward silence. "Been missing you at cards lately."

"I've been busy." Earl looked away when he said it.

"I understand that. Retirement can keep you hopping more than employment," Harold said, sliding into the seat opposite Earl and making himself at home. "Walt's been asking about you, too, you know."

Earl scowled. "Walt can ask all he wants. I'm not asking back."

Harold pshawed at that. "You know, Earl, it's a free country, last I checked. Which means if you don't go after what you want, someone else is free to go after it."

"Unless someone doesn't want you going after it," Greta said to Harold. "The first clue should be the no trespassing signs."

"She's in love with me," Harold whispered. "She just doesn't like to admit it out loud."

At the next table, Pauline covered a laugh with her menu. Esther took out her knitting and started clack-clacking away.

Greta ignored Harold. Instead, she grabbed Daisy and pulled her to the side. "A little birdie has told me that you booked Olivia's wedding at the Hideaway Inn."

"Yep. We're all set for three weeks from Saturday."

"Wonderful." Greta beamed. "I assume that means that you'll be staying in town, settling down? Maybe setting up house with the mister?"

Daisy glanced around, but no one seemed to have overheard Greta. Letting the town know she was married to Colt didn't scare Daisy as much as the little thrill that had run through her for a second when Greta asked the question. What was wrong with Daisy? "I'm here to get the inn reopened. We'll see after that."

Greta patted Daisy's hand. "My dear, if you believe in happily ever after, you're much more likely to find it. I always told my grandson that only those who believe will receive."

"Sort of like with Santa Claus?" Daisy laughed.

"Well, hopefully, your happily ever after is a little leaner and younger than the *ho-ho* guy, but yes." Greta winked.

"Right now, my focus is on the inn. But I appreciate the warm words, Greta." One of Daisy's favorite parts about being in Rescue Bay was the way the residents had welcomed her with open arms. It was like the family she'd always wanted. No matter what happened in the future, Daisy knew she would always treasure her days here.

"Speaking of the inn," Pauline said, setting her menu on the corner of the table, "did you consider advertising at the town festival on Saturday? Most everyone who's got a business in Rescue Bay will be there, and it's a great way to get the word out."

"Why we're even thinking of having a booth for our crafts," Esther said. "Imagine a table filled with nothing but quilts and pillows. It would be—"

"Suffocating," Greta muttered. "We are not sponsoring a craft table, Esther. If we do, someone is going to get seriously injured with a glue gun."

Esther pursed her lips. "I think it's a good idea. For those of us who aren't secret craft haters."

Daisy bit back a laugh. Earl had told her about Greta's ongoing attempts to sabotage Esther's craft binges. "I'll look into the festival, Pauline, thank you." It would be a prime opportunity to test the local market for the Hideaway. A festival would require brochures, which would be a reason for Emma to take some pictures, maybe stay a few extra days to help put the brochure together.

Everything was coming together. Earl was doing better, the inn was getting business, and Emma was finally smiling and laughing again.

But as Daisy ran down that mental list, she realized everything was getting better and falling into place—except for her. That internal battle still waged inside her. When all this was over, would she leave and move on, as if she hadn't been affected by this town, these people, and those late-night conversations? Or stay, and risk heartbreak a third time?

Nineteen

Ever since Daisy had moved into Colt's house, her sleeping pattern had gone to hell. She couldn't fault the super comfortable double bed, or the soothing sounds of the surf outside her window. Her body refused to relax, not until she knew he was home.

Colt had taken to coming home later each day, often not walking through the door until everyone else was in bed. He'd turned down her offers for family dinners and outings, saying he was too busy working.

She lay in bed that night, tense, wide awake. Major had opted to sleep in her room tonight, and had curled up a few feet from the window, where the incoming breeze would keep him cool. Above the dog's gentle sleepy snarfles, Daisy listened for the sound of the door opening.

Around midnight, she heard the click of the latch. She told herself she was going to stay in bed, and not go out to the kitchen like a worried wife, to make sure Colt had made it home okay. Because she wasn't really his wife—not in the true sense of the word—and she wasn't worried.

Yeah, right.

Five seconds later, she was putting on her robe and

heading down the hall. She found Colt sitting at the kitchen table, his head in his hands. There was something forlorn about his posture, something that said he was battling a war alone. He rarely opened up to her, rarely shared any of the burdens on his heart. She was tempted to leave him be.

Then he sighed.

"You okay?" she said, coming up behind him to lay a hand on his shoulder.

She'd meant the touch to be a quick comfort, nothing more, but when Colt covered her hand with his, her heart melted. He held her hand for a long moment, then turned to look at her. "Yeah, fine. Thanks for asking."

"It's okay." She almost added, *That's what wives are supposed to do*, but stopped herself. Because she wasn't playing the role of Colt's wife. Not really.

He glanced at the clock on the stove and let out a curse. "I'm sorry if I woke you when I got home."

"You didn't wake me, Colt." She raised a shoulder, let it drop. "I don't sleep that well."

Concern filled his face. She half expected him to feel her forehead for a fever. "I can prescribe something for that, if you want."

How could she tell him there was no prescription for what kept her up at night? No magic pill that would keep her from lying in her bed, rehashing the what-ifs? She stepped away, so he wouldn't read the truth in her eyes. "No, it's fine. I just have a lot on my mind."

"The renovation project?"

"Yeah." That worked for an excuse. Far better than admitting the truth. That she couldn't sleep, wondering why a guy she had stopped loving fourteen years ago still occupied her thoughts. She poured a glass of water, then slipped into a seat across from Colt. "I'm not just renovating the inn, I'm sort of renovating me, too."

"Don't tell me you're thinking of cosmetic surgery."

She laughed. "God, no. Though, taken literally, I guess I can see where you would get that." She pressed a hand to her chest. "I meant interior renovations. Sort of a restart on my life, my goals, all that crap I should have figured out at eighteen."

He scoffed. "Does anyone figure any of that stuff out at eighteen?"

"You did. I mean, you did when you came back here and went off to medical school. Me, I just floundered for a while. Got my act together enough to get my GED, but I never really figured out what I wanted. I only figured out what I *didn't* want."

"And what's that?"

"To be like my mother." She stared out the back door at the endless ocean of sparkling moon flakes, rising and falling with the waves, as if the moon itself was sailing away. She stared at the sea and the sky, and finally faced a few truths about herself. "As much as I tried to avoid that, in the end I became just like her. Never staying in one place for long, never committing to a job, an address, a person. Exactly what you accused me of the other day."

"I was out of line, Daisy. You're committed to the inn, to helping your cousin and your aunt. That's something. A huge something."

"I don't know if I'd call it that. More like . . . self-preservation." She wrapped her hands around her glass. "When I sat next to my Aunt Clara in the hospital, she was talking about the Hideaway Inn, about how it had been in her family for so many years, and how she had all these memories centered around it. She talked about the inn being part of Rescue Bay's history and charm. It all sounded so . . . grounded. I only spent one summer here, that summer I met you, but it was the best summer of my life. I felt like I belonged, if that makes sense. I was a part of the frame and structure of the Hideaway Inn, helping my aunt with the chores around the place, giving her input on planning the meals and hosting events, and then staying up way too late at night, talking with Emma about you and the guy she was dating. It was the longest time I ever spent in one place, with the same people, and it was . . . awesome."

All these years, she had never really talked about her life, not in an honest way, at least. When she was younger, she'd made it sound like fun to have a flighty mother who didn't believe in a traditional life. Daisy had always claimed that she loved having no ties, nothing to hold her down. But that was a lie.

The woman who had run off and eloped had been seeking the very thing she'd never had—dependability and stability. Irony at its best.

"I can't even imagine what that was like for you," Colt said. "My life may not have been perfect, but it was predictable. Annoyingly so."

Even his clothes echoed his words. He had on another variation of the shirt, tie, and khakis tonight, as if his clothes had cloned themselves. A part of her wanted to rip all the stuffy business casual right out of him, and replace it with the leather jacket, battered jeans, and soft-as-butter T-shirts he'd worn when she met him.

"Which is what had you so anxious to break all the rules." She thought of what Earl had told her, about all the expectations heaped on Colt's shoulders. Colt hadn't talked much about his father when they'd been dating, but she'd gotten the sense that theirs was a difficult, strained relationship, filled with high expectations, the complete opposite of Daisy's childhood. No wonder he'd craved her world.

"It was also what attracted me to you," he said. "You didn't live on a timetable. You just . . . lived. Take off in the middle of the day and go to the beach. Eat breakfast for dinner—"

"Still one of my favorite things to do."

He grinned. "Mine too."

Their gazes met, held, and smiles curved up both their faces at once. A shared memory, a snippet of the past, filling the space between them, knotting another thread. "If you have eggs and bacon, I have mean frying skills."

He grinned and got to his feet, hauling her up, too. "You read my mind, Daisy May."

Hot tears rushed up her throat, behind her eyes, damn it. Had to be the late hour or the reminiscing. Not the way he said her name. "No one's called me that in . . . fourteen years."

He took a step closer, and reached up to whisk a lock of hair away from her brow. "No one?"

She shook her head. "No one else calls me by my middle name. Just you."

"Then I should do it more often."

Oh, this was dangerous. This was the kind of moment that made her fall for him. There'd been so many of those when she'd first met Colt. The way he looked at her—really looked at her—when they had a conversation. The way he'd sit back and listen to her talk, or meet her eyes and tell her she was beautiful. The way he made her feel like she mattered.

No. She wasn't falling for that again.

"Let's, uh, get those eggs in a pan before midnight breakfast becomes early morning breakfast." She crossed to the fridge and pulled out the necessary ingredients, then put two frying pans on the stove and turned on the heat.

Colt slid into the space beside her and dropped four slices of bread into the toaster. "O.J.?" he asked.

"Of course." She set two glasses on the counter, before adding bacon to the first pan and sliding two eggs into the second one. Within seconds, breakfast was sizzling, filling the kitchen with the tempting aroma. Coupled with the dim room, the ebony night outside, the whole scene seemed to whisk her back in time, to that tiny fifth-floor walk-up apartment they'd had. Cheap on rent, bare on furnishings, but for three weeks, filled with life.

"Here's a clear sign that we're older and more risk averse." She held up the package. "Turkey bacon."

"And free range eggs." He grinned. "I like to call it being smarter, not older."

She put her back to the counter and waved at him with the spatula, while the eggs fried and the bacon crisped. "Don't tell me you're worried about aging."

"Not at all. If I can age as well as you have." He caught a tendril of her hair, and let it slip through his fingers. "How is it that you look more beautiful now than you did when you were eighteen?"

"High-dollar cosmetics."

He chuckled, then sobered. "Seriously, Daisy, you are a thousand times more beautiful now. You have an edge about you that you didn't have at eighteen."

"It's called graduating from the school of hard knocks." The self-deprecating words gave her an excuse to break her gaze away from his.

Dozens of men had told her she was beautiful over the years, but there was just something about the way that Colt said it that made her feel shy, as if she was seventeen all over again and sitting on those steps, sharing a package of Oreos with the cute boy who had stopped to talk to her.

From the second she'd climbed into bed tonight, her plan had been to stop thinking and fantasizing about Colt. Stop letting him invade her sleep and her thoughts. To look at her time here as just another job. Except Colt Harper wasn't some sweaty manager in a greasy diner telling her to hurry the hell up, and he wasn't some drunk customer refusing to pay for the meal he'd finished eating. He was Colt, the only man she'd ever fallen in love with, and the one man she'd never been able to forget.

With so many other people, she could throw on the mask of sassy defiance, and turn the tables back on him. She had to be sleep deprived to be so easily undone by a few sweet words.

"You don't believe me?" he asked.

"The . . . eggs are burning."

"Let them." He captured her jaw with his hands and waited until her gaze connected with his. Behind them, the bacon sizzled and spat and the eggs crinkled along their edges. The toast popped in the toaster. But all Daisy saw was Colt's hypnotic blue eyes, eyes that seemed to see past her walls and defenses, deep into the pit of her soul, in the places she kept hidden from everyone else. "You are a beautiful, amazing woman, Daisy, and sometimes, I think I forget to appreciate that."

"Colt, I—"

He put a finger to her lips. "Repeat after me. Thank you."

Silliness. But it made her smile anyway. "Thank you."

"Now don't say another word to negate that or disagree, just hold on to that compliment and believe it." He waited a second. "As I was saying, you are beautiful and amazing and I appreciate everything you have done with my grandfather. You've been here a handful of days and you have changed . . . everything."

"I didn't—" She saw the warning look in his eyes, which made her laugh. "Okay, thank you. He's a wonderful man, Colt. I don't mind spending time with him at all. You should join us more often. I think it'll really help whatever went wrong between you two."

A shadow dropped over Colt's face. He turned off the burners and moved the eggs off the heat. "Maybe. It's been years since he sat around and joked with me. Or hell, wanted to do anything with me besides throw a coffee cup at my head."

"He misses you, Colt. He really does. I know that sounds silly since he lives here, but when we were talking about you—"

"You were talking about me?"

"I asked him what you were like as a little boy." She danced a finger along his button-down shirt, wrinkled now at the end of the day, but still as buttoned up as ever. "He said pretty much like you are right now, all scheduled and organized."

Colt slid the eggs and bacon onto their plates, then flanked the protein with buttered toast triangles. He handed Daisy one of the plates, then took a second for himself. Instead of sitting down at the table, they both leaned against the counter and began to eat, just as they had years ago. "Life is easier that way."

"Is it?" She held a bite of egg in his direction and gave him a teasing, sassy smile. "Or is it better to mix things up once in a while and have breakfast for dinner?"

He leaned over, and ate the bite off her fork. "Maybe a little of both. Best of all worlds."

"I do believe we're rubbing off on each other, Mr. Harper. You're getting a little loosey-goosey with those rules, and I'm getting a little more organized and traditional." She stacked her toast until all the points aligned.

He chuckled, then plucked a slice of bacon from her plate. "Like that?"

"Hey, no! That was my bacon. You're going to pay for that." She reached for his plate, but he whisked it away.

"You want my bacon?" He dangled a piece in front of her, but kept yanking it out of her reach. "You'll have to work for it."

She propped her fists on her hips. "And how exactly do you want me to work for it?"

His eyes turned dark, his smile sexy. In an instant, the mood between them shifted from playful to charged, the air sparking with electricity. "I can think of one very, very good way."

"If I remember right, it's what followed breakfast for dinner, every single time."

Oh Lord, did she remember. Making love with Colt had never been boring, never been anything short of amazing. An ache started deep inside her, stoking embers that had never died.

Colt came closer, holding the bacon between them. He brushed it against her lips. "Every. Single. Time."

She took a bite, watching him, while she chewed, swallowed, then opened her mouth again. Her heart raced, her pulse pounded in her head.

"More?" he asked.

She nodded. "Much . . . more."

He dropped the bacon onto the counter and kissed her instead, soft and sweet for one long moment, then harder, hungrier. She wrapped her arms around him, and he grabbed her waist, pressed her into the counter. She arched against him, fire burning deep inside her, as if Colt had flipped a switch.

He grew hard against her, and his kiss deepened, his tongue dancing with hers, a wild, feverish pace. He anchored his palms on the counter on either side of her, and she reached up to claw at his back, the breakfast forgotten. He hoisted her onto the counter and slid into the space between her legs, his cotton khakis rubbing against the bare skin of her legs. He reached a hand between them, parted the flimsy fabric of her robe and nightgown, then lowered his mouth to her breast, drawing her nipple into his mouth.

She arched, gasping his name. Her pelvis met his, heat against heat, throbbing need raging through every ounce of her body. She scrambled to wrest her arms out of the robe, the nightgown, to bare everything to him, to ease the hunger for more, more, more. At the same time, he reached for her robe, and their arms collided, knocking into one of the glasses on the counter.

It toppled onto the floor. The glass shattered on the tile, spraying them both with juice and tiny shards. Colt jerked back. "Damn it. Sorry."

"It's fine. Let me—"

He stopped her from hopping down. "Stay right there. I'll get it. You're barefoot and I'm still wearing shoes. I don't want you to cut your foot open."

"Hey, if I do, at least I have a doctor readily available for some stitches."

He grabbed a broom and some paper towels and set to work cleaning up the mess. By the time he was done, Daisy had straightened her clothes, and begun cleaning up from breakfast, as best she could by reaching from the countertop to the sink. When Colt was done, he hoisted her off the counter. "I'm sorry our breakfast is cold now," she said. Not just the breakfast, but the passionate moment, too. She wasn't sure she was sorry about that, because every time Colt touched her or kissed her, her brain short-circuited and she forgot all those wise arguments she'd had with herself about staying away from him.

"It's fine. Besides, you should get to bed. I can finish this up." His voice was cooler now, platonic.

She put a hand on his. "Or you can just let it soak. The

world won't fall apart if you go to sleep with a sink full of dirty dishes and an overflowing trash can."

He looked back at the mess, then at her again. "Okay. But if I wake up in the morning in a *Day After Tomorrow* scenario, you're cleaning the kitchen."

She laughed. "Deal."

As they walked down the hall toward Daisy's bedroom, she debated inviting him in, asking him to spend the night, to finish what they had started. Oh, how she wanted that, but then she thought of the broken glass, its timing like a warning bell heading off a bad decision.

What if she fell in love with Colt again, spent three weeks or three years with him, and in the end, he shut her out just as he had a thousand times before? Her wary heart cautioned her to keep it light, and to keep her door shut—in case she was tempted to run upstairs to his room.

"Sunday, there's a big festival in downtown Rescue Bay," she said. "I'm setting up a table to advertise the Hideaway Inn, and your grandpa is planning on going to help out. Do you want to go? If Emma works the booth with me, then you and I can take some time to walk around the festival. There's supposed to be a band and everything."

"I . . . can't. I have plans."

"Surely not all day." She leaned against her door and gave him a grin. "Come on, you say you want more family time with your grandpa. You have to actually *make* some time to have that, Colt."

"I know. And I will. I just . . . can't this weekend."

"What could you possibly be doing that's more fun than hanging out downtown with us?" She grinned, teasing him, trying to ease past that wall he kept in place. Even as she told herself not to open her heart to him, not to invite him into hers, stubborn hope kept pushing her forward. "Come on, Colt, we'll have a good time."

"Thanks for the offer, Daisy. Maybe another time."

She realized he hadn't told her why he couldn't go. Or what he was doing instead. Maybe he did have a girlfriend.

Or maybe he wasn't interested in anything approaching a real relationship with her. She should have known. What was that old saying about past history predicting the future?

She never thought she'd be so grateful for a broken glass. She turned the knob and opened her door. "Forget I asked."

"Daisy—"

"Good night, Colt." Then she slipped inside and shut the door before he could hear the disappointment in her voice.

Twenty

"So give me one good reason why you're here with my ugly face instead of at home with Daisy." Nick signaled to the bartender for a second beer, then plunked a few dollars onto the worn oak bar. Above their heads, a trio of big screen TVs showed two baseball games and a tennis match, the sound muted, while the closed captioning scrolled the commentator's words across the bottom of the screen.

"Because she drives me crazy." Colt was still nursing his first beer. He'd been nursing it so long, the liquid had gone warm. Didn't matter. He wasn't here to drink. He was here to avoid going home, avoid dealing with everything that conversation on the beach and that midnight breakfast meal had stirred up.

And avoid dealing with the flicker of jealousy that ran through him when he saw his grandfather joking with Daisy after Colt walked in the door late last night. For years, Colt had been struggling to reestablish his relationship with his grandfather. Daisy had managed to connect with Grandpa Earl in a matter of days. It was what Colt had wanted—and why he'd hired her—but damned if it didn't make him wonder why he couldn't do the same.

"Sometimes crazy can be a good thing, you know," Nick said.

Colt scoffed. "Trust me, with Daisy, it's not. She's everything I *don't* want in my life."

"Beautiful, sexy, funny, nice. Yeah, I can see why that would be a drag." Nick took a long pull off the second beer, then turned to Colt. "So have you told her yet?"

"Told her what? That she drives me crazy? She knows I'm not interested in her."

Nick snorted. "Right. Because your body language around her is so monk-like, right? Just like when you slept with her a few months ago?"

"That was . . . an aberration." He was using that word a whole lot lately, his go-to explanation for everything that happened with Daisy Barton. Because admitting otherwise would mean admitting that he still longed for her as much today as he had fourteen years ago. That she still made him want to run away and find a private beach where all they did was explore each other for days, or even better, hole up in some snowed-in cabin in the woods for weeks on end.

He took a sip of the warm beer, but all it did was upset his stomach, not erase the thoughts of Daisy lying on a bearskin rug in front of a roaring fire, wearing nothing but a pair of boots and a smile.

"I meant," Nick said quietly, "have you told her about Henry?"

Colt scowled. He didn't want to talk about that. Hell, he didn't even want to *think* about that. "She doesn't need to know."

"You know, I love you like a brother, Colt, but you are one stubborn mule. What's that old saying about the doctor never taking his own advice? You gotta talk about the things that weigh heavy on your mind or they'll weigh down your soul. Or some such new-age truth."

Colt spun on the stool and rested an elbow on the bar. "Have you told Maggie you're interested in her?"

"Hell, no." Nick paused, then chuckled. "Okay. Touché."

"Yeah, giving advice is a hell of a lot easier than taking it."

Nick nodded, then sipped at his beer for a little while. On the center TV, the White Sox were handily beating the Oakland As, with three innings left. The announcers were already talking World Series potential for the White Sox, who had just signed a new, superstar pitcher. "Daisy told me today that Olivia booked her wedding at the inn, which means Daisy's going to be in town at least another month. So either you're going to have to start going home and dealing with her sleeping in your guest bedroom, or start paying rent for that stool."

"You are a pain in the ass, you know that?"

Nick chuckled. "I'll take that as a compliment. And agreement that you still want her."

Colt didn't reply. He didn't trust himself not to tell the truth.

Nick sat there, quiet, while he fiddled with the beer bottle. Above their heads, the White Sox had three men on base, and the close-up of the Oakland As pitcher showed a nervous guy wiping sweat off his brow. "I know you probably don't want to hear this, Colt," Nick said after a while, "but I think you were a better person when you were with her."

"A better person? Nick, I quit my job, bought a motorcycle, and ran off to Louisiana to elope. How is that being a better person?"

"You're a hell of a doctor. The kind that dots all the i's and crosses all the t's. In healthcare, it's important to keep track of the details, to be anal retentive and dispassionate, and all those things. But in real life . . ." Nick shrugged. "It can make you a pain in the ass."

"Gee, thanks."

"I'm just saying that letting loose once in a while is good for the soul. Don't be so worried about the rules and regulations and little things."

"Now you sound like the title of a self-help book."

Nick raised the bottle in his hands. "It's the beer. Makes me smart."

Colt chuckled. "I'd like to see that study."

"You are seeing it. It's called real life." Nick signaled to the bartender for a fresh brew for Colt. "Try it yourself, and you'll see."

"You're a bad influence on me, you know."

Nick grinned, then toasted Colt's new beer with his own. "Then I'm seriously rocking my job as best friend."

Daisy took her time getting ready, switching dress options three times before finally settling on a sky blue sundress with white trim. She paired it with white flats, then curled her hair and let the tendrils hang down her back. Nerves churned in her stomach. This was it, her big chance to try to drum up enough business to ensure the Hideaway's future. With enough potential customers, she hoped to convince Emma that reopening the B&B would be a good idea not only for just Luke and Olivia's wedding, but also for the long term.

Not to mention, the income from future events would help pay for the renovations. Colt paid her well to take care of Grandpa Earl, but it wasn't well enough to repay the loan. Which meant they needed dozens more events, just to break even.

Though that wasn't what had her fretting over her dress choice or spending thirty minutes fixing her hair. It was the tiny possibility that Colt might take her up on her offer after all, and turn the festival into a family event. He had barely been home in the last few days—she could count on one hand the number of times she'd seen him since that midnight breakfast—and had been noncommittal when she mentioned the festival again yesterday.

As soon as the Hideaway was functioning again, Daisy could move out of this house, move on, to somewhere that didn't make her feel like she needed to repair all that was broken. Heck, she could barely straighten out her own life. What made her think she could change the lives of two grown—and very stubborn—men?

Focus on the B&B. On Emma. Leave the rest alone. A good mantra, if only she could follow it.

Daisy flipped out her cell phone and pressed Emma's number. "Good morning. Are you ready for today?"

"As ready as I'll ever be." A pause. "Do you think the pictures look okay in the brochure? I was thinking last night that maybe we should—"

"It's perfect. You're an awesome photographer, Em. You managed to not only capture the spirit of the Hideaway Inn, but crop the photos just enough to hide the construction." Daisy had loved the pictures Emma took, each one of them strategically lit and angled to give the Hideaway the appearance of its former glory.

The other reason Daisy was grateful for the festival and the brochure project—Emma had agreed to stay an extra few days, to handle the design and printing, then help at the Hideaway's booth. Emma hadn't mentioned Roger or her job back in Jacksonville, and every time Daisy brought up the subject, Emma deflected to something else. Either way, it was clear Emma needed a break from her life. In the last few days, her mood had lightened and she'd become more like the old Emma.

"Glad you liked my creative photographic skills." Emma laughed. "I'll meet you at the festival in a little bit."

"Bring the coffee. I think we're going to need it." After the last few nights of tossing and turning, Daisy could use an IV drip of caffeine. Colt had come home late every night, often long after Earl had gone to bed, leaving again in the morning before anyone got up. She'd stayed in her own room, avoiding him as surely as he was avoiding her.

He'd called her a coward, and he was right. She didn't confront him, didn't go see him, because she didn't want to have him break her heart again. She'd opened her heart to him that night—okay, not a whole lot, but it was a start—and in the end, he'd shut her out again. The real coward, Daisy decided, was Colt Harper. The question was why. The man she'd married had been adventurous, spontaneous. This one was cautious and guarded.

She hung up with Emma, then headed out to the kitchen. "You ready?" she asked Earl.

"As ready as I'll ever be." He had on sneakers and jeans, and a T-shirt advertising the garage he used to own. But it was Major Pain—Major, she corrected in her thoughts—who looked the most ready to tackle the day.

Earl had brushed the dog until his coat shined, then tied a big red bandana around the dog's neck, matching the red leash already attached to Major's collar. Major sat on the tile, tail swishing, tongue lolling, ready to go.

"Okay, great. Where's Colt?"

Earl shrugged. "Said he had to go somewhere. Didn't say where or when he was getting back."

Daisy cursed under her breath. She'd really thought Colt would make time for this. For a man who kept complaining about the distance in his relationships, he sure was a big part of the problem. "Well, maybe he'll meet us there."

"Maybe." But Earl sounded as doubtful as Daisy.

Daisy and Earl headed downtown, walking slow so Earl wouldn't get winded. Major pranced beside them, excited to be outside, or just plain excited. The downtown festival event was in full swing by the time Daisy arrived, with several local Rescue Bay businesses advertising on banners and little pop-up awnings spread throughout the park. An eighties-style cover band played on the gazebo stage in the center of the park while people drifted from booth to booth.

People milled about the festival, starting with the food vendors handing out free samples, then working their way down toward the businesses lining the park. It was a sunny day, bright and warm, with the scents of fresh-cut grass and salt water mingling in the air. The rest of the country might be starting to bundle up and think about comfort foods for fall, but here in Rescue Bay, it still felt like summer.

"You need any help?" Earl asked.

"Nope. I have it under control." She bit her lip, shifted her weight from foot to foot. "Emma should be here soon, too."

Earl's light blue eyes softened. "You look nervous, Daisy."

She bit her lip again and nodded. "A lot is riding on this. If we don't get a lot of interest in the Hideaway Inn reopening, then we'll go bust before we even make our first dollar. And we owe a whole lot of dollars to the bank."

"If there's one thing I've learned now that I'm an old man, it's that worry is a lot like sitting in a rocking chair," Earl said. "It takes a lot of energy, and doesn't get you a damned bit further down the road. So don't waste your energy on sitting in place. Focus on the road ahead, and the rest will work out."

She laughed, and just like that, her nerves eased. "Thanks, Earl. I needed that."

He nodded, then thumbed toward the food vendors. "I'm going to go get a hot dog."

"Earl, you shouldn't—"

He winked. "Just kidding. They're selling some of that chicken on a stick. I figure anything on a stick can't be too bad for you." He gave her a little wave, then headed across the park with Major.

Daisy slipped behind one of the small white tables that Olivia, as the organizer of the festival, had set up for the exhibitors. Down the road maybe she could buy a stand-up display, invest in an actual booth—

She stopped herself. What was she doing? Making plans to stay and be what . . . the marketing director for the Hideaway?

That meant a long-term commitment. Something Daisy had arrived here sure that she wanted, but as she got more of a feel for the homespun life of Rescue Bay, she wondered if she was deluding herself. Baking a turkey or setting fresh flowers on the kitchen table didn't qualify her for domesticity. For stability.

Or was she rushing to hand off the reins to Emma because she was more afraid of something else, something bigger. Something like . . .

Falling in love with Colt again.

That would be the biggest mistake she could make. Believing that a few tender moments, a couple of midnight conversations, meant that he still loved her.

His absence spoke the truth. She needed to pay better attention to Colt's actions, and stop putting stock in words that held about as much weight as the wind. Then maybe this constant ache of disappointment would disappear.

A few minutes later, Daisy had spread the table with a bright red tablecloth, added a pile of business cards, some brochures Emma had designed and run off at a local copy shop, and flanked it all with a collage of photos of the Hideaway Inn that Aunt Clara had sent to the girls. Daisy reached into her bag and pulled out a few other items, then set them up on the right side of the table, arranging and rearranging until she was satisfied with the setup.

"Hey, great marketing idea," Emma said. Her cousin had her hair down today, long dark brown waves curling over the straps of her pink sundress. "Makes me want to head there right now for a weekend away. And I've been there a thousand times."

Daisy grinned. "You think so? I wasn't so sure about the satin sheet set."

"It says romance and getaway, all in one." Emma ran a hand over the soft fabric, then danced a touch across the twin champagne glasses and bottle of Asti. "It's really romantic."

Emma's voice sounded sad and lonely. "Hey, you okay?"

"Yeah, sure. Just fine." Emma shrugged. "Just thinking it's about time I headed home."

"Already? But I love having you here. If Roger's busy at school every day, why not stay? Take a nice long solo vacation." Daisy adjusted the wine bottle, and laid a red rose across the top of the sheets. A few scattered paper red hearts added a little more romance to the tableau. Hopefully it was enough to draw in some customers, and spread the word that the Hideaway was reopening.

Emma wrapped her arms around her chest and looked

out over the bustling park. "Maybe I will. But just a few more days. Okay?"

"I'll take it."

"If I stay, it doesn't make sense to keep paying to stay at the horrible motel. Maybe I can move into the inn on Monday. Nick got one of the bedrooms done, and the up-stairs bath is all repaired. It gives the place a little se-curity, too."

"That's a fabulous idea," Daisy said.

"If you ever get tired of staying with Colt, you could join me. Just like old times." Emma smiled. "I've missed that."

"Me too." Daisy glanced at the park entrance, as if just mentioning his name would make Colt appear, but he wasn't among the people she saw.

"And maybe then you'd stop looking like someone ran over your puppy every time his name comes up."

Daisy jerked her attention back to Emma. "I do not."

Emma arched a brow.

"It's just tough," Daisy said with a sigh, "living under the same roof with a man you used to love."

"Yeah, that's something I know well," Emma said softly.

Before Daisy could ask Emma what she meant, Olivia strode up to the table. "I'm so happy you got the brochures done in time," she said, picking one up. "Now I can show everyone the awesome place where we are holding our wed-ding. Wow, these are fantastic photos."

"Emma took them." Daisy gestured toward her cousin, who had a shy smile on her face. Emma had always been an amazing photographer, but had never really seen her own talent. Maybe that was why she'd never fully made the leap into self-employment. "Emma is our resident Ansel Adams."

"These are fabulous photos," Olivia said. "Hey, if you're going to be in town, will you do the photography for my wedding? I want something like this, with a natural, homey feel. None of those staged, stiff, family portraits like every-one's doing a lineup with the bride and groom. I want our pictures to be relaxed and fun, like Luke and me. And the crazy family I'm joining."

Emma glanced at Daisy. "I don't know my future plans, but I'll make sure I'm back in town to cover your wedding either way."

Things were finally coming together. The renovations were on target, Emma was getting involved, and their first event was only a few weeks away.

Then why did this empty feeling linger in Daisy's chest? She shook it off, then refocused on Emma and Olivia, who were discussing possible shots for the wedding. "By the way, the renovations are right on target for your wedding," Daisy said to Olivia. "We'll have the lobby open for a small reception and restrooms, stuff like that. But if it rains, I don't think we'll have the space for a big crowd."

"That sounds perfect. And, no worries about a big crowd. Luke and I want a small gathering. If it was up to us, I think we'd just run off and elope, but Greta would never stand for that." Olivia chuckled. "And I have to say, there is something about walking down an aisle in front of your friends and family that's nice."

"I eloped, so I never got any of those big romantic, feel-good moments. I kinda wish I had a traditional wedding." Daisy fiddled with one of the paper hearts. The wind caught it and blew it away. A sign? Or just a coincidence? "But we were in such a rush, we got married in a courthouse, in the middle of the day. Nothing fancy, nothing blue or old or whatever the saying is."

Emma stood beside Daisy, mute. Odd. Emma was one of those girls who'd loved talking about weddings, watching wedding shows, debating bridal gown choices. Unlike Daisy, Emma had a romantic streak running deep in her veins.

"Well, if you ever get married again, you should have the ceremony at the Hideaway," Olivia said. "I think it's going to be perfect for Luke and me. Since that wonderful place is part of your family history, it would be even more perfect for you and . . . you know"—Olivia lowered her voice and leaned in—"Doctor Harper, should you ever retie the knot."

Daisy froze. Olivia knew, too? Of course, Luke was engaged to Olivia. He would have told her about Colt.

She didn't want to tell Olivia that she'd never gotten unmarried in the first place, and the chances of another marriage to Colt were slim to zero. The finalized loan papers were now in Daisy's hands, which eliminated Daisy's need to stay married to Colt.

And that, she knew, was what had tainted this sunny day ever since she woke up. For days, she'd avoided thinking about it, as if burying her head in the sand would change anything. Instead of being relieved that she would finally be free of the bond to a man who had broken her heart, the thought saddened her. It wasn't just about letting go of Colt forever, but more about a bone-deep craving in Daisy for the very thing she'd gone her whole life thinking she didn't want.

Family. Home. A place in the world, all her own. A place where she could set down roots, make memories, build lifetime bonds.

The question was whether she was brave enough to dive in and embrace that kind of life on her own. Especially a life where Colt would be living just down the beach.

Mike Stark entered the park, hand in hand with a woman who could have been Olivia's twin. Two young girls skipped ahead of them, beelining for the shelter dogs sitting in a large pen to the right of the table set up for adoptions. The littlest girl darted to the table next door, offering up a winsome smile, which earned her a cookie from the ladies representing the Rescue Bay Bakery.

"Those adorable girls are my nieces," Olivia said, with clear love in her voice. "Or will be, once Mike and Diana get married. The older one is Jenny. I swear, she's going to grow up to be a vet. She's at the shelter and Diana's practice more often than I am. The little one is Ellie. She's a firecracker, but she has pretty much everyone in this town wrapped around her little finger."

The whole scene was so . . . domestic. So ordinary. Like something out of a TV show. Bone-deep envy filled Daisy. All her life, she'd said she was glad to be single, on her own, no one relying on her or wanting her to make dinner. But now, just watching Mike and Diana with Jenny and Ellie, Daisy wondered—

What if she had stayed with Colt? Would they have two kids like Mike and Diana? Would they be holding hands as they walked through the park? Splitting cookies with each other and sharing laughs?

Good Lord, what was wrong with her? She kept running hot and cold—one foot turned toward the Betty Crocker world that surrounded her, another stepping outside the door, ready to run like a rabbit back to the no-commitment world she had left in New Orleans.

Olivia noticed a few people heading for Daisy's table. "I'll let you get back to selling. Good luck, Daisy." Olivia reached over and gave Daisy a quick hug, then hurried off to the Rescue Bay Shelter table.

Daisy drew in a sharp breath, surprised at the tears such a simple gesture could bring to her eyes. Every time she convinced herself she wasn't cut out for this home and hearth world, something like a hug from a person she barely knew to a few kind words of advice from a cantankerous old man brought her back around again.

As the morning wore on, Daisy and Emma shifted into work mode, tag-teaming to answer the questions about the Hideaway Inn and the status of its renovation from the people who stopped by the table. There was a general consensus of support for the B&B's return to Rescue Bay, which Daisy took as a good sign for the road ahead. That, and the way Emma joked and smiled with the visitors to the table. For a little while there, Emma was her old affable, warm self, which told Daisy she'd made the right choice in bringing Emma here. Maybe with enough time in Rescue Bay, Emma would ease whatever heartache she held inside.

And maybe Daisy would, too. Her attention kept straying to the park entrance, scanning the people milling about for Colt's tall frame and wide smile. He hadn't arrived, hadn't texted or called. Not a word.

A little after eleven, there was a lull in activity so Emma took a break for lunch, and Greta came over to Daisy's table, handing her a napkin and a frosted cookie, as if she'd read Daisy's mind and knew she was long overdue for a sugar rush. "Looks like this town is growing on you," Greta said. "You fit this place like a nut with a bolt. I think you should plan on settling in here for a good long time. Like forever."

Perhaps. But staying here, when Colt was living just a few streets away, would be the epitome of painful. "I don't know. We'll see what the future brings."

Greta nodded toward the clipboard holding a list of potential customers for the Hideaway Inn. "Looks to me like the future's bringing some bright prospects your way. Be a shame not to see where they lead you."

As more people began wandering toward the table, Greta moved away, heading over to chat with Esther and Pauline, who were standing beside a table for a craft store. Esther had an I HEART KNITTING bag slung over her shoulder, with a big thick brown knitted thing sticking out of the top and two giant knitting needles stuck into the mass of yarn, like a voodoo doll. Daisy saw Pauline send a wave in Earl's direction. He gave her a nod, then went back to his conversation with Olivia at the shelter's table. But his gaze kept straying to Pauline, even if he pretended to be looking elsewhere.

"Wow. The Hideaway Inn." A middle-aged woman came over to the table, picked up one of Daisy's business cards, flipped it over, then glanced up at Daisy. "I remember that place."

Daisy put on a bright smile. "We're renovating and hoping to reopen in a few months. So if you're interested in booking a weekend getaway or a—"

The woman glanced at the card again. Then up at Daisy. When their gazes connected a second time, a flicker of recognition ran through Daisy.

"Wait. Daisy Barton? I remember you." The lady pointed. "You're that girl."

That girl? She tried to place the other woman, but drew a blank. "Uh, I'm not sure who you mean, but I'm—"

"The girl who had that party in that abandoned house. Only it wasn't abandoned. Just vacant. Temporarily."

Then Daisy remembered. The party that had exploded. She'd wanted just a quick, end of summer celebration with the friends she'd made in Rescue Bay. And Colt. But the party, like parties were apt to do, became a monster of its own. She'd chosen that place because someone had told her it was empty. Sold, foreclosed, something. Daisy had thought no one would care if they had a party. Back then, Daisy hadn't thought much about consequences or damages—she'd wanted a party and she'd had one, figuring she'd deal with the mess later.

"A hundred teenagers in my house, spilling beer and alcohol everywhere," the woman went on, "trashing my pool and tearing up my lawn. Took me three years to get those tire tracks totally filled in, and a few thousand hours of hard work to fix the damage to my house. Not to mention what it cost me to repair the damage to the walls, the carpets."

The police had been called, the owner—Jane Mellon, a snowbird living in Indiana or Iowa or something—had driven down the day after the party, showed up at the Hideaway Inn, and ranted at Daisy for a solid thirty minutes. At the time, Daisy remembered being defiant and disrespectful, more interested in protecting her friends from trouble than making amends.

Now Daisy's face heated. She swallowed, and wished the space would open up and help her disappear. She wasn't that teenager anymore, but she doubted Jane would see that. Nor could Daisy blame her for still being angry. If the roles were reversed, Daisy would have been raising the roof. "I'm very sorry, Mrs. Mellon. I was young and stupid and truly didn't mean to do any of that." Daisy wished she had better words to express her regret, to explain how idiotic and selfish she had been back then. Everything she said felt . . . inadequate. "It just got out of hand."

"Yeah, it always does, doesn't it? Thank God your family at least paid for the damages."

"My . . . family?"

Jane shrugged. "Your mother dropped off a check one

day. Said she was taking you out of town that afternoon. She apologized up and down, which is far more than you did."

Willow had paid for the damage that Daisy had done? No wonder she'd yanked Daisy out of Rescue Bay so quickly, zipping her back up to Jacksonville. Daisy's mother had never said a word, never a condemnation or a lengthy lecture. Nothing. Maybe her mother hadn't been as uninvolved or self-absorbed as Daisy had thought.

Maybe Daisy had been the one too busy condemning Willow's actions to notice when her mother actually did do her best to raise a responsible daughter. "I am very, very sorry, Mrs. Mellon," Daisy said again. "I know that doesn't make up for everything, but I hope you accept my apology, even though it is late."

Jane leaned in, her eyes narrowed and her face pinched. There was no forgiveness in her features. "Weren't you the one who ran off with Colt Harper, too? I remember the town was all abuzz, about you two dating, then about him running away on that motorcycle. And after what happened to his little brother . . ."

"His little brother?"

Henry?

Dread filled Daisy's chest. *After what happened.* Those words were never followed by anything good.

Like gears shifting into place, the silences, the troubled sighs, the sentences left unfinished, all clicked together in one horrible picture.

"What happened to him?" Daisy asked, praying, praying so hard, that the answer was anything but—

"Oh, don't play innocent. You know he died."

"Died?" Even though her heart had known the truth before Jane spoke, the word hit Daisy like a brick. Henry? That sweet little boy? *Died?* "But how . . . when?"

Jane ignored her and barreled on, her voice laced with sarcasm, anger. "Such an awful tragedy, too. People talked about it for years. And it all would have been avoided, they say, if Colt had been here."

If Colt had been here? "I don't understand. Henry worshipped him," Daisy said in a soft, small voice. "He followed Colt everywhere. He used to call him his shadow. He never would have let anything happen to Henry."

Died.

No wonder Colt hadn't said anything. No wonder there was that pall of emptiness hanging over Colt's house, over his relationship with his grandfather, over every conversation.

"I . . . I didn't know."

"Don't bullshit me. Of course you knew. You were his girlfriend."

Wife, Daisy started to correct, then stopped herself. She was never really Colt's wife, not in the true sense of the word. Never a partner in anything but irresponsibility. For years, that had never bothered her. She'd never worried about being accountable, about what people thought of her. But now, standing beneath Jane Mellon's scathing glare, Daisy did care.

Because if she'd truly been Colt's wife, if he had truly loved her, he would have told her. And she, in turn, would have been there for him.

"I'm sorry," Daisy said.

"I don't care." Jane flung the business card at the table. It pinged off the champagne glasses and fluttered to the ground. "Why are you even here in this town? Haven't you done enough damage for one lifetime?"

Jane stomped away. The wind caught Daisy's card and tumbleweeded it across the grassy lawn, around the corner, and finally, out of sight.

Twenty-one

Earl stood to the side of the festival, the dog by his side. Funny thing about a dog. It provided friendship, without demanding much in return. A man could while away the hours with a dog, not having to say or do a thing. Major just waited, turning his head from time to time to look up at Earl, as if to say, *We staying put? Or moving on?* Every so often, Earl would give the dog a pat of reassurance, then Major would go back to waiting. Patient and loyal.

Across the way, Earl saw Walt Patterson and Harold Twohig enter the park. The two men were laughing at something. Earl took a step forward, then stopped himself. If he went over and talked to the guys, they'd ask him why he wasn't coming to their card games anymore, and he'd have to explain himself.

Earl was in no mood to explain. The trouble was, he missed his friends. Missed their camaraderie, and their terrible card playing. But he wasn't about to go back to that old folks' home and listen to everyone whining about their bum hips and worn-out tickers. All it did was remind him of his own worn-out ticker, and he had enough reminders of his mortality when his joints staged a mutiny every morning.

Earl's gaze lingered on Pauline, who was standing under the shade of a tree, sipping lemonade. She had on sunglasses, which hid her pretty green eyes from his view. She turned toward him, flashed him a smile, and he gave her a half nod in return. Major looked up at him, as if saying, *That's it? That's all you got, old man?*

"It's complicated," Earl said to the dog. "And it's all because of that damned Walt Patterson."

Major wagged his tail.

"No, I'm not going to forgive him for stealing Pauline out from under my nose."

Major barked, got to his feet, his tail wagging at a furious pace.

Earl sighed. "You are a stubborn dog."

Major cocked his head, as if saying, *Look in the mirror, mister.*

Greta Winslow passed by Walt and Harold, ignoring Harold's how-do-you-do. Greta kept right on trucking, with Esther and Pauline flanking her on either side. Walt and Harold brought up the rear, with Walt stopping Pauline to talk to her, aside from the others. Damn that Walt Patterson. Man claimed to be his friend, when really, he was just a wolf.

Earl made a little *ch-ch* sound, and Major snapped to his feet, tail wagging, ready to go wherever Earl went. He didn't go far, just a few feet to the right, to the cookie table. He might not feel like socializing, but he sure as shooting felt like eating cookies.

It was merely a coincidence that the ladies had also ended up at the same table. He had a chocolate chip halfway to his mouth when Pauline came up beside him.

"Morning, Earl."

He gave her a little nod. "Morning, Pauline." He tried to work up something a little more conversational, but all Earl could see in his mind was Walt Patterson, the damned fool, grinning and whispering in Pauline's ear.

She hovered over the cookie display, debating between

a peanut butter cookie and a frosted sugar one. "Nice day for a festival."

"It's Florida." He harrumphed. "It's always a nice day for a festival."

She slid into the space between him and the cookies, and put her hands on her hips. "Who threw mud in your eye today? You're a grump and a half. Which I'd say is normal, except today you have that extra half a grump."

"Go talk to Walt Patterson." Earl nodded in the direction of his former best friend. "He's always got a sunny disposition."

Pauline snorted. "Is that what this is about? I compliment Walt and suddenly, you and I are enemies?"

"You didn't just compliment Walt, from what I heard."

Crimson filled Pauline's cheeks. Regret filled Earl's gut.

"Sorry, I shouldn't have said that," he said. "I was out of line."

"Yes you were. And for your information, what I do or don't do with Walt Patterson is my personal choice. Last I checked, you and I weren't anything more than friends."

"Friends?" He scoffed and looked away before she read anything else in his face. One would think at his age that he wouldn't get so discombobulated by a woman, but blast it all, every time he got around Pauline, he was a sixteen-year-old stumbling fool all over again. "You're blocking the cookies, Pauline."

"Earl Harper, you are a stubborn man. Fine. Have your cookies. I hope they keep you warm at night." Pauline walked away, with a determined, unhurried step. Earl turned away before he saw if Walt caught up to Pauline.

The festival began to wind to a close. Vendors packed up their booths, families gathered their children and headed out of the park. Earl snagged one last cookie from the booth, then grabbed Major's leash and walked over to Daisy's booth.

"Did you have a good day?" she asked.

"Just peachy." He wasn't about to explain about Walt and

Pauline and the little soap opera in his life. All that did was give him indigestion anyway.

She stacked the brochures in a pile and wrapped a rubber band around them, then did the same with her business cards. "Emma and I were going to go get some dinner. Maybe some takeout, since it's getting late. Do you want to go with us?"

Earl had done enough socializing for the day. He didn't want to be here, didn't want to be anywhere. He wanted to be alone. "Some of the guys invited me to a card game," Earl said, and instantly felt bad for lying to Daisy. "I'm going to go there, and catch up with you later."

"Are you sure you don't need a ride? Do you want me to pick you up later?"

"No, no, I'm fine." He even put on a smile, to give his words a little extra believability.

"Okay. Well, have fun." Daisy turned back to talk to someone who had stopped at her table, and Earl walked out of the park.

Just him and the dog. And a whole lot of regrets and heartache that hung heavy on his shoulders, like a winter coat on a summer day.

The festival wound to a close. Still no Colt. It was Sunday, for Pete's sake. Where could he be all day? Daisy told herself she didn't care that he'd let her down, that he avoided all the family outings she planned. Colt kept saying he wanted one thing—a family, relationships—and did everything to work against that. That was what she needed to remember every time she got swayed by a kiss or a late-night conversation with him.

"I can take this stuff back to the inn," Emma said, lifting the box of cards and brochures and wine glasses.

"Thanks. You want me to pick up some food and meet you over there?" Daisy said. "Chinese? Pizza?"

"I . . . have a headache. I think I'm just going to get something at a drive-thru and turn in early. Sorry."

Emma's happy, light mood from earlier had evaporated, and her face had gone back to being troubled, her green eyes filled with sadness. "Are you okay?"

"Yeah, yeah, it's just been a long day."

"Okay." Daisy gave Emma a quick hug. "Call me if you need anything, and thanks again for helping today."

Emma headed out of the park and Daisy picked up the few pieces of trash that littered the ground near her feet. Except for the encounter with Jane Mellon, the festival seemed to have been a success for the Hideaway Inn. They had several people interested in future events, and three appointments to meet with possible customers next week. All good signs for the future of the inn.

The encounter with Jane had left Daisy shaken. Maybe staying here, where her past mistakes would haunt her, wasn't such a good idea.

It was more than that. It was the hurt that had washed over her when she'd realized Colt had kept Henry's death from her. Hadn't he realized that she had cared about Henry, too?

Mike Stark crossed the park toward her. "Hey, need some help with the table? I can take it down and bring it back to Olivia's shelter for you. I have a truck."

"Definitely. Thank you. I appreciate it." Daisy ran a hand through her hair, then scanned the park entrance again, but no one came through the gate. Disappointment washed over her. "I was hoping Colt would be here to help Emma and me clean up, but he never showed."

Mike gave her a quizzical look. "He said he'd come to this?"

"Well, not in so many words, no, but I thought since it was Sunday, and he had nothing to do—"

"What do you mean?" Again, the confusion on Mike's face. "He's busy every Sunday."

"No. He has Sunday off. Sometimes he does rounds on Saturdays, but . . ." Her voice trailed off. "What do you know that I don't?"

Mike hesitated, then let out a breath. "Listen, I have to

head over there anyway. Let me just load up the table, then we'll go."

She touched his hand to stop him. "Go where?"

"You'll see. It'll make sense later." Mike broke down the table and carried it to the bed of his truck. Daisy followed, trying not to show how hurt she was that Colt had kept a secret from her. They weren't really married, and never really had been, so his life was his own. It shouldn't bother her that he went other places or saw other people. But it did because today had hammered home once again how she lived on the periphery of Colt's life. And maybe always would.

A half hour later, Daisy sat in the passenger's side of Mike's pickup truck, with his daughter Ellie between them, as they rode out of Rescue Bay. Ellie chattered a mile a minute, about kittens and horses and dogs and pretty much anything that popped into her head. She was an adorable four-year-old, but Daisy's mind was on where they were going.

And what she'd find there. Mike hadn't explained and she hadn't pressed him. Daisy wasn't so sure she wanted to know.

The sun was just starting to kiss the tops of the trees when Mike pulled off the main road and headed down a worn, rutted road. The road curved to the left, then ended in a dirt-packed circle, right beside a beautiful lake that spread out like a deep, dark blue blanket. A few boats bobbed on the placid water. A heron flapped his wings and made a graceful exit from one side of the lake to the other.

The three of them climbed out of the truck just as Mike's other daughter, Jenny, came running up to the truck. Her muddy jeans and T-shirt were topped by a ball cap that said HOOK, LINE AND THINKER CLUB. "Daddy, I caught three fish today!"

"Awesome, Jelly Bean. You're turning into quite the fisherman." Mike ruffled his daughter's hair, then turned to Daisy. "I suspect you'll find Colt right down there. He comes here every Sunday, runs a fishing group for kids. Teaches them all about water safety, and how to bait a hook. It's all catch and release, which teaches the kids to respect the water, and the creatures who call it home."

She would have been less shocked to hear Colt was jetting off to Mars on the weekends. Of all the things she imagined him doing on Sundays, this didn't even make the list. "He does?"

"Yup. Been doing it for years now." Mike pointed at a well-worn path that wound between the trees and down to the water. Colt's car was parked beside the path.

Daisy thanked Mike, then headed in the direction he had pointed. Behind her, she heard Mike start up his truck and head down the road. Quiet descended over the woods, broken only by the rustling of some squirrels and the occasional chirp of a bird.

She grabbed a sapling to steady her steps as she climbed down the embankment, her shoes skidding a little on the smooth path. At the bottom of the hill, Colt sat on a stump, his back to her, a fishing pole propped against a nearby tree. A matching cap to Jenny's hung from the handle of a pale blue tackle box.

"Colt?"

He turned at the sound of her voice. Surprise filled his face. "How did you find me?"

"Mike brought me here."

Colt scowled, then turned back to the lake. "You might as well catch a ride back with him. I'm not leaving yet."

Daisy crossed her arms over her chest. "I'm not going anywhere. And Mike already left."

"Fine." Colt cursed. "I'll drive you home."

He started to get up, but she stepped in front of him and put up a hand. "No. Not until you tell me why you lied to me about where you've been every Sunday."

"I didn't lie to you. I just . . . chose not to provide details."

"Why? What are you doing? Illegally poaching fish or something?"

He shook his head. A slight smile flickered on his face for a moment before it was gone. "You can't poach fish,

Daisy. And it's nothing illegal. Just not something I want to talk about."

She wasn't going to be swayed by his smiles or his attempts to deflect the question. In all the time they had been together, the two of them had never done much talking. A lot of sex, but not a lot of conversations deeper than *What do you want for dinner.* Even now, when she was living in his house, taking care of his grandfather, their conversations had been mostly superficial. Coming here and finding out Colt was running a fishing club—something that he could have told her—made it clear that he didn't want to include her in his life. He hadn't even told her about his brother, never even mentioned it, and she wondered if any part of their relationship had been real. "Well, I'm sick and tired of you and your grandpa and everyone I know not wanting to talk about what hell is bothering them."

He scoffed. "You're reading *me* the riot act for not opening up? Hell, Daisy, you weren't exactly an oversharer yourself."

"You're like a *vault*, Colt." She threw up her hands. The outburst startled a bird in a nearby tree, and he took off with an impatient squawk. "We were married and you still didn't share anything personal with me. You still don't. How hard is it to say, *Hey, I'm busy today, taking some kids fishing*?"

"We never had a real marriage, Daisy."

The truth hurt. Maybe because a part of her had always hoped that in Colt's mind their marriage hadn't been just one short honeymoon. That it had been more. But what more could she have expected from three weeks together? Did she think that just because their marriage date had a fourteen-year run, that it made them closer? Obviously not, if she had been excluded from the biggest tragedy in his life.

"A real marriage requires opening up," Daisy said. "Something you have never done, Colt."

"You know everything about me, Daisy. Hell, we were friends before we . . . well, before we slept together."

"Were we? Really?" She turned away and looked out over the placid blue expanse before her. The reflections of trees and a far-off cabin shimmered on the water, and the ripples of a slow-moving pontoon boat created gentle kisses against the shore. "Because a friend would know that the reason you ran out on your wife was because your brother died."

The air between them stilled. As soon as the words left her mouth, Daisy wanted to take them back. Not because they didn't need to be said—they were about fourteen years overdue—but because of how coldly and callously she'd said them. God, what was wrong with her? When was she going to learn to think before she acted?

She reached for his hand. "I'm sorry, Colt, I—"

He jerked away, his face stony and cold. "Let it go, Daisy." Then he yanked up his fishing supplies and charged up the hill. She hurried after him, scrambling for branches to steady her footing.

"I didn't think, Colt. I just reacted. I was so mad at you for not coming today, and then this woman came up to me at the park, yelling at me about that party I had in her house years ago, and she talked to me like I was the reason your brother died, and Colt—" Her heart broke seeing the pain in his eyes, the cold set in his shoulders. "I . . . I never knew. I'm sorry."

"Yeah, me too." He turned away from her, took a couple steps, paused. "Just leave me alone, Daisy."

"Colt—"

"I said, leave me alone, Daisy." His voice was raw, scraping past his throat.

"Please don't shut me out. Please tell me." She reached out to touch him, but her hand hovered inches from his back. "What . . . what happened?"

He whirled on her. "It doesn't matter what happened or how it happened or how I was too late to save him. Talking about it won't bring my brother back, won't get my grandfather to forgive me, won't make me feel any less guilty. Talking about it won't help me one goddamned bit."

"But—"

"I said I don't want to talk about it." His features hardened, his voice sharpened. "Which part of that sentence said *please keep bringing it up*?"

She shook her head and swiped at the sudden tears in her eyes. "No wonder you had to hire me to spend time with your grandfather," she said, partly to herself, partly to him. "No wonder he's so mad, he throws coffee cups and plates at you and you just lecture him. Neither one of you talk about what happened, what's going on, or say that you need each other. Don't you think this hurts him, too? He'd be there for you, Colt, because that's how family works."

"Don't tell me how family works, Daisy. You told me yourself you never really had one. So that does not make you an expert on mine or anyone else's."

She stepped back, jaw agape. The harsh words hung in the hot air between them, slicing at her with the precise swath of truth. "You're right, Colt. I have no idea what it's like to truly be in a family. To have someone who is there for you, all the time. Or how to do that myself. I've always been out to protect number one, to take care of me. I never stopped to see how the people around me, the people I loved"—at that, her voice caught—"were being hurt. Or left alone."

He nodded, his gaze on the trampled ground. "It doesn't matter. It's too late. Just let it go."

"I'm sorry, Colt. I really am. I loved Henry, too." She swiped at her eyes again. "And . . . damn it all, I loved you. Even if you're too stubborn to realize that all I wanted then, and all I want now, is to help you." She turned and headed up the hill, cursing the branches that hindered her path, swatting at leaves and twigs, because her vision was blurry and her chest tight.

He caught up to her just before she crested the hill and put a hand on her arm. "I'm sorry. I was out of line for saying that. It just . . . it hurts so much to talk about Henry. So I don't. I keep it all inside and I come here and I wish . . ." His lower lip trembled, his breath shuddered out of him, and she wanted to just wrap her arms around him and make everything better. "I wish I could do it all over again."

The truth dawned on her, as she stood there, watching the man she had once loved, the man who had left her and never returned, the man with a bone-deep pain that still hobbled his life. She thought of the club he had started, the way he dedicated every Sunday to a group of kids about Henry's age. Colt, who was one of the most caring men she had ever met, trying to make up for a sin he didn't even commit. "Did it happen here?"

Colt didn't say anything for a long time. He just stared out at the lake, watching the water glisten under the bright sunlight, golden diamonds twinkling in the ripples.

She took his hand, held it tight, and waited. If he didn't talk, that was fine. She was here either way. The lake began its evening song of birds settling into trees and fish giving one last flip of the tail to a waning sun. Far across the lake, mothers called their children in from the shore.

Colt let out a long, painful breath, then he started to speak, his voice as quiet as the lake below them. "Henry loved the water. You'd take him to the beach and he'd swim until he could barely stand. Take him to the lake and he'd spend all day exploring the shore or leaping off the rope swing." A slow, sad smile stole across Colt's face. "But what he loved most was fishing. My little brother had no patience when it came to Christmas or dinner or building sandcastles, but put him in a boat with a fishing pole in his hands, and he could sit for hours."

She thought of the rambunctious eight-year-old she'd known, who had never sat still for anything, except this lake. "It sounds peaceful."

"It was. And the one time when my brother and I could spend time with Grandpa. He was always working, always at the shop, seven days a week. But pretty much every Wednesday and Sunday, he'd take us boys fishing. Didn't matter if Walt Patterson needed a transmission installed that day or Harvey Michaels had a broken down pickup, my grandpa would take us boys fishing."

How she wished she'd had a grandfather like that, a brother like Colt. Her admiration of Earl Harper went up another notch. "What a wonderful tradition. I bet you enjoyed that a lot."

"I did. Both Henry and I looked forward to it all week.

Even when I was seventeen and too cool for fishing, I'd still manage to get in those fishing trips."

She thought back, but of all the days she and Colt had spent together, he'd never said a word about this lake or the fishing trips. "I don't remember you ever mentioning any of this."

A wry smile crossed Colt's face. "That was part of the adventure. My grandpa said this was a special guy thing, a man's club, so to speak, and so we didn't tell the girls about it. The girls being my grandma, my mom, and of course, girlfriends. Henry loved the idea of a secret, and so we kept the location and the time to ourselves."

It made it all sound so much sweeter, more special. Daisy thought of a teenaged Colt, not above indulging his eight-year-old brother's requests, treating the fishing trips as sacred events. The bond between the three of them had to have been steel strong. No wonder losing Henry had left such a gaping wound between the Harper men. "Didn't your mother wonder where you were or why you were bringing home fish?"

"We rarely brought home fish. Grandpa taught us to respect this lake, to respect life, which is why we did catch and release, and now I do that with the fishing club I run. As for my parents, I think they welcomed the break from two busy boys. My parents worked so much, we could have backpacked to Antarctica in the middle of the week and they wouldn't have noticed until Saturday."

Daisy thought how sad that was, how the two of them had grown up with absent, distant parents. Her mother, always following one whim or another, Colt's spending their hours at work instead of with their sons. "I know how that feels. I could have dropped off the face of the earth for a month and my mother wouldn't have noticed. My mother wasn't much for putting down roots. I guess that's why I never have, either."

"You're putting down roots here, though, by reopening the Hideaway."

She didn't want to tell him that she was thinking about

leaving as soon as Emma took over. Speaking the words aloud would make them true, and right now, with the day winding to a close while she and Colt stood on the hill above the lake and bared their souls, she didn't want to think about leaving. "And you returned to your roots."

"What else could I do?" Colt said, taking a seat on an overturned log and looking out at the lake. "This is where Henry was. At first, I wanted to leave. To hop on my bike and blast out of town and never come back. Never drive by this damned lake again. Never see Henry's picture on the mantle. Never be reminded of how I let him down, and how—"

He shook his head. Cursed. She sat down on the log beside him, laid a hand on his back, and waited. The birds kept up their chirpy conversations, the boats on the lake motored slowly past with quiet *glub-glubs*, and the day marched from afternoon to early evening.

"How it was my fault he died," Colt said finally, in a soft, ragged voice.

"Your fault? Colt, you weren't even here. You were in New Orleans with me."

"And that's why he died." Colt turned to her, his eyes wide and full, his face a mask of anguish. "Did I tell you he called me? Asked me to come home, not to miss our fishing trip. I told him I was married now, and I didn't know when I could go again and . . . shit." He looked away and his body shuddered.

"Oh, honey, you can't blame yourself. You were eighteen, Colt. It was okay to have a life of your own."

He wheeled on her, his eyes filled with unshed tears. "I wasn't here, Daisy. Don't you understand? I didn't show up. I wasn't here. Because I was . . ."

His voice trailed off. Daisy filled in the blank in her head. *Because I was with you.*

No wonder he hadn't returned to her. No wonder he'd never told her about what had happened. Their marriage had been built on a sandy foundation, and when Colt's life fell apart, he'd retreated to what he knew, instead of returning to a wife who was barely a friend. A wife who reminded him of why he had been far, far away when Henry needed him most. "Colt . . ."

She reached for him, but he jerked to his feet, as if he could charge out to the lake right now and stop what had happened fourteen years ago. "I wasn't here. So Henry took the boat on his own, and there was a storm and—" Colt cursed again. "They found his body the next morning, and I think that damned near killed my grandfather. My parents moved away, my grandpa stopped talking to me, and I've been trying like hell to make up for it ever since."

In that moment, Daisy could see the entire horrifying moment in her mind. That exuberant, confident little boy, climbing onto the boat, sliding it out onto the beckoning, blue water.

Colt, getting a call from someone and rushing home, leaving Daisy only a note. *Headed back to Florida. Will call later.*

Colt had never called. She'd tried to call him, left a dozen messages, but he hadn't called back. Instead of going after him, she had moved on, moved to a different apartment, a different job. When Colt had needed her most, she had left him alone.

"Oh, Colt. I'm sorry. I'm so sorry." She wrapped her arms around him, as tight as she could. Tight enough to wash him with forgiveness, tight enough to tell him she was sorry for leaving him alone all those years ago, and tight enough to hold him together now.

They stood there for a long, long time. The sun set behind the trees, and the boaters chugged back to the dock. The birds settled into their nests and the crickets began their evening song.

Daisy drew back, and took both of Colt's hands in her own. "Come on, let's go."

"Where?" he asked.

She smiled, and gave his hands a gentle squeeze. "Home, with your wife."

Twenty-two

With your wife.

The words rang in Colt's head long after they got into his car and headed back to the house. He liked the sound of them—very much—but didn't want to ask if it had just been a turn of phrase or a purposeful sentence.

The kind that said *I'm staying for a long time.*

He reached across the console for her hand. Daisy's palm fit against his, snug and perfect. What if they had had this conversation fourteen years ago? Would it have been enough to keep them together? Would she have been here, to help him wade through those horrible months and years after Henry died? He liked to think so, but he wasn't so sure. They were different people then, and with the passing of more than a decade, they had changed. Maybe this was the Daisy he was meant to be with, not the headstrong, impulsive one from years ago. "Thank you."

"All I did was listen, which is what I should have done a long time ago."

"Just like I needed to talk a long time ago. It doesn't make it easy, but a little easier, if that makes sense." All these years, he'd kept what happened to Henry bottled in his chest, as if doing so would keep him from remembering, from hurting.

Physician, heal thyself. It was a standby saying because it was true. How many times had he encouraged patients to go see a therapist or just sit down and have a long-delayed conversation with a loved one, because he could see the physical toll their mental anguish was taking? And here he'd been doing the same thing.

Him, and his grandfather. Somehow, Colt needed to break down that wall between himself and Grandpa Earl. Maybe then they could restore a semblance of their old relationship.

Colt and Daisy pulled into the driveway and got out of the car. Night had fallen, and the street was lined with lit porches, beckoning like friends. "You know what we need now?" Daisy said. "Ice cream."

He chuckled. "I take it there's a gallon in my freezer?"

"There is indeed. But don't worry, it's actually frozen yogurt, and it's marked 'For Emergency or Special Occasions Only.'"

"And which is this?"

"Neither. Which makes the dessert all that much more decadent." She grinned at him, then ducked inside the house.

Colt followed her and dropped his keys in the bowl by the door. The house was quiet, lights off, TV off. No dog lying in an inconvenient spot. "Huh. My grandpa's not home yet."

"Oh, I forgot to tell you. He said he was going to go play cards with the guys."

Colt arched a brow. Maybe he wasn't the only one making mental leaps forward today. "Really? That's great. It's been months since he did that."

"I think he's feeling a lot better. He stayed at the festival all day today. Talked to a lot of people, and mostly ate healthy. I think he even had fun." She swung open the freezer door, grabbed the container of frozen yogurt, then snagged a pair of bowls out of the cabinet. "One scoop or two?"

"I'll live on the edge. Two."

She laughed, then began working the scoop into the frozen dessert. "You run enough miles every week to work off this entire container."

"It wasn't to work off the ice cream," he said, slipping into place beside her. Daisy just grinned, and added an extra scoop to his bowl. "It was to work off a certain woman in my system."

"Couldn't be me. I'm sweet. Easy to live with."

"Sweetly deluded," he said, giving her nose a tap.

"Chocolate sauce?" she asked.

"Is there another way to eat ice cream?"

Daisy smiled again, then retrieved a small bottle of chocolate syrup from the fridge. Clearly, she'd been doing some grocery shopping because Colt didn't remember any of these decadent treats in his refrigerator from before. He didn't mind so much, though. She mitigated the sweets with healthy dinners and warm breakfasts. Colt realized he was starting to like having her influence on his life. Not the same hell-raiser influence of their youth, but more of a tempered, balanced Daisy flavor. It made him crave her more, want to know more about her, to fill in all those gaps he'd never taken time to fill before.

"You started telling me about your family back there at the lake." Colt leaned on the counter beside her and watched her work on the ice cream. "What'd you mean when you said your mother never put down roots?"

Daisy shrugged. "It was nothing, Colt, really."

"Come on, I spilled my guts to you. Tell me."

She handed him his dessert. "There's nothing to talk about. I had a crappy childhood. I survived. End of story."

Which was the same thing she'd said fourteen years ago. Maybe he was wrong about how much Daisy had changed. "I'm no psychologist, but even I know your childhood influences who you become as an adult, why you make the choices you make. Look at me. I had a father who put a thousand rules on me, had expectations higher than Mount Everest. I rebelled, but eventually found a happy middle ground."

"Are you happy?" she asked.

"I'm getting there," he said quietly, taking her hand, and wondering why he had waited so damned long to talk to Daisy. Why he'd been so stubborn, thinking he was better off on his own. She hadn't turned away from him after he told her about Henry—she had understood, and comforted him. The weight lifted from Colt's shoulders had to weigh a thousand pounds. "And I'm a lot closer today than I was before."

"I'm glad. I really am." She stepped back, put the cover back on the frozen yogurt, and stowed it in the freezer. She started to scoop up a bite, then stopped when there was a sound at the door. "Is that a dog?"

"Must be Grandpa. Must have been a long card game. I figured he'd be home a while ago." Colt glanced at Daisy when the dog started barking.

"Did he forget his key or something?"

"I didn't lock the door." Colt darted down the hall and pulled open the back door. Major hurried into the house and straight for the water bowl, lapping up the liquid with furious movements. Colt stepped onto the porch, then came back in. "Grandpa Earl isn't with the dog."

"There's no way your grandpa would lose track of that dog. Where do you think—"

Colt's cell phone rang. He jerked it out of his pocket and pressed the button. "Colt Harper."

In an instant, the expression on Colt's face changed from frustration to worry. His features went stony. He listened for a while, then nodded. "I'll be right there."

Before Daisy could ask, Colt was grabbing his car keys, and reaching for her hand. "We have to go. My grandfather is in the hospital."

Colt Harper had walked the halls of the Rescue Bay Hospital a thousand times. He'd visited patients, consulted with other doctors, even interned here when he was in medical school.

But never had the walls seemed so sterile, so cold, so dead as they did tonight.

Guilt weighed his steps, as if he was running through mud. Once again, someone he loved had been hurt when he'd been elsewhere. He shouldn't have taken Daisy's word on where Grandpa was. He should have followed up, picked Grandpa up from the card game.

Daisy hurried alongside Colt, into the building, down to the information desk, and then up to the third floor. For a second, he couldn't remember if Room 308 was to the left or the right, and he hesitated at the T outside the elevators.

"This way," Daisy said, taking his hand and turning to the right.

Three doors down, the placard outside Room 308 read HARPER, E. in thick black Sharpie. Colt halted just outside the door, then forced himself to turn, to enter, to take in that disinfectant smell that managed so often to mingle with death and hope.

"Grandpa?"

Grandpa Earl lay in the big white bed, the light dimmed above his head. His eyes were closed, his lips pale and a little blue, his hands still upon his chest. Oxygen tubes snaked into his nostrils. The television above his head played some inane sitcom, the sound lowered to almost a whisper. The heater kicked on, sending a rattling burst of forced hot air into the room.

Colt stepped forward. He barely noticed Daisy's hand on his shoulder, her presence by his side.

"Grandpa?"

There was no movement, no response. Panic climbed Colt's throat. *He's dead*, Colt thought, *he's dead, and it's my fault*.

"He's sleeping," Daisy whispered, as if reading his mind. "That's all."

Colt pressed forward until he reached his grandfather's side. It took a solid minute of concentrating to convince himself that yes, indeed, Grandpa Earl's chest was rising and falling. The cardiac monitor machine beside the bed kept a steady track of his blood pressure, heart rate.

The clinician in Colt made a sweeping assessment. A furosemide drip, inserted into a basilic vein. Blood pressure 110 over 70, heart rate steady, but a little high at 140. Colt picked up the chart on the end of the bed, and flipped through the ER assessment.

Dehydration. Elevated heart rate. Light to moderate confusion. Hypertension.

Colt sank into the bedside chair. "It wasn't a heart attack. He just pushed himself too hard and too fast."

Daisy's hand returned to his shoulder. "That's good news, then. Isn't it?"

Colt nodded. "I think so. I'll know more when the tests come back."

"There aren't going to be any goddamned tests."

Colt got to his feet and hovered over the bed. Relief replaced the irritation and worry in Colt's chest. "Grandpa. What happened?"

"I just got a little worn out. That's all." Earl opened his eyes and shifted toward Colt, as if daring his physician grandson to disagree. "Nothing to get worried about."

Colt wanted to throw up his hands and yell at his grandfather. Instead, he kept his voice low, and controlled his frustration. What was it going to take for Grandpa to realize he had to take care of himself? "You're in the hospital. That's something to worry about. You should have let me drive you home. Should have—"

"I know what I should do. Doesn't mean I'm going to do it." Earl patted the bed until his hand hit the attached remote. He fumbled with the buttons and started flipping channels. "Now are you going to let me get some rest or are you going to keep on lecturing me?"

Colt sighed. "Do you need anything?"

"A nap. And for you to feed my dog. The damned doctor's keeping me overnight. Told him I was just fine."

"Dr. Boyle is one of the best cardiac specialists in Florida, Grandpa. You're lucky he was here when you got admitted. If he wants you to stay overnight, then you should listen to him." At least listen to somebody, because Lord knew Grandpa wouldn't listen to Colt.

Grandpa just harrumphed. He lay back against the pillows and turned up the volume on the TV. That, apparently, passed for agreement.

Colt sat back in the chair, feeling helpless, as if his hands had been tied behind his back. "Did they do an EKG? You know your last one was three months—"

"Are you going to yap through my show about medical crap?"

Colt got to his feet. "Fine. If you don't want me here—"

"I don't."

"Then I'll go home. I'll call Doctor Boyle in the morning and ask him—"

Grandpa Earl waved his hand in dismissal. "Call him, talk medications and CAT scans and EE-whatevers and all that stuff you enjoy so much. Just leave me the hell out of it."

Colt stared at his grandfather for a long time, but Grandpa Earl kept his attention on the images flickering on the screen. Daisy stood to the side, looking from Colt to Earl, as if asking Colt to do something, to figure this out somehow.

Instead, Colt turned on his heel and left the room. There was no prescription for this situation, and the sooner he accepted that, the better.

Twenty-three

Two a.m.

The clock ticked past, flipping the digital numbers from 2:00 to 2:01. Daisy gave up on trying to sleep—she hadn't closed her eyes since she'd gone to bed anyway. She'd been just as worried about Earl as Colt, but tried not to say anything, in case it made Colt's stress level higher. Finally, she gave up on trying to sleep, tugged on a robe, and padded down to the kitchen.

Outside the screen door, she saw a figure standing on the back step, his tall silhouette standing black against the dark gray night. The moon hung heavy and full in the sky, casting a white river down the center of the ocean. In the distance, a boat cut through the water, the red light of the bow aiming toward Clearwater or Tampa or maybe down to the Keys. It was a dark, supernatural sight, with a storm brewing off the coast, adding a hint of danger to the air.

The door creaked a protest as Daisy stepped outside. Colt turned. "Hey. What are you doing up?"

She shrugged. "I couldn't sleep."

"Me neither. It's been a hell of a day." He stared out at the surf. The storm hovered far out to sea, reaching toward

Rescue Bay's shore with strong winds and frothy waves. The palm trees clacked together like skeletons in a bag, an eerie, powerful sound that crept down Daisy's spine.

"Worried about your grandpa?"

He nodded. She went to him, and just opened her arms. He hesitated, then stepped into them, and she wrapped an embrace as tight around him as she could. Colt stood stiff and unyielding for one long second, then, like a girder succumbing to too much weight, he leaned into her, his head on her shoulder, his arms circling around to her back.

"He'll be okay, Colt. He's in good hands."

"I know." He drew back and let out a sigh. "But it doesn't stop me from worrying. That's the bad part about being a doctor. You know all the worst case scenarios, and it's hard not to let them torture you."

She slipped her hands into his and gave him a grin. "Then let's do something to take your mind off it."

"Do something? Daisy, it's two in the morning."

"A perfect time for a walk on the beach, don't you think?" Major snapped to attention at the mention of the word *walk*. His tail wagged, and he started panting with excitement. "And Major agrees."

Colt glanced at the dark, rolling sky. "There's a storm coming in tonight."

"And what is the worst that could happen? We'll get wet?" She shrugged. "So we'll bring raincoats."

He shook his head, but a smile had curved up his face. "You have an argument for everything, don't you?"

"You know it." She ducked back inside the house, grabbed the dog's leash and two jackets from the hook by the door, then returned to Colt's side. "Come on. It'll be fun."

He leaned down close to her, his breath warm against her neck. "The last time you said that we ended up married."

Damn. How could he light that fire in her belly with just a few words? She let out a shaky laugh to cover for the desire he'd awakened. "Well that won't happen today. I guarantee it."

"Of course it won't. Because we're still married."

"So there's no danger of you falling in love with me and running off into the sunset."

"Not a chance."

She laughed, but the words still sent a ribbon of disappointment through her. What was wrong with her? She was signing the divorce papers soon. Ending this whole pseudo-relationship.

If that was so, then why was she delaying? Why hadn't she just up and signed them already? Every time she saw the envelope on top of her dresser, she told herself it was because she wanted to make sure the loan was secure. That the bank wouldn't have some last-minute second thoughts and yank the financing. Except the loan papers had long ago been approved, signed, sealed, delivered.

Done.

There was no reason to stay married to Colt Harper any longer. No reason—except she didn't want to let him go. Not yet. Not tonight.

"Watch your step," Colt said, reaching out a hand to steady her on the rickety wooden steps leading down to the beach. A strong breeze rippled down the beach, bending the sea grass to its will, making the bell on the end of the dock sing its deep clanging song.

"Thank you." She took his hand, and didn't let go, even after their feet met the sand and she kicked off her sandals. They walked barefoot on the cold beach, while the surf crashed against the beach and the wind swirled along the coast. It was a wild night, edged with danger and suspense, as if anything could happen. She took off Major's leash, and the dog ran up ahead, darting in and out of the water, barking at the waves, the wind.

"Careful, there's a dip there." Colt tugged on her hand, and she tumbled into his arms, her bare feet sliding on the silky sand.

She tipped her chin to look at him, trying not to think how good it felt to press her hand to his chest, to feel the strength and solidity of Colt beneath her palm. He'd always been like that, the one that she could depend on, to be calm and rational and strong when things got crazy.

She should have been that for him, years ago. Maybe then they wouldn't have lost each other for fourteen years, lost that magic they'd had. Seeing him today, hurt and vulnerable, had added another dimension to Colt. She'd always thought he was a rock, but now she saw he was more like a willow tree, stronger than anyone knew, yet also human enough to bend when the pressure got too much. The kind of man a woman like her could fall in love with, if she wasn't careful.

"Thank you again," she said.

"You have to be careful," he said, his eyes deep and dark in the moonlight. "There's a storm coming in."

"I know." There was a storm inside her, one that had been gaining steam ever since she'd rushed into his office. Heck, that storm had been building since the day he'd sat down and shared her Oreos with her. It wrapped her in a whirl-wind, displacing her thoughts, her plans, her intentions.

He lowered his hands to her waist, his mouth to hers. A fraction of an inch separated her from him, a fraction too far, too much. She could feel the warmth of his breath, whis-pering across her skin. "We really should stop before we get caught in the worst of it."

"That would be the wisest course to take."

His blue eyes were as dark and deep as the roiling waters beside them. "We've never taken the wisest course, have we?"

She shook her head. Slow. She wished she could stand here forever, with him looking at her with heat and intention, with that delicious anticipation of something more delicious and wonderful to come, if only she let it happen. "Never. Why start now?"

"Because someone could get hurt."

"Oh, Colt, hasn't anyone ever told you that dancing in the rain is so much more fun than watching the rain?" She tangled her hands in his hair, drawing him closer, until her breath mingled with his. She wanted him—hell, she'd

always wanted him—and didn't want to go on pretending.
She wanted the heat and magic, the fire and rush, that came
with everything she did with Colt. She wanted to lose herself
in him, today, tomorrow . . . forever.

"What if we get struck by lightning?"

Her heart hammered in her chest. "That's a chance we'll
have to take."

"I'm not a risk taker, Daisy, not anymore."

"You're here with me," she said, her voice dark and
husky. "That's a risk already."

A smile curved across his face. His lips brushed against
hers as he spoke, so intoxicating, so sexy, she wanted to melt
into him. "Are you saying you're dangerous?"

"I'm saying that you and me"—she took a breath, let her
mouth dance across his—"is dangerous."

His eyes caught hers, held. A heartbeat passed. Then he
pulled her closer, bringing her body against his so tight and
so hard, not a whisper of wind could slide between them.
"I don't care," he said, the words a growl.

Then he cupped her head and kissed her. Hard, fast, deep,
the way she loved to be kissed by him, as if he was con-
suming her, drowning her soul with his. There was no gentle
in this kiss, just a fire to have each other as fast and furious
as the approaching storm.

"Daisy, I want you," he groaned. "Now."

Hot agony brewed inside her, a fire torched by the need
in his voice. "Then take me, Colt."

They tumbled to the sand in a frenzied rush to jerk off
jackets, spread them across the beach, then reach for fasten-
ers and buttons. She grabbed at his shirt, tugging the fabric
up, over his shoulders, his head, then she attacked his shorts,
yanking them down, off and away. Boxers followed, and she
paused only long enough to curl her hand around his length
and hear him moan against her cheek. Then it was her turn
to lean back, let him fumble with the buttons on her shirt.
Frustration, cursing, when the tiny buttons snagged. She put
her hands over his, and whispered, "Just tear it off."

He rent the shirt in two, and the fire inside Daisy reached

a fever pitch. Before she could think, could take a breath, he had shoved aside her panties and plunged inside her. He reached between them, pushing her bra up and over her breasts, then lowered his mouth to suck one of her nipples. She groaned and arched, clawing at his back with one hand, trying to unfasten the damned bra with the other. The clasp sprang free, and she tossed the scrap of fabric to the side.

Above them, thunder rumbled and lightning crashed over the ocean. The rain began to fall, pelting them with warm, slick water. Daisy didn't care. She curved beneath Colt, fingers digging into his back, his buttocks, while he plunged into her again and again, harder, faster. He was hot, he was hard, and he was so damned good, she wondered why she had ever let him out of her bed.

Colt's flexed arms braced them on either side, but his mouth, oh holy hell, his mouth, was back on her breast, and she thought she was going to die or self-detonate as the orgasm hit her like a tsunami, spiraling her up, up, up, sending lights behind her eyes.

She rolled him to his back and climbed on top of him, feeling wanton and sexy as the storm began to whirl, and she rode Colt. His hands cupped her breasts, thumbs sliding across her nipples, then he flexed beneath her, driving him deeper. She arched backward, riding the wave as the next orgasm took control and she jackhammered her body against his. A moment later, he cried out her name, and stiffened, and she rode with him, shifting her hips to catch him as he came.

When they were done, she rolled to the side, and curved into Colt's arm, laying her head on his chest, listening to the still frantic beat of his heart. "I don't think we've ever made love slow and easy," he said.

She laughed. "That's for the movies."

"None of that fluffy romantic stuff for you, huh?"

"Not on your life." She said it as a joke, instead of admitting the truth, that the kind of slow, easy, romantic love others had was the very kind that scared her to death. Slow and easy meant exposing her soul, opening her heart, letting

Colt get close to her for more than a few minutes. She wanted hard, fast, in, out, and over before she risked something foolish—

Like falling in love with him. Again.

Tears sprang to her eyes. Damnable, vulnerable, weak tears, and she tried to will them away, but they brimmed in her eyes. Then the rain began to fall and mingle with her tears until she couldn't tell which was Mother Nature and which was her.

The rain started coming harder then, pelting the sand and their bare skin. Major dashed up, barking before doing a fast shake that sprayed them all with a new storm. "Let's get out of here," Colt shouted above the growing volume of an angry wind.

Daisy slid on her jacket, while Colt tugged on his pants and gathered up the rest of their clothes. They dashed along the beach, laughing, stumbling, catching each other, until they were back on the safety of his porch. They stood under the roof and shook off the worst of the water. Major paused on the top step, and before Daisy could stop him, the dog gave another vigorous body shake.

"Major, no!"

Colt grimaced and swiped the water off his legs. "Major Pain fits him."

She laughed, then grabbed Colt's hand. "Come on, let's get inside and make something warm to eat."

"Or . . ." He held her gaze, and a smile curved across his face again. "We could take a nice long, hot shower together. And find other ways to warm up."

She wanted that, oh, how she wanted that. But something had shifted inside her tonight on the beach, something that told Daisy she wasn't as in control of her emotions as she thought. Nor was she as over him as she had thought. Maybe she never had been over Colt. There was a new softening in her heart for Colt, and that—

That was the true danger. The one she had done her level best to avoid all these years. There was something in the way he worried about his grandfather, the way he took such heavy responsibility and wore it like it was nothing more than a cotton shirt, that touched her.

And made her want to stay. To try again. To be his wife again, in every sense of the word.

"Rain check?" she said, then laughed at the pun. "I, uh, have to be up early to meet with Mike's construction crew."

"I'm glad the loan worked out," he said. "I think you're going to do a fabulous job with the inn."

A flicker of doubt filled Daisy. Such a huge responsibility, resurrecting a business. "I'm going to do my best. Either way, I'll make sure I repay the loan so you don't end up on the hook for it."

He waved that off. "I trust you, Daisy."

I trust you. The words held such weight. She thought about how far they had come since that day at his office a few weeks ago.

Okay, maybe they'd come a long way in terms of financial agreements, but as for a relationship . . . No promises had been made, and there was no more of a tether binding them to this sham of a marriage than there had been before.

"I guess this means we don't need to stay married anymore." She turned and grabbed the door handle before any of the emotions fluttering in her chest belied her light words. "You'll finally be free of me."

His face clouded. "Then what was that back on the beach?"

"That was"—she pulled open the door and forced a smile to her face—"a storm that hit us before we could run."

Twenty-four

Grandpa Earl was his usual sunshine and rainbows self the next morning when Colt arrived at the hospital to take him home. "Where do they find the idiots who run this place?" Grandpa said, glaring at the orderly who helped him into a wheelchair and plopped the bag of Grandpa's belongings on his lap. "They're making me use this damned thing, like I'm some kind of an invalid. I can walk my own damned self out of here."

"Think of it as red carpet service," Colt said, waving off the orderly so he could slip in behind Grandpa's chair. Grandpa had good color, his blood pressure was down, and he should be fine as long as he did what Colt had been harping on for months—ate right, exercised regularly, and took his medications. They wheeled down the hall, and around the corner toward the patient pick-up area.

"Red carpet service, huh?" Grandpa said. "If that's the case, there should be dancing girls and champagne at the end."

Colt chuckled. "I can wrangle some ginger ale, and maybe a cute candy striper."

Grandpa considered that for a second, rubbing at the stubble on his chin. "I'll take it."

The electric doors opened, letting in a nice warm burst of Florida air. Colt pushed the chair outside and over to his car, parked against the curb. He helped Grandpa into the passenger's seat, then backed away, rather than caving to his instinct of hovering to make sure Grandpa buckled his seat belt. Baby steps.

After Colt returned the chair to the lobby, he slid into the driver's seat. "Did they treat you okay in there?" he asked Grandpa.

"Treated me like the damned King of Sheba. Do you know every single person who works at that hospital?"

"Not everyone. But a lot of folks."

Grandpa harrumphed. "Well, you must be doing a good job because all they did was talk about you."

Colt chuckled. "If that's a compliment, I'll take it."

They rode for a while, not saying anything. The air conditioner pumped cool air into the car. Palm trees slivered shade through the windows. "You know, I've been thinking," Grandpa said. "I don't want you to get all worked up or anything, but maybe I can try one of those veggie meals you were talking about. Daisy says some of it's so good, you can't tell the difference. Like the yogurt she told me was ice cream, and that fake beer you gave me. Tasted the same, more or less."

Colt kept his face calm, impassive, trying not to show his surprise. "Sure. We can do that. How about we compromise, and start with a veggie pizza?"

"They make those? Well, I'll be." Grandpa took a moment to think about it, then nodded. "Veggie pizza sounds like a damned good idea. Especially after eating the crap the hospital serves. A man could die eating that stuff."

Colt arched a brow and flicked a glance at Grandpa's belly. "Doesn't look like you suffered too much."

"I did, too. I was forced to live on pudding and applesauce."

"Oh, the inhumanity. Just pudding and applesauce?" Colt grinned. "I'll be sure to file a formal complaint for you with the board."

Grandpa Earl chuckled and Colt joined in. It was the first real laugh the two of them had shared in months, maybe even years. And it was good. Really good.

A little while later, Grandpa Earl was settled in the battered La-Z-Boy with a thin crust veggie pizza—and not complaining about the taste of the broccoli florets. Colt wondered if the hospital had given Grandpa a whole lot of Prozac, or if the tide was really changing in their relationship.

Daisy hadn't returned from her meeting with the construction crew at the inn, so Colt grabbed a slice of pizza and changed into his running clothes. When Colt came back into the kitchen, the dog tagged along. Colt reached for the door handle, and the dog barked.

"Seems he wants to go with you," Grandpa said.

"Hey, he's your dog."

"And I just got out of the hospital." Grandpa flipped out the footrest and sat back in his chair. "I'm supposed to take it easy for at least ten minutes."

"All right, all right." Colt retrieved the leash from the hook by the door and snapped it on the dog's collar. "Okay, you can come, but keep your opinions to yourself."

Major Pain barked, and wagged his tail some more as they headed out the door. Outside, the storm from the night before had disappeared, leaving in its place a bright, warm, sunny day. Broken palm fronds and chunks of tree bark littered the beach, but otherwise, everything was quiet and still. Waves sung a gentle *shush-shush* song, reaching into the shore and back again.

Colt wondered if there was still an imprint in the sand from Daisy's glorious body last night. That had been an amazing night, one he knew he'd never forget. Hot, sexy, edged with danger—pretty much all words that encapsulated Daisy Barton. Maybe tonight the two of them could take another walk—or he could take her up on that rain check for a long, hot shower, followed by a long, hot night in his bed.

"Nice day," he said to the dog, because if Colt didn't start thinking about something else, he wasn't going to be able to walk straight.

The dog didn't answer. Just kept on walking, his tail beating a happy, frantic beat against the air. The dog was amiable and easy, walking on the leash without pulling or detouring. He seemed genuinely happy just to be outside with Colt.

"You know I didn't want you," Colt said to the dog. "But you're kinda growing on me. Don't tell my grandfather."

Major Pain looked up at him and wagged his tail. With the way his ears perked and his tongue lolled, one might even say he was smiling. Or saying *I told you so.*

"Maybe you'd even make a good running buddy. What do you think? Would you like to run?"

Major Pain let out a little bark and wagged his tail some more. Colt took that as a yes, so he broke into a slow jog. The dog kept pace easily, and the two of them ran a mile down the beach, then another, then a third. The dog trotted along beside him, as if he'd done this a thousand times before.

Colt rounded the corner to the Hideaway Inn, and caught sight of Nick, working on some gutters on the backside of the building. Colt slowed his pace, and turned to the dog. "Probably not a coincidence I ended up here, is it?"

The dog didn't answer. Colt took that as agreement.

He climbed the sandy path to the inn, scanning the building for any sign of Daisy. He hadn't seen her since last night, since that incredible moment on the beach that had changed everything. It wasn't just about finally opening up to her about Henry, it was about finally letting her into his heart.

Falling for her in a way that went far deeper than the lusty infatuation he'd had at eighteen. That thought had him hastening his pace, taking the wooden steps to the inn two at a time.

"Hey, Colt. Nice surprise to see you here," Nick said. He climbed down from the ladder and swiped the back of his hand across his forehead. Then he reached in a nearby cooler and pulled out a water bottle. "Want one?"

"Yeah, thanks." Colt unscrewed the top, then grabbed a plastic lid off of Nick's makeshift workbench, and poured some water into it for the dog. "Have you seen Daisy?"

"You just missed her. I think she was heading for your place."

"Oh, okay. Just thought I'd ask."

"Just thought you'd ask? Bullshit." Nick grinned. "You're interested in her. I can tell."

"She's still my wife, Nick. Of course I'm interested."

"In a purely legally connected way?"

Colt took a long drink of water. "Well . . . I wouldn't call it purely." Actually, not a single one of Colt's thoughts lately about Daisy had been pure. "Or legal."

Nick laughed. The back door of the inn opened and Maggie came outside. She had on a dark blue tank top and cutoff denim shorts. Nick's attention jerked to her legs, then her breasts, then her legs again. Colt half expected his friend to start drooling.

"I'm going to grab some subs for lunch," Maggie said to Nick. "You want one?"

Nick was still staring at Maggie's legs, and didn't respond. Colt gave him a jab. "Oh, uh, yeah, sure," Nick said.

Maggie grinned. "The usual?"

"Yeah, that'd be great. And some chips."

Maggie put her hands on her hips and shook her head. "You know what happens when you order chips? I end up eating half of them. You are one bad influence, Nick Patterson." Then she turned and went back inside.

"Don't I wish," Nick mumbled.

"You are a pitiful excuse for a man," Colt said.

"What the hell do you mean by that?"

"You keep telling me to go after Daisy, in a non-purely legally connected way, and here you are, having to pick your jaw up off the concrete after a conversation about subs with Maggie."

Nick shrugged. "I get excited about lunch."

"You get excited about *her*." Colt nodded in the direction Maggie had gone. "When are you going to ask her out?"

"Never. I work with her." Nick swiped at the sweat on his brow and took another drink of water. "Do you know what a disaster that would be?"

"So you're saying you're planning on breaking her heart?"

Nick scowled. "Don't make me regret giving you that water bottle."

Colt laughed. He took a seat on an overturned five-gallon bucket, with Major curling into the shade beside him. "Speaking of women who make a man weak in the knees, I think you're right about taking things beyond a purely legal interest. I'm going to go for round two with Daisy."

"If this is going to lead into a discussion about your sex life, at least wait till I have my lunch."

"I meant round two of our marriage. Not sex. Though the two do go hand in hand."

Nick leaned back and gave Colt an assessing glance. "You two are back together? Didn't you tell me a few days ago that she drives you crazy? Now you're rocking the Kasbah over there in *chez Harper*?"

Colt laughed. "I am not even going to talk about that mess of a sentence you regurgitated."

"You, my friend, are avoiding the question."

"Okay, yeah, we are back together." A goofy, silly grin filled Colt's face. The same grin he'd woken up with and had yet to shake. "I'm thinking of making it permanent."

"More permanent than already being married?"

"More permanent, as in, making it a real marriage."

Nick chuckled. "You just want an excuse to have her sleep in your bedroom."

"Well, that is one of the many perks of marriage." Colt grinned again, then sobered. He toyed with the water bottle, peeling at the label. "Seriously, though, she's different now. *I'm* different now. And together, we're better than we were before. She makes me want to be a better person, a better man, and I don't want to let go of that. But I still worry about it not working out." He tore off the label and tossed it in the trash. "Maybe I'm doing the wrong thing and I should just let us get divorced."

Nick wagged a finger at him. "You, my friend, are afraid. You are an excellent doctor, but maybe you're too good."

"There's no such thing as being too good of a doctor."

"There is when you keep thinking you're responsible for the whole world. You can't fix everything or everyone."

"I know that." It was part of the tragedy that came with being in medicine. Sometimes those you fought really hard to save still didn't make it. Even those you loved. "You can't force somebody to take your advice. They have to want it for themselves."

"Yeah? Then why are *you* the only one you haven't fixed? You take the cautious road, the one most traveled, instead of going after what you really want. You're all talk, no follow through. If you ask me, I think it's because you're afraid of losing someone else you love. And hell, that risk comes along every time you open your eyes."

Colt thought about that for a second. Was that what he had done? Why he had let fourteen years go by before seeing Daisy again? Why he had taken off after that night they'd had three months ago, and sent her the divorce papers? "You're awfully wise for a man who barely beats me at basketball."

"That's just part of my charm." Nick grinned.

"Thanks, Nick." Colt finished off the water, and tossed the bottle into a nearby recycle bin. Nick was right. It was time to stop worrying about the what-ifs and just take the leap. "I'm going to head home now and see if my wife wants to go out to dinner tonight. And every night for the rest of our lives."

Daisy clutched the envelope to her chest. It was done. She didn't know how she felt yet, other than . . . numb.

A few swipes of a pen, and the last bit of silly, girlish hope in Daisy Barton had dissolved. She had made a vow this morning to stop being starry-eyed and impetuous and instead approach her decisions with calm, reasonable rationale.

She had just started scribbling out a note when the back door opened. Major barreled through first, followed by Colt.

Her heart stuttered when she saw him, and she wondered if that reaction would ever stop. It didn't matter if he was in shorts and a T-shirt or wearing those damned khakis and ties, just the sight of him made her pulse race.

He smiled when he saw her, and her heart did that silly little flip again. "Just the person I was looking for."

She put down the pen and crumpled up the note. "I didn't know you'd be back today."

"I took the rest of the day off. Thought maybe we could go on one of those picnic lunches you've been trying to talk me into. And tonight, dinner out, just you and me. A real date. What do you say?"

She bit her lip and studied the tile floor. The envelope seemed to chafe her skin, as if the documents inside were trying to climb out. This was the right decision, she knew it was. She just had to say the words, and it would be done. *Tell him. Tell him before you start believing in the impossible again.* "I won't be here tonight, Colt."

"No problem. We'll go tomorrow night."

"I won't be here then, either." She lifted her gaze to his. "I'm moving out."

The light in his eyes dimmed, and the smile on his face dropped. "Moving . . . out?"

"Emma already moved into the Hideaway Inn because Nick got enough of the electric and plumbing repaired for us to stay there. So I'm going to go there, too."

"You don't have to stay with her. You can stay here." He moved closer. "With me."

How tempting those words sounded. *With me.* She could tear up the papers in her hands, and just slide into life with Colt all over again. She clutched the envelope tighter and shook her head. "Come on, Colt. We both know this isn't going to work. For one, your grandpa needs a real nurse to be with him, not me. And I can't stay here and keep . . ." She bit her lip and shook her head. "Keep thinking this is going to turn into something more. Besides, my cousin needs me at the Hideaway. After all, someone's going to have to answer the phone to handle all those new bookings."

She gave him half a smile, then dropped her gaze again because it hurt too much to look at Colt's face.

"That's an excuse, and we both know it."

"It's easier than saying I signed the divorce papers." She held out the envelope.

He stared at the package for a long time, then took the envelope and looked inside, as if he couldn't believe she had really done it. "Why?"

She tried another smile but it hurt her face. "We both knew this was a temporary deal. Quid pro quo, right? I have the inn on the path to restoration and you . . . have your freedom."

"Happy ending all around?" His voice was harsh and cold.

Just push through this, she told herself. Once she was moved out and living at the inn, it would be easier. And it was the best decision for all of them. "I already talked to your grandpa and told him what I was doing. He agreed to let a visiting nurse come in every day until you find someone else."

"You thought of every detail."

"I didn't want to leave you in a bind."

"How thoughtful."

She heard the hurt in his words, and averted her gaze before he saw the tears in her eyes, and she was tempted to undo all she had done. "I'm going to go pack."

"Daisy, wait." He grabbed her arm and spun her back to him. "Why are you really doing this?"

"One night together doesn't change the fact that we are two different people, Colt. We always have been."

"Are we? Really? Because I see two people who have been let down by the people who love them. Two people who are scared to trust each other. But if we do, we can make something great."

She wanted to believe him, wanted it more than anything in the world. But they'd been down this road before and she could already predict the ending. "We're oil and water, Colt. They don't mix."

He took her hand, and waited until she looked at him. "I think we're more like tinder and a spark together. Sometimes we come together and create an explosion, something that is really hot and awesome to watch. But the problem with us is we never took the time to let the fire die enough to see what was beneath it. I'm willing to try, Daisy. Because I think what's underneath will be even better than the fire above."

She shook her head, and the old familiar fears chased up her throat, tightened her airway. "I can't, Colt. I just . . . can't. I'm no good at staying in one place or making commitments. I thought I wanted that when I came here, I really did. All my life, I've looked at my cousin and her family and wanted what she had, what I've missed out on by flitting from here to there and never settling down. A family. A sense of belonging. Something permanent."

"We can have that together, Daisy."

She swallowed and kept talking. "Then I realized I'm not that sort of person. I don't even know how to be. I don't put stock in people, and I don't put stock in places, because most of my life, I lost it before I could even get attached. Until I came here. Now I have something I want to hold on to, but I'm scared as hell to put down roots, to stay here and run the Hideaway. To be honest, half the time I think about packing up my car and heading anywhere. Just . . . away."

"Why? Why not stay? You love that inn."

"What if I do? And I screw it up? Colt, I've been a screwup most of my life. I dropped out of high school, eloped with you, and I've never had a career, just a lot of jobs serving burgers and scrambled eggs. That's not the kind of person people should be depending on." She waved in the direction of the inn. "Emma's the one with experience, the one with staying power. She's the one who should be running it, not me. She worked at the inn for several summers, she's got her degree. She's married, settled down. Dependable."

"And you don't think you're dependable?" He took a step closer. "Because you've been here for me, and my grandfather. And you're here for your cousin."

"All temporary, Colt. I've never held a job for longer than a few months. Never lived in one place for longer than a year."

"But you've been married fifteen years. Today, in fact.

It's our anniversary, in case you forgot." He gave her a cock-eyed grin.

"Not anymore."

The truth sat there between them, cold and harsh. Their marriage, such as it was, was ended. A few swipes of a pen, and it was over.

She raised on her tiptoes and placed a kiss on his lips. "You are a good man, Colt. You always have been. I wish I was the kind of woman who would stay around and appreciate that."

Twenty-five

"You coming in with me?" Colt pulled into a parking space outside of Golden Years and parked the car. He was on his fourth cup of coffee of the day, after spending most of the night tossing and turning and resisting the temptation to run over to the Hideaway Inn to try to talk some sense into Daisy. In the week and a half since she had left, the house had become more and more empty and cold without her. She'd been resolute in her decision to leave, and so he'd let her go.

He had yet to file the divorce papers. The envelope sat on the kitchen counter day after day, like a lead weight.

"Hell, no, I don't want to go in with you," Grandpa Earl said. He sat back against the seat and crossed his arms over his chest. "Why would I want to go in that place? Nothing but a bunch of old geezers who sit around and complain all day."

Colt arched a brow. "And what makes you think you wouldn't fit right in?"

"Hey, I don't complain."

"I thought you went and played cards with the guys the other day. After the festival."

Grandpa looked away. "I didn't go. I said that because I

didn't want anyone pestering me. I just needed some time alone. I ended up at the Shoebox Café, had a little . . . episode and they panicked and called in the ambulance."

"Next time, please let me know where you are. If something happens and I don't know where you are—"

"I'm not five years old, Colt. Stop treating me like I'm gonna break."

Colt didn't say a word, just turned off the car. Ever since the friendship with Walt Patterson had gone south, Grandpa Earl had found one reason after another to skip the weekly card games the guys had been holding at Golden Years for three years now. Colt had hoped that bringing Grandpa along on his rounds would encourage him to stay, hang out with his friends again. No dice. Maybe things between them weren't going as well as Colt thought. "All right. Well, I'll be a couple hours. If you get bored—"

"I know how to keep myself occupied." Grandpa waved toward the building. "Just go. I don't need you hovering over me. For God's sake, you were like a mother hen back at the doctor's office."

Colt bit back an argument, because he knew it would just be the same one he'd had last week and the week before that. Grandpa didn't want to take *any* doctor's advice—and especially not his grandson's. Colt was the one taking notes, asking questions, double-checking the prescriptions. Grandpa acted as if the entire thing was one major inconvenience. At least he'd gone to this appointment. He'd canceled the last three behind Colt's back.

"Grandpa, I love you," Colt said and turned in his seat. "But I'm tired of this battle we keep having. I miss you and I want to get back the grandpa I had . . . before."

Grandpa Earl didn't say anything. He just stared out the windshield. His lower lip trembled, but he shook it off. "When you go, leave the keys so I can at least listen to the talk radio station."

Colt sighed. Why did he keep trying? It was clear that Grandpa was never going to forgive him. "Fine."

Colt headed inside and spent the next hour or so

completing his rounds, checking on patients who had been sick, others who were recovering from surgeries, and popping in to see the ones who didn't always follow his recommendations. Ending with the most contrary patient of all.

Greta Winslow.

Colt entered the morning room and crossed to the round table by the window. "Good morning, Mrs. Winslow. How are you?"

Greta looked up from the table where she was sitting with Pauline and Esther. The ladies had a pile of papers spread out on the table before them, along with a stack of newspapers and a couple legal pads. Pauline scooped up the papers and swept them under the newspapers. Colt bit back a laugh. Must be the ladies' newest letters from the lovelorn requesting advice. Greta had told him about the column the ladies did their best to keep secret from everyone else in Rescue Bay, lest it mess with their "process," whatever that was. Greta hadn't explained and Colt hadn't asked.

"Why, Doc Harper," Greta said. "Back again so soon?"

"Here every Tuesday at two for rounds. Just checking to make sure people are taking my advice, following their prescriptions."

"Well, I would do that if I had a prescription from you. But unfortunately, I left your office before you could write out that little memo. The one for my gastrointestinal health." She jerked her head in the direction of the table at the back of the morning room, where four men were seated. Joe Hardy, Reggie White, Walt Patterson, and Harold Twohig.

Colt chuckled. "Mrs. Winslow, I assure you, you don't need a prescription."

She harrumphed and sat back in her chair, arms crossed over her chest. Esther leaned forward and put a hand on Greta's arm. "If you are having a little . . . intestinal issue, Greta, I have some Pepto-Bismol in my medicine cabinet. Or if it's stuck the . . . uh, other direction, I have a year's supply of Metamucil. I knew there was a reason why I entered that contest on the back of the jar."

Greta rolled her eyes. "I don't need either, Esther. For goodness' sake, I have the constitution of a horse."

"Horse? I was going to say goat," Pauline said. "Seems a far more appropriate comparison."

Colt laughed. "You ladies all seem as healthy as can be to me. I'm going to check on the gentlemen, then be on my way."

"Doc, hold up a minute." Greta got to her feet and tugged him to the side, out of earshot of Pauline and Esther. She peered up at him, her pale blue eyes as alert and incisive as a lie detector. "I wanted to ask how things are going with a certain young lady."

"Mrs. Winslow, I don't discuss my personal life—"

She waved off his words. "I know, I know. But since you are my *personal* physician, I don't think discussing your personal life is anything different than you discussing mine. Besides, if you're happy, that's good business. When the doctor's happy, everyone's happy." She wagged a finger at him. "That should be a needlepoint on your wall. Esther, the crafting fool, would be glad to stitch you one, if you ask."

Happy. It wasn't a term he associated with his life. Content, perhaps. Predictable, yes. But happy? No. That word wasn't in his vocabulary right now. For a brief moment in time, it had been, but then he thought of the envelope on his counter and that moment passed.

"I'm fine, Mrs. Winslow," Colt said. "Just fine."

"And I'm the Easter Bunny." She put her hands on her hips. "Now, listen, I know you're the one used to giving advice, but I think it's time you took some."

"Mrs. Winslow—"

"You are an excellent doctor. And if you tell anyone I said that out loud, I will steal all your stethoscopes and put super glue on the earpieces."

He chuckled, then made a zipping motion across his lips. "I'll never tell a soul."

"Like I said, excellent doctor, but an idiot man." She put up a hand to ward off his protest. "A little birdie told me that Daisy moved out and is now living at the inn. I can't believe you let her get away."

"I didn't *let* anything happen," Colt said, then wondered

why he was explaining his love life to his eighty-three-year-old patient. "We just decided to separate."

That sounded better than divorce. Less final. Less un-doable. Yeah, then what were those signed documents in that envelope saying?

"She's just scared." Greta waved a hand. "A woman like that needs a grand gesture. Something bigger than life, to show that you are serious."

"Are you telling me to rent one of those biplanes and scrawl something across the sky or throw a proposal on a Jumbotron?"

"Goodness, no. Those have all been done before. Do something . . . special. Just for Daisy. Something that she'll be unable to resist." She patted his arm. "Be adventurous, Doc. Love is a risk, and you have to show you're a risk taker, too."

Earl Harper lasted about ten minutes in the car. He'd never been the kind of man who could sit around and do nothing. Truth be told, that was what drove him craziest about living with Colton. That sense of . . . nothing.

At least when he'd had the repair shop, he'd had something to occupy his mind every day. It had kept him from dwelling, and ever since he'd sold his business to Gator Lee, Earl had done altogether too much dwelling.

Dwelling on mistakes. Dwelling on regrets. Dwelling on the holes in his life, holes that would never be filled again.

He glanced at the retirement home. He could go in there, sit down at the scuffed table in the back of the morning room, and play a couple rounds of poker with the guys. It would pass a few hours, maybe even ease the heaviness in his mind. But going in there would mean delivering an apology to Walt Patterson, and if there was one thing Earl wasn't in the mood to do, it was apologize. Or explain.

He glanced at the keys dangling from the ignition. Then again at the entrance to Golden Years. Earl tugged on the door handle and got out of the car. He stood in the parking lot for a good long second while the Florida sun beat down on his thinning hair, until the decision he needed to make cemented some resolve in his heart.

Joe, Reggie, Walt, and Harold still left an empty seat on the right side of the table, even though Earl Harper hadn't been at a game in more than six months. Colt slid into his grandfather's chair, and waved off Joe's offer to deal him in. "I think there's something in the Hippocratic oath against playing poker during working hours."

Joe put a finger to his lips. "Don't use the *P* word around here. Nurse Ratched"—he nodded in the direction of the tall, thin woman who often patrolled the morning room—"will kick us out."

"Then what are you guys playing?"

"A shell game." Walt winked, then dropped a trio of shells into the pile in the center of the table. "I raise you two scallops and one pear whelk."

Joe rubbed his chin. Then he raised his gaze and studied Walt. "I think you're bluffing. I'll see your bet and raise you one King's Crown." He added a giant curved shell to the pile.

"Too rich for my blood," Harold said. He folded his hand and tossed it onto the table. "Gentlemen, it's been great. But I see my sweet petunia is leaving, and I want to talk to her."

Walt scoffed. "Harold, you are either a fool or a glutton for punishment. Greta Winslow hates you."

"That's just a front. She doesn't want her friends to know she's hot for this eighty-four-year-old body."

Walt snorted back a laugh. "Then she's either blind or desperate."

"Says the man who's got his eye on a certain bachelorette in this room himself."

Walt ignored the jab, and added his shell to the pile. "Whatcha got, Joe?"

"Three ladies." Joe laid his cards on the table and displayed a trio of queens.

"Sounds more like your love life than a hand of cards." Walt grinned, then laid his own hand on the table. "I've got a whole handful of diamonds. Read it and weep, Joe."

"I thought you guys said this was a shell game," Colt said. "Not p—"

"It is a shell game." Walt winked. "In the strictest sense of the meaning of shell game."

"As in, our pathetic attempt to fool Nurse Ratched into thinking we're playing a simple game of cards and trading shell collections," Joe explained.

Colt laughed. "And how's that working for you?"

"Working just . . ." Joe let out a low whistle. "Well, would you lookie there. That's not a sight we see around here nearly often enough."

Colt turned. His breath caught, and his chest tightened. If he hadn't known better, he'd swear his heart was stopping.

Daisy stood beside Greta, talking to the three ladies. The rest of the room dropped away, and all Colt saw was Daisy's curves, luring his attention in a clingy green dress that skimmed her knees and dipped in a V above those amazing breasts. She had part of her hair pinned back, which left dark bangs skimming across her brows and long curls brushing her shoulders. She laughed at something Greta said, and something in Colt's gut tightened.

"Seems Harold isn't the only smitten man in the room," Joe said.

"Gentlemen, if you'll excuse me . . ." Colt got to his feet, started toward Daisy, then stopped when Walt tapped him on the shoulder.

"Forgot your bag, Doc." Walt handed him his black medical bag. "A pretty woman will do that to you."

"I'm on rounds. I have to . . ."

Walt chuckled, then gave him a little nudge. "Yeah, whatever. Go on over there. Just remember to close your mouth first. Don't want to drool all over her, you know."

Colt cleared his throat, and shifted the medical bag from one hand to the other. The action helped shake off the temporary stupor brought on by Daisy's presence and bring him back to planet earth. Where he was a doctor, not an infatuated fifteen-year-old. Still, he wondered if she had come here to see him. He hoped like hell that was the case and quickened his pace.

"And every week we pick a letter to answer, giving advice culled from decades of experience," Greta was saying as Colt approached. "We are always looking for someone who needs our advice. Or helpful . . . nudges."

Colt came up behind Daisy, resisting the urge to put his hands on her waist and spin her into his arms. She sensed him behind her and pivoted. For a second, a smile lingered on her face and his heart stuttered. Then the smile died and his heart fell.

"Colt. You startled me."

"Sorry." He felt as awkward as a teenager at his first dance, especially with the ladies of Golden Years watching his every move. "I'm surprised to see you here."

"I came by to meet Olivia and Greta to talk about the final details for the wedding on Saturday."

"It's going to be lovely. On the beach, at the end of the day. The Hideaway Inn provides the perfect backdrop for a sunset wedding." Pauline sighed. "So romantic."

Harold came up to table, and sidled into place beside Greta. "Wedding? Well, I can think of one lovely lady who is going to need a date." He put out an arm, and patted the elbow, gesturing for her to link hers. "Greta, dear, would you accompany me to Olivia and Luke's wedding?"

"I can accompany my own damned self." She jerked her arm away. "Besides, it's almost flu season. I have no idea where your hands and nose have been. I wouldn't take a chance on infecting myself by coming into contact with possible contagion."

Harold just chuckled. He leaned over, and before she could stop him, pressed a light, quick kiss to Greta's cheek. "They say the best way to avoid the flu is to get exposed. Call that your Harold vaccination."

"Would that there was such a thing," she grumbled.

Colt chuckled. "Don't knock it. There are advances in medical science every day."

Greta scowled and gave Harold a little shove. He took a half step back, but didn't leave. The other men got up from the poker game and came over to the table, flanking Harold like a backup team.

"Where's your grandfather?" Daisy asked, peering around Colt. "I'd like to say hello to him. Is he doing okay?"

"He's his usual self." Colt nodded toward the exit doors. "Refused to come with me and said he wanted to stay in the car."

Walt frowned. "You mean he's here, and decided not to see us?"

"He's still licking his wounds, Walt." Colt put out his hands. "What can I say?"

"Let me go talk to him. Straighten this thing out once and for all."

The three of them headed out of Golden Years, with Walt leading the way, a man on a mission, it seemed. Before they even reached the parking lot, lead sank in Colt's gut. He saw an empty space between two yellow lines. "My car is gone."

"Who would take . . ." Daisy's voice trailed off. "Grandpa Earl?"

Colt nodded, his posture calm, but his mind a wild whirlwind. He'd never thought Grandpa would do something like this, and wondered for a second if maybe the other cruel partner to Parkinson's—dementia—was starting to set in. Had Grandpa forgotten where he was? Why he was in the lot? And just driven off to somewhere far, far from here?

Colt had left the car with a half a tank of gas. That gave Grandpa a good two hundred miles before the tank ran empty—enough mileage to get pretty much anywhere in the state of Florida. "Damn it. I never should have left the keys in the car."

"I'm sure he didn't go far, Colt. Is there a friend he might go see or a church or something?"

Colt scoffed. "No. Not my grandpa. He probably got pissed at me for bringing him here or for taking him to the

doctor or for criticizing his breakfast choice, and decided
to strand me. He didn't use to be like this and no matter how
hard I try, it doesn't get better between us. I swear, I have
no idea how to get him back."

"He's gone through a lot the last few years, Colt. Losing
Henry, and then Nancy . . ." A sad smile filled Walt's face.
He looked out over the road, empty now, quiet. Then back
at the space where Colt's car had been parked. "I think I
know where he went."

Daisy drove because it kept her from having to look at Colt,
and focusing on the road kept her from wanting to hold
Colt's hand. Walt had given Colt a strong, man-to-man hug,
then gone back inside. She sensed that whatever Walt wanted
to talk to Earl about was going to wait, and that right now,
Earl's friend realized his grandson should be the one to bring
him back from wherever he'd gone.

Save for "Take a right here," and "Left at the light," Colt
didn't say a word on the ride. Daisy tightened her grip on
the steering wheel and told herself she wasn't hurt.

But she was.

She'd asked for this, though. By keeping him out of her
own life, by keeping her own cards close to her chest. Colt
had opened up and told her all about that heartbreaking day
his brother had died, and what had she done when he asked
her about her life?

Divorced him.

"Take this turn," Colt said, the words soft and sad.

She did as he said, then wove her way down the curving
road and around to the back, past the lines of trees, the
manicured shrubs, the well-tended flowers, until she saw
Colt's Honda parked beside a low white concrete bench.

Earl's hunched body filled the center of the bench. He
had his elbows on his knees, his head down, and a paper-
wrapped cone of flowers drooped from one hand. Daisy
parked, then shut off the car. Colt didn't say a word, just got
out and crossed to his grandfather.

The two of them sat there a long time, not saying a word, as still as figures in a painting. In the distance, Daisy heard the sound of a lawnmower roaring to life. Some birds calling to each other, and far, far away, the traffic on the freeway progressing at a steady hum.

Earl stared straight ahead at the two oval headstones before them. The first had a slight green tint to the concrete, and a trail of ivy curling up the side and over the top. The second, newer, gleamed in the sun, and the letters for NANCY HARPER, BELOVED WIFE AND MOTHER, shone where the granite had been chipped away.

But it was the first headstone that held Daisy's attention. HENRY HARPER, SON, BROTHER, GONE TOO SOON.

And then the date, a date Daisy knew well. It had been a sunny spring day in New Orleans, and she'd been coming home from the store, groceries in her arms, a smile on her face, ready to make dinner for her new husband and to settle into this life of domesticity. She'd gone upstairs, and found empty drawers, an empty closet, and a note. Her heart broke for Colt all over again, for the tragic, horrible loss of that little boy with the infectious laugh.

The two men sat there a long time. Daisy stayed in the car, the windows down to let in a breeze, giving them space, privacy. And she whispered a silent prayer that this time, these two men she was beginning to care very deeply about, would find a way to bridge the rocky gulf between them.

Earl Harper wasn't a man who opened up a vein and let it bleed. He was raised in a time when men kept their emotions buried and sucked the hell up, whether they'd lost a finger in an accident or a grandson in a tragedy. He'd done a damned good job of sucking it up, years and years of burying every emotion he ever had. Where'd it get him?

Sitting on a cold stone bench in a cemetery. Next thing he knew, he'd be part of the ground here, and Lord help him, he didn't want to have his time come before he lost a second grandson to his own stubbornness.

"I've been a shitty grandfather," Earl said.

Colt turned on the bench. "No you haven't. Why would you say that?"

"Because it's true. I've treated you like crap. Resisted your medical advice. Called you an idiot—"

"Only a couple times." Colt grinned.

"A couple times too many." Earl tore off a long blade of grass and tossed the pieces onto the ground. "I wasn't raised to be a huggy kind of guy. Hell, I don't even like to smile."

Colt chuckled. "You're grumpy, but you're not that bad."

"Okay, maybe not." Earl looked down at the two granite slabs that marked the graves of two of the people he'd loved most in the world. Maybe it was time to quit being so damned stubborn. Nancy would have read him the riot act for the way he'd been acting lately, and rightly so. She'd had a way of bringing out the best in him, and with her gone, it was like he'd lost that side of him. "I've been blaming you, because it's easier than blaming myself."

"For what?"

"For not being there that day." He shook his head and let out a curse. "Eight years, I never missed a fishing trip. Eight goddamned years, I went with you boys, twice a week, like clockwork. That day, though, I told Henry I couldn't go. My business had been hurting the last few weeks before, and I had a rush job come in. Some snowbird, needing his car fixed after it broke down coming down here. Offered me double just to get it done that night. I told Henry, hey, we'll go tomorrow."

"But he didn't wait."

Earl sighed and shook his head. "I'd taken him fishing the last two weeks before, when you were . . . away. Just him and me. He kept telling me he was older now, *Let me drive the boat, Grandpa, let me throw out the anchor.* So I let him. You know, that's how boys learn. You let them try, let them fail, and they learn. I thought I was doing the right thing."

Colt put an arm around his grandfather's shoulders. Earl seemed ten times more frail, a hundred times more heartbroken. "You were. You couldn't have known he would try to go out by himself."

"I never should have shown him. I should have made him wait till he was older. Ten, eleven." Grandpa's voice cracked and when he turned to Colt, his eyes were filled with tears, his face washed with regret, sorrow. "He was too young, Colt, too damned young."

"I know. I know." Colt's voice broke.

"I miss him, like somebody tore off my left arm and just left me to bleed to death. Every day since that boy died, I've felt like that. Hell, half the time I wanted to die myself. The only thing that kept me going was Nancy. Then she died and . . . I didn't see the point anymore."

"So that's why you won't take your medicine or go to the specialists. Just let it happen." Colt shook his head. Tears burned at the back of his eyes, but he didn't give a damn. "Didn't you ever think that maybe I need you, too?"

Earl scoffed. "You don't need me. Hell, you're ten times smarter than I ever was. You always have been."

"Every boy needs his grandpa," Colt said softly. "You're the one who taught me everything I know."

Earl scoffed again and shook his head.

"About girls and engines and fixing broken water pipes. But most of all, Grandpa, you taught me that it's a good thing to find a job you love and be the best damned one at it that you can be. People come up to me every day and tell me what a good mechanic you were. How you fixed their car when they were out of work, and wouldn't take money from them. How you rebuilt an engine or pulled out a dent late on a Saturday night because someone needed to go out of town on Monday to visit their sick sister. I can only pray I turn out to be half the man you are."

"You really mean that?"

"Hell, yes. You're my hero, Grandpa. You always have been."

Earl dropped his gaze. A tear puddled on his leg. He swiped at his face. "Thank you, Colt, but I don't deserve that. I just fix cars. You fix people. Save their lives. If any-one's the hero here, it's you."

"The only life I care about saving is yours, Grandpa."

Earl raised his gaze to his grandson's and held it a long while. His vision blurred, his throat closed, but he let those words sink into him, before he nodded and said, "Okay, Colt. Okay."

Colt drew his grandfather into a long, tight hug, the kind that reminded him of when he'd been a little boy and had grabbed his grandfather at the end of those Sunday fishing trips, wanting so bad to stay in that warm maple-syrup-scented house with his indulgent grandparents, instead of going home to a pristine world of rules and expectations. He held on to his grandfather for as long as he could, because it was all he could do, and all he'd ever really wanted.

Twenty-six

Emma had spent two weeks at the Hideaway Inn. Her quick weekend away had turned into an extended stay, and now with bookings starting to fill the calendar, Daisy was going to need Emma even more. The renovations were nearly complete, and there was a crew working on the patio today, setting up chairs and tables for Luke and Olivia's wedding later today.

She had called her mother a couple times, keeping the conversations upbeat and short. Still, half her mind was back in Jacksonville, knowing that she eventually had to return and make a final decision about her marriage.

A car swung into the circular drive of the Hideaway. It took her a second to realize it was Roger's sedan, dusty from the four-hour trip from Jacksonville. Her heart leapt to her throat. Was he here to tell her in person that he'd filed for divorce?

Roger stepped out of the car, sunglasses hiding his eyes. He started toward the front steps of the Hideaway, then saw her standing on the beach and detoured in her direction. As he approached, she saw that he wasn't dressed in the neat, perfectly pressed clothes he normally wore. Instead, he wore rumpled shorts and an old faded T-shirt she remembered buying for him years ago. She stayed where she was, cemented in place, until Roger reached her.

"What are you doing here?" she asked.

"Looking for my wife."

The words caused a little hitch in her breath. "I'm not your wife, Roger. We're separated. You made the announcement yourself."

He sighed. "I did it because I was frustrated. I felt like we weren't going anywhere and I might as well accept the inevitable."

"Inevitable? You're the one who moved out. You're the one who gave up. I'm the one who kept trying." She turned away, cursing the tears that burned at the back of her eyes.

He circled around to stand in front of her. "You're right."

The two words hung in the air between them. Said so simply, so sure, that the argument she'd been bracing to launch died in her throat.

"I'm sorry," Roger said. "I let us slip away, a little at a time. I got consumed by my job, by that book contract, by all the things that I thought would make me happy. Then we had that night together . . . and then you proposed the weekend away, and I blew it. I thought I couldn't have both."

"Both what?"

"Both the career I'd always dreamed of and the marriage I'd always wanted. So I moved out, and moved on, and then I was sitting there in my apartment by the campus, spending two full days wandering around like a lost puppy. I couldn't understand what was missing, why I felt so . . . derailed. And then I realized something."

She couldn't read his face. "What?"

He took off his sunglasses and tucked them in his pocket, then clasped her hands in his own. His dark eyes met hers, and held, for the first time in forever. "That the career didn't matter. Didn't mean a damned thing. Not without you by my side." He shook his head, and sadness filled his features. "How did we get so offtrack, Emma?"

"We stopped trying. Both of us." She'd been just as guilty as Roger, letting her marriage wither away rather than fighting the inertia that had crept in like a slow flood. "We never should have quit."

A sad smile stole across Roger's face. "Quitting's so much easier."

"So . . ." She let out a breath. "What now?"

"I unload my car and set up my computer." He brushed the bangs off her face and rested his palm against her cheek. "I booked a room at the Hideaway Inn for the next twelve months."

"You . . . what?"

"I took my sabbatical, packed up my car, and came here to be with you, Emma. I'll write and help you, and we'll try again. If . . ." He hesitated, and Emma realized she had never seen her driven, confident husband so unsure before. "If that's okay with you."

She drew in a breath. "Before I answer, I have something to tell you."

His touch fluttered. "Okay."

"Remember that night a couple months ago? Well . . ." She exhaled the breath. "I'm pregnant."

Roger's dark eyes searched her face. Confusion filled his eyes, then yielded to joy. "Really?"

She nodded. "Listen, I understand if this changes things. I know you didn't want kids while you were still trying to build your career at the university and—"

He pressed a finger to her lips, silencing her. "None of that means a damned thing without you. And"—he dropped his hand to her belly—"our future."

They stood there a long time, enjoying each other, kissing, talking, laughing, then Roger told her to stay where she was while he unloaded the car and got them both some ginger ale for a toast.

When Roger was gone, Emma stood on the beach and looked out at the ocean. She wrapped her arms around herself and smiled. The sun warmed her face, her hands, and filled her chest. She watched the water wash in and out, in and out, and for the first time in months, felt . . .

Peace.

It wasn't perfect, and there were still a lot of unanswered questions and decisions that lay ahead of them both, but for now, this would do. She'd have to call her mother and tell her that she wasn't coming back to Jacksonville. If there was one thing sure to cheer Clara up, it was being told she'd been right all along.

"There you are," Daisy said, coming up beside Emma. "I can't believe we've finally reopened this place."

"You did it, Dase. It was all you."

She waved that off. "It was Nick and his crew, and you, and a big fat loan."

Emma turned to face her cousin. "None of this would have happened without you. You believed in it, you believed in me, and there were times when you believed enough for all of us. You got that first event booked, you managed to get that loan, and you brought the Hideaway Inn back to life, and in a way, you brought me back, too. Don't discount that. It's a big deal. A really big deal."

Daisy watched a sailboat cutting through the water, as easily as a knife through melted butter. "I never imagined I would do anything that mattered. I mean, I've been a waitress most of my life. I never served anyone a cheeseburger that changed their life." She laughed a little. "But I'm glad this changed things for you. I've been worried about you, cuz."

Emma drew in a long breath and let it out. "I'm better now. Or I will be. And if you still want me to run the inn with you, I'm going to stay."

"Really? But what about Roger and your job in Jacksonville?"

"I hated my job in Jacksonville. I never liked working at that insurance company. And my photography business can go where I go. As for Roger . . ." She watched the water for a while more, then a smile bubbled to the surface of her face. "He's here. He wants to stay and try again. He took a sabbatical, so we have a whole year to figure this out."

Daisy draped an arm around Emma's shoulders and drew her close. "That's wonderful. I'm so glad for you."

"Are you staying here, too?" Emma asked.

Daisy shrugged. "I'm thinking about it. You know me and settling down in one place. I don't do it well."

"That's because you've never tried. And you've never had the right incentive."

"Incentive? Right now, all my incentives are telling me to leave." She glanced down the beach, in the direction where Colt's house lay.

"Well, what if I gave you an extra reason to stay and help me?"

"Extra reason?"

Emma drew in a breath again, and faced Daisy. The joy in her heart threatened to burst. "I'm . . . pregnant."

Surprise dawned in Daisy's face, followed by a giant smile. "Really? I can't believe it. Oh, when, how? Never mind, it doesn't matter." She drew Emma into a tight hug. "I'm not going anywhere. I'm staying right here with my best friend."

"And running the Hideaway Inn together? Resurrecting a little of the past?"

"While also changing our futures." Daisy gave Emma a happy, goofy smile. And in the conviction in Daisy's eyes, Emma found hope.

Either Daisy was hormonal or she was getting sappy in her thirties. Late on Saturday afternoon, when Olivia stepped barefoot onto the flower-strewn trail on the beach and walked toward a beaming Luke, something caught in Daisy's throat. The music swelled, then Olivia and Luke took each other's hands as the minister called for everyone to be seated.

True to Olivia's word, there were only about fifty people in attendance at the wedding. Greta and the girls, Walt, Harold, and the rest of the poker gang, as well as Diana and Mike and his daughters. Earl had arrived just a few minutes before the ceremony and taken a seat with Daisy, Emma, and Roger in the back row. She'd asked him where Colt was, and Earl just shook his head.

She tried not to think about Colt, tried to pretend she didn't care that he wasn't here. She had divorced him, and that meant she was supposed to let him go, not let every word the minister spoke to Luke and Olivia remind her of her own wedding.

The sun kissed the horizon just as the minister pronounced them man and wife. Luke cradled Olivia's face in his hands, then leaned in and kissed her, slow and sweet, like she was a treasure he had waited a lifetime to find.

Daisy looked away, and told herself it didn't hurt her heart. Didn't make her want to dive into the ocean and lose herself in the deep blue nothing.

When the music swelled again, Daisy forced back the lump in her throat, plastered a smile on her face, and rose to give Olivia a hug as she and Luke headed back up the aisle. The guests began to mingle and head toward the reception on the patio, while Emma and Daisy picked up the flowers. Roger kept his eye on his wife, as if he couldn't believe she was really here. It was such a sweet sight, and one that sent another lump into Daisy's throat.

"Beautiful wedding," Emma said.

"Absolutely."

"And it made you miserable the entire time." Emma put a hand around Daisy's shoulder. "Why don't you just tell him that you are madly in love with him?"

"Because I'm not. He's all wrong for me. All rules and organization and permanence."

"Sounds to me like a list of things you've been looking for all your life, all rolled up into one handsome package."

"I miss the man I did fall in love with. The risk taker. The motorcycle and the leather jacket. That Colt was the one who understood me."

"Just because a man trades his motorcycle for a suit and tie doesn't change who he is inside. I think you're just scared and looking for an excuse."

"I think I better get these flowers up to the reception before they wilt." Daisy started forward, then hesitated when she heard a guttural roaring sound, thudding like a heartbeat, increasing in volume, rumbling the air, the ground. A low-slung black motorcycle prowled down the circular drive of the Hideaway Inn, then came to a stop. The driver kicked out the stand on the side, then swung his leg over the silver and black beast.

"I'll take those flowers," Emma said. She gave Daisy a nudge. "And you better go see who's late to the wedding."

She walked up the path that led to the front of the building, waiting, her breath caught in her throat, for the driver to take off his helmet. He just leaned against the bike and waited for her. He had on dark-wash denim jeans, a thick black leather jacket, and—

A button-down shirt and tie.

Daisy started to laugh. She shook her head, sure she was seeing things, then he took off the helmet and gave her a grin.

"Sorry I'm late," Colt said.

"You're not late. You only missed the wedding, not the reception." She tried not to read anything into his appearance. After all, Olivia and Luke had invited him, so that didn't mean he was here for any other reason than to celebrate a friend's marriage. Except . . . he was riding a motorcycle and wearing a leather jacket, as if she'd conjured up the old Colt by talking about him. "What are you doing with all . . . this?"

"Showing you that I'm not just a khakis guy." He flicked at the Windsor knot. "Though I didn't give up the tie."

She grinned. "It is a wedding, after all. Ties are appropriate."

"That's what I hear." He hung the helmet on the handlebars, then closed the distance between them. "So, too, is having a date."

So he had come for her? Joy burst in her heart, chased by the familiar fears that had ruled her life for so many years. "Oh, Colt, I'm working and busy and . . ."

Her voice trailed off when he took her hand, put something in her palm, then closed her fingers over it. "Remember when you made me buy you one of these? Maybe we both should have taken that promise to heart. Always remember to take chances, Daisy."

She opened her fingers. A pair of black and white plastic dice dangled from the ring holding the motorcycle's key. Plastic and cheesy, and just like the pink ones that she had kept all those years. "Colt . . . I don't know what to say to this."

"Come for a ride with me. Just for a little while."

She flicked a glance at the inn. "There's the wedding and—"

"I have it all under control," Emma said, coming up behind them.

Roger stepped into place beside her. "And whatever she needs help with, I'm here to do."

Emma grinned. "So go, you two. But be back before they serve the cake, or I'll eat your piece."

Daisy laughed, then turned back to Colt, and handed him the keys, because right now she was trembling, whether from fear or elation, she wasn't sure, and in no condition to drive a motorcycle. "You heard the woman. I'm serious about my cake, so only a few minutes."

"Hopefully that's all I need." He climbed back on the bike, settled the helmet on his head, then handed an extra one to her. A moment later, Daisy had her arms wrapped around Colt's waist and they were flying down the road, while the wind whipped at them and the heat of the bike wafted over their legs.

It was just like the old days and if she closed her eyes, she could pretend they were running away, off to a new life filled with unknowns. A life that had included a whirlwind courtship, marriage, and ending.

This time, there wasn't going to be a marriage at the end of the road. She had divorced him—the papers were signed and all Colt had to do was file them with the court—so there was nothing left to bind them. Yet she had climbed on his bike anyway, her thighs anchored against his, her arms locked across his chest, her cheek pressed to his back, and she wasn't quite sure why.

He turned off on a side street, and brought the bike to a

halt in a small shaded park. They got off the bike, set down the helmets, and crossed to a grayed picnic table, scarred and dented from years by the seashore. "Why are we here?" she asked.

"Because I wanted a moment alone with you, to prove to you that I can change. That I can be more than just a tie, more than just a motorcycle. That I can be the kind of guy you want."

She shook her head and realized that for all her arguments about wanting the old Colt back, she had been lying to her cousin, to him, to herself. It wasn't about the Harley or the khakis. It never had been. "Colt, I don't need you to buy a motorcycle or a leather jacket or to wear a tie."

"Then what *do* you need, Daisy?"

He came closer, and a part of her wanted to just dive into his arms and stay there. At the same time, her heart began to race, and she fought the urge to run out of the park. "I don't know what I need, but I do know the thought of being in one place longer than a few months terrifies the crap out of me."

"Why?"

"I just don't settle down. I'm not that kind of person." She shook her head and looked away from him.

"Yet you came here, took on a giant mortgage and an even bigger project. If that's not settling down, I don't know what is. All I'm asking is for a chance for you to settle down with me, too."

She backed away, shaking her head and putting up her hands. "You're going to want me to be this perfect doctor's wife. Cooking dinner and making pies for the town fair, and dressing our kids in matching little outfits, and that's just not me, Colt."

He laughed. "Where did you get the idea that I wanted any of that? I love you just the way you are, Daisy. I love you when you burst into a room and yell at me, I love you when you climb on top of me outside and make my head spin. I love you when you bring home a dog that I didn't expect and I love you when you make me break the rules."

He strode forward, caught her chin, and lifted her gaze to his. "What are you really afraid of, Daisy?"

She broke away from him and walked across the small lawn. A chill ran through her, even though the day was warm and sunny, a nearly perfect blue sky with only a smattering of clouds. Daisy wrapped her arms around her chest and took in one breath after another, fighting the urge to just leave instead of having this conversation.

A hundred times before, she had walked away—heck, run away—when the conversation got tense and difficult. She'd stomp out of their apartment, slam the door, and not come back until after Colt had gone to sleep.

Avoid and duck. Two things that Daisy did well. Two things she had been doing since the day she arrived here. How easy would it be to just tell Colt to take her back to the wedding and avoid this entire conversation?

"Colt, I don't know what you want me to say."

"I want you to talk to me, Daisy. To really talk. Like a wife talks to a husband who is a part of her life. Not like a woman talking to an unwanted guest who overstayed his welcome."

"I never—"

He came closer, until mere inches separated them. "You never let me in, Daisy. We could run away, we could get married, we could have mind-blowing sex, but when it came to talking about anything deeper than what kind of takeout we were ordering, there was a distinct line in the sand."

"What did you want me to talk about?" She threw up her hands. "My sucky childhood? How my mother would take off, just because she got bitten by some whim, or she'd get tired of living on this street or with that neighbor, and *wham*, we'd move. How I came home from school one day and she was gone? The house was empty, the locks were changed. She'd forgotten to tell me where we'd moved to and I spent the entire day tracking her down." She shook her head and cursed the tears that sprang to her eyes. "Who wants to hear me complain about that?"

"I did," he said, his voice low and quiet. "I did."

The truth in his voice stopped her cold. All those days she'd slammed the doors, walked away. What would have happened between them fourteen years ago if she had just stayed? Her heart broke and she wondered if it was too late, too many years passed, too much damage done. "How did we live with each other and so completely miss each other?"

"I don't know, Daisy." He sighed and met her gaze with his own. "I don't know."

Earl Harper was having a perfectly good time sulking at Luke and Olivia's wedding when Walt slipped into the chair beside him. He didn't say a word to his friend, just grunted in his general direction.

"You done being pissed at me?" Walt said.

Earl crossed his arms over his chest and watched the bride and groom swirl around the dance floor. They looked happy, a couple of young kids in love and banking on a long future together. "Nope. I figure I got at least another six months left."

"If that's the way it's gonna be . . ." Walt started to rise. Earl clamped a hand on his arm.

Earl sucked up his pride, and decided he'd wasted enough of his life. It was no fun being a hermit when your only company was your own grumpy self.

"I've been an ass," Earl said to Walt. "I let a woman come between us, and I shouldn't have."

Walt nodded. "For what it's worth, I never dated Pauline. Took her to lunch once, but there just wasn't any chemistry."

"Are you blind?" Earl gestured toward Pauline, standing on the other side of the patio, in a pale blue dress and low heels. She had her hair pinned up today, with a few curls dangling along her face, making her look softer, younger. Even the sun seemed to like Pauline, the way it scattered golden light along her skin. "She's a beautiful woman. Any man worth his salt would be head over heels for her."

Walt chuckled. "Sounds like there's already one man in

love with her." He got to his feet and clapped Earl on the shoulder. "I'll see you back at cards next week."

Earl nodded, and just like that, a many-decades-old friendship was restored. That was the good thing about true friends. A spat could come between them, but eventually it would pass, like a summer storm. He'd go back to the card games, and maybe add a few woe-is-me medical issues to the table. He did, after all, have a recent hospital stay he could milk for sympathy points.

Just as Earl was thinking about getting in the buffet line, Pauline strode up to him. "I want a word with you, Earl Harper."

He gestured toward the empty seat beside him. Seemed everybody in Rescue Bay was wanting to talk his ear off today. Though this particular somebody was a welcome change. "Have a seat."

She stood. "I am at a wedding. Which means I have a rare opportunity to dance. So I am going to talk to you and you are going to dance with me."

He cocked his head. "You think you can just order me around like that and I'll jump to my feet and do the fox-trot?"

"Yes, I do. Because you are interested in me and you are being too pigheaded to show it. So somebody has to take the lead in this relationship, and I guess it's going to be me."

Earl got to his feet. "Since when do we have a relationship?"

"Since you asked me to dance at Luke and Olivia's wedding."

"I did no such thing. You *ordered* me to dance."

She put her fists on her hips and glared at him.

Earl shook his head and laughed. Never had he ever met a woman more stubborn than himself. That was what he'd liked about Pauline from day one. Earl Harper needed a woman who would keep him in line, and this one did that in spades. She was awfully fiery for an old woman, and that, Earl thought, would keep them both young. "Pauline, would you do me the honor of dancing with me?"

"Why, I would be delighted, Earl. I thought you'd never ask."

He just laughed some more and took Pauline's hand. Hers felt right in his, smaller, more delicate, but soft and warm. They made their way past the tables and chairs and out to the center of the patio. A boom box played a Michael Bublé tune on the speakers, one of his covers of a Frank Sinatra hit. Earl put out his arms and Pauline stepped into them, fitting into the space as if she had been made for him.

"Now would be a good time to compliment me," Pauline said.

He arched a brow. "Are you always going to tell me what to do?"

"Are you always going to be difficult?"

He chuckled. "Probably."

"Then, yes." She smiled up at him and did a nice sashay to the left, twirling her skirt around her legs. She sashayed to the right, then gave him an expectant look.

"You look lovely today, Pauline. That . . ." He paused, scrambling for words that didn't make him sound like a fool. "That shade of blue looks nice with your eyes."

"Thank you, Earl." She stopped dancing and rose on her toes, planting a soft, sweet kiss on his lips.

"Hey, the guy is supposed to do that."

"I was tired of waiting. I'm an old woman, Earl Harper. I don't have a lot of time to wait for you to make the first move."

"Then at least let me kiss you right," he said softly. He stopped in the middle of the dance floor, placed his palms on her cheeks, then pressed his lips against hers. It was a soft, tender kiss, the kind that melted like butter on a man's heart, and when Pauline let out a little sound and wrapped her arms around his neck, Earl knew he was a goner.

Twenty-seven

Daisy was halfway to the motorcycle when she stopped. What was she going to do? Hop on the bike and roar out of here, leaving Colt in her dust?

The part of her that had done that a thousand times before wanted to go, wanted to run, wanted to put as much distance between herself and the fear that had ridden her shoulders all her life. Colt wanted her to stay, to put in the grunt work that being in a real relationship took, to give all of herself, and risk that he would be there once she did. This wasn't some spur-of-the-moment runaway idea they'd had. This was staying in place, building a fence, and putting azaleas in the front yard.

Risking failure. And that, when Daisy boiled down all her fears and worries and bad decisions, was what sat at the core. Fear of failure.

She hung her head, then drew in a deep breath and turned around. "Do you want to know why I never wanted to make love with you?"

The question came out of the blue and his brows knitted in confusion. "I thought that's what we did the other day on the beach."

"No. That was *sex*. Hard, fast, dirty, and good. It wasn't making love." She took a step closer to him, and thought no one in the world had eyes as blue as his. "We've only really made love once. It was that night after we ate at that little café on Bourbon Street, do you remember? I stumbled on the sidewalk, and I twisted my ankle, and you carried me home. Up all five flights."

He took a step toward her, the smile of memory playing on his lips. "I put ice on your ankle, and propped it up with pillows in our bed."

"I didn't want you to leave, so you curled up on the bed with me, and you held my hand, and it was so sweet"—tears sprang to her eyes, but she let them come this time, instead of hiding her emotions from Colt, because hiding hadn't gotten her anywhere but alone—"and the next thing I knew, we were kissing, and then a lot more than kissing. It was slow and sweet and easy. And . . . beautiful."

"I didn't want to hurt your ankle, so I tried to be gentle."

The memory washed over her, so real, she could almost hear the trumpets jazzing in the New Orleans air, smell the crisp, sweet fried dough from the bakery underneath their apartment. "I remember feeling like . . . a baby bird. Like something that would break if you weren't very, very careful."

He brushed away her bangs, then let his fingers trail down her cheek. "Because I loved you, Daisy. I still do."

The words beat a tattoo in her heart, caused a hitch in her breath. "And that's what scared me."

"How can me loving you, making love to you, scare you?"

"Because you left, Colt. You left that next morning. And you never came back. And . . ." Her throat clogged and tears sprang to her eyes. "It broke my heart."

"So you think I might do it again? Leave you, break your heart?"

"Everybody leaves, Colt. But that's not what this is about, not really. I thought it was. Did a darned good job convincing myself I was afraid of being alone, but I'm not. I'm afraid of finding out I suck at being a good friend, a good wife, a good anything. I mean, look at me—I'm a high-school dropout whose only skill in life is waitressing." She tried to shrug it off like she didn't care, but that fear sat at the crux of everything in Daisy Barton's life. The girl who had never had a home that was permanent enough to celebrate two birthdays in a row had grown up terrified to become someone, to settle in one place and bloom there, because she had learned how fragile everything around her was. And how easily she could screw it up. So she'd cut the ties before she lost them forever. Then she'd taken a risk and fallen in love with Colt Harper—and he had walked out the door when she wasn't there, proving correct her misguided philosophies.

"Oh, Daisy. You are a success in a thousand ways. You're smart and determined and strong, and the bravest woman I know. You take risks all the time and I . . . I don't." He sighed. "Do you want to know why I left and never came back? Because I realized pretty quickly that I wanted more. More than just sex. More than just fun. I wanted something real and lasting and true, but I was just as scared as you to take a chance on that and totally screw it up. I was running from the very thing I wanted most."

She chuckled at the irony that they'd had the same fears all this time, and never said a word to each other. "Join the club. I'm a charter member."

His eyes danced with laughter. "Maybe we should start an organization. Commitmentphobes Anonymous."

"As long as you don't serve crappy coffee at the meetings, I'll be there."

"I promise, no crappy coffee," he said. "But there will be dessert." A car went past the park, and from far down the street, she heard the sound of children playing.

Colt's features sobered and his mouth thinned. "Deep down inside, this commitmentphobe really wants someone in my life that I know is going to be there when things get rough, like you have been for me this last month. Someone who understands when I need to talk and doesn't let me hide behind work. Someone who challenges me and makes me want to be more than I already am."

She wanted that, too, and if there was one thing that Colt Harper had done for her since she returned to Rescue Bay, it was challenge her. To reach further, to try harder, to trust more.

"Call me a sap, or tell me I'm getting soft in my old age," he went on, "but I don't want just a good time in bed. I want more, Daisy. Either you do, too, or we're just wasting our time here."

"I do, Colt. I want all that, and more."

He lifted her hands to his lips and kissed them. He held on to her, and the tender look in his eyes wrapped a spell around her heart. "I love you, Daisy May. I always have. I just wasn't smart enough to come back for you the last time. I won't make the same mistake twice."

"I love you, too, Colt," she whispered, and a tear fell onto her cheek. "I'm just scared." Scared to trust. Scared to give him her heart. Scared to let him deep inside her, where she was vulnerable and small. "Scared that we'll try again and it will all fall apart. And it'll hurt ten times more when it does. I've taken so many other risks—coming here with no real plan or financing to resurrect an inn that had been closed for a long time—but I never took the risk on coming after you."

He chuckled softly. "I don't know about that. You came after me in my office that day. All fire and sass. Any man would be a fool to resist that . . . or let it go a second time."

The earth beneath her feet was solid, strong. She loved this place, this town, and most of all, this man. Having all of those things meant taking a giant leap off the cliff of faith, handing the controls of her fragile heart over to another with no guarantee. It was the scariest leap she'd ever taken, but she knew if she didn't jump now, with both feet, she would lose something special and true. "Kiss me, Colt," she said. "Slow and easy. I don't want to rush anymore."

"Me either." He lifted his hands to cup her jaw, whisking away the tear with his thumb, as tenderly as he had cradled her ankle all those years ago. He lowered his mouth to hers and their lips brushed, once, twice, three times, then he opened his mouth and kissed her, as gentle as kissing a china doll. This wasn't a hard, fast, demanding kiss, it was a slow, musical concert against her mouth, playing strings and percussion with his lips, his tongue, his hands. She swayed into him, her eyes closed, letting the kiss wash over her like sliding into a warm pool of water.

He drew back, then captured her gaze with his own. "Are you scared now?"

"Terrified." A grin played at the edges of her mouth. "I'm terrified that if we wait one more minute to make love, someone might disturb us."

"Here?" He glanced around. "It's risky."

"Isn't that our new motto?"

"Absolutely. Then I think we should do this"—he kissed her—"again and again, until you're not scared anymore."

She smiled. "Immersion therapy, Doctor Harper?"

"Something like that," he murmured.

He kissed her a second time, until her knees went weak. Then he slipped out of the leather jacket, led her to a secluded area behind a thick copse of trees, and spread the jacket on the ground. Colt lowered her to the grassy bed, slow and easy, and took his sweet time kissing her mouth, her throat, her neck, her shoulders, her breasts, her belly. The languid tease stoked the fire inside her, made her writhe in agony beneath his tongue, his fingers. She stroked his erection, nipped at his shoulders, rubbed her legs along his. When neither of them could stand the sweet torture another second, he slid into her, holding her hands above her head and watching her, his blue eyes warm and full, as his strokes seemed to reach the deepest parts of her that Daisy had always kept hidden.

She had never felt so treasured, so special, so delicious. And when the orgasm finally came, it washed over her with a power that threatened to take her breath away. It rolled in waves through her body, lingering long after they were done and she had curled up against him.

"So that's what I've been missing all this time," she said

as they slipped back into their clothes and walked back toward the motorcycle.

"You and me both, Mrs. Harper."

Mrs. Harper. She shook her head, and cursed the tears that came again. "I'm not Mrs. Harper anymore, Colt."

"You are if someone 'forgot' to file the divorce papers again." He reached inside his leather jacket and pulled out the envelope. He gave her a sheepish grin, which she swore had a touch of devil in it, too. "Seems you're still married to me."

"You didn't file the papers? Organized, scheduled Colt Harper forgot something as important as that? Why?"

"I don't know. Guess it was an aberration." The grin widened, became a full-out smile. "I broke the rules, Daisy. I think you've rubbed off on me. In some very good ways."

She danced her fingers down his black leather jacket, skipping across the unknotted tie, the button-down shirt, still partly undone. "I'd have to agree. And you've done the same with me."

"Then what are we going to do with these?" He tick-tocked the envelope.

Once, she would have seen those divorce papers as freedom. As escape. A direct path to the nearest exit. But now she realized that they were really about loss. Losing the one man, the *only* man, she had ever loved. Losing her best chance at the happiness and family she'd desired all her life. And most of all, losing herself to the fears that had controlled her far too long.

She hesitated only a second before she grabbed the envelope, tore it in two, and let the pieces fall into the trash. As the papers fluttered away, a weight dropped from Daisy's shoulders, and her heart lifted with joy. "Seems you're stuck with me."

"That was my plan all along." Then he reached inside another pocket and produced a small velvet box. "And so was this." Colt pulled back the lid, and revealed a set of rings. The sun caught them from above and made the bands glisten.

Daisy gaped. "Wedding rings?"

"We were too broke to buy them when we first got married. I told you, I won't make the same mistake twice." He slid them out of the box, then took her left hand in his. "Will you be my wife, Daisy May?"

"I always was, Colt. I always was." The ring slid onto her finger as if it had been made for her. She took the matching band, then slipped the thick gold band onto Colt's finger, and closed her palm over their joined hands. They stood there for a moment, in a private little grove with birds and squirrels for witnesses, and celebrated the marriage they should have had all along.

"I think we better get back on that bike," Daisy said, as the last bits of sunlight disappeared. "We have a wedding to get to."

"And after the wedding?" Colt asked.

"I believe we better start planning." She rose on her toes, wrapped her arms around his neck, and kissed him. A light, gentle kiss, but one that came with her whole heart. "We missed our fifteenth anniversary, after all. What's the time limit on celebrating?"

"As long as it takes"—Colt grinned—"to find a pretty amazing gift."

"I already have everything I ever wanted, Colt." Then she climbed on the back of the motorcycle, leaned into his back, and they rode off into the sunset, like a fairy tale. Only better.

Greta Winslow dabbed at her eyes several times, as she watched Luke and Olivia spin around the patio of the Hideaway Inn as man and wife. The wedding ceremony had been perfect, right there on the beach she had loved all her life, with the beautiful, restored inn as a backdrop. She spied Edward on the sidelines, talking to Lydia Charleston, a local seamstress. Lydia said something that made Edward laugh, and a second later, her uptight son was leading her onto the dance floor. Then Greta damned near burst into tears like a baby when Luke came over to the sidelines and asked her to dance. The music segued from a fast beat to one more like a modern waltz tempo. "I'm so glad you married that girl," she said to Luke.

"I am, too. Maybe now my grandma will stop trying to hook me up with the neighbors." He grinned.

She swatted at his arm. "It was only one neighbor and it turned out mighty well, if you ask me."

"It did indeed." Luke pressed a tender kiss to her cheek. "Thank you, Grandma."

"You can thank me with some great-grandkids. And quick, too, because I'm not getting any younger."

Luke shook his head and laughed. "I'll see what I can do. In the meantime"—he stopped dancing and put out a hand—"it seems there's someone else who wants to take you for a spin on the dance floor."

Before Greta could run away, Harold Twohig stepped into Luke's place and fitted his hands on her waist, as if he owned the space. He had on a tuxedo, and she wasn't sure if it was because he liked to overdress for a beach wedding or he thought she was serious when she mentioned the tux the other day. Either way, Greta figured Harold had a couple screws loose. Even if he did look uncharacteristically handsome today.

"Don't stomp on my feet or claw out my eyes, Greta dear," he said. "This is just a dance, not a lifetime commitment."

"More like a life sentence," she mumbled.

"Well, if you're that unhappy about it, I can always go dance with Patty Simon." He lifted his hands and made like he was going to walk toward that troll of a Welcome Wagon president standing on the sidelines.

"You'll do no such thing," Greta said, cementing Harold's hands back on her waist. "That woman will have you hogtied and branded by the end of the day."

He laughed. "That could be fun."

"Play your cards right and I'll do it to you myself."

"Promises, promises, Greta dear." He turned her to the right, then waved at the entrance to the patio. "Speaking of things you do and do well, check out our latest project."

Daisy and Doc Harper stepped onto the floor, hand in hand. The torches surrounding the patio lit them with a golden glow, but even from a thousand miles away, Greta could have seen the smiles on their faces and the gold bands on their hands. It warmed her heart, from the inside out.

Harold wrapped an arm around her waist and leaned in to whisper in her ear. "You and I could be that happy, too."

"Only with the help of a lot of pharmaceuticals."

He chuckled. "Is that all you got, Greta dear? No backhand to my head, nothing meaner?"

"It's a wedding. I'm in a good mood for once." A good mood helped along by seeing Pauline dancing with Earl, and Diana dancing with Mike, Emma with Roger, and Edward with Lydia. Good Lord, one would think it was Valentine's Day, what with all these couples. Which was just the way Greta liked things. With the people in her life happy and settled. Kept her from worrying all night, and if there was one thing Greta Winslow liked more than bourbon in her coffee, it was a good night's sleep.

"Maybe I should take advantage of that good mood," Harold said, then quickly, before she could stop him, he cupped her face with his hands and gave her a good long kiss.

Greta sputtered and jerked away from him. "What the hell was that, Harold Twohig?"

"A token of my affection."

She wagged a finger at him. "Don't you ever do that again. Or you'll be gumming your food for the rest of your life." Then she straightened her spine and raised her chin. "Now that Colt and Daisy are happily married again, our alliance is done. We go back to the way things were. Neighbors with very big boundaries. Barbed wire and electric fences, if necessary."

"What if I want more? What if I want lasagna on Friday nights and cookies on Sunday mornings?"

"Then hire yourself a live-in chef." Greta spun on her heel and walked off the dance floor. Where did Harold Twohig get these crazy ideas? Have one dinner with the man and he considered it an invitation to be her new best friend.

Doc Harper stopped her as she passed. "Mrs. Winslow. Where are you going so fast?"

"To find some Listerine. I just tasted something horrible."

Daisy and Doc Harper laughed. "Remember what you told me a few weeks ago?" he said. "Eat more broccoli, drink less bourbon, and most of all, don't be afraid of love. Because in the end, it's sure as hell better than the alternative."

Greta glanced back at the dance floor. Harold was still standing there, the old fool, waving at her. She shuddered. "I've tasted the alternative. Frankly, I'd rather have the broccoli."

Doc Harper reached in his pocket and pulled out a pen and a piece of paper. He scribbled on it, then handed the slip to Greta. "Here. That prescription you wanted."

Greta glanced down and read the few lines. "One dose of true love, taken daily. For a healthy heart." She crumpled the paper up and tossed it at his chest. "I swear, sometimes I think you got your medical degree off the back of a Cracker Jack box."

Then she walked away, but slowly. Harold Twohig was trailing along behind her, like a little lost puppy, and she didn't want to make him think that capturing her heart was as easy as that. The man could make an amazing lasagna, after all, and maybe it would do her diet some good to keep him around awhile.

Read on for a special preview of the
next romance from Shirley Jump

When Somebody Loves You

Coming Fall 2015 from Berkley Sensation!

When Elizabeth Palmer's mother died in 1992, she left her only daughter three things: a fake ruby ring she'd bought at a garage sale, a tattered apron with a plastic nametag hanging askew from the corner, and one piece of advice—*Never bet on a losing horse.*

The trouble with that advice was figuring out ahead of time which horse was going to lose, and which one was going to have a final kick at the end. Something Winnie Palmer had never quite gotten the knack of doing. She had, however, wasted nearly every dime of her diner paychecks at the track, betting on everything from dogs to ponies, searching for that elusive ticket that would drag her out of a life of poverty and set her down smack-dab in one of the mansions she cut out of the Sunday real estate section and tacked onto the fridge with little horseshoe shaped magnets.

Elizabeth's mother had been like Delta Dawn, that helpless romantic in the song immortalized by Bette Midler. Standing there in her Sunday best every spare minute of the day, hoping for some miracle to bring her to the castle in the sky. In the end, all it had taken was a few thousand

Marlboros to give Winnie the gift of emphysema and a one-way ticket to a castle-less plot in Whitelawn Cemetery.

Whenever Elizabeth hit a crossroads, she would think. *What would Mom do?* And then she did the exact opposite.

Until yesterday, when she'd quit her job, giving up medical insurance and a bi-weekly paycheck for a chance at pursuing the only dream she'd ever allowed herself to have. Now she was stuck in the middle of Nowhere, USA, and trying not to hyperventilate.

She needed something to eat. And a bathroom. Maybe then she could take a few deep breaths and convince herself that throwing away job security was a smart move for a thirty-year-old with bills to pay.

What had she been thinking?

That she needed a way out of a dead-end administrative job that was heading down a hellish road of bad fluorescent lighting and endless reams of computer entries and a boyfriend who told her via text that, whoops, sorry we wasted two years together, but he was in love with the fifty-year-old cougar on the second floor.

Elizabeth glanced again at the assignment sheet from the horse breeding magazine that had given her a chance with her first-ever freelance job. A "quick, easy assignment," the editor had promised, about a topic Elizabeth knew nothing about—breeding and training quarter horses. But after three hundred and seven query letters and two years of trying to break into a national magazine, Elizabeth wasn't about to say no. So early that morning, she'd stowed an overnight bag in the trunk of her Honda, then headed out of New Jersey and down to Georgia. She had called the Silver Spur Ranch yesterday afternoon, talked to some woman named Barbara Jean, and made an appointment to meet Hunter McCoy at seven that night. An initial meeting, she thought, gather a little background information, do the formal interview the next day, and be back on the road by lunchtime.

Then she'd hit Atlanta at rush hour and spent an ungodly amount of time trying to get through the city center. By the time she got to Chatham Ridge, she was ravenous. She hadn't spied anything resembling a drive-through in at least a half an hour. Damn. She should have stopped when she was on an actual highway instead of these rural roads that ran through Georgia like veins in a bodybuilder.

Even though it was close to seven, the temperature outside had gone from hot to holy hell in a matter of hours, and the sunny day she had welcomed when she'd stepped outside this morning had become a torturous descent into the depths of Dante's inferno.

Otherwise known as Chatham Ridge, Georgia. Population: Not Nearly Big Enough.

The sun was just starting to wane when there was a low, menacing rumble from above and the skies opened up. Rain began to fall in thick, heavy sheets that pummeled her windshield and taunted her wipers. Elizabeth drove slowly down Main Street, peering through the veil of water, looking for something—anything—that would sell food and have a clean bathroom. The lights were off at the little white building with a hand-painted sign that read Bob and Mary's Sundries. There'd been a single gas pump out front, a pile of cordwood stacked and bundled with a handpainted sign that read THREE BUCK BUNDLE. But they were closed, as was the hardware store, the art studio, and the bank.

Finally, she spied lights and a tiny neon OPEN sign outside a brick front building on the corner of Main and Pecan. She pulled in, then parked and made a break for it. She'd left her umbrella at home and the storm lashed at her white dress shirt and dark blue pants with fat, soaking slaps. Too late, she realized she hadn't run into a restaurant but rather a bookstore/coffee shop. She stood in the entryway, dripping a puddle onto the hardwood floors and trying to catch her breath. Outside, the storm raged, whipping against the windows and door.

A buxom woman with a pile of gray hair swirled onto her head in a loose bun came bustling forward, her arms outstretched, her face bright with greeting. Before Elizabeth could react, the woman had wrapped one arm around Elizabeth's shoulders and was tugging her into the store and over to a small café in the corner.

"Darlin', you look about half drowned. Come on in. Let's get something in you and dry you off before you catch your death." She swung a bar stool away from the counter and pressed Elizabeth into it. "You sit tight and I'll be right back with a towel."

Then she hurried away, disappearing behind a swinging door. Elizabeth swiped the damp hair out of her eyes and looked around the bookstore, really a converted Colonial Revival home. She could still see the home in the décor, much more so than the store. It just had that feeling of walking into somebody's house, the kind of house where you'd stay a while and not be worried about putting your feet on the coffeetable or dropping a crumb. The hardwood floors gleamed, their darkened planks worn and dented from years of tread. A dozen bowl-shaped chandeliers hung over the space, casting a warm bright light into the nooks and crannies. The walls were a pale straw color, with thick wood molding that had the occasional hiccup flaw marking it as handhewn. A sign above the café counter read HAPPY END-ING BOOKSTORE, in a bright pink curlicue script. The shop was large but cozy, with rows and rows of bookcases stuffed with books that formed a rainbow of straight lines. At the back of the store, a six-pack of wingback chairs ringed a small circular table set before a fireplace with a tiny flickering flame teasing at a pile of logs. Was that what you got with a Three Buck Bundle?

"Here you are, sweetie." The woman draped a fluffy white towel over Elizabeth's shoulders, gave her a firm squeeze to cement it in place, then went back to the other side of the counter. "I'm Noralee Butler, no relation to Rhett."

Elizabeth couldn't help but smile. "Nice to meet you. I'm Elizabeth Palmer."

Noralee cocked her head and studied her. "Let me guess . . . New York?"

"New Jersey. Born and raised in the lovely city of Trenton."

"Can't say I've ever been there. I hardly ever leave my little corner of paradise. I figure the Lord planted me here so I could bloom, and that's what I been trying to do for near on sixty-two years now."

Elizabeth had exhausted her repertoire of small talk. "Do you serve food? I stopped in just to grab something to eat. I'm supposed to be out at the Silver Spur Ranch by seven and it's already past that."

"Hunter McCoy's place?" Noralee waved a hand. "Oh, I know Hunter. I'll give him a call. He'll understand."

Before Elizabeth could stop her, the woman was dialing, talking to Hunter, saying something about giving this poor creature a sandwich and a sweet tea, then she covered the phone and looked at Elizabeth. "You got a place to stay, honey?"

"I was planning on finding a motel." Yet another reason why spontaneity wasn't Elizabeth's strong suit. She hadn't even thought to go on Expedia and book a stay before she left. Damn.

Noralee's brows wrinkled. "Motel? In this town? You won't find one, not for another twenty miles, and believe me when I tell you their idea of a *sleeping establishment* is pretty light on the sleeping and the establishment. In this storm, you'd be lucky not to get washed off the road, straight into a ditch. Don't you worry, honey. We'll get you something to eat and then you can head over to Hunter's. He's got a house big enough to hold a Boy Scout Jamboree, so I'm sure he can put you up for a day or two."

"I can't stay—"

"Hunter?" Noralee said into the phone. "This girl needs a place to spend the night, too. Oh, she's no trouble at all. You got that big old house. . . ." A pause. "Okay, good. I'll let her know."

This had already gotten out of hand. A journalist didn't spend the night at the house of the person she was supposed to be interviewing. "Mrs. Butler—"

"Oh, I'm not a Mrs., and nobody 'round here calls me anything other than Noralee. 'Cept for Cooter Whitman. That man's full-time job is giving people nicknames. Now, don't you worry about Hunter. He's as fine a gentleman as they come. I'm not even sure they make gentlemen like him anymore. So, honey, if you want to catch him—"

"Oh, no, not at all. I'm here to interview him, for a magazine. Nothing more."

"Well, won't that put a feather in the town's cap? I'm just sayin' Hunter is the most eligible bachelor in Chatham Ridge right now and I haven't met a woman yet who hasn't fallen half in love with him from the minute he said *ma'am*." She waved toward the corner of the room. "Now you go get yourself freshened up and by the time you come back, I'll have something warm waiting for you."

Elizabeth ducked into the tiny one-stall ladies' room at the back of the store. She washed up and tried to do her best to clean up the raccoon eyes of her mascara and the wet tangle of her dark hair, loosening it from its usual clip and letting it hang around her shoulders to dry. She peered into a reflection that screamed *needs a good night of sleep*. That hadn't happened in a long time and she doubted it would happen today. Elizabeth sighed, washed her hands, then headed back to the counter.

Noralee stood there, as proud as a peacock, beaming at Elizabeth. "Glad you had a chance to get the drowned rat off you. Now you sit right down and enjoy yourself." She patted the chair.

Elizabeth wanted to say she'd get the food to go, but then she looked down at the plate and saw a muffin as big as a grapefruit sitting there, warm and welcoming. The scent of blueberries wafted up to tempt her. Butter pooled in the crannies of the halved baked treat, and before she could think twice, she'd eaten the whole muffin and washed it down with a full glass of sweet tea. "That was delicious."

"Why, thank you. It's my grandmama's recipe. Lordy, that woman could cook a porcupine and make it taste like something from a fancy French restaurant. You come by here on a Tuesday and I'll have her praline cookies. They're usually gone within an hour. My most popular treat, next to the books of course."

"It's a very nice bookstore."

"It was my mama's. Course, it was a dress shop when she owned it. She was always saying to me, *Noralee, you get your head out of that book and live your life.* Now I'm living my life, with my head always in a book. Funny how things work out like that." Noralee leaned in, curiosity sparking in her green eyes. "Tell me what you're reading now."

"Oh, I don't read much."

"Well, that is just a crime. I will make it my mission to find the right book for you. In fact, I'm going to talk to the Southern Belle Bookclub tonight and see what they think. That's why you caught me here after hours. It's about time for those ladies to come on in and fill this place with chatter."

As if on cue, the door to the shop jingled and a quartet of women came inside, laughing and talking as they doffed their umbrellas and shook the water off. For a second, Elizabeth felt a stab of envy at the easy roll of conversation between them, the kind that marked lifelong friendships. They seemed happy, at ease in their place in the world, and at that moment, Elizabeth wanted to stay.

She shook her head and cleared her throat. "I, uh, should get going." Elizabeth slipped out of the bar stool and reached for her purse. "How much was the muffin?"

"Oh, honey, you don't owe me a dime," Noralee said. "You just promise to come on back sometime soon. I guarantee I can find you something to read that'll change your life." She drew out the middle syllable of *guarantee*, as if the word was running away.

Elizabeth had no intentions of returning. She was here long enough to get the story, then get back to Trenton. With one last thank you to Noralee—who insisted on giving Elizabeth directions to the Silver Spur Ranch—and one last glance at the bookclub, already settling into those wingback chairs by the disappearing Three Buck Bundle, Elizabeth headed out into the rain again and down the road toward the Silver Spur Ranch.

She found it twenty minutes later, tucked at the end of a long, dark road. The rain seemed to have increased since she left, attacking her car with fat droplets that hammered a one-two punch at her windshield. The wind had kicked up

and buffeted her little car. Elizabeth flicked on the high
beams, and concentrated on the road between quick swipes
of the wipers. The ranch itself was dark, but the main house
at the end of the drive was ablaze with lights that flanked
the front door and either end of the wraparound porch. Twin
rockers swayed back and forth on the porch, as if beckoning
someone to sit and stay awhile.

No matter what Noralee had said, Elizabeth wasn't staying here tonight. It wasn't professional for one, and for another, one woman's word that Hunter McCoy was a
gentleman didn't make it a fact. She'd get the initial meeting
out of the way, then find someplace else to stay the night.
Her phone had lost its signal a while ago—apparently Chatham Ridge, Georgia, wasn't big enough to be in the all-
coverage-all-over plan she had—but once she got back to a
main road she could pull over and find something.

Elizabeth took a deep breath, then got out of the car,
using her notepad as a shield against the rain. She charged
up the steps and raised her hand toward the doorbell. The
door opened before she touched it.

A tall man filled the doorframe, literally. He was at least
six-two, with broad shoulders and a commanding presence
that charged the air, made Elizabeth draw in a breath. His
brown hair curled a little at the ends, as if he'd gone too long
between haircuts, softening the look of command his body
wore. One lock of hair fell over his brow, emphasizing eyes
so blue they could have been oceans all on their own. He
had on worn, comfortable jeans, a thick cotton white button-
down, and a glare colder than the biggest glacier in Alaska.

So this was Hunter McCoy.

"Sorry you've come all this way," he said, "but I want to
make one thing clear before we go any further. I don't know
what Barbara Jean and Noralee told you, but I'm not interested in being in a magazine."

That was a curveball Elizabeth hadn't expected. "I'm
sorry, Mr. McCoy, but I thought my editor spoke to
you—"

"She did. I told her the same thing I'm telling you. I'm

sorry, but I don't want to be in the magazine. You can stay here tonight, especially since this storm isn't gonna lighten for at least another couple hours, then be gone in the morning."

Elizabeth tucked her hair behind her ears, but the wind picked it up and plastered it against her cheek again. "But Barbara Jean said—"

"Barbara Jean means well, but she thinks our DNA allows her to make my decisions for me. I don't want to be in a magazine. I'm a private man, and that means I like my privacy."

"But it's a wonderful opportunity for people to find out about your breeding operation and—"

"If people want to find me, they know how. It's a small town, and I'm the only quarter horse breeder in the county." He gestured toward the open door behind her, and the wind whipping around them both, howling its anger at the world. "Are you done letting the storm into my house?"

She debated telling him good-bye, and just hitting the road again. But that would mean she had failed at her very first freelancing job on her very first day. Did she have it in her to send another three hundred and seven query letters, just to get a second chance? "I appreciate your honesty, Mr. McCoy," she said with a smile, as if she had no problem with his refusing the interview, "and you know, you're right. It is a long drive back to New Jersey. So if it's okay with you, I'm going to take that offer of hospitality and stay here. I just need to grab my bag out of the trunk." She started toward the car before he could change his mind.

"Wait."

She turned back.

He put out his palm. "Give me your keys. You get inside, dry off, and I'll grab your bags."

Elizabeth stared at him. Was this perfect stranger offering to do the chivalrous thing and get her overnight bag out of the car? In this Noah's Ark storm? She thought of all the men she had known in her life and couldn't list a single one who would do the same thing.

"Keys?" Hunter said again.

"Oh, oh, yes. Sorry." She fished her keys out of her pocket and dropped them into his palm. "It's just . . . I didn't expect you to do that."

"My momma raised me to be a gentleman, and not just when it's convenient or I'm trying to impress a pretty lady. Now you wait here, ma'am." Then he gave her a grin that transformed his face and filled her gut like drizzling honey on toast.

Holy cow. Noralee had been right. The way that man said *ma'am* set off a riot of fireworks in Elizabeth's belly. She fanned at her face, suddenly feeling ten degrees hotter.

He ran outside, and a minute later, was back with her small overnight bag and her briefcase, shiny new leather, bought for this very occasion. He set them by the door, then turned back to her. His gaze dropped and lingered for a moment. "I . . . uh . . . should get you a towel or something. You're . . . soaked."

She glanced down and realized that her shirt, which had been merely damp at the bookstore, had gotten so wet by her second run in the rain that it plastered the thin cotton to her chest, outlined the lacy scoops of her bra and soft peaks of her nipples. She yanked the briefcase up and pressed it to her chest and tried not to look disconcerted. "That would be great. Thank you."

Hunter disappeared down the hall. Elizabeth leaned against the wall and let out a sigh. Great. So much for making a professional impression.

Her gaze landed on a small table to the left of the door. An empty crystal vase sat to one corner, behind a small framed photograph of Hunter and a pretty blond woman. She was leaning into him, one hand possessive and protective on his chest, and looking up at him with a smile so wide, it seemed to last forever. Hunter had a cowboy hat tugged down on his forehead, masking his expression, but Elizabeth could see that his attention was locked on the woman in his arms. He had his hand over hers, their wedding rings glinting in the sun.

It was a picture of love. Pure, unadulterated love. The kind Elizabeth had only seen in movies, and didn't believe really existed. Heck, maybe it didn't for Hunter and this mystery woman, either. For all Elizabeth knew, they could have had a big fight five minutes later over taking out the garbage or what to eat for dinner.

Hunter returned and Elizabeth jerked her gaze away from the photo. "Here's a towel. Guest bedroom is at the top of the stairs on the right. I don't get many guests, so it's clean, but probably a little dusty. Breakfast is at six, on the dot. You miss it, you're on your own. Goodnight."

Then he turned on his heel and disappeared down the hall. Apparently, that was the extent of his hospitality to unwanted reporters camping in his guest room. For an easy, quick assignment, Elizabeth had a feeling she was in for a Herculean effort.

Hunter McCoy stood on the front porch of the small white farmhouse that sat at the edge of the Silver Spur, sipping a cup of coffee and watching the sun rise. He'd watched near every sunrise behind his property, for as long as he could remember. 'Course, when he was a boy, he'd watched the sunrise with a mug of chocolate milk, standing tall and straight next to his dad and his granddad, pretending he was holding a cup of coffee like the men he'd so admired. Now it was only him, running the Silver Spur. But that hadn't stopped the morning tradition. In Hunter's mind, it was a way to commune with his father and grandfather, maybe soak in a little of their wisdom as the sun crested over the trees at the far side of the land that had been in the McCoy family for as many generations as the state of Georgia had been in the union.

The sun started like a shy child, peeking between the trees, washing a slight gold over the long, squat stables, the smooth circle of the training corral, the old red barn, then finally reaching tentative fingers across the lawn, up to the steps of the porch. The birds chattered in the trees, rising in volume as the land went from dim to bright. The horses nickered in their stalls, and from far down the road, Joey Barrett's rooster crowed.

For years, this land, this place, had filled him with peace. But as he stood on the porch for the ten thousandth time, sipping another coffee he barely tasted, peace eluded him. He dumped out the coffee, then laid the cup on the railing and headed out to the stables. Work, that was his salvation. The only thing that kept him from drowning in a pit of his own misery.

He noticed the reporter's car still sitting in the driveway, caked with mud now that the rain had stopped. She was a tiny little thing, that Elizabeth Palmer, one of those take-charge women from up north who didn't take no for an answer. Hunter made a mental note to talk to Barbara Jean. He'd made it clear, hadn't he, that he wasn't interested in the magazine article? He wanted his peace, and by God, if he couldn't have that, he'd at least have his days uninterrupted, one after another following until they became a blur and his mind stopped whirring.

He greeted each of the horses in turn, running a hand along their velvety muzzles. He stopped at the last stall, and waited at the gate, but the mare inside didn't move from where she stood at the back of the stall. He clucked his tongue. "Hey, Dakota. Wanna come see me today?"

Diamond Heel Dakota's tail flicked left, right, and she shifted her hooves, but didn't move. The mare had been here for a week now, and had yet to warm up to anyone. Hunter never should have bought her—she was long past her best breeding days and according to Billy Ray, Dakota was long past her barrel racing days, too, especially since that accident last spring. But there'd been something about the horse, something that tugged at Hunter, and when Billy Ray said he was just going to send her off to the slaughterhouse, Hunter had pulled out his wallet and taken her home.

Hunter reached in his pocket and withdrew a small red apple. "Got a treat for you, Dakota."

The horse didn't turn around. Her tail flicked, left, right. Hunter stood there a while longer, then set the apple on the gate. "I'll be back tomorrow, Dakota. And the day after that."

The stable door opened, casting a shaft of light down the long wooden corridor. A single shadow followed, the long, thin figure of Carlos, who had been the right hand man at the Silver Spur for forty years. "Hey, boss. Our girl talking to us today?"

"Nope. Maybe tomorrow."

Carlos cast a doubtful look toward the last stall on the right. "She's stubborn, that one. There's a reason Billy Ray unloaded her on you."

"She's difficult. Not impossible."

Carlos chuckled. "You're always the optimist."

"I don't know about that. I just see talent in her. And I want to get my money's worth."

Carlos shook his head and clapped a hand on Hunter's shoulder. "You can pretend all you like that this is about dollars and cents, but I've known you a long time, boss, and you run this business like it's a family."

Maybe because it was pretty much all the family he had left now. The horses, the workers, the hay in the stalls, the beams above his head. It was what got him out of bed in the morning, what kept him putting one foot in front of the other. Without the Silver Spur, Hunter would have curled up into a corner a long damned time ago. "We got work to do," he said to Carlos.

"We always do." Carlos grinned, then headed off to feed the horses.

Hunter started toward the water troughs, then stopped when the front door opened and the reporter from yesterday stepped out onto the porch. She stood there, her face up-turned to greet the sun, wearing a pair of black dress pants, high heels, and another of those silky shirts—this one dry and dark blue, which sent a ribbon of disappointment through Hunter.

He shook it off. He wasn't interested in her. Hell, he hadn't been interested in anyone for so long, he wondered if maybe he should add monk to his job title. He had his work, and that was all he wanted, all he needed. This little spit of a thing standing on his porch was another complication—and Hunter was going to handle her like he handled all other complications.

By shaking her off like a burr stuck under his saddle.

FROM *NEW YORK TIMES* BESTSELLING AUTHOR

SHIRLEY JUMP

The Sweetheart Rules
A Sweetheart Sisters Novel

Veterinarian and single mom Diana Tuttle wants a long-term relationship. But it's hard to resist temptation when a one-night stand from her past shows up in town.

Coast Guard Lieutenant Mike Stark is doing his best to become a family man ever since his ex-wife left their kids on his doorstep—and reconnecting with Diana is the best part of his new life. But can he handle one more commitment?

Luckily the Sweetheart Sisters have the perfect scheme to make this second chance last a lifetime...

"Shirley Jump weav
from th
—*Coffee*

shirl
facebook.com
facebook.com
pe